Chris Else was born in the UK and came to New Zealand age thirteen. He was educated at Auckland Grammar School, University of Auckland and Auckland Teachers' College, none of which fitted him for a settled career. He has worked as postie, storeman, publisher's rep, bookseller, computer programmer and information consultant. He also teaches both creative and technical writing and, with his wife Barbara, runs TFS, a literary agency and manuscript assessment service. He has, for many years, been active in literary politics through such organisations as the New Zealand Society of Authors.

Chris has published three novels and two collections of short stories. He can be contacted through his website: www.elseware.co.nz

Other books by Chris Else

Novels
Why Things Fall
Brainjoy
The Beetle in the Box

Short Stories
Dreams of Pythagoras
Endangered Species

on river road

CHRIS ELSE

V
VINTAGE

National Library of New Zealand Cataloguing-in-Publication Data
Else, Chris, 1942-
On River Road / Chris Else.
ISBN 1-86941-623-6
I. Title.
NZ823.2—dc 22

A VINTAGE BOOK
published by
Random House New Zealand
18 Poland Road, Glenfield, Auckland, New Zealand
www.randomhouse.co.nz

First published 2004

© 2004 Chris Else

The moral rights of the author have been asserted

ISBN 1 86941 623 6

Cover design and illustration: Matthew Trbuhovic, Third Eye
  Design & Graphics
Design: Katy Yiakmis
Printed in Australia by Griffin Press

ACKNOWLEDGEMENTS

A number of people have helped in the writing of this book. I began it while I was working on a different project during my tenure in the 2003 Foxton Fellowship, generously provided by Diane and Peter Beatson. A period of full-time work to complete it was made possible by a Creative New Zealand project grant. In between I had a lot of help from people who provided background information: in particular, Jim Chipp of Wellington Community Newspapers, Johnny Levesque from the Williams Garden Centre and Ian McMeeking of the Wellington CIB. They are not, of course, responsible for any errors of fact in the text. Finally, I would like to thank my editor, Jane Parkin, and my three most perceptive of readers — Barbara Else, Emma Neale and Harriet Allan — for their guidance in helping this novel reach its potential.

For my daughter, Taibi

1.

YOU STUPID MAN. YOU stupid, stupid man. You don't think. You don't feel. You feel nothing for no one but yourself. You are insensitive. You play games. You manipulate, manipulate. You stupid man. Always, always you manipulate me. You are nice, you buy me presents, then you go quiet, you say nothing for hours, or else you shout because I don't do what you want, because I have my own life, and you think what I do is nothing. You hate what I do because it's mine. So would it be a surprise if I go with someone else? Someone who listens? Someone who understands me? Would it be a surprise? We have no life any more. We don't make love. You ruin it because you drink too much. You drown yourself in wine and in whisky until there's nothing left, until it's all gone, all finished. And I can't stand it that you hate what I do, because if you hate that, you hate me. So what choice do I have? You give me no choice. I have to have a life. So I don't want you. Go away! Get out! Get out! Just leave me alone!

2.

HANNAH CRESWELL'S NEXT APPOINTMENT was a man called Tom Marino. He was small and well formed and wore a navy-blue pea jacket and blue jeans. He had black hair and eyebrows, a trimmed black beard, black fuzz at his throat and curling in tendrils from the open neck of a white shirt. The black sheep, she thought, although there was nothing ovine about him. He was wilder than that. Standing at her door, looking up at her with amber eyes, long dark lashes.

Hannah was taller than many men, and the doorstep made her taller still. She watched him from her height, a moment's hesitation as her intuition felt for him. He smiled but it was only with his mouth and teeth, white teeth in the dark beard. His eyes gave her nothing. He was wary. She felt that he would spring away if she moved too quickly.

'Tom?'

'Yes.'

'Come in, please.' A gesture to draw him forward. He mounted the step and entered her house. She took his coat and felt the heat of him against the backs of her fingers, caught the scent of soap. It seemed incongruous, untrustworthy, a mask of cleanliness. She hung the jacket on the hooks beside the door and ushered him down the hallway towards her office. His shoulders in the white shirt were square, his back straight. The shadow of his torso lurked beneath the cloth.

'Sit down,' she said.

He went to the usual chair, the patients' chair, black leather, in the corner beside the window, but he didn't sink back into the cushions. Instead, he perched on the edge of it with his hands in his lap and his legs stretched out and crossed at the ankle. His shoes were brown, expensive-looking and polished bright. They had pointed toes and leather soles.

She sat down opposite him.

'Welcome.' She smiled to help him feel at ease.

Immediately, he moved, leaning forward, drawing his feet back towards the chair, his elbows on his knees.

'Hi.'

She let the pause lengthen. She could feel his resistance, his uncertainty beneath the push of his confidence.

'I'm just here to listen,' she told him, 'and to make suggestions maybe. This first session is an exploration, to see if we can work together. At the end of it, we can decide if we want to go on or not.'

'How do we start?' he asked. She remembered the voice from the telephone when he made the appointment. Deep and soft, seductive.

'Just tell me a bit about yourself.'

'What sort of thing?'

'Whatever seems relevant.'

'My name's Tom Marino. You know that. I'm forty years old. I run Greenwise, the garden centre in Hammer Road. I'm . . .' He had turned his head and was looking out of the window into the trees that pressed close up against it. 'Last year, six months ago, at the end of November . . .' A flick of his eyes. 'My daughter was killed in a hit-and-run accident.'

Hannah thought she remembered it. A teenager with a bicycle, hit by a car. She waited.

'I guess, in a sense, indirectly, that's why I'm here,' he said.

A pause.

'Indirectly?'

'My partner, Lisa, thinks I'm not coping with things very well. She thinks I'm in denial.'

'What do you think?' she asked.

'Me? I just want to know why it happened. Not in the Meaning of Life sense. That's bullshit. I want to know in a practical way. How Carla got hit. Why she was there. She was supposed to be going to the library. Somebody must know something. Somebody other than the one who did it, that is. I just think that if we had a little bit more information, then we might catch the driver. That I might understand it better.'

A pause. He was very still, very tense.

'How old was Carla?' Hannah asked.

'Sixteen.'

She felt a wave of sadness, grief and rage surging into her as if something had broken and it was pouring out of him. The word sixteen was the key, the loss and waste in that word. The anger startled her but she knew why it was there. He needed it to protect him. And his partner was wrong about one thing. However poorly he was coping, he wasn't in denial.

He was looking out of the window again. The trees there were part of the therapy. She had let them grow to form a shield but they were not impenetrable. Like a forest, they drew you into them and tempted you away into a space where strange things were possible.

'Maybe understanding it, or trying to, is a means of dealing with it, working through it,' she said.

He nodded, agreeing with her or just allowing the comment. 'It's different for Lisa. Carla's not her daughter. Not that she doesn't care. Of course she does. She and Carla were really close. It's . . .' He looked at her, a wry expression. 'I should explain. We have one of these modern families. I've got, had, two kids. Carla and Vincent, who's nineteen. Lisa has a daughter, Imogen. Imogen lives with us most of the time. Vincent did too until he started university. Then he went to his mother, in Winston. Carla used to live with her mother and come to us on weekends and in the holidays. Until last year, when she moved in permanently.' He glanced back out into the trees. She let the pause lengthen and draw him on.

'Annabelle, that's Carla's mother. Annabelle and I split up eight years ago. I was working in computers and . . . well . . . a life crisis all round, I guess. I decided to get out of that and do something different, so I moved up here and bought the garden centre. Annabelle couldn't understand it. She still can't. We don't communicate very well. We hardly talk at all since Carla died.'

She watched him, saw the signs of blame, the bitter twist to his mouth. And the guilt, the inevitable guilt. She was tempted for a moment by Annabelle's story but she let it pass.

'Lisa and I have been together seven years. She works on the local paper. The *Advocate*. That's how we met. She interviewed me when I took over Greenwise.' Another pause. He was remembering, perhaps, that first encounter, or feeling the space of the relationship.

'I'm not really answering your question, am I?' he said suddenly.

'Which question?'

'About how well I'm coping.'

'Do you have a different answer to the one you've given?'

'Am I coping?' He looked down at his fingers, which had formed themselves into a rounded cage, strangely delicate for such a fierce nature. 'Yes and no, I guess.'

'Tell me about the no part.'

He did not answer immediately. He was uncertain, she could see. He was on the point of decision. Slinking back and turning away or stepping out into the open.

'I suppose the thing that troubles me . . .' He looked up at her. 'I guess . . . I don't know . . .' Another glance out of the window as if he might escape through the trees. 'I'm having an affair.'

His gaze flicked to his left and he sat there, very still, waiting for her judgement, the moral judgement. She had none to make, of course. She was not interested in right and wrong. She believed that human beings were creatures of the wild, with instincts, needs, desires that drove them. Judgement was an instinct. Like revenge.

'Tell me about it,' she said.

'It's been going on a couple of months now. It just happened, I don't know why. And I don't seem to be able to do anything to stop it.'

'Do you want to stop it?'

'Yes. No. I guess I just don't care any more. And I guess, in a way, I'm obsessed.'

'You're obsessed with this relationship?'

'Yes. And with other things. Other possibilities.'

'What sort of possibilities?'

'I don't know. When I think about it now, at this moment, there doesn't seem to be anything there. It's like a desert, empty, dry. Cold. But then, when I'm with someone, anyone I find attractive and even some I don't find that attractive, I feel I have to . . . I want to say "make love to them", but love isn't the word . . . I don't know what the word is.'

And do you confess to them? she wondered. Is that what happens? But she couldn't ask him that. It wasn't meaningful just yet. Instead she said, 'And this is different from the way you usually feel?'

'Yes. I mean, it's normal to think about sex, to be aware of other people in that kind of way. I suppose the difference is that I need to do something about it.'

'That's what troubles you? Needing to do something?'

'Yes. I don't think it's right. It's not responsible. I don't want to hurt people.'

'Lisa?'

'Yes. And other people. They don't need any grief from me.'

An interesting word to choose, she thought.

'Has anything like this ever happened to you before?'

'When I left Annabelle. But that was different, too. I wanted to find somebody.'

'And you found Lisa?'

'Yes.'

'So you're saying you don't want to find anybody now.'

'No. Nobody real.'

'Somebody unreal?'

He didn't answer. He was looking at his hands again. The left one held the right wrist. Right palm opened and then closed, testing his grip, feeling the sinews move.

It is all unreal, she wanted to say. The world we see, the people we love. We paint the desert with our urges. But it would not help him if she told him that.

The pause lengthened and she began to consider the possibilities that had opened up, the paths she might point out to him. Perhaps the best one was the most obvious, the most direct.

'Is this situation, this obsession, connected with Carla's death, do you suppose?'

He looked up at her, a little flash of hope, gone in a moment.

'I guess it must be,' he said. 'But I don't see how.'

'Is that what you want to find out? How?'

3.

LISA CAIRNES OF THE *Durry Advocate* opened the door of her four-wheel drive and stepped down into the cool morning air, the pale light, smell of dew-soaked earth. The scents crept over her and into her head. She closed the car door softly, stood there, looking round. A dog was barking, an old dog, somewhere ahead of her out of sight. She was in a clearing, trees on both sides and, in front, a view out to the north-east, the Kaimohu Hills, grey in the distance. To her left was an old ute, mud-spattered, and beside it a corrugated-iron shed and a water tank on a wooden stand and then a battered caravan, half-covered in creeper, a dead-looking mass of tangled stalks trailing over the black roof and down the dirty-yellow sides. Rust streaks bleeding from the window frame.

The dog was coming slowly over the far side of the knoll. It was black, with a white muzzle, floppy ears and a round barrel of a body. A mongrel, mostly labrador, wagging its tail now. She waited for it, watched it thread its way through what looked like a garden, ragged zigzag paths between the clumps of growth. There were vegetables and ferns and stout seedlings — baby shrubs and trees. The dog lumbered on, doing its job. Stiff lift of arthritic legs and rolling hips. Your call, dog, your territory. It stopped in front of her, looked up, seeking her out with breathing nostrils. Scent of me? You'll smell cat, she thought. She held out her hand for it to sniff.

'Hello, dog.'
'Hello, lady.'
She started.

A man was standing a few metres away to her right, watching her. He was tall and lean, his lined face half-hidden by a floppy, stained hat. He wore a faded shirt and a shapeless jersey, khaki wool with a hole in the left elbow. Baggy grey trousers, tied at the waist with twine and tucked into black gumboots. In his right hand, upright like a spear, he held a garden hoe.

'Hi,' she said. 'I guess you're Max.'

'I am.' He was squinting at her from under the brim of the hat, his eyes bright, deep in wrinkled sockets. He had a nose like a wedge and bushy white eyebrows. There was a mist of white stubble around his cheeks and chin.

'I'm Lisa Cairnes. From the *Advocate*.'

He didn't answer, just looked at her. She felt an urge to move, to walk away, to pace the ground, but she resisted. Thrust her hands deep into the pockets of her jacket. Looked down to her left, at a clump of arum lilies, one white trumpet curled at the lip and the thick golden stamen. She felt hungry suddenly. A growl in her belly. Remembered she had had no breakfast. Stupid woman.

'You've got a nice spot here,' she said, for something to say, glancing up at him.

'Nice?'

She indicated the garden. 'The ferns and so on.'

'That's what I do,' he said. The dog had gone to him and was nuzzling his knee. He ignored it.

'How long have you lived here?'

'Seventeen years.' He moved then, a quick shift of the hoe to his left hand, swinging it to the horizontal. 'This piece you're going to write. What's in it for me?'

'Depends what you mean,' she said. 'We can't pay you

anything. But it might help in other ways.' She took a step towards him. 'I understood you have a problem, a legal dispute.'

'Might have.' A quick wriggle of his shoulders as if something had bitten him there.

'And that's why you wanted to talk to me?'

'Might be.'

Good God, what is this?

'Look,' she said, 'if I'm wasting my time, tell me now.'

'Wasting? Hm.' He pulled a face, a bad-smell face. 'You talked to them next door?'

'The Kerringtons? No.'

'You going to?'

'I'm a journalist. I get the facts. I tell the truth, the way I see it.'

'I don't want any cutesy-wootsy stories about this crusty old bloke that lives in a caravan and grows native plants.'

'I don't write that kind of story.'

'Somebody at your paper does. I've read 'em.'

He turned away suddenly, began to walk towards the open side of the clearing. Lisa followed him, picking her feet along the zigzag path, feeling the brush of leaves against her ankles, damp soak in the fabric of her jeans. Max was soon way ahead of her. He had the rhythm of it somehow, striding forward with his hoe like a quarterstaff. He seemed to lever himself over the ground. She felt heavy in comparison.

But then there came a shift in the sky, the cloud breaking smoothly, quickly. The light flowed down in a rush of warmth across her cheek and the back of her neck, and all around her the green things throbbed with a sudden pulse of colour. She felt her muscles stretch to meet the sun, and then she was out of the maze of paths and striding through the grass. A lift in her chest, a need to run, to leap and shout, a savage stab of joy.

At the edge of the knoll the view stopped her. The ground fell steeply away. Ahead the farmland stretched out to the grey hills in the distance. The sunlight was racing like a breaking wave across the fields. Below to the left was a loop in the stream, just visible, with the light sparkling on the water, and to the right a house, surprisingly close.

It was a house she knew. It might once have been her own. She had passed it on the road coming here, of course, but it was hidden then down a long drive, behind a grove of half-grown trees. She had been to it many times over the years, pulling up at the front door, dropping off her daughter, Imogen, and picking her up again, stepping inside sometimes, just for a moment or, even longer, for a cup of coffee. But now, having it there, below her, she was startled by its presence: walls of yellow brick with colonial windows and a dark tiled roof, the long spine of the nearby greenhouse with its thin ribs beneath the glass, the beds where Heidi grew her dahlias, the garage like a flat box with its doors open. She could see the 4WD inside. She could even make out the garden furniture on the back terrace, white wrought-iron.

She stood there, looking, breathing. Every out-puff was a little gust of fear. But that was stupid, unnecessary. The house was nothing. Someone else's ground. She had never had a right to it or wanted it. God, no.

'Are you coming?' Max was to her left, below her, on a path that led down the slope.

'How do you get on with your neighbours this side?' she asked, pointing.

'Good. Good as gold.' He took a step or two back up

towards her. 'I go and have a chat to her sometimes. She doesn't mind.'

Do you know him, then? Colin Wyte? She might have asked that. I was married to him once. She might have said it lightly, casually. He's the father of my child. He's a bastard, an idiot. But you know what? We're still friends. We socialise together. He's the best mate of my best mate's husband. Correction. He's the best mate of both my best mates' husbands and he's the business partner of one of them. And I'd rip his throat out if I didn't feel so guilty.

The dog was there, its head beside her thigh. It gave a little whimper.

'Come on,' Max said. 'I haven't got all day.'

She followed him, with the dog behind her. The path curved around the knoll and, to her right, the view opened up over the flats, a paddock with a herd of cows and the stream. It flowed in lazy loops through a cutting that curved away to the west. There was a line of poplars on its southern bank and a single clump of pines to the north, too, on a little rise.

Max stopped.

'You own this place?' she asked him.

'This here . . .' He jabbed the ground with the butt of the hoe. 'Too right I do. This is mine.' Then he raised his free hand and pointed. 'That there's the Kerringtons' place, the other side of the creek. You can see it there.' He pointed towards the poplars. The grey iron of a pitched roof and the white spike of a finial were just visible. 'They own everything on the left-hand side as it is from here. Bloke called McCracken owns the other side. That's his stock you can see down there. In between there's a public roadway. It's supposed to be along the creek bed. Look at the map down at the council. It's clear enough.'

Lines on paper marking out our claims. This is why we are called civilised, she thought.

Max went on. 'In the old days, the path ran along the right-hand side of the creek. If you look there, though —' he pointed towards the pines — 'you'll see you can't get through that way. That bend's right up against the cutting. Didn't used to be like that. The creek shifted in the big flood. Thirty, forty metres. If you surveyed down there now, you'd find the roadway actually crosses the stream about there —' shift of his finger — 'and goes up the left-hand side, right round that slope under those poplars. Now beyond where you can see is the back end of the Kerringtons' place.'

She leaned forward, following his finger, caught a whiff of him then. A smell like dried blood, old meat. She moved back.

'And you use the path round there?'

'I do.' He lifted his hand and pointed further. It was a big hand, creased and folded, with a thick yellow nail at the end of the finger. 'It's the quickest way through to that stretch of bush. There's possum in there and hare along the fringe of it. Good dinners. I mean, this was a bloody stupid place to try and put a road, but it's legal. It's there. It's even got a name. Little River Lane. That's my legal address.'

'So when did the trouble with the Kerringtons start?'

'Six or seven months back. When they moved in. Old Mountford never bothered, but they've got this notion of making it all beautiful so they can have a nice view from their living room. I can understand that.'

'So what happened?'

'We argued about it. I ignored them. They put up a

fence. You can see it. Down there . . .' He pointed, but Lisa could not make out where he meant. 'I cut a hole in it.'

'Was that wise?' Of course it wasn't wise.

'It was on public land! I know bloody well it was on public land!' A quick flash from his mad old eyes.

She grinned at his ferocity. 'What happened then?'

'They got me arrested for trespass. Took injunctions out. Kerrington's got plenty of money. He impresses people.'

'So what are you going to do?'

'Stand up for my rights. What else can I do?'

What else can anyone do except knuckle under, give up, bow to the inevitable?

4.

WELCOME TO DURRY, POPULATION 15,000, tucked away in the Durry River valley, forty-seven kilometres north of Winston. It's a town with an air of optimism, although it hasn't always been that way. The history of Durry traces a minor theme of the twentieth century, the fall and rise of middle-class self-confidence.

A hundred years ago it was a vigorous trading centre on the main road north, smug with the profits of beef and timber. The trees were all felled by the First World War, however, and by the Second there was a new highway over to the west. Durry was bypassed and in decline. The Depression had shaken its faith, and no amount of hard graft and determination seemed able to revive it. The boom times of the fifties and sixties drifted past, and by the middle of the seventies there were empty shops in its main street and a feeling that life was elsewhere and had been for a long time. No one who attended the town's centennial in 1978 could have guessed what would happen next, for no one understood that Durry's greatest asset was not the fertility of its fields nor the diligence of its citizens but something else less obviously bankable.

It was a pretty place. It had always been pretty, with the hills shielding it from the worst of the nor'westers, the air fresh, and a sense of peace; an oddly spiritual feeling, as if the sky bestowed a blessing on the land. Hard to put your finger on, the source of this quality, but it was real enough. How else would a town with no beach and ten kilometres from the main road suddenly become a haven for commuters?

A horde of accountants, lawyers, bankers and stockbrokers descended on it. They were hungry for the fresh air and for open spaces that the kids could grow in, and they began to spend up large in the local economy. High Street was bustling again, lined with boutiques that were rich on credit. There was a new mall and car park in Victory Road, and Hardy's, the department store that had served the Durry farmers since there was a pavement here to walk on, had transformed itself into a kind of rustic Harrods. Nothing you couldn't buy in Hardy's, if you had the means to pay.

One person who had the means was Sylvia Hannerby, wife of hot-shot Winston barrister, Larry Hannerby, and best friend of Lisa Cairnes of the *Durry Advocate*. The Hannerbys lived on The Rise, to the west of the town, in a two-storeyed house of white weatherboards, with a red-tiled roof and gabled windows, built to catch the best of the sun, morning and afternoon. It had seemed a huge financial commitment when they bought it seventeen years ago, although it was dirt cheap by Winston standards, but now the mortgage was paid off and there were two BMWs in the garage and the family took holidays in Queenstown or Japan and the wine on the dinner table cost forty dollars a bottle.

Sylvia was not easy with this affluence. It made her nervous to be burdened by things she didn't need, and while she would have struggled to define her requirements she had a sneaking sense that they fell far short of what she had. She was an odd person in that she liked the cold, the crunch of snow under her feet, the nip of frost on naked skin. She wanted to live like that, not physically but spiritually — with a clarity of being that could sense things over great distances. Instead, she was distracted by the clutter of the proximate world: looking after Larry and their two children, working fifteen hours a week at the local library in a job she did only because she felt she ought to be useful somehow. She did not resent any of this but she wondered why it was necessary and why she couldn't rise above it. Was it habit or a sense of duty? Was she ungrateful or neurotic? Was it just that she was badly organised?

Thus, she dwelt in the shadow of her own disquiet. It gave her an air of nervousness as if she half expected someone to shoo her away. She thought that people might object to her because she was false to herself, and she tried hard to be honest and straightforward. Her hair was grey but she refused to have it tinted. She welcomed the little lines that had appeared between her eyes because they were the marks of authenticity. What she failed to appreciate was the startling quality of the eyes themselves, the long dark lashes, the clear whites and the irises the colour of forget-me-nots. Sylvia's eyes, together with her fine cheekbones and pale complexion, caught people's attention and moved them to ask her where she came from — a question that always disconcerted her. Winston, she would say, Thomas Street, Highwick. Any mention of her ancestors, who had lived for generations in a tiny village in the Urals, would have seemed irrelevant. Sylvia didn't care about her lineage any more than she valued her own good looks. She wanted to be here and now and inconspicuous so that she could move about in secret and find what she was looking for.

There were maybe a dozen people in Stratos, in pairs or small groups. No Lisa yet. No Maddy. Sylvia was tempted by the fresh air on the terrace, but the others would think it too cold out there so she took her coffee to the usual table in the window. It was a bay window that looked out onto the lawn in front of the coffee shop, the gnarled grey trunks of the pohutukawas, the cars parked along the kerb. The view was diced into little rectangles by the leaded window-glass. An autumn morning, sunshine now.

Stratos was in the Esplanade, an old street along the river, full of buildings from the beginning of last century when Durry was in its heyday. Fat cats in their top hats, carriage wheels with iron rims, the clop of horse's hooves. Perhaps the window brought these antique thoughts. Perhaps it was her melancholy mood. She sat there staring, not at the scene outside but at the bright panes. Each pane was like a page in a notebook ready to be written on. Who was it wrote a poem on a window? She couldn't remember and then she thought that if it had really been a notebook, one of her own, the pages wouldn't have held poems anyway. They'd have been full of lists. But then maybe a poem, especially a modern poem, was just a list held together by associations. But so was a sentence, in that case. It was a list of associated words with some rules attached to tell you how to build it. But then the rules were just sentences too, weren't they? So they were lists as well. So what exactly was it that held the words in a sentence together?

The idea intrigued her. She felt she had stumbled on something interesting, but then, suddenly, it was all gone because there was Maddy beyond the pages of the window, walking down the pavement, plump and bustling on her little feet, her mass of brown curls bouncing with the rhythm of her stride. She was wearing a scarlet coat with a big floppy collar, a black leather bag in her black-gloved hand. She turned into the path that led to Stratos and, catching sight of Sylvia in the window, smiled and waved, a little twinkle of her fingers. Smiled again as she entered the room before she headed to the counter. She ordered her coffee, a trim latte, no doubt, and chatted to the girl there while it was made. Head toss from side to side. The girl, half-turning from the machine, smiled back at her. Everybody smiled at Maddy, who, in any case, was the wife of a town councillor and a tireless worker for the local community. She peeled off a glove and delved in her bag for the money.

And, of course, she knew some of the other customers as well so she had to pause and say hello, make a joke, move as if to touch someone on the shoulder, although she had a plate in one hand and teetering coffee cup in the other.

'Oof!' she said, sitting down, squeezing into the bench seat. 'How was your weekend?'

'Difficult,' Sylvia said. 'The cat got Josie's praying mantis.'

Maddy gave a little wince. 'Oh, yuk. Where was it?'

'In her room. She was feeding it flies to see how big it would grow.' The memory of the argument, Josie's fury, came with a rush of anxiety. Anxiety and guilt, because she was the one who had opened the door and let the cat in.

'Urgh.' Maddy took a bite from her lemon slice. Little tip of a pink tongue licked a crumb from her upper lip, perfect lip, the bow red, scarlet to match her coat. Then, as if she suddenly thought she was being impolite, she held the slice out to Sylvia.

'Have some. It's yummy.'

'No thanks.' Sylvia sipped her coffee, thought about the argument. *That's three months of my research programme completely wasted!* Larry had gone and hidden in his study so Josie wouldn't see him laughing. Sylvia couldn't afford to laugh. It was better to look remorseful, under the circumstances. *I told you to stay out of my room! Why can't you do as you're told?* Should a mother let her fifteen-year-old daughter speak to her like that, especially with James, her younger child, standing there listening, wide-eyed at the drama of it? She supposed not. At least the cat hadn't got into the spiders.

'It was my fault,' she told Maddy.

'Poor you.'

'And I don't know why I did it. I mean, *consciously* I was thinking maybe there are rats or mice in there. But, on another level, it was one of those moments when you're in a kind of dream and you just do something, knowing full well it's going to be a disaster.' A kind of dream, she thought. Like just now, looking through the window. 'Has that ever happened to you?'

Maddy laughed. 'All the time. It's the state I live in.'

Sylvia laughed too, of course. Because she knew full well how organised Maddy was, despite her carefree air. 'So what have you been up to?' she asked.

'Oh, God. We had the first meeting of the Arts Festival Committee yesterday. What a bunch of geriatrics! Plenty of time! Plenty of time! This thing's supposed to be on in September and they don't have a blind clue what they're doing. And let me tell you, David Langden's the worst of the lot. You should be there instead of him.'

'Me?'

'Yes! The library needs decent representation. Somebody who doesn't fall asleep in meetings.'

'Maddy, I'm a part-time library assistant. I shelve books.

He's the Head Librarian.'

'Yes, but he's useless. Like the rest of them. Durry Arts Festival Team. I actually called them that yesterday and no one had the wit to figure out the acronym. No, what I've decided is that they can maunder on however they like and I'll put some sub-committees together to do the real work. I want one for the Writers' Weekend and I want you on it.'

Maddy took a mouthful of coffee, swallowed.

Sylvia waited. Maddy hadn't finished.

'We need people who read,' she said. 'Literate people. Otherwise it'll be the same old, same old. You know, Angela Paine.'

'What's wrong with Angela Paine?'

'Tired. Passée.'

'She's sixty. Not exactly on a walking frame.'

'But she gets wheeled out year after year. It's like an annual unveiling. Where's the new talent? There has to be someone young and exciting who's got connections with the town. Or maybe one who hasn't. Who cares?'

Sylvia thought about it. 'Helen Talbot?'

'Who's she?'

'A poet. She won the Grenville Prize last year. Her aunt and uncle have a farm out Baledon way.'

'How old?'

'I don't know. She looks Josie's age but she's probably late twenties.'

'She'll do. See? I knew we needed you.'

This was how it went. The cost of knowing Maddy, of being gifted with her love and attention, was the occasional demand that you serve on a committee. Not that Sylvia minded. When it came to the actual doing, she quite enjoyed it, working with other people towards a shared objective. As long as it didn't take too long. Big projects with distant goals made her nervous. It was like being shut in a room when you could be outside wandering the hills.

So she didn't reply to Maddy's request. Just drank her coffee. Maddy didn't say anything more on the subject either. This was Maddy's way. She didn't pressure you. She let you decide for yourself to do things for her.

'So how's Larry?' she asked, after a moment.

It was a question before a question and it brought Sylvia up with a start. 'Fine. He's fine.'

'When's the verdict?' That question.

'The end of the week, most likely. The prosecution case finishes today or tomorrow.'

'We saw him on the news last night. He looked tired.'

Yes, Sylvia thought. He is tired. It's not just that, though. He's caught up in this case more than usual. It's got its teeth into him.

'She should get off,' Maddy said.

'She should. But she won't.'

'Didn't Larry say he was going for manslaughter?'

'Yes.' Polly Drafton, who killed her husband with a kitchen knife, a single blow to the chest so powerful, so firmly wedged between bone and cartilage, that she couldn't pull the weapon out again, although she tried.

'Ghoulish, isn't it, this preoccupation with another person's misery?' Maddy said. 'I don't really approve of people who get interested in such things, but I'm just as bad as the rest.'

'It's human nature.'

'Yes, I suppose so. Like gossip. I read somewhere that

people gossip in all known cultures. They say it's genetic.'

'They say everything's genetic these days. Nature versus nurture. Nature wins.'

'You think so?'

'I don't know. It doesn't really make much difference, as far as I can see. Genetic or not, you still have to decide whether to have another piece of chocolate, don't you?'

'Not me. The answer's yes!'

Maddy's laugh was a whoop, a scoop of high, sweet sound, and Sylvia felt the tingle of it in her skin, remembering or at least realising all those years of Maddy's friendship, the ease and simplicity of the trust between them. Because her relationship with Maddy was the longest of her adult life, going back to the beginning of their adolescence, the two of them giggling with their heads together in the playground of Highwick Intermediate School. When Maddy's your friend, she stays your friend. You don't get away without a fight.

The quick rush of feeling took Sylvia by surprise. She turned away, looked across the room towards the counter and felt another surge of the same strange combination of need and love and gratitude, for there was Lisa, ordering coffee. She'd come in without them noticing. Tall, slim figure in a black jacket, smooth cap of black hair. She turned, moved across the room between the tables with a loose-limbed, awkward kind of grace.

Maddy saw her too and gave her a little wave. Lisa smiled and Sylvia thought, as she sometimes did, what a lovely smile she had.

Thus, the three of them together, like always. Maddy teased Sylvia by telling Lisa about Josie and the praying mantis, although maybe it was just to give herself an excuse to talk about her own kids, or at least Damien who had scored the winning try on Saturday and you should have seen Ward, puffed up like a pouter pigeon. Not just Ward, of course. The pride in Maddy's voice was clear enough and her delight, too. Because although she wasn't interested in sport, not really, well, not the brutal macho kind, there was just something about a child succeeding that you couldn't help but be pleased about and who would have believed that Ward and Maddy Lorton, Mr and Mrs Chubby, could have ever had a son who was a sports star?

Lisa might have been interested but she was chomping through a sausage roll with hungry bites, a scattering of pastry flakes about her plate. When she had finished, she didn't ask Sylvia how Larry was, although she was no doubt curious about the Polly Drafton case, just like everyone else. Instead, she told Maddy she had heard a rumour that Ward was starting a campaign aimed at lowering the speed limit on River Road. Was that right? Maddy said, yes, he was, and her tone went quiet and serious all of a sudden because the thought of Carla had touched all three of them and their eyes turned down to the table for a moment or into the depths of their coffee cups. The death of a child was something too awful to contemplate, except you had to when it happened, right there, to a child you knew, a child you loved. Sylvia felt an impulse to ask Lisa how Tom was but she didn't, perhaps because it might be better to have that conversation when the two of them were alone, although she did not know quite why she felt that way. Instead of saying anything, she leaned over and put her hand on Lisa's wrist, squeezed it.

Lisa glanced at her, knowing what she meant.

Maddy changed the subject then, as only Maddy could.

'Isn't it strange,' she said, 'how different things are?'

'How do you mean?' Sylvia asked.

'I was just remembering, I don't know why, about the way we used to live. The things we put up with. Scuffed paint and old furniture.' Maddy gave a little laugh. 'Do you remember that sofa in Phoenix Street? The one Ward and I bought at the Boy Scout auction for five dollars?'

'The blue one?' Sylvia remembered it well.

'Yes. The springs were so collapsed, it was like a hammock.' Maddy's hand swept through the concavity.

'An instrument of torture,' Sylvia said. She had liked Phoenix Street, the way the wind howled and the barge boards rattled when the southerly blew. Maddy had hated it, though.

'God, that place was disgusting when we moved in. Do you remember the cockroaches in the oven?' Maddy shuddered at the thought.

'Cockroaches?' Lisa asked.

'Yes. You saw them. You and Colin helped us move. The inside of the oven was crawling. Larry lit the gas and shut the door and it was months before anyone would use it because of the roasted cockroaches.'

'We could never understand why you took that place,' Lisa said. 'Or why you stayed so long. How long were you there?'

'Three years,' Maddy told her.

'Really?'

'Yes,' Sylvia said. 'The four of us moved in just after Larry and I got married. Twenty years ago.'

'You've been married twenty years?' Lisa looked surprised. 'Yes, I guess you have.'

'May ninth.'

'That's next week. When? Friday?'

'That's right. Friday. Twenty years next Friday.' She wanted to say it felt like for ever, but the others would laugh at her, not thinking she meant it seriously, in a good way.

So they drank their coffee and talked about other things, like Maddy's plans for the Arts Festival, although Sylvia noticed that Lisa wasn't asked to be on a committee. Perhaps Maddy had other plans for Lisa.

Stratos filled up with the mid-morning crowd, the room got warmer, stuffier, and the noise lifted to a buzz of people being people, just together. And it was quite pleasant sitting there, just for a little while, before you moved on, before the restlessness got to you, although Sylvia didn't understand how it worked, really, how anybody could actually like anybody else. Why Lisa and Maddy, for example, didn't hate each other: they were so different, but they talked and they laughed and they smiled at one another. Sylvia remembered the tension there had once been, when they were all at high school together, and how surprised she had felt when she realised that her two best friends were jealous of each other because of her. So strange to think that she mattered to anyone that much.

Lisa was asking about the Kerringtons, the people who had bought Clisserford, the big house down Cox's Line, did anyone know anything about them. So Sylvia said the woman had used the library a few times when they first arrived last year and had been a bit of a bitch, and Maddy said she hadn't met either of them, they seemed to keep themselves to themselves, although Ward had plans to get them involved. The male Kerrington was being put up for membership of the Businessman's Club and someone on the Cultural Committee had wondered if Clisserford might be used for a celebration on Waitangi Day, because wasn't the house built on the site where the Treaty was signed with the local tribes in 1840? Mountford had been such a crusty old fart and the place had got so run down that nobody would have thought of asking before, but maybe the new owners had a different attitude. A garden party on the lawn there. What do you think? Because, of course, by then, by next February, they would have had the local elections and perhaps, just perhaps, Ward would be Mayor. And Maddy? A big, beautiful smile from our Lady Mayoress on our National Day! Was it possible? Of course it was. We hoped it was. We all hoped.

Twenty years, crammed with life. All the things done and things not done and things that ought to have been done and things that would have been better if they were left undone. None of it could be changed, though. It was like stone, like ice. Frozen. The beginnings and the endings. Like Polly Drafton's blow to her husband's heart and Carla Marino's encounter with a car on River Road.

'Are you busy tonight?' Sylvia asked suddenly.

Lisa and Maddy looked at her, glanced at each other.

'No,' they said, almost in unison.

'Would you like to come over for a drink then? You know, everybody together? I think Larry would really appreciate it.' And she thought, that's the problem, isn't it? That's why I'm being so melancholic. I'm scared for him. For us.

5.

TOM DIDN'T MEAN TO stop. Of its own accord, the ute just seemed to swing the change of angle into the lay-by, gravel popping under the tyres, a slide as he applied the brakes. He sat, hands drooped over the steering wheel, staring up into the driving mirror, the little rectangle like a photograph of the scene. Stones and dirt, a clump of weeds, a wire-and-batten fence. A slim white cross nailed to a post. There was a wreath of flowers, tattered, faded. Imogen and Lisa had put it there a week ago. The twenty-second of April, the six-month anniversary. Tom couldn't face it — not that, not any kind of ceremony. Let her be, let her rest. But he couldn't explain why he felt that way. He remembered Lisa's pained look as she resisted her urge to comment, saying everything with her eyes. *Talk to me.* What to say? What is there to say?

It was strange, though, having to drive past it like this on the way to Astra's. Was Hannah Creswell right? Had he picked Astra just because she lived here?

The bike was found there, on the edge of the lay-by, Carla's body a few metres further back. Was she riding it? The police didn't seem to know. The back wheel was bent and there was white paint scuffed into the rubber of the tyre. He tried to picture how the bike had lain, and Carla, too, beyond it from this position, half in the grass verge, her legs out on the road. In the rain. Was that how it was? He didn't know. She was still alive when Martin Wraggles drove along and found her and called the ambulance, still alive when the ambulance got there. She didn't have her helmet on. It was lying in the bushes, halfway down the river bank. Why was that? Why wasn't she wearing her helmet? He knew nothing except her body at the hospital, covered to the neck in a grey sheet, the bruises, swelling blue and shiny, deep gash across her forehead. Her face was so puffed up he might not have recognised her but for the streak of blue neon in her dark hair. The other injuries he did not see: the broken arm, the smashed leg, the lacerations to her left thigh and the chunk of glass buried in the flesh. Just her dead and battered face. And nobody knew how or why. Except the driver of the white car (two-door, late-model) heading south.

Hannah Creswell was supposed to be good at her job. And she had a method. Talk. We'll talk about it. Talk about your thoughts, your feelings, dreams, yourself, your situation. Dreams? You want my dreams? I have none, never did have many, just a fright or two from long ago, a childhood nightmare best forgotten. But, then, you're the expert. You know about this. You've been here before, with other people. Well, not quite here, perhaps. Not exactly. Because nobody has ever been here, at this moment, looking through these eyes. *If you had the answers. If you had all the facts. Would it make a difference?* Yes! He had wanted to yell that at her. Except the vehemence, the force of his impulse, was its own denial, like a recoil, kicking back and bouncing off the walls with the echo of a different answer. No; what difference could it make, in the end? What difference could it possibly make? Except that somebody knew. Somebody killed her. Somebody saw her in the last seconds of her conscious life come flailing over the bonnet, thump against the windscreen. Thoughts like that just wound him tighter, cold and hard.

Astra's place was on the eastern side of the road with the river at the end of the garden. A chilly spot, damp on the winter mornings when the valley filled with mist as if the water were on fire. The house was old. It had an iron roof, a bay window, a veranda and a flowerbed at the front. The long gravel drive ran down past a stretch of unmown grass, a child's swing, a slide and a seesaw, painted red, rusting.

He let the ute roll under its own momentum, his foot on the brake to hold it against the pull of the slope. Around the back of the house into the yard. He stopped in front of the garage with the little brown Toyota parked inside, got down from the cab and stood for a moment breathing the air. The sun was bright but a breeze from the valley took the heat of it away. If I feel the cold, he thought as the cool current brushed his forehead, I must be warm. The conclusion seemed strange, a paradoxical discovery that he couldn't quite believe. He felt nothing, really, nothing inside, but the surface of his body was still alive.

The workshop door was open. He went and stood there, leaning with his forearm against the jamb. She was at the bench with her pokerwork iron in her hands. A red T-shirt, blue denim overalls, a blue and white bandanna tying back her frizzy ginger hair. She looked up, saw him.

'Hi there, lover,' she said, smiling. Fair face, rosy cheeks, blue eyes. Astra always looked so warm and healthy. Maybe that was what drew him to her.

'Hello.' He moved around to her side of the bench. She put down the iron and turned to face him, lifted her arms as he reached out to her. Mouth to mouth, her lips and tongue.

He wanted her at once, the ache of it flooding through the numbness in him. Hands explored her back and buttocks through the thick cloth. Then he tried to drag the strap of the boiler suit down so he could get at her breast.

'Hey,' she said, pulling away. 'You're in a hurry.'

'Shows how much I missed you.' Holding on to her as she leaned back, looking into her eyes. She was grinning, pleased to be wanted.

'I'm trying to finish your order.' She tossed her head towards the bench. A scattering of wooden plaques in various shapes and sizes. Pokerwork texts and tendrils of design like flower stems entwined, little spots of colour for the blooms. *You are nearer to God in a Garden than anywhere else on Earth.*

'That's all right. It means I can come back tomorrow as well.' The words sounded hollow, false. He wanted her now.

She laughed. 'Anyway,' she said, 'you're the reason I'm late. I was making you a present.' She broke his hold and reached under the bench, took out an oblong strip of wood about five centimetres by twenty. It had a fluted edge and lots of scrollwork, little red flowers, a message. *To the Sexiest Man Alive.* 'Just so you know I appreciate you.' She held it up under her chin, like a number in a prison mug shot. Looked at him, eyes bright. She was awkward, blushing. Such a silly message.

'You're wonderful,' he told her. Leaning forward, he kissed her on the brow.

She turned away, moved over to another bench, pulled open a drawer.

'This is a reverse present,' she said over her shoulder. 'First you see it, and then it gets wrapped.' Her hands busy with a sheet of purple tissue paper and a pair of scissors. 'I know it's stupid giving you this. I mean, don't feel obliged to keep it or anything. You can throw it away if you like. I guess you'll have to. Just so long as you don't tell me if you do. But you wouldn't, you're not that kind of person.'

Words in an awkward rush, like a child. She needs protecting, he thought. She needs looking after. What on earth do you think you're doing to her?

'There!' Turning back to him, holding out the plaque wrapped in the purple paper with a silver ribbon, little silver rosette. He took it from her.

'Thank you.'

'I have a terrible confession to make, too. The real reason I'm late with the other stuff is that I had to do that one twice. You know how lousy my spelling is? Well, the first one of those I did, I missed the second E out of sexiest. Awful, eh?'

'Freudian slip,' he said.

'No! You're not sexist. I know sexist. I've been there. Have you had lunch?'

'No.'

'Do you want some?' Stepping closer to him.

He put his arms round her, kissed her again, felt the desire lift in him, and something else, too, something deeper, an opposite, guilt or fear, except that whatever it was made him want her more, somehow.

Afterwards, together in her bed, she began to talk about the accident.

'I asked around. Like you wanted. The people down the road. They didn't see anything. Not until the ambulance arrived.'

Too late by then.

'There's a woman lives by Scanty's Corner saw a white car going south,' he said.

'Mrs McIlroy?'

'Yes.'

'It scares me the speed people drive down here. I worry about Brad and Timmy all the time. I mean they're responsible kids, they know the danger, but there's always a risk. And Brad wants a bike now. What am I going to do about that?'

'It's hard,' he said.

She sighed. Fingers in his hair raking slowly back from his forehead. He stroked her hip, the outside of her thigh, the smooth, complex curves of her body. Made it better, all better. Not only that, though. There was more to it than that. He bent his head and kissed her belly, licked her, felt her chuckle, smelt the smell of her. Every woman had a different smell. And taste. And Astra's body was pink and white, her skin a little dry, a sandy quality. Like beaches and summer. Like hot sun and kids playing. Vincent and Carla, running to the water's edge and out into the waves. He and Annabelle sitting together in the sand. And Carla's shrieks so high-pitched, like a bird. It would be her birthday in three weeks.

'Kids . . . I don't know,' Astra said. 'It's awful, isn't it, how they can get you hurt.'

'Hostages to fortune.'

'What does that mean?'

'Just what you said. All the things that can happen to them and you're helpless to stop it.' He stroked the inside of her thigh and she lifted her leg to let him in between.

'Don't you really want lunch?'

'I don't need to eat,' he said. 'I have you.'

'You think you can live on sex?'

'I can try.'

Suddenly, she was twisting away from him, sitting up.

'Men are so stupid sometimes,' she said, walking to the door. She pulled a dressing gown from the hook and slipped it on. 'Soup and toast all right?' She pulled the belt tight, knotted it.

'You shouldn't be spending money on me,' he said.

'Soup and toast? Are you crazy?' Amazement, annoyance in her face. 'I can look after myself, you know. I do.'

'I'm sorry.'

She sighed, then grinned at him. 'That's all right. Come and talk to me while I make it.'

6.

GREENWISE GARDEN CENTRE IN Hammer Road, proprietor Thomas Anthony Marino. Monday and Tuesdays were busy times, cleaning up, ordering in after the weekend, except that these days the boss seemed to take less interest than he used to. He was distracted — you know, after the accident and that — and he left more and more of the daily running of the place to Billy Ryan, his right-hand man. Not that Billy minded. He was from Yorkshire — Hull, to be exact — and he had left school at fifteen, run away to sea, been here since he jumped ship in Winston, 1965. Billy was a plain man and he liked being busy. He took a plain man's pride in his knowledge, hard won over thirty-five years working in the gardens of the Winston City Council. There wasn't much about growing things that Billy didn't know, whether it was roses or rhododendrons, rhubarb or radishes. People now? They were a different matter. Weird buggers most of them. So when the boss came back from one of those long lunches, freshly showered with a far-away look in his eyes, Billy felt awkward, embarrassed, as if he'd done something wrong himself.

Standing there, the two of them, in the barn of the main building with its concrete floor and fret of steel beams up above. Indoor ferns and garden furniture, the racks of fertiliser, pesticides and herbicides, the seeds, the artificial waterfall that trickled in the quiet. They were in the middle of a problem with the rose order, when the woman walked in.

'Ay-up,' Billy said.

Tom looked too, saw her coming towards them. A

blonde, in black leather pants and jacket, a white shirt and a red scarf around her neck. Long slim legs, high-heeled shoes, a slinky movement to her hips. Not your average Greenwise customer. More like somebody in Hardy's, ordering people about, buying perfume and handbags. She was heading straight at them. Billy took fright. Did a runner.

Not Tom, though. Tom stood his ground.

'Do you people give advice?' she asked, stopping in front of him. Shift of her body, and a ripple, a sheen of light in her leather skin.

'It depends what you're looking for.'

Blue eyes, red mouth, cheekbones touched with rose. A long narrow nose with a flare to the nostrils. She was taller than he was by an inch or two but that was mostly the heels.

'My landscape architect's done me a plan but I'm not happy with it. I need a second opinion.' Eyes fixed on his, her face expressionless.

'Yes. I can do that for you.'

'You personally?'

'Yes.'

Her attention shifted, flicked over his shoulders and chest, the tag, with his first name, pinned to his jersey. Then back to his face. He was being examined, critically. For signs of competence.

'How much?' she asked.

He said nothing, deliberately held back, looked at her, met her gaze. He felt the stretch of the silence, the growing threat of the snap that would make their little struggle conscious. The tip of her tongue came out and flicked her upper lip.

'Forty-five dollars an hour,' he said, just in time.

She glanced away. 'All right. When can you come?

This afternoon?'

'Friday.'

'No. Friday won't do. Tomorrow.'

'What time?'

'Two.'

'Let me check.' He moved to the till and pulled out the appointments book. Tomorrow was Wednesday. He was free all day. He knew that without looking, but he didn't want to seem so immediately at her beck and call.

'Three-thirty,' he said.

'All right.'

He was about to ask her name but already she was handing him a card. It was white, printed in gold and black, a flowing, cursive font. Laura Kerrington. A land-line number and a mobile.

'Clisserford. It's the second place down Cox's Line. Well . . .' She blinked, correcting herself. 'Let's say it's the second house of any significance.'

'I'll see you at 3.30.'

'Fine.' She turned and walked away.

He watched her go, the sway of her hips, the little swell in her blonde hair, bounce with each stride. The electric eye caught her, and the doors opened. She stepped through into the open air, moved to the left. Bright writhe of light on her black back.

Tom slipped the card into his pocket, wrote the appointment in the book. For no good reason. There would be no others by tomorrow afternoon. Billy came scuttling back again. He hovered, twitching with curiosity, but he said nothing. Of course not. Billy wouldn't think it was his place to ask a question.

7.

LISA CROSSED THE LIVING room, kicking off her shoes, sat down in the armchair by the window and put her gin and tonic on the table beside her. The cat jumped onto her knee immediately. It had been waiting for her. She picked it up, her hand around its ribcage, and lifted it to her face, buried her nose in the soft fur behind its ear, felt the beat of its heart as she breathed in the smell of it, a dry, musky, dusty odour, big lungful like a drug. It didn't like that indignity, of course, and squirmed in her grip. She let it go and it gave a twitch and a wriggle and lay down in her lap, needle claws for a moment through the fabric of her jeans. She stroked it and it settled. Relaxed. Why not?

She leaned her head back on the cushions of the chair and closed her eyes. Heard the thud of her own heart then, felt the smooth warmth of the cat under her hands, the ripple of its purr. Black cat, soft and cruel. Are we cruel, cat? Moving as the mood takes us, needing no one. Except we do need, of course. More than we think.

She opened her eyes, slowly, looked at the room with its wood panel door in a blue frame, its off-white walls, the sofa and the other chair (oatmeal colour, buttoned cushions) and a big painting of a West Coast lake that Colin had given her for her thirtieth birthday. It was a small room and inconvenient; a narrow rectangle arranged around a fireplace in the long wall, a fireplace they never used. She and Tom had plans to gut the whole house and redesign it but they had never got around to it. Just as they had never got around to shifting the pine cones with the red ribbon and the string of fat silver beads that had been in the grate since Christmas.

A noise. The door opening. Thin, oval face between drapes of straight dark hair.

'Hi,' Imogen said.

'Hello, sweetheart, how's it going?'

Imogen came in, still in her school uniform — white blouse, grey tunic, black stockings. Tall and skinny, just a bunch of sticks. Yet she ate like a horse and, as far as Lisa knew, she wasn't in the habit of poking her fingers down her throat. She sidled into the room, her shoulders hunched. Stand up straight, Lisa wanted to tell her. Be proud of your body! But she kept quiet. What fourteen-year-old was ever proud of her body? What forty-three-year-old was, if it came to that?

'Well,' Imogen said, sitting down on the sofa. 'It's pretty average, I guess. I got an A in English but then we had PE. That's always a bummer. Humiliating.'

'Don't worry about it. Think about the English. That was good.'

Imogen nodded. Serious. Far too serious.

'Vincent called,' she said.

'Oh? Is he okay?'

'Fine. We talked. It was nice. You know, it's a weird thing. We never used to talk.'

'Sometimes it works that way,' Lisa said, thinking about the room across the corridor that no one opened any more, Carla's room stripped bare of everything that meant her except the single photograph on the bedside cabinet.

Imogen was staring at her shoes. She had her left foot on top of the right, heel on toe, as if they were the first two stages in a tower.

'What's incest?' she asked.

'Well.' Lisa was taken aback. Thinking, doesn't she know? 'I guess it's when members of a family have sex. Who shouldn't.' Feeble answer.

'I know that,' Imogen said. 'I want to know what combinations aren't allowed.'

'Well, father, daughter. Mother, son. Any combination where one person is descended from another. And then there's other combinations like brother and sister, half-brother, half-sister, things like that. I guess it's got to do with how many genes you have in common.'

'What if you have no genes in common?'

'Like what?'

'I don't know. Like me and Vincent.'

'That's illegal because you're under age.'

'What if I wasn't?'

'Are you serious?' She didn't quite shout it. She was glad she hadn't shouted it. You had to keep calm and cool and clear at such a moment.

'Don't be horrible,' Imogen said, turning on her big, moony, dark eyes. 'I was just wondering.'

'Well, don't!' It was a shout this time, or nearly, but she managed to stop herself, took two, three deep breaths. 'Just think of Vincent as your big brother, okay?' But that was no answer. You couldn't retreat into your own feebleness. She took another drink, finished the glass.

Imogen was slouched back now with her backside on the edge of the sofa, her legs stretched out, arms folded across her stomach.

'I'm sorry,' Lisa said, more calmly. 'I don't mind talking about it. If you want to.'

'It's okay. I was just thinking, before, about what's a family and what isn't. About Vincent and Carla. Last year, when Carla first came to live with us, I hated it, you know? I just wanted her to go away again. And then, after a while, I thought she was really great. And it was like, wow, here I am, I never had a big sister before, and now I've got one and she doesn't hate me. She likes me. And she's so cool. And now . . .' Imogen's eyes squeezed tight shut for a moment and then opened again.

'God, sweetheart, I know. It's the worst thing ever.' Lisa began to move, to go to the child and comfort her. The cat leapt from her lap. But then . . .

'Now it's just me and you and Tom. Are we a family?'

'Well.' Sitting back, pushed back. 'Yes, of course we are.' We're all there is, she wanted to say, but that wasn't quite true. 'And there's your father.'

'Yes, but that's not what I mean. The people are great, you know, as separate bits but . . . What is a family? Really?' The stare again, the big, helpless eyes.

'I guess it's complicated in the modern world. I guess it's partly biological and partly social, people living together, loving one another. I guess it's a matter of commitment. Any group of people can be a family if they want to.'

'But it isn't a matter of choice, is it? I don't have a choice. I don't have a choice that you're my mother and Dad's my father, and I didn't have a choice that you and Tom got together.'

'You could have made it really hard for us. You and Carla and Vincent. I'm very grateful you didn't.'

A shrug in response, an indifferent shrug, it seemed. Have I failed her? Lisa wondered. Of course. Because even if

I knew what her question was I couldn't answer it. Perhaps you always failed them on the hard questions. Like why you couldn't keep living with their father. Like why someone had to die. And thinking of Carla again made her realise that she might owe Imogen an apology.

'I've got something I need to talk to you about,' Lisa said. 'I've written a story about the accident.'

'That's okay.'

'You're sure?' Too late now, if it wasn't okay. 'There'll probably be a photo of the cross we put up. And the flowers.'

'Who cares? Everybody knows, anyway.'

'It's just that Ward's organising a road safety campaign. I thought I could help.'

'It's okay. Really.'

Was it? Something about the story made her feel uneasy. Was it her own reaction or Ward's? She remembered her conversation with him this afternoon, his hesitation, as if he felt bad about his interest in the subject. A road safety campaign would be good for his public profile, of course. Was he ashamed of exploiting their grief? No. Ward was always so open, so honest, so unlike a politician. It was the main reason he was successful. And he'd been deeply upset by Carla's death. She remembered him at the funeral. Ashen. Appalled. As if he could hardly bear to be there, it was so painful.

The door again. It was Tom, of course. The sudden sight of him, his dark hair, his beard, brought a twitch of relief. To know he was safe.

'Hello,' he said. He looked tired. There were bags under his eyes.

'Hi.' Imogen was standing up, twisting, unfolding. She looked at Lisa. 'Can I get you another gin?'

'Thank you, sweetheart, that would be really nice.' Lisa knocked back the last drop and gave her the glass, watched her turn to leave. 'Tom might like something too.'

'No,' he said. 'Not right now.'

He sat down in the chair, on the other side of the fireplace. Where he always sat, the two of them together.

The door closed behind Imogen.

'She hasn't forgiven you,' Lisa told him.

'For what?'

But she could tell that he knew for what. The cross by the roadside. The ceremony. Even now she felt angry that he hadn't joined in. It wasn't much to ask, was it? He couldn't still be so deeply bound up in his own feelings that no one else's mattered at all. Yet, how could she say that? How could she even think it?

'I should apologise to her again,' he said. 'Would it do any good?'

'It might.' Lisa sighed. 'How are you?'

'Stuffed.'

He looked stuffed but also relaxed somehow, sloppy, his limbs falling about as he laid his head back against the cushions of the chair. As she had done. She was tempted to ask him how his session with the counsellor had gone, but she held back. He would tell her if he wanted to. It was none of her business.

'You got my message?' she asked. 'About this evening?'

'Yes. What's the occasion?'

'No occasion. Sylvia just suggested we go round for a drink. Do you want to come?'

He scratched the back of his head, rubbed his palm over his face before he answered. 'I don't know. Maybe.'

'I'm going.' Although she wasn't sure why, now she thought about it. Colin, her ex, would probably be there, lapping up the booze, as if every gulp were an accusation. He and Larry winding each other up, getting sillier by the minute. Both of them teasing Ward, making him look lumbering and stupid when, in fact, he was essential to their lives and had been for thirty years. A strange business, the three of them together. Beyond friendship. They were more like lovers, a folie à trois. She knew it had to do with that camping accident in their teens but she had never understood it fully. And then, for a moment, she could hear Ward laughing. Huff, huff, huff through his thick moustache, his body bouncing up and down, his blue eyes watering, lift of his crippled hand to cover his mouth, as if he were ducking down behind it. Ward the hero, our most unlikely hero.

'Ward's running a campaign to get the speed limit on River Road reduced to 50.' She hesitated. The same flinch of fear she had felt with Imogen. 'I'm doing a story on Carla to support it. There'll be a photo of the site. Front page, I hope.'

'Great,' he said, as if he meant it.

The door opened. Imogen with the glass of gin. She had filled it too full and was gripping it in both hands, her attention on the brimming rim.

'Thank you, sweetheart.' Lisa took it from her.

The girl turned and went out again. Lisa watched Tom watching her go. The expression on his face, a look of doubt and pain. He doesn't deserve to be stuffed around by a teenager in a mood, she thought. But, then, that isn't fair to Imogen either.

'I'm sorry about the story,' she said.

'Why? If it does any good, write it.'

'I should have checked with you first.' Was that it? Was that what niggled her? Carla's death was private property and not some scrap of gossip to be swatted about in public places.

'What difference does it make?' he asked.

Lisa sighed. 'God, life gets complicated. Imogen was asking me before if we were really a family.'

'What's a family?'

'You, too?' She sipped her gin. It was way too strong. Thank you, sweetheart!

'I suppose a family is an evolutionary strategy for ensuring the survival of the species,' Tom said, in his best pontificating tone.

'Yeah, right. And on that basis, we're not a family, are we? Imogen isn't your kid, so why should you care about her? And why should you care about me, given that I'm not going to have any of your babies?' It felt dangerous to say that, to offer him the option of not caring, but the words were out before she could stop them.

He looked at her for a moment as if he were uncertain what to do. Then he gave her that grin of his, the teasing, sexy grin that made her squirm inside. 'You're still of child-bearing age.'

'Get real, buster!' A scornful laugh but then she thought, Good God, he might be serious. Fixing that permanently was just one of the things they'd never got around to doing. Maybe they could have a child, if they wanted to. And, just for a moment, the thought of it made her want it very much.

8.

WARD AND MADDY LORTON, wrapped up against the cold of the autumn night, walked the two blocks from their own house to the Hannerbys'. Safer to walk if they were both going to drink, and drink, after all, was the whole point, wasn't it? Ward felt the anticipation, his hopes for the evening, drawing him on like a scent in the air, like fresh-baked bread or roasting beef. You wanted to be there, to taste it, and the walk, in the cold, made it all the more desirable.

Larry and Sylvia's. The room with the white walls, the paintings, the bookshelves, the ranchsliders that opened, on a summer's day, to a terrace and the garden. Shut now, shadowy reflection, like a ghost out there of the world in here. There were three leather sofas and two chairs around a big low table, bottles and glasses and nibbles on the wooden surface. Colin and Heidi were here already, on opposite sides. Larry sitting in his usual spot, in the chair with his back to the windows, long legs stretched out, a whisky in his left fist.

Smiles and greetings as they came in, words like pats of reassurance. Ward felt a wrench in his chest, a little stab of happiness. His friends, warm and welcoming and all together, coming together, to the centre, which was this place tonight although it could have been anywhere that everyone agreed on. He would risk a lot for the chance of this, even the possibility of facing his own conscience. He stood at the table, looking down at the bottles. Help yourself. That was the rule.

A passable Aussie red and a white of some kind stuck in a plastic wine-cooler. The Gar Valley Sauvignon. Not too chilled? Beads of water on the green glass. He poured for Maddy, one for himself, felt the little flush of expectation around the root of his tongue. Maddy was sitting in the sofa, facing the ranchsliders, with Sylvia in the chair to her right. He lowered himself down beside her, gave her her glass, and then he lifted his own, sniffed at it, nostrils wide, huffing up a big dollop of the freshness. Sipped, rolled the liquid round his mouth. Nice and clean, lime pushing up against the gooseberry. Let it slide down. Long, smooth finish. Smacked his lips. Not bad. Yummy.

'So how are things with you?' Maddy said, looking round the room. She turned to Sylvia. 'How's Josie?'

'Oh, God!' Sylvia said.

'She is sick?' Heidi looked worried.

'She's a clever little minx,' Larry said.

Sylvia started explaining to Heidi, something about a praying mantis.

'We've just concluded a negotiation,' Larry went on. 'A hundred dollars' compensation and a lock on her room.'

'Maybe she should be a lawyer.' Ward was half listening to Sylvia, trying to get the gist.

'Ha!' Larry raised his voice. 'Ward reckons she should be a lawyer, Syl.'

'God no. One in the family's enough.'

'Keeps you in the manner to which you refuse to become accustomed.' He turned to Colin. 'Are women less corruptible than men? Or is it a class thing? I mean, here I am, a ragged-arse from South Shields, and as soon as I get a sniff of money I'm into it like a randy ape, whereas Sylvia, who's your average upper-middle-class doctor's daughter, born to privilege, gets desperately embarrassed because she has to drive a BMW.'

Larry leaned forward, picked up the bottle of Scotch, sloshed another measure into his glass, reached out for the water jug, just a touch to cut the spirit. Good old Larry. Face and bald head flushed already, gluey look in his eyes.

Ward sipped his wine and let his mind drift off into a vague contentment. Hazy images and blurred connections, something indistinct beneath the fuzz of satisfaction, something about his schooldays in the third form at Winston Grammar when he had first met the boy from South Shields, a thin kid with a floppy mop of blond hair, skinny legs and knees like cricket balls, an accent so thick you couldn't tell if he was swearing or not but you guessed he was, most of the time. Ward, the stumble-foot, the lumpy boy, had spotted a fellow outcast and taken his chance. And the two of them teamed up, against the world. A perfect pair. A pair of opposites. Fat and thin, slow and quick, dumb and smart. But it worked somehow. And then Colin came along and they were three. And it wasn't a crowd. Oh, no. It was better than ever. How had it happened?

He leaned forward to the table, to the little bowls of food there. Nuts and crackers and dips and olives. Corn chips and guacamole. Sylvia's guacamole? Ah! A scoop of a chip into the green paste, lifting to his mouth, the scrunch, the cold, the slide and sharp taste, smooth of avocado, twist of garlic, feather of paprika. That was it, maybe, the flick of paprika on the end of the vinegar. He should talk to Maddy about that.

'Justice?' Larry was in full flight, waving his drink-free arm. 'Justice is a ritual, that's all. It's like getting married. Blah-de-blah-de-blah-de-blah. I now pronounce you guilty of murder.'

'That can't be right,' Heidi said.

'Why not?'

The doorbell rang. Tom and Lisa. Ward felt a sudden panic. But no, it was all right. It would be perfectly all right.

Sylvia put her glass down on the table, stood up, started moving towards the door.

'He's just being cynical,' she said over her shoulder.

'If I wasn't a cynic, I'd have to be a fool,' Larry called, grinning, supping his whisky, a lip-smacking sup.

'But for truth?' Heidi gave a kind of shrug, like it was obvious.

Larry laughed. 'There's no truth in a court of law. There's only evidence. And evidence is a story told by a witness.'

'Forensic fiction,' Colin said.

'That's right, my friend. The Law is literature.'

Through the door came Lisa, tall, wearing jeans and a sweatshirt. Casual and confident and sexy in a rangy sort of way. Ward stood up to greet her, wondered, as always, quite how things would work with Colin and Heidi here in the same room, whether anything would happen.

'Hi,' Lisa said, scanning the group.

The greeting was for everybody, and Ward felt a bit foolish because he was the only person on his feet. But that was for a reason, of course. His awkwardness. He wanted forgiveness. But how could they forgive him if they didn't know what he'd done? Tom, coming in behind Lisa, making it worse. 'Good to see you,' Ward said, stepping forward. 'Great to see you.' Offering his hand, his bad hand. What else could he do? And everything in the room seemed to disappear except Tom's eyes.

Tom shook the hand carefully, a considerate touch, but there was still a little flare in the flesh, all the same.

'Ward, how's it going?'

'Good, good.' Ward found it hard to look at him but he managed it. Tom's eyes were difficult. They seemed to stare right into you and Ward had to remind himself that Tom couldn't really do that. He couldn't see and he wouldn't know.

Lisa was sitting down beside Maddy in the place Ward had left. Of course. She wouldn't sit next to Colin or Heidi. And Tom and Colin couldn't sit together. Ward picked up his glass from the table and moved around, lowered himself down beside Colin. 'How's it going?' he said.

'Lovely, mate. Just lovely.' A grin, a sarcastic sort of grin, that Ward didn't really understand. Colin and Heidi were sitting on opposite sides. As far apart as possible? A tiff there? Heidi was wearing a white blouse and black pants, her blonde hair tied back in a ponytail. Severe-looking. Serious. Ward didn't like the thought of the two of them fighting.

Tom and Heidi were sitting together, carefully not touching and not talking, although neither of them was conscious of the care they took. They were the odd ones out here, the interlopers, the Johnny-and-the-Jenny-come-lately, so it was perhaps appropriate, or ironic, that the two of them should be paired, however awkwardly, and listening now, as Colin told a joke.

It was a joke he had picked up from the Internet and he was telling it with the natural skill of a raconteur who found himself the centre of a group: the words coming easily, the tone rising and falling to match the rhythm of his story and the voices of his protagonists, his eyes flicking round his audience without actually seeing them, just touching their attention, feeling their attention, as a dog might stretch itself in the nourishing warmth of a fire. He was drunk by now, of course, his face flushed with wine. The flop of hair that he combed over his bald spot had begun to come awry. He was comfortable, confident. A creature in its element.

'So, the blonde in question goes into a shop and asks the shopkeeper if she can use the phone because she wants to call her mother urgently.

'"Fine," says the shopkeeper. "But it'll cost you five dollars." He is a grasping little swine, you see.

'"Oh, dear," says the blonde. "I've got no money and I really need to call my mother."

'But the shopkeeper insists.

'"I'll do anything," says the blonde, "only just let me make the call."

'"Anything?" says the shopkeeper.

'"Anything at all."

'So the shopkeeper locks his door, puts a Gone-to-Lunch sign in his window and takes the blonde into the back room.

'"Kneel down," he says.

'So she kneels down.

'"Unzip my fly," he says.

'So she unzips his fly.

'"Take it out," he says.

'So she takes it out.

'"Now do it," he says.

'"Do it?" The blonde looks at him a bit puzzled.

'"Yes. Do it!"

'So the blonde leans forward and she says, "Hello, Mother, are you there?"'

Laughter. They all laughed, even Sylvia, who had precipitated the joke by claiming that nothing could be dirty or prejudiced and, at the same time, funny. They all laughed except Heidi. And Tom. Tom had begun to laugh but then he sensed the tension next to him, the coolness. Was it physical, that shift in temperature? He turned his head a little to take in Heidi's profile. Her face was still, blank. No angry compression in the lips, no knot of tension over the bridge of her nose. The smooth cap of her golden hair gleamed in the light.

After a joke there is always silence, a second or two of silence, no more, because a joke is a story, like a trial, with a beginning, a middle and an end, and after an end you must pick yourself up and start again. At the stretch of this particular silence Tom turned to Heidi more obviously and said, 'What are your plans?'

She did not answer immediately, didn't move. The pause was long enough for him to look where she was looking. At Colin. But Colin was oblivious. He was leaning towards Larry, bending his head to catch a whisper. He was grinning. He seemed pleased with himself.

'Plans?' she said then, turning to Tom.

'How're the dahlias?' He was not sure why he had used the word 'plans'.

'I am not so busy at the moment. But I think I start lifting next week.'

A bit early? Perhaps.

'I can take more this year,' he said. 'If you have them.'

'That's good. You want them like last time? In the pots, when they bloom?'

'Yes.'

'We will talk about it. Colours etcetera.'

He noticed her eyes, how blue they were, and the length of her lashes. When she blinked they were like little golden awnings coming down. He was struck by her strangeness — not the fact that she was foreign but the sense of her being, warm and conscious and alive, as if the scent of her reached out and curled around him.

'I think I have a good one,' she went on. 'A semi-cactus. Red. Very big. Very dark.'

'I like the semi-cactus best. I always think they are the true dahlia.'

'It's not for sale this year because I don't know if it can divide. It's a wonderful colour, like blood. Of course, I can't show you. It is just a tuber right now.' A shrug of her shoulders, right hunched higher than the left.

'A baby.'

'Ah, yes.'

'To the baby.' He lifted his glass and she followed suit, a little clink, barely audible. She was grinning and he felt a quick touch of sadness, just the stroke of a feather. Was it hers or his own? He wanted to lean over and kiss her there, where the dimples showed at the corners of her mouth, the double-curl in the flesh at the side like quotation marks at the end of her smile.

'I have a photo,' she said. 'You can come and see my photo, if you wish.'

'I wish.'

'And I must thank you. I'm grateful that you take my stuff. It makes me feel like a professional grower.'

'You will be one day.'

'Of course. My Empire of the Flowers.'

This is the circle, these people around this table. If you look at it from the outside, you can see it for what it is, but from the inside, if you're a member of it, you know only the others filling your field of vision. Take Lisa, for instance. Right now, she looks across at Larry, grinning with his loopy grin and a mad glint in his eye, and at Colin, leaning towards him, eager with the urge of his own wit. She sees (does she notice?) that the top of Colin's polo-neck is not rolled properly. There is a diagonal ruck in the black fabric along the side of his throat. In the old days, she might have fixed that, perhaps as they stood in the hall before they went out. She might have reached up and straightened it, and maybe he would have put his hand on her shoulder as she did it. Maybe he would have said, 'Where would I be without you?' or something equally meaningless. Well, they both know the answer to that one now, although Lisa doesn't think it out consciously. Not at this moment. She sees but she isn't aware. She feels a kind of sadness but she doesn't know why. What she misses, in some part of her, is the right to touch. Not sex but the little moments that came with living close, the intimacy. These days she can kiss anyone in the room, except Colin.

The feelings play within the circle. The bonds have settled in over the years. None of it is realised but all of it is real. Lisa's relationship with Larry, for example. Way back then, when they were eighteen, they were in the same English tutorial and he asked her out. He was tall and narrow, like a reed, with shoulder-length blond hair and that same wicked grin, ironic and self-effacing, designed to draw you in and hold you off against the chance you might reject him.

Black leather jacket and blue jeans tight on his pipe-cleaner legs. And a motorbike. She didn't like the bike. It was too big, too fast, too much like giving up control. But she went to the movies with him, clinging on behind him like a monkey. *The Invasion of the Body Snatchers*. No memory of it now. No memory much of anything, even the kiss goodnight, his lips cold and smoky. Could there ever have been more to it, if she'd wanted to pursue it, if it hadn't been for her best friend Sylvia, wide-eyed and eager? My boyfriend? No, he's not my boyfriend. You can have him. But don't forget that I introduced you to him. Just as I won't forget that he introduced me to his best mate, Colin Wyte, who had a car, let me tell you. A Daimler Dart. Always a touch of class, our Colin.

But she wasn't thinking of such things. She didn't feel them even. They were no more than the murmur in the background of her everyday, the fabric of her mind, the tone of consciousness. Because even at the tender age of forty-three we forget more than we remember.

She sipped her wine and realised that Ward was looking at her, watching with that mournful way of his. He brightened up when she met his eyes and grinned at her hopefully, wanting attention in his usual way — a little obligation that drew her to him automatically. She leaned over towards him and he to her, his elbow jutting over the arm of the sofa, his scarred right hand resting stiff wristed on the leather, the last two fingers knuckled tight. She didn't really think about the hand, hardly saw it these days.

'Front page,' she said. 'With luck.' The sounds she made tasted strange, thin and sour, like a lie.

'Great!'

'I hope it'll help.'

'Oh, yes. For sure.' He nodded and swallowed, his larynx crawling upwards into the flab beneath his chin. He was pleased. She could tell he was pleased, but she did not know whether pleasing him was something she cared about.

'The police made a recommendation,' she said, because it seemed she had to go on speaking. 'In their report on the accident. A 50 k limit, all the way to Nick's Creek.'

'Did they? Who told you that? Your cop friend?'

'My cop friend.' Stan Andreissen. Was he a friend? She remembered his chuckle when she told him what she wanted, because he knew that she knew that even if the information wasn't exactly classified it was against policy to reveal anything at all except through official channels, in the proper form and wording. But Stan, of course, had the instincts of a spin-doctor. No other cop she knew could be quite so judiciously indiscreet in a good cause. And he was in love with her. She was aware of that, although she never could have said it, even to herself.

'Deep throat, eh?' Ward said.

And because of what she never could have said, she took offence, feeling an innuendo, something sleazy there. But, of course, that couldn't be right. This was Ward, the harmless one who never had a nasty thought, so decent you always felt obliged to him. The ambiguity brought a hesitation that stretched into awkwardness and the awkwardness into a need to pull away.

'So,' she said, sitting back. 'We'll see.'

'Yes.' A little hurt look on his face, as if she'd rejected him.

How could such a bumbling man be so sensitive? She didn't understand him or herself at this moment and it didn't matter. Or it wouldn't matter, in the long run, because all these little ripples in the force field of their feelings were without importance. Or, at least, without an ultimate significance. They were like weather in this tiny microclimate.

Larry was holding forth: ' . . . but you don't need any deep psychology to figure it out. Booze and linguistic poverty are at the root of most of it.'

'Linguistic poverty? What is this?' Heidi asked.

'Inability to express your feelings. I had somebody lose it with me the other week. Total apoplectic rage. What does he start screaming? "Fuck the fuck you fucking fucker. Fuck your fucking fuck, I'll fuck your fuck to fuck." And, believe me, this bloke's articulate compared to some of them.'

'This is like animals,' Heidi said.

'Well, that's right, Madam.' Larry grinning. 'Whip 'em into shape. Get 'em under control.'

Lisa was alert to this. She felt an expectation, waiting for the next absurdity. To judge? Or just to laugh?

'Law and Order,' Colin said.

'Ah!' Larry turning to him. 'Lawn Order? Keep off the grass?'

'Exactly, mate. This is the trouble with the modern world.' Colin rising to it, as he always did. 'We spend millions on a police force but instead of doing what they're meant to do, instead of keeping our lawns tidy, they're chasing criminals and dishing out speeding tickets. Speeding tickets, I ask you. Anyone would think a bloke didn't have the right to kill himself if he wanted to.'

The scream of an ambulance. The thought of it appalled her. Insensitive prick! Lisa looked across at Tom, but he didn't seem to care. Maybe he wasn't listening.

'Anyway,' Ward said loudly, grabbing the attention. 'Isn't it all supposed to be the end of the world? Didn't Quo Vadis say so?'

'Quo Vadis?' Sylvia asked.

'The one who made all the predictions,' Ward looking puzzled.

'You mean Nostradamus. Quo Vadis means "where are you going?" in Latin.'

'Well, that's right,' Ward said, looking confused.

'Ah, my friend!' Larry laughing. 'My pet, my monster. My dear old ignoramus. *Ignoramus ponderosimi*. I drink to you!'

And poor old Ward just sat there, grinning like a loon.

9.

THE NIGHT AIR WAS COLD, the sky clear. Maddy slipped her hand under Ward's arm, his good arm. He crooked it, giving her somewhere to rest her wrist as they walked. She liked it, that feeling of solidity, something to lean on that would not give way. She liked that he was big. Sometimes she worried that he carried too much weight, that he might have a heart attack at the office or the club, but these were momentary fears. For the most part, she had the same easy confidence in him that she had in herself. They had a good life, the kind of life she had always wanted, although she had never known she wanted it until she had it. Even now, perhaps, it was not exactly knowing. It was more that she didn't question any of it, didn't stop to wish or speculate that it might have been different. Other people tied themselves in knots over things like that — Sylvia, for example, and Lisa, too. Maddy could never understand it, although she cared too much for either of them to be critical.

The street was empty. Noise of their two pairs of heels along the pavement. Pale pools of light from the street lamps merging, dark shadows among the trees in the gardens. Yellow. Everywhere the light fell was a pale, dim yellow. Dirty yellow. A mucked-up colour.

'Is Lisa doing the story?' she asked.

'Yes.'

'Good.'

'The Progressives will want to take the credit.'

'Well, don't let them.' She gave his arm a little shake. It

annoyed her when he wasn't given his due. Of course, some of that was his own fault.

'Larry was in good form,' Ward said.

'Yes. Although I think he's a bit down. You know. I think that's why Sylvia asked us all over.'

'Why's he down?'

'Don't know.' Although the thought that came to mind was Polly Drafton, beaten by her husband till her bones cracked.

'Do you . . .' He paused, looking for the right words. 'What do you think Larry thinks of me?'

'You're his friend. You're his best friend. You and Colin.'

'Sometimes, you know, he says things. They hurt a bit.'

'Oh, Pookey, I know.' She squeezed his arm, for comfort.

'I'm not *that* stupid,' he said.

'You're not stupid at all!' She stopped suddenly and his momentum tugged at her, pulling her up on to her toes, swinging her around so they were facing one another. She reached out for him and hugged him, pressed herself against the mass of him, which seemed bigger than ever with the padding of his coat. She felt his hesitation for a moment as he wondered, as she did, whether anyone could see them, and then he was wrapping her up in his arms and holding her. She lifted her face and she closed her eyes, waited, and then the familiar brush of his moustache descended. It was damp and cold from the night air but then his lips came quickly after, warm and wine-tasting, and she felt the wanting inside her, deep down.

'He doesn't mean it,' she said, when her mouth was free again.

'I know.'

'He's got a hard streak, that's all. It's his background.'
'Background?'
'The way he was treated when he was little.'
'He doesn't remember when he was little.'
'That's what I mean,' she said. 'It would have to be really tough to force you to forget it.'

It was impossible to imagine where Larry came from. It was so different from what she had known herself, what any of the rest of them had known. Larry was reinvented. No sign left of the child he had been. No sign of the accent even.

'It's their wedding anniversary next week,' she said.
'Who? Larry and Syl's?'
'Yes, their twentieth. Next Friday.'
'Really? We should celebrate.'
'Yes.'
'We should put on a dinner for them, for the whole Tribe. At The Little Frog.'
'Yes.' A rush of feeling, love and gratitude and respect for his generosity, his great good-heartedness. 'You're wonderful,' she said.
'Oh, Poppet. Thank you. You're all I've got. You and the boys.'

For a moment she thought he was going to cry, which would have been a very strange thing for him to do.

The hill in Castor Road swept down to the traffic lights at the end of High Street. Amber. Colin planted his foot, felt the power, the smooth surge of the V6. The pull of the curve towards Victory Bridge.

'The light was red,' Heidi said, beside him.

'"Twas yellow.'

'It was red when you go through.'

That prim tone, always right, made him cringe a little.

'Hey, lighten up,' he said. 'It's after midnight.'

'And people are bad drivers after midnight. And you would fail the breathalyser, I think.'

'Takes more than a few wines to make me a bad driver.' Glancing at her, sitting with her head back against the rest, her face pale, calm, staring ahead. Relaxed, unruffled. Not bothered at all, was she? So why was she nagging if it didn't bother her?

Over the bridge and into the dark. The full-beam headlights splayed along the hedgerow on the left, the grass verge, the power poles, flick and flick and flick and flick, as the Jag slid down the booze-smooth tunnel.

'About some things I am more seriously than you,' she said.

'Serious.' He couldn't resist correcting her. '"I am more serious."'

'Don't pick my words. I mean there are things you do. Like driving too fast.'

He didn't answer. Didn't slow down, though, either. Damned if he'd slow down just because she said so. Keep the mood, the happy mood. But it was already slipping away.

'Like sexist jokes,' she continued.

'I'm sorry you didn't enjoy your evening,' he said, articulating carefully with just a soupçon of sarcasm. Un petit peu.

'Oh, I enjoyed. They're my friends. Nice people. I think you were not nice, though.'

'Get over it. It was a joke.'

'No, I don't mean the silly joke. I mean . . .' A lift of her hand, a gesture, caught it in his side vision. 'You drive too fast. You say it doesn't matter. You make jokes about the cops give speeding tickets. But they are chasing people who drive too fast, people like you. And it is somebody like you who killed Tom's daughter.'

'I did not kill Tom's daughter!' The bark of rage was a shock, like a blow to the head. Good God, where did it come from? Slow down! But he didn't want to. Couldn't. Not now. 'Anyway.' Fighting for control. 'How come you're so friendly with Tom, all of a sudden?'

She shrugged. 'We talk.'

'For half the evening.' They'd been very intimate, too. Little clinks of the wine glass? 'Don't you have any consideration for my feelings?' What feelings? What were his feelings exactly?

'We talk business.'

The corner coming up. He braked, felt the loss of power. Turned the wheel and the car swung smoothly into Cox's Line. The long stretch home towards the hills. He put his foot down. Ran for it.

'I can't help you,' she said. The same calm tone.

What was she talking about? 'I don't need help.' He needed consideration and loyalty. Just a little bit of loyalty.

'No, I mean I can't help when you are jealous,' she went on. 'Whatever I do, if ever I talk to a man, or even a boy who does not yet shave or even maybe a woman who is not entirely ugly, you are jealous. So, either I live only talking to the plants or I don't care.'

'You don't care? Well, fine. That's fine by me. You're a

free agent. Have it off with whoever you like.' As long as it's not Tom Marino.

'Maybe if we do more I would not need.'

What? What was that supposed to mean? 'Are you complaining about my sexual performance?'

'Complain? Oh, no. I am a grateful person.'

'What the fuck's going on, then?'

'Ah,' she said. 'Linguistic poverty. I understand it now.'

Larry sat sprawled in the chair, the glass still in his hand nearly slopping. Head back. Sylvia thought he had passed out or gone to sleep, but when her shadow fell across him his eyes opened.

'You okay?' she asked.

'They all gone?'

'Yes.'

He sat up, swayed, sighed with a lip-trembling splutter, lifted the glass, guzzled at it.

'Wonderful evening, was it?' he asked.

'What do you think?'

'Wonderful evening, wonderful, wonderful.' He sounded vague, empty. Drunk, of course. But he had many forms of drunk. He was drunk more ways than he was sober.

She touched him on the shoulder and he lifted his eyes, familiar eyes with that self-ironic twinkle — except this time there was something else, something behind them that frightened her. She sat down on the sofa nearest him, leaned forward, elbows on her knees.

'I haven't asked you how today went,' she said.

'Good.' He nodded. 'Good. Jackson's still trotting out the Holy Riverites. We must have done half the bloody congregation by now. Clones for Jesus. The men in their Hallenstein suits. The women in cotton frocks and cardies buttoned up to the neck, with those triangle scarves on their heads. And they all say the same thing.' His voice shifted into a quoting tone. 'Pastor David Drafton was a good man, a tower of moral strength to his flock. Could he have beaten his wife, then? Could he have raped her? No, no, no. Impossible.'

'How do you deal with them?'

'Oh, the jury doesn't have much sympathy. Bible-bangers like that are too weird. All you have to do is let them say what they believe. Polly's evil because the pastor said so. She has a falling sickness because the pastor said so, and the sickness accounted for her bruises. How else would she have got bruises like that?' He shrugged. 'No sensible person's going to believe them ahead of the medical evidence.'

'How's Polly holding up?'

'She just sits there. You've seen her on TV. Head bowed, dressed like them, the way that scarf makes her ears stick out. I was talking to her today. I was asking her why, why he called her a whore. It was a whore of the spirit, she says, not the flesh. Did he really stand her up in front of the congregation and call her that? Yes, she says. So did she think she was a scapegoat? Ah! And suddenly she comes alive. She looks at me and she smiles. God, you should have seen it. A slow lifting of her face except that the left side doesn't move as far as the right so that her expression twists into a travesty. The eyes and mouth of a pretty young woman, a simple girl, but here —' his hand lifted to his left cheek and jabbed there with open fingers — 'here the nerves are broken and the muscles are half dead and so her face is full of pain, a leering pain. It would've frightened kids. It would've set dogs barking.'

The words, the images they conjured, made her feel ill, as if that world, with its secret savagery, had suddenly become real to her. Human beings did this to each other. Creatures like herself, like Larry. She felt implicated somehow.

'How can you stand it?' she said.

He looked at her, a weary look, and then he gave a puff of a sigh. 'Don't know, to be honest.'

And she heard, in that helpless tone, the reason that he so often made mock of it, treated it like a game.

'Anyway,' he said. 'I can't win this one. The best I can do is get the poor bitch three years instead of fifteen.'

'That's better than nothing.'

'It's weird,' he said. 'She makes me think of my mother.'

How could that be? He always said he never knew his mother.

'You remember something?'

'No. No, no, no. It makes no sense at all.'

10.

FRESH. THE BLUE SKY. The lawn still white with dew. Colin stood on the terrace, the coffee cup in his right hand, saucer in his left, looking out over the garden and the paddocks beyond towards the hills in the distance, the band of mist and then the darker blue-grey peaks above. Every day this view was different, depending on the time he got up, the sunrise, the cloud cover, the moisture in the air. Every day had its own mood, its own colour. *What's today, then, Colly? Is it a blue day? Is it a black day, darling?* No, no. Today's not black, Mum. Today is a YELLOW! day. A big, fat smiling YELLOW!!! day. *Now how did we manage that?* Hard to say, given the general situation, but don't knock it. Just enjoy. On a yellow day, there's a special little ritual. We open the French doors and we step out here with bated breath, keep our eyes lowered until we're in position, feet apart, cup and saucer hoisted to the chest, and then lift — the cup and the gaze at the same moment. Sip and look. The coffee and the view.

Heidi made good coffee and today the fact of her making it was a good sign, an extra bit of yellow, because he could take it to mean that she forgave him, that last night's snapping didn't matter. The coffee and the view were proof against doubt and disapproval. Because a man can do anything on a yellow day. He can stand his ground and fight the fight. He can win the treasure *and* the princess. He can conquer the world — was doing so, in fact, as the view attested. Because a good chunk of what was spread out there was owned by guess who? That's right. Yours Truly, Colin Wyte. Gent. No, not 'gent', not precisely, because a gent didn't work and he'd worked bloody hard to get what he had. Ten and a half hectares, most of which was making money, leased to a dairy farmer further north. *Mustn't brag, though.* Why not? *People don't like braggers, Colly.* Oh, come on, now, who's to know? Isn't a chap entitled to a little brag, a teensy-weensy brag, as long as he does it in the privacy of his own home, contemplating his own view? Because the view was like a mirror, like a plate-glass window in which your shadow floated. It was like the look in the eyes of guests at a social function when you arrived with Heidi on your arm.

So enjoy the yellow while you can because it never lasts. It gets taken away and dealt with. The world is black and the joy of yellow is a fleeting thing, like the pulse of an orgasm in the dreary dark, and after it the suck of emptiness that drags you down, drown. Silver bubbles rising, blip, blip, blip. *Quiet, now, Colly. Your father can't concentrate if you make a noise.* He can't concentrate on what he's doing, doing nothing, staring at the newspaper. Why doesn't he turn the pages? *Shush, Colly. Shush now.* The memory tripped a need to act, an impulse not to duty and obedience but to love, a spasm of responsibility.

He drained the last of the coffee and, with a half-turn, bending at the knees, placed the cup and saucer on the small wrought-iron table to his left. Then he reached into the inside pocket of his jacket for his phone, flipped it open. Speed dial 22. He lifted his eyes back to the hills as it rang.

'Hello?' Imogen's voice, light and rising. A little roundness to the O, as if in special emphasis.

'Hello, darling.'

'Hi, Daddy.' A fall in tone. Disappointed? Hoping for

someone else? A friend? A boyfriend, maybe?

'What are you doing?' he asked.

'Hanging around. Waiting for my ride.'

'You're early, aren't you?'

'I've got music practice.'

'Well, I just called to ask you what you want for your birthday.'

'A horse,' she said. She didn't even have to think about it.

'A horse?'

'Yes.' The lightness back again, a breathlessness like the gasp of cold in a mountain lake. He could hear the unspoken plea floating there. He waited for it to rise to the surface. 'Please, Dad. Would that be possible?'

'Well,' he said. 'I don't know.' What would Lisa think?

'Just say it would be possible. Pleeeeeease. I'll love you for ever.'

'I'll think about it.'

'Great!' She took his answer for a yes, of course. Did he want that? 'Oops,' she said suddenly. 'I gotta go now. Seeya.'

He had meant to offer her a lift. Who was taking her to school this early? Tom? The thought was grit in a wound. He stole my wife. He's stealing my daughter. No. That was dumb. That was not a productive thought.

Colin closed the phone, slipped it back into his pocket, took a deep breath, looked once more at the distant hills. Feel the power, feel the clarity, he told himself. Because it was obvious. There was one thing Tom and Lisa couldn't do. They could not give Imogen a horse. They couldn't afford it. So who had she asked? Her Daddy. So, why not? She was his girl, his baby, and she should have what she wanted. Especially on a yellow day. A little growl of satisfaction lifted in him.

'What d'you reckon?' Stevie looked up from the monitor to Dart, the editor, who was hovering at his shoulder. Dart bent forward and peered at the front-page layout. The photo of the roadside with the cross and the garland, the flowers caught in a little lift of wind, forlorn-looking. Lisa had almost cried when she first saw the picture.

'Hmm,' Dart said, 'give me full page?'

Stevie moved the mouse, clicked an icon. The layout shrank. The banner appeared at the top, the ads down the left and across the bottom. Lisa was tense with the waiting.

'Yes,' Dart said, 'that's good.'

Gotcha! she thought.

Dart stood up, glanced at her, his black brows knotted in a frown. She wondered if she'd said something inadvertently, made a noise out loud. But then Dart often glowered for no reason that anyone could see. He turned away, back to his desk.

'Right on!' Stevie was busy with the mouse.

She felt strange, a lightness in her head, a slow cold creeping through her. For a moment she was scared she was going to faint, so she started walking, one pace, two, towards her desk. Lifted her hand to her face. It was shaking, a shudder through her spine and shoulders. She stopped, leaned forward, hands on the top of the stationery cabinet to support herself. She was going to throw up. No!

'Are you all right?' Tracey was beside her, arm around her.

'Yes.' The nausea began to ebb.

'Do you want something? Water? Let me get it for you.'

'No, it's all right.' She closed her eyes, swallowed, deep breath, let it out again. Fine.

'Menopause,' she said, grinning at Tracey. 'It must be.'

'Hot flush, was it?'

'More like a cold one, actually.'

'Is there such a thing?'

Lisa looked across the newsroom: the workstations crammed together, the view through the high windows of the western sky, grey like half-cooked meat. Tracey was talking about her mother and hot flushes. How old was her mother? Fifty-five?

Lisa stood up straight. The fizz of whiteness smeared her vision briefly at the edges. Ignore it, she told herself. It's nothing. So she walked a steady walk back to her desk and sat down. Tracey was watching her. Smile, then. She managed it. Everything's just peachy, see?

Everything was normal. Dart on the phone, leaning back in his chair, his foot resting on the bottom drawer of his desk left open for the purpose. Stevie, busy with the layout, peering at the screen. Tracey back in her place now too, her blonde-brown head just visible above the bookshelf beside her workstation. What could you do, where could you go, except the next story?

On the side frame of Lisa's computer monitor was a yellow stickie with the initials, L K, and a phone number. She pulled the steno pad towards her, picked up the pen. Dialled the number.

'Good morning. This is Laura Kerrington.' A cool, well-modulated voice, formal but welcoming at the same time.

'Hi. This is Lisa Cairnes from the *Durry Advocate*. I'd like to have a chat with you, if I may.'

'Oh?' A shift in tone. Suspicious?

Lisa felt the lingering dizziness, like a cloud of gas

diffusing slowly. 'Is this a good time?' she asked.

'For what?'

'To talk. We're thinking of doing a piece on Little River Lane.'

'For heaven's sake!' The scorn was mild, amused, curious that anyone would be concerned with such a piece of trivia.

'I thought perhaps you and your husband would like the opportunity to give your side of the story.'

'You don't need to involve my husband.'

'Maybe you could give me your view then.'

'No, I don't think so.'

Well, stuff you, Lisa thought. 'I understand you have a boundary dispute with Max Hosche,' she said quickly before the woman could get away.

A pause then. Go on, hang up, if you dare.

'No,' the woman said. 'I don't believe we do. I believe we have a trespasser.'

'His argument is that the course of the river has moved and that part of what you claim as your land is actually public property.'

'I know what his argument is.' A little huff of a sigh. It was all too, too tiresome, darling. 'Look, if it were really just a matter of one side of a river bank versus another, then, of course, we would come to an accommodation. Like good neighbours. However, it isn't as simple as that. He's a Peeping Tom.'

A little pause. Lisa stared at her steno pad, felt only confusion. Carefully, in her best shorthand, she wrote Peeping Tom. She thought of Max Hosche, his hand dry and scaly but warm, too, when she shook it at their parting. Wicked glint in his eye.

'Tell me more,' she said.

'He has binoculars. In fact, I think he has two pairs of binoculars. One for seeing in the dark.'

'Infra-red?'

'If you say so. He's quite blatant about it. He stands on the bank above the river and watches our house. And, in addition, I found a muddy footprint on the veranda by one of our windows. It wasn't my footprint. Or Monty's. And it wasn't the gardener's. So?' A verbal shrug, case proved.

'When did this behaviour start?'

'A few months ago.'

'Was it before or after you got into a dispute about the boundary?'

A little laugh. 'Oh, I see. You think his behaviour is retaliation.'

'I was wondering why he did it so blatantly, that's all.'

'And of course he's an interesting old man, a character, and we're just a couple of newcomers from the city, moving out here, buying up land. Obviously, he's the victim. Local Hero stands up to the Townies. Isn't that the story?'

Lisa felt a surge of irritation, but it was defensive, she knew. She couldn't deny she was on Max's side. The insight hurt, especially when it came from someone who sounded like an ad for Revlon.

'How would you like it,' the voice went on, 'if someone was watching you through binoculars?'

'I could draw the curtains.' Oh, God, no! Lisa thought. Why did I say that? I'd kill somebody who said that to me.

'Well, I don't want to draw the curtains, as it happens. One of the reasons for coming here was so I don't have to draw the curtains.'

'I'm sorry,' Lisa said. 'That was out of line.'

'Good. I'm glad you think so. Look, this is just a stupid situation. I don't want the old man arrested. I mean, he's untidy but he's kind of quaint, in his way. But I won't have him interfering with my quality of life. That's just it, as far as I'm concerned.'

Click. The line went dead.

Lisa spun in her chair, leaned back. 'Aargh!' she said.

'Problems?' Dart was looking at her.

'Bitch!' she said, 'fucking toffee-nosed bitch!'

'Language, darling!' Stevie now, wide-eyed, mouth down. Tracey, too, peering over the bookshelf.

'Why is everybody looking at me?' Lisa demanded.

'Perhaps because you're making an exhibition of yourself,' Dart said.

On the steps of the Durry Branch of the National Bank, Tom Marino bumped into Martin Wraggles, the man who found Carla as she lay dying. Martin was thin and grey-haired. He had a big nose and buck teeth and was taller than Tom by a good six inches.

'Tom, hello.' He offered his hand. These two were strangers before November. Now their lives were for ever tied together by a knot of memory. And because they lived in a small town they met from time to time and came face to face with what was real.

'Martin. How are you?' They looked at each other but they didn't see what you or I might see if we looked at them — the pain in their eyes, the cast of their mouths. They didn't see anything, except a flash of recall. For Martin it was that moment when the thing near the verge on the opposite side of the road suddenly became a foot, in a black shoe. He felt the horror that he felt then. He felt the guilt that he could do nothing for the girl as he waited for the ambulance, as the paramedics tried to revive her, as the police took his statement and then suggested firmly that he should go home now. Was he capable of driving? For Tom, it was the time when Martin introduced himself at Carla's funeral to which he had been drawn by that same sense of helplessness, and Tom, too, felt what he felt then: a gratitude that there was someone with her to hold her hand and a fierce stab of jealousy that it was Martin Wraggles and not himself and, then, after a brief delay, a burning need to know.

'I'm okay,' Martin said. 'Not looking forward to winter, though. Can't seem to take the cold these days.' He put his hands in his jacket pockets, shivered, turned his head, looked along Cross Street towards the hills on the other side of the river.

'Thanks.' Tom didn't even realise what he'd said, that it made no sense as a response to Martin's words. The questions in his head, like a bag of spiders' eggs, were hatching quickly. Have you remembered anything more? Did you see the white car? You must have seen it. You were travelling north. It must have come towards you with its smashed-up headlight. Maybe the windscreen broken, too. How could you have missed it? . . . Did he speak the words out loud or only think them?

Martin looked at him and shook his head. 'I'm sorry, Tom.'

And Tom felt shame. His thoughts had been importunate. He'd lost it there, just for a moment.

11.

THE CENTRE OF THE world was Maddy Lorton in her conservatory with her telephone, her Organiser, her list of calls. She sat on a wooden sofa stuffed with blue cushions, a cane table beside her with a copy of *Cuisine*. Around the sofa and the table was the red-tiled floor, the wrought-iron stands with the pot plants, bromeliads and ferns, the whole space soaking in the pale sunlight through the glass panes. And outside was the garden, lawn and shrubs, the plum tree with the remnants of the swing that the boys hadn't used since Donovan was how old? And beyond the garden came the neighbourhood, the houses on The Rise, the suburb and the town itself, the town of Durry, and beyond that again the country, the nation and the circling sea, the planet Earth with all its troubles, and then the rest of it, whatever it was, however big it was. Because for practical purposes (and 'practical' here means the basis of our thoughts and actions) the world is just the reach of a mind.

On this particular morning, Maddy's reach was maybe ten square kilometres to the town and its immediate environs and to the sundry rooms containing telephones with their attendant people waiting for her call. Well, not exactly waiting, of course, but most times when you make a call you assume that the other person is there and available to take it otherwise you wouldn't bother, would you? On this particular morning she had been doing well. Eight of the people on her list were ticked off and six of them had said yes. She had the beginnings of her three sub-committees: Art and Craft, Performances, and Literature.

'Good morning, Trevor. This is Maddy Lorton.'

'Ah, Maddy. How are you?'

'I'm well Trevor. Have you got a moment?'

'For you, Maddy? Of course I have.' Silly idiot.

'Do you know what's happening with the theatre in late October?' she asked.

'October? Arhm.' His response was guarded. 'Nothing definite. Caroline wants to do *Private Lives* later in the year but Marshall's desperately keen on *Noises Off*.'

'Have you thought of doing something for the Arts Festival?' Her sweetest, naivest tone.

'Arhm.' A fumbling pause. 'Well. You know, after last year . . .'

'Oh, Trevor. Absolutely. It was a shambles and the theatre was treated really badly. Especially you and Marshall. But I just think it's so sad if we have a cultural festival in the town and there's no drama in it, don't you? I mean, the theatre is so very active. It makes a fantastic contribution. And we have everything else.'

'Well . . .'

'What would it take for you to be involved?'

'Maddy, I swore I'd never be involved, ever again.'

'Not even if you were a member of the Performances sub-committee and could really say your piece?'

A pause, as he thought about it.

'Who else is on this committee?' he asked.

'So far? Meremea Pettisen, Jilly Dace, Peter Harringday and me.'

'Jilly who?'

'Dace. She's young. Very smart. Very up-front. She has connections with the Youth Group and the Marae.'

'You're casting your net wide, aren't you?'

'Art and culture isn't just watercolours and recitations, is it? I want to get everyone involved, the whole community. Rock concert, chamber music, the Marae. Let's make it really vibrant and exciting.'

'Hmm.'

'What have you always wanted to do in the way of theatre?'

'Well . . .'

Caught him now. Don't let him suggest anything, though. It might be way off beam. Like Artaud in French. 'Whatever it is, this could be the opportunity,' she said. 'We're just on the point of working out the programme.'

Something, a movement at the corner of her eye. She looked up.

Donovan, her youngest, was in the doorway, his grey shirt hanging half out of his shorts and his hair mussed. There was a graze on his left knee.

'There are any number of possibilities,' Trevor was saying in her ear. Was that what he said? She was fighting her instinct to leap up and fuss over her son, who was standing there, staring at her. But no, he was moving now, turning away.

'Let me call you,' she said to Trevor. 'When I've got the rest of the committee. All right?'

A reply. It was something about being unwieldy. The committee?

'I think six is the right number, don't you? I thought of asking . . .' Who? She couldn't think who for a moment. 'Alistair. Alistair Oxeley, you know him?' Go away. Please, go away.

'Well, yes,' Trevor said. 'That's a good idea. He's very busy, though.'

'We can only ask. Shall I call you then? For a meeting? Early next week?'

'Monday or Tuesday.'

'Fine. I'll get back to you. You know, I'm sure we can make this thing really hum.' Hanging up. Was he hanging up?

'Jolly good.'

Push the button, turn the phone off.

'Donny!' She got to her feet, hurried after him. But Donovan hadn't fled. He was in the living room, with his back to her, staring straight ahead of him.

'Are you all right?'

'Yer.' Except he wasn't, was he?

'Why are you home at this time of day?'

'I got a headache.'

She moved around him, so that she could see him better. There was a puffiness, a touch of blue in the pale skin above his left cheekbone.

'Have you been fighting?' She could hardly believe it was true.

He didn't answer. Turned away.

'Donny, darling.' She touched his shoulder, felt the damp sweat, chill in the fabric. Where was his jersey? 'What happened?'

'I hit my head,' he said, lifting his hand, fingering the back of his skull.

She touched him there herself, felt the lump. He winced. She tried to look, but he was as tall as she was these days and she could not see clearly.

'Lovey, what happened?'

'I fell over.'

She didn't believe him. 'What about your eye?'

No response.

'Did you black out?'

'No.'

He was not concussed then. Probably not.

'Look,' she said. 'Go and lie down. I'll bring you something for the headache.'

He turned, moved away, doing what she told him, which was a worry in itself.

So she made a cup of tea and took it to him on a tray, with a couple of paracetamol, a glass of water, a big piece of chocolate for comfort. Knocked on his door. She remembered to knock.

He was lying on the bed, fully clothed still, but at least he had taken his shoes off. She put the tray on his bedside cabinet, sat down beside him. He rolled his head on the pillow, looked at her with sad, blue eyes. He seemed like he was about to cry. The bruise on his cheek was more obvious now.

'Here,' she said, picking up the glass and the painkillers, feeding them to him as he lay propped on his elbows. One and a gulp of water, two and another gulp. He lay back down, closed his eyes.

'This happened at school?' she asked.

He nodded.

'At morning break?'

Another nod.

'And it wasn't a fight?'

'Please, Mum. Don't make a fuss, okay? Don't do anything.'

'What would I do?'

'Complain. Go down there.' I know you, he might have said. He was right, of course. She was already thinking of what she would say to the headmaster when she confronted him.

'Did you talk to anyone, any teachers?'

'No.'

'You just left?'

Another nod.

'They'll wonder where you are,' she said. 'They'll need to know.'

He didn't answer.

'Drink the tea. It'll make you feel better.'

She got up, went and opened the cupboard above his wardrobe. Reaching up on tiptoe, she pulled down one of the spare blankets, took it back to the bed. She was about to cover him with it when she noticed his knee again. Black marks on the white skin, little smears of red where the blood had dried. So she went and fetched a bowl of warm water and some disinfectant, cotton wool and a box of band-aids, big ones. He was drinking the tea when she got back. Good, she thought.

'You don't have to tell me,' she said, 'but, of course, if you don't, I'll only invent something. I mean, people have to have explanations, don't they? Even if they make them up.'

He didn't answer. Just gave a twitch as she bathed the graze.

'So what I think happened is some yobs got hold of you. Bullies.'

It had happened before, when he was smaller. He was not like Damien, quick and athletic. Popular. He was a pudgy boy, like his father, and he had knock knees. She was realistic enough to see these features clearly and to know that other people thought them unfortunate or pitiable. She could see how they saw him, but she didn't agree. Looking at him now, she felt that churning feeling, love and fear and anger, that always came when one of her boys was hurt.

'Am I right?' she insisted.

After a second or two, he nodded, not looking at her.

She stripped the covering from the band-aid and spread it over the graze.

'Does it happen a lot?' she asked.

'What?'

'Bullying. Does it happen to other kids?'

'A bit.'

'And who does it? The older ones?'

'Sometimes. Not always. There's a bunch of kids.'

She unfolded the blanket, spread it over him, tucked it round his legs.

'I think we should encourage these people to stop, don't you?'

12.

THE HOUSE WAS IN the grand style: two storeys, each with a veranda sweeping away from the central tower of the entrance. The weatherboards were white with grey trim, not a garish, dazzling white but a smoothed-out tone, a touch of green in it. Tom stopped the ute in front of the wide grey steps, got out on to the gravel of the driveway, looked around. Sniffed the air. Cool air, the smell of rain. To his right, between the house and the road, was a patch of lawn dotted with azaleas and rhododendrons, tight pale leaf buds just visible on the bigger trees. And all above a grey sky, with the clouds moving in a brisk nor'wester. He thought of Martin Wraggles. Can't seem to take the cold these days.

'Over here.' Laura Kerrington was standing in the driveway by the corner of the house. She wore a maroon anorak and jeans. Hands in her jacket pockets. He walked towards her but she turned away and headed off out of sight.

So he followed her, round the corner and down the side. Trees on his left, fruit trees in rows — apples and pears and plums, by the look of it — and two long wire-strand fences measured off with the stumps of grape vines. Behind the house, the drive ballooned into a turning circle before a row of garages, an extension to the building — maybe it had been a stable once. At the end of the row was a lean-to with a grey concrete step and a grey-painted door. She was there already, mounting the step, opening the door. He followed her inside.

A space, about two by four metres, and a smell. Blood and bone. On the back wall there were floor-to-ceiling shelves stacked with equipment and chemicals: fertiliser, Bordeaux mixture and Derris dust, a back-pack sprayer and a chainsaw on the bottom shelf. A roll of plastic weed-matting stood in one corner leaning against a cardboard tub of lime. Opposite the shelves, down the other long wall, was a bench with a row of windows above it. A view over the paddocks to the hills in the distance.

She had unzipped her jacket but her right hand was still in her pocket. Her left rested on a big sheet of paper, the only thing on the bench.

He stepped forward. 'This is the plan then?'

'Yes.'

It was not so much a plan as a drawing. A curving band — the bed of the stream — cut off the top right-hand corner. Below this was a shaded area labelled 'Existing Garden' in a spiky script. To the left, covering most of the paper, a sketch of curving paths and beds and two roundish shapes labelled 'Mound 1' and 'Mound 2'. Cross-hatching of different textures indicated plants. At the bottom of the page a series of elevations: north-west to south-east, and north to south through each of the mounds. The planting notes were rudimentary: ferns, flowers, shrubs, trees.

'This is the area, here,' she said, pointing out of the window. 'Directly in front of us.'

The ground sloped gently down to the stream about two hundred metres away. It was marked by a line of scrub and rushes, angling off to the north-west. Nothing in front of it but grass. Nothing beyond it but more grass, green that layered into the misted grey of the hills.

'It bores me to death,' she said. 'I want something to look at.'

He examined the plan, trying to envisage what its implementation would mean. Two mounds. The one to the left was six metres high. The other, to the right, would be closer and smaller. Between and in front of them a kidney-shaped lawn and curving paths. A gazebo in the lee of the larger mound.

'Who did this for you?' he asked.

'My architect. I asked him for some ideas. This is the one I like best.' Her hand, on the bench beside the paper, had red nails. There were rings on three of the fingers, flashy rings with gold and diamonds.

'This is a big project,' he said.

'Yes, I'm aware of that.'

'You're going to excavate to build the mounds?'

'Yes, I believe so.'

'Then you need to be careful. These elevations look a bit extreme to me.' He tapped the plan. 'The water table's quite high here, so if you dig too deep out towards the stream you're likely to create a bog, especially in winter. You wouldn't want that too close.'

'Couldn't we plant it? Make a feature of it?'

'Sure, if you have a liking for mosquitoes.'

'Hmm.' The hand lifted, disappeared back into the pocket.

'But really,' he said, 'it looks fine. And you could always truck in some of the fill if you had to.'

'I need someone to take care of this for me. Do you want the job?'

'As project manager?'

'Call it what you like.'

He looked at her. She met his eyes directly, neither frank

nor dismissive. There was a stillness in her face like a mask, the nose finely carved, the lips at rest, a dark seam in the red wax. No hint. No offer. Strictly business.

'Why me?' he asked.

She blinked. Long lashes. Maybe the question disconcerted her.

'Because you're local, on the spot.' She paused for a moment. 'Because you seem to say what you think. And because what you say sounds sensible.' The suggestion of a smile then. 'And lastly, I suppose, because at forty-five dollars an hour you seem to be value for money.'

'When do you want it done by?'

'When can you do it by?'

'Depends on the weather. Three months minimum.'

'Two.'

'It depends on the weather. And I have a business to run. I can't do this full time.'

'No, I appreciate that. Let's say July the fifteenth.' The same pale smile. 'Depending on the weather.'

'Do you want to draw up a contract?'

'Do you?'

'Do we trust each other?'

'Ha!' It was a laugh like a little gulp. A lift of her chin, showing her throat and the underside of her jaw. 'This is a business arrangement,' she said, eyes on his. 'Why shouldn't we trust each other?'

'So how would we work it?' he asked.

'You tell me what you need, how much it'll cost and when it's going to happen. I'll agree, or not, as the case may be, and I'll pay the bills. You charge me for your time every month.'

'Every fortnight.'

'All right.' Watching him still. 'When can you start?'

'As soon as I can find someone to do the excavations.' He looked back out of the window. 'It's going to be a mess for a while.'

'That's why I don't want it to take three months.' A pause to reflect on the arrangement, to allow it the dignity of reconsideration. 'So?' she said. 'Will you do it?'

'Yes.'

'Good.' She held out her hand and he took it, small, warm from her pocket. Smooth and dry.

Looking at him with her head on one side, an oddly girlish expression. 'I think it'll work out fine,' she said.

Of course. Why not?

Say you're a man and you have a daughter and she's sixteen. Her hair's done differently these days. It's asymmetrical, short on the left to show the black-fuzzed skin, the bony skull behind her ear, long on the right so that it hangs in a thick screen over her forehead and halfway down her face. She's dyed that bit blue, bright blue like an electric spark. When she goes out now, to the movies or to parties at her friends', her face is pale, the health painted out of it, and her lips are darkly red. Wide, dark mouth that tries to keep its cool but can't help jumping into grins or gasps or twists of disapproval. So you look at her, the way she's changed, the way she moves now, skinny limbs becoming graceful, and you're frightened, you're appalled. You try to take comfort in all the things she still does, like her homework or going to the library on a Saturday afternoon, like turning to you with her eyes full of that puppy-dog appeal when she wants something, but none of it helps. Because she's beautiful. Not in the way she's always been, not merely because she is your child, the offspring of your being, focus of your love and care; she's beautiful now in a different way. She's beautiful now in a way that other people can see, that men can see, young men and old, and you know that because you can see it too, looking at her as a man might look. You can't help seeing it and, therefore, you can't avoid the implications. Because you can't now treat her as you used to, even a few years ago, when you could grab her round the waist and throw her in the air and make her scream in protest and delight. And it's not just her size or her new-found dignity or the fact that she menstruates and is technically a woman. No, there's something else. An ambiguity, a confusion. It's there in the sudden shift in her expression as she checks her impulse to fling her arms around your neck and hugs you more discreetly instead. It's there in your doubt, in your fears for her safety, in your growing sense that she has a right to her freedom. And the world at large is loud in its condemnation of incest and child abuse, and all that stuff annoys you because it feels like an unjust accusation, a prurient insistence that you think about the unthinkable. Because the fact remains that here you are, hovering round her life like a hopeless lover, feeling inadequate and rejected and jealous of any male who looks at her. Because she's beautiful and you can see it.

Not always, of course. She can be a pain in the arse sometimes. She can be wilful and stubborn, and she has a sharp tongue on her and enough intelligence to make it hurt when she decides to use it. She can see right through you. Why not? She's known you long enough, all her life, and she's grown enough in her independence to feel the first cold seep of disillusion. But the sarcasm and the sulking are ambiguous, too. They're irritating and they're tedious but you also feel relief in them because they show she's still a child, protesting at her powerlessness, pushing at her boundaries. One day she'll realise she doesn't have to take any of this shit any more, that she can just walk out, if she wants to. And knowing that, seeing it could happen and, indeed, that in some sense it ought to happen, you begin to make a new adjustment. You begin to imagine what it might be like to have an adult daughter, to watch her from a distance, to see her move through the world with the intelligence and the serenity and the confidence she shows in her better moments, to take pride in her achievements, to see her happy and fulfilled in whatever endeavour she chooses to pursue. She'll go to university. She'll have a career. She'll marry. Will she? Perhaps. Perhaps she'll have a child. Your grandchild, strange to contemplate. Not something you've ever thought about before because you've never had a sense of dynasty or continuity, flesh to flesh, atom to atom. But if we truly are just creatures, just one of the many species on this planet, then that's what it's all about, isn't it? Whether we like it or not. So you hold that thought. You hold it lightly, secretly. It's not a hope, because it isn't something you could say you wanted or, even less, needed. You still feel your justification should be here and now and not there and then in a future time that someone else (your daughter) has control over. And yet the thought helps you to make sense of it. Her interest in boys, their interest in her. She will need love. She deserves it. She'll find someone. She'll have a child. So what will her child be like?

Impulse is just an action that we cannot quite explain, although there may be good reasons for it, like the possibility of improving the business, of cutting costs by finding cheaper sources of supply, and bad reasons, too, like her golden hair and the warmth of her thigh next to yours as you sit on a sofa talking about her dahlias, or the two little hooks, her dimples, at the corner of her mouth. Whatever the case, driving back, down Cox's Line, it might be very easy to turn off at the house with yellow brick walls. It might even be inevitable.

'Tom. Hello.'

'Hi.'

'Come in. I'll make some coffee.'

And doubtless, as she ushered you into the kitchen, you wouldn't need to ask yourself what you were doing. There. Then. You could just be in a space that smelled of fruit and clean wiped surfaces. Cream paint and a brown-tiled floor. The skylight cast an angled shaft of brightness, big beam like a sloping stone. There was a rimu table and a set of chairs with raffia seats. So sit.

She was at the sink with the kettle. Her body slim and straight, a cream-coloured sweater, blue jeans, bare feet on the tiled floor.

'It's so strange,' she said, glancing at him. 'I was thinking about you.'

'Oh?'

'And then you are here.' A little smile, but then immediately she turned to the coffee grinder, drowned out any chance of a reply. So he waited, watching.

'I've been at the Kerringtons',' he told her, when the noise stopped.

'What are you doing there?'

'Landscaping.'

'Ah. Laura has big plans, I think.'

'Big plans.'

'What would you like? An espresso?'

'Please.'

She reached up to a cupboard to take down cups. The stretch of her arms, the curve of her breast under the sweater. She turned to the machine. A hiss of steam. Standing there, still, in the shaft of sunlight. Hair like an angel. Or the sleek, golden feathers of a bird.

She came towards him, a cup in each hand, placed them on the table, sat down. A bloom of rose on her cheekbones, faint dust of freckles over the bridge of her nose. A healthy, natural look. Like Astra. Not like the other one, Laura, with her mask. She smiled again. Is that why I'm here? he wondered. For a smile.

'Thank you,' he said, picking up the coffee.

'So?' A light tone. Watching him over her cup, her eyebrows raised. But if she had been thinking of him, she must have had a reason. Why couldn't they use her reason? 'How's business?' she asked.

He shrugged. 'I'm getting bored. I need more to do.'

'Oh? What?'

'Expand maybe.'

'You decide?'

He laughed. 'No. I don't decide. Not yet.' Spreading his hands to offer up the alternatives. 'All things are possible.'

'Ah.' A tension in her, eagerness held back. Was this her

reason, then? A sniff of something interesting.

'It's complicated,' he said. 'Do I expand using wholesalers or do I get into growing myself? That's the first question. If I'm not going to be a grower, then expansion is more risky because I have to do it on a smaller margin. If I start growing, then I have to do two things, not one.'

'You need help, maybe.'

'Maybe I do.'

'Land.'

'Yes.'

'How much?' she asked.

'Not so much, perhaps. A quarter of a hectare would be plenty. I mean, just to focus on the low end, high turnover, that would be a help.'

'Flowers?'

'Pansies, violas, alyssum, viscaria. We can sell two hundred punnets of that sort of stuff in a weekend. Vegetables, too. Lettuce and so on.'

'I have the land,' she said simply. 'I have a greenhouse also.'

'Yes.' He looked at her. She dropped her gaze, stared into the white cup tilted in her hand.

'How do we do it?' she asked.

'I could lease off you.'

'That's no fun for me.'

'What do you suggest then?'

'We could be partners.' She was moving the cup as if there were something small and alive in it that was trying to escape.

'A company?'

'Sure, a company.'

'It's possible.'

'Why not?' Glance at him, sharp blue eyes.

Because they both knew why not. An impediment. Did it matter? Ought it to matter? If it ought not, did they have a right to do what they wanted? Of course. They were rational beings. He would focus on the business and then he wouldn't need to see Astra so much. He could resolve all that. He could end the relationship in a civilised manner, without fuss, without mess. He could go back to his real life. And maybe he would stop obsessing about Carla, too. So, it all made sense, didn't it? Except that reason and focus meant an act of will, a determination to take charge of the future, when he didn't want a future. If there was a future, there had to be a past and if there was a past then the future was worthless. Better to be here in the present, watching. Waiting. Ready to fight or run if they tried to hurt you again.

'We could make it work,' she said. 'If we wished.'

13.

'WHAT'S FOR DINNER?' JOSIE asked, hovering at her mother's right elbow, peering at the raw ingredients on the kitchen bench. She had an apple in her hand, half eaten.

'Fish,' Sylvia said.

'When will Dad be home?' James, on her left, looked up at her.

'I don't know. He might stay in town. He has another client.'

'What client?' Josie demanded.

'He didn't say. I think it's a rape.' Another tale of misery and brutality, no doubt. He would tell her about it, when he was ready. He might tell the kids about it too, probably over dinner when he sometimes liked to wind them up over his work, egging them on to argue the merits of a case while he fed them scraps of evidence and pointed out the defects in their legal logic. 'You can watch him on the news, if you want,' she said.

'Nagh,' James answered. 'They never let you see anything. All the witnesses have their heads chopped off or their faces fuzzied out. If they show Dad at all, it's just him asking a question, and they don't even give the answer.'

The case for the defence would have started today. Had Larry put Polly Drafton on the stand yet? It would depend on how long the medical evidence took, the experts talking about her state of mind, her bruises and her broken bones.

'Rape is the only crime you can't justify,' Josie said, the words sloshing round the chew of apple.

'What?'

'It's true. You can justify murder, under certain circumstances. You can justify torture, maybe.'

'How can you justify torture?' James asked.

'What say that someone had information that could save the whole world and they absolutely refused to tell you?'

James didn't answer.

'You can't justify rape, though,' Josie went on. 'On the other hand, it's the only crime that has direct reproductive consequences.'

'Rape isn't about sex. It's about violence and control,' Sylvia said. She scraped the chopped onions into a bowl, got a last whiff of fumes that squeezed her eyes shut, made her flinch.

'It might be about sex, too. People get pregnant. Especially in the old days. In the Pleistocene. It might be a gene that got selected.'

'It wouldn't make you very popular with the rest of the tribe, though, would it?'

'What about other tribes? You know, like there's a lot of tribes in the same area and they're always fighting each other. It would make sense then.'

'It's just wrong!' It was almost a shout.

'That's what I said. You can never justify it.' Josie looked at her, calm and reasonable. Then she took another bite of the apple, white teeth crunching through the cream flesh.

Sylvia sighed. It astonished her sometimes that she had this alien, intellectual being for a daughter, someone who took such an objective view of the most disturbing subjects. She remembered how delighted Josie had been to get her first period because she could get to examine the blood for intrauterine cells.

'Scraoul!' The cat, down by her ankles, rubbing itself against her leg.

'Get away!' Josie stepping back, peering at it. 'I haven't forgiven you yet.'

Have you forgiven me, though? Sylvia wondered.

'Feed him, please. Someone,' she told them.

James turned, moved to the pantry, swung open the tall wooden doors. Head tilted back as his gaze lifted to the higher shelves.

'He should starve,' Josie said. 'Make the punishment fit the crime.'

'He didn't eat it,' James told her. 'He just sort of chewed it.'

'He killed it. Destroyed it.'

'But it wasn't a total waste. You said so.' A whirr from the can opener as the blade engaged the metal.

'What *did* you do with it?' Sylvia asked, bending to the cupboard under the sink, reaching for the frying pan.

'I dissected the head and thorax,' Josie said. 'The mandibles looked really cool under the microscope. They're not like mammal jaws, you know. They're two sets, jaws inside jaws.'

'Like in *Alien*,' James said.

She grabbed the olive oil from the bench and poured some into the pan, twirled it so that the thick liquid rolled in a spreading loop over the black Teflon.

The cat was smooching James's leg, back and forth, as he hunkered over its bowl, spoon in one hand, can in the other. A thin child, dark-haired. The sinews of his neck stretching up from the curve of his collar. Vulnerable. Heart-wrenching. It reminded her, suddenly, of the phone conversation she'd had with Maddy earlier.

'Josie,' she said. 'Is there much bullying at school?'

A pause. Josie looked at her. A serious look. 'A bit. Yes. I guess so.' Interesting that she took the question so seriously.

'Is it older kids on younger kids? Or what?'

'It just happens, you know? It kind of comes and goes.'

'Is it happening now?'

'Right now? I'm not sure. Why?'

Sylvia turned to the stove, took the frying pan off the heat. Something about Josie's attitude made her feel . . . what? She wasn't sure. Alarmed? Not quite.

'Maddy called. Donny came home from school today. Before lunch. He was a bit knocked around.'

'Really? What happened?'

'He wouldn't say. Except that he got picked on.'

A pause. 'That's Donny, though, eh?' Josie said.

'What do you mean?'

'Well, he's got a sort of victim mentality.'

'That doesn't make it right.' Sylvia felt a nip of anger, hurt, in Donny's defence.

'No, no. Of course not.' Josie looking at her, blue eyes wary.

'And it shouldn't be allowed to happen. Something should be done about it.'

They were both watching her. Two pairs of eyes, round and worried. Yet she wasn't that angry. She hadn't snapped at them. Maybe they were reacting to the subject. Maybe bullying played a bigger, more serious part in their lives than she had realised.

'Does it happen at your school?' she asked James.

He shrugged. 'A bit.' As if he were embarrassed.

'Has it happened to you?'

'No.' Quick flash of his eyes.

She believed him, yet that made his awkwardness more puzzling. Was it shameful to be the victim? Was it embarrassing to have people think that other people bullied you? Like rape, she thought. The victim's fault.

'It's just a few kids,' Josie said. 'You know, a few sickoes. Most people are just fine.'

'Pretending it doesn't happen.' She regretted the sarcasm in her voice as soon as she'd spoken.

'No!' Josie said, offended. 'Some people are really down on it, you know. They really try hard to stop it.' She looked at Sylvia, pleading. That hurt look of a child who wants to be thought well of but doubts she deserves the affirmation she needs. Sylvia felt her anger melting but then Josie said, 'Like Carla.'

'Carla?'

'Yes. Carla used to get seriously mad about it. She'd just blast out anybody who picked on other kids. Especially little kids. And she'd protect people. You know, look after them.'

'Really?' It was a side of Carla she had never guessed at.

'Yes. That was what she was doing by the river that day. There was this year nine kid she was taking care of, someone who was getting a seriously hard time, and there was some talk that they were going to take her down to the river.'

'What for?'

'I don't know. They were just being stupid, probably. They didn't go.'

'But Carla did?'

'Yes. I think so. I think that's why she was there.' A stricken look on Josie's face, the feeling they all got thinking about Carla.

'Do the police know about this?'

'Maybe. I don't know.'

'Why didn't you mention it before?'

'I didn't know it before. I only found out about a month ago. Some kids were talking.'

'You should have mentioned it.'

'Why? It won't bring Carla back, will it?' Suddenly her expression was twisting up, the tears threatening.

'Oh, darling.' Sylvia reached out, hugging her daughter in reassurance, even though her hands were smeared with fish and onion. Arms about the thin shoulders, wrists pressed on to the bony spine.

Josie pulled away, sniffed loudly, took a deep inward breath, her face stretched downwards, mouth open in a gasp. Then she gave a little sigh. Conquering her emotion. Seeing her do it, watching her fight back the tears she did not approve of, was almost as heart-rending as the tears themselves.

'I guess I should have told you,' she said.

'Well, you know. People need information like that. Especially Tom. It's really hard for him not knowing what happened.'

'Yes, I guess.'

'So who was it? Who was involved?'

'Merry Gibbitson, that was the little kid. I don't know the others. The usual suspects probably.'

'Who are they?'

'Margot Riley and Tina Greene.'

'Only girls?'

'Yes, of course. Girls pick on girls and boys pick on boys.' A look of scorn, as if everybody knew that, didn't they?

Nice to have her bounce back so quickly, Sylvia thought, with only a little irony. She glanced at James but he was over at the refrigerator, peering into it, as if it held the answer to an abiding question.

Section 169 of the Crimes Act 1961 defines provocation.

Any thing said or done (a) that in the circumstances of the case was sufficient to deprive a person having the power of self-control of an ordinary person, but otherwise having the characteristics of the offender, of the power of self-control — and — (b) that did in fact deprive the offender of the power of self-control and thereby induced him to commit the act of homicide.

Larry could have a lot of fun with this one. How on earth can we know what the power of self-control of an ordinary person might be in the circumstances of the case? Does it even make sense to ask how you or I would have reacted if we had been in Polly Drafton's shoes? How could an ordinary person be in those shoes and at the same time still be ordinary? How, moreover, do we assess the self-control of a woman who stabs her husband through the chest with a kitchen knife? The issue is a minefield, a can of worms, a Gordian knot (to triple-mix the metaphor), and it is made more complicated by the fact that deciding if the circumstances are sufficient to deprive that ordinary person of self-control is a matter of law (something which can be ruled on by a judge) whereas deciding if the accused was so deprived is a matter of fact (something for the jury to determine).

The case comes down to this, then. Larry must satisfy the court that anyone in Polly Drafton's situation might have lost their self-control. The prosecution must prove that, even if the court is so satisfied, Polly did not in fact lose her self-control on this occasion. Larry must cast enough doubt on the prosecution's argument to persuade the jury that it did not constitute an adequate proof. There is not much logic in any of this. There are few rules and precious little procedure. The only thing to work on is emotion, subtly, instinctively. Larry knows about such things.

And, of course, he must put Polly on the stand. The pastor has dozens of people to testify to his good character. Polly has no one but herself. She will tell her story clearly, humbly. Her whole demeanour will breathe remorse and truthfulness, a simple sense of the horror of what has happened. She won't break down, though. She'll shed no tears. She'll show no overt signs of being deeply moved. Larry might be tempted to push her, but he would not dare. Unless his own behaviour stays within the bounds of sympathy and careful consideration for the feelings of his client, he might give the impression that the two of them are playing parts; that the manner of her testimony is a put-up job. This is the balancing act between competing judgements: sympathy versus principle, feeling versus thinking, our sense of natural justice against the requirements of the law.

14.

LISA, MY GIRL, YOU have to watch yourself. You have to watch your temper. Shit! Because you have no right to be annoyed. No reason but your animosity. She looked at Tom, sitting in his chair with the calm, the stillness, that she sometimes found infuriating. Take a deep breath. Get the voice right.

'And you said yes?'

'Yes,' he said.

'Why?'

'Because it's money and it's a challenge. I haven't done anything like that, a project, for a long time.'

She might have pointed out to him that the reason he got out of the computer business was because he was sick of projects: the hassles, the deadlines, the way people stuffed him around. He thought Laura Kerrington wouldn't stuff him around?

'You have an objection?' he asked, looking at her.

'I don't like her.'

'You know her?' He sounded surprised.

'I talked to her on the phone this morning.' That voice. A telephone voice. Of course. She's a jumped-up receptionist. Batted her eyelids at the boss and married him. 'She gives me the creeps. She's not human.'

He didn't answer and she wondered, for a moment, what Laura Kerrington looked like, especially through a man's eyes. Peroxide and botox, was she? Tom wouldn't fall for that. He would have more sense, she hoped. He would be too much of a realist. Or perhaps not.

'What will you do at Greenwise?' she asked.

He shrugged. 'Billy's there. And Annie and the others. We can get some part-time help if we need it. I'm not exactly rushed off my feet.'

'You know we might be on opposite sides of a story?'

'Wouldn't be the first time.' He gave her a grin that was meant to be disarming. It almost worked. When she didn't reply, he asked, 'What story?'

'You know someone called Max Hosche?'

'Sure. I've bought stuff off him occasionally. Natives.'

'He and the Kerringtons are having a boundary dispute. They're trying to keep him off what is probably public land.'

'And you're defending the little bloke against the evil rich folks?'

His tone pricked her. She had started having doubts about Old Max. The Peeping Tom. Did she believe that story? No. But then her dislike of Laura Kerrington might be her only reason for rejecting it. She had no facts either way.

'I don't know,' she said. 'I might be.'

He didn't respond. Not directly. 'I just think I should do something new,' he said. "Expand the business. Like the consultancy side. Or growing. Or I could even open another outlet somewhere.'

'Where?'

He shrugged.

She felt confused. Her instinctive reaction to any plan was to tear it apart. This time, though, she was scared to criticise. It felt so strange to have him talking about the future again.

'Kaimohu?' she suggested.

'You think so?'

No, she didn't think so. Kaimohu was too small, surely.

But she had to say something, to encourage him. For the moment at least.

'You'd need a loan,' she said.

'Yes. Especially if it was a new outlet. I wonder if growing isn't a better option.'

'Why don't you talk to Ward?'

'Yes.'

His attitude seemed strange. She sensed a lack of enthusiasm. All the speculation was just words, something to say to pass the time. Sitting there, leaning back in his chair, looking at her, although not quite looking at her. Looking nowhere really. Hello? Can you see me? Can you see anything at all? Are we real here? Are we alive?

She stood up, moved over to him, bent down and took his hand, pulled at him.

'Please.'

Looking up at her. He gave a little rueful smile.

'Please,' she said, pulling again.

He got to his feet and she put her arms around him, hugged him close, felt his touch on her back, but it was tentative, provisional.

'I'm sorry,' she said.

His hands stiffened for a moment. 'What for?'

'I'm not nice to you.'

'Yes, you are.'

No, don't say that! Fight me. Fight and laugh like we used to do.

'I'm a catty bitch,' she said.

'Contradiction in terms.'

That's better! She leaned back, away from him, and began to unbutton his shirt.

'What's that for?' he asked, a little bit of mocking now.

'I'm going to demonstrate. Do you want it where everyone will see?' Peeling the cloth back from his shoulder. Mouth on the smooth skin, warm muscle, licked him, tasted faint tang of salty sweat, the man-smell. Opened her jaws then, and bit him. Hard.

He grunted. And then he was alive, arm around her, squeezing her close against him, hand in her hair and pulling her head back. She laughed but his mouth came at her and shut her up, his lips hard, bristle of the beard. Suddenly the need opened in her, a hot, melting hunger that made her shudder. Twisting her head away.

'Come to bed,' she said.

'Where's Imogen?'

'In her room. Come to bed. I want to eat you seriously.'

Betrayal. In the dark now, the physical bit of it done with, lying there, skin to skin, in spoon fashion. Arm about her, hand on the smoothness of her belly. A betrayal. And the more they wanted each other, the more intense the pleasure, the more their bodies strove to get at one another, the greater a betrayal it was.

He understood that, felt it, and at this moment he was sure the other thing, the cheating, would not go on. Lisa was his life. Astra was an aberration, an unreal episode. She seemed as distant now as a creature in a fairy castle. She had never been real. Or, at least, it was not her reality that mattered. It was not that person in the house by the river, with the two small boys and the rusting seesaw in the yard.

It was the idea of her. But not that either. It was the feeling when he touched her, the coming alive, like a rampant chemical charging through the brain. But it was finished with.

He needed Lisa. He couldn't live without her. When he made love to her it was all there, everything. Not just the lust of the moment, but their whole life together: all their loving from the past, the nights when the wanting wouldn't let them sleep, the fights they had, their plans, the kids and all their problems too, the future. And that was hard, of course. Real life. But somehow he had to go on with it. He had to sleep and wake and eat and drink and go to work and get and spend and talk and love and care and do his duty. Even if he had no claim to any of it. Even if he felt that going about his business as if nothing had happened was another kind of betrayal. Which it was, wasn't it? Because if you pretend that nothing has happened, it's like your little girl is still alive or she never existed. Well, she's not alive and she did exist.

The toss of her head to keep that designer flop of hair from her eyes, the lipstick so dark it was almost black.

— Crankshaft? They're just a band.
— What kind of band?
— Loud and raucous, the usual kind.
— You mean like Led Zeppelin.
— No, Dad. I do not mean like Led Zeppelin!

Chuckle. The baby chuckle that she never quite lost. Because sixteen was fifteen was twelve was nine was five was three.

— Daddy, Daddy, where are you?
— I'm coming to get you!
— No!
— Boo!

Yes, girl. Boo. That's the way it goes. One minute we're having fun and the next the world blows up in our faces. As it blew up in your father's face that Saturday afternoon when he went to the door and found a cop standing there, bareheaded, the breeze stirring in her soft dark hair. Boom, like a letter bomb. And he's left there helpless with no eyes and no hands. So what can he do, this cripple? He has to learn to live with it, of course. He has to go on, minute by minute, day by day, with the self-control of an ordinary person. Everybody says so. And they're right.

They want you to help him, sweetheart. Do you see that? They want you to say goodbye. Can you do it? Can you let your Daddy go?

He was on River Road, standing in the lay-by looking for Carla and he could hear the water running down below, down the slope of the bank, and he knew there was something strange down there, something scary. There was a car coming from the south, a big car, white, and as it drove towards him he could see that it was gradually falling to pieces, crumbling, bits dropping off it, and collapsing in on itself until, as it passed him, it was no more than a big pile of mangled metal, sliding along with its own momentum.

Then he was in a theatre looking at a stage and there was a spotlight, yellow, illuminating someone, a figure in a clown costume, with a white face and red spots on its cheeks and it was wearing a small red hat, conical, with a white pom-pom on top, and for a moment he thought that it had two heads, both identical, but then he saw that it was not a person at all but a cartoon, like Disney or Looney Tunes, and it was singing.

> *Promissory magic, promissory magic*
> *Your promissory days are done*
> *For I'm all ready for a three-day corpse*
> *That is standing out in the sun.*

He woke, in the dark, tumbling out of the dream and feeling frightened, but at the same time wondering, surprised. Because his dreams had never been like this before. Not since then, not since the days in the night when he was nine years old. And along with this thought he was also puzzled, because in the dream the white car came from the south and that was wrong. It came from the north, didn't it? It was someone leaving town, heading towards Winston. The opposite direction to Martin Wraggles. That's what Mrs McIlroy saw.

15.

IMOGEN WAS SITTING AT the breakfast table in her grey school uniform, the tunic with its pleated bodice, a white blouse underneath. The yellow tie with dark blue stripes was done up in a clumsy, flat, fat knot. Like Carla used to do it.

'Good morning,' Tom said.

'Hi.' She was eating cereal, her bony wrist half-cocked as if the spoon were too heavy. Head bowed, not looking at him. Her dark hair was tied back at the nape of her neck, a few strands loosened already, dangling at her cheekbone. She hated her hair, complained about it constantly. She hated him at the moment too, maybe. And he her. Because she was alive and Carla wasn't.

He put two slices of bread in the toaster.

'You want coffee?'

'No thanks,' she said.

Beans in the grinder. He pressed the button and the noise slammed through the silence. Apologise, he told himself. It's a good time. The thought brought a sick feeling, a memory of the day she and Lisa had put up the cross. Why hadn't he gone with them? Because their grief was too small. Because nothing could match his own sense of loss. How dare you, how dare you pretend to feel what I feel. He was ashamed of it now.

He remembered Annabelle at Carla's funeral, her refusal to speak to him, and Vincent, confused, awkward, standing by his mother and looking at him with a mute appeal, wanting the help that Tom couldn't give him. Annabelle's accusation:

if she hadn't been living with you, she'd still be alive. Maybe that was what made him close off to both of them, to everyone. The guilt.

I have a son, he thought, I barely think of him.

The kettle boiled. Coffee and water in the plunge pot. He set it on the table, together with his mug. Fetched a plate from the cupboard. Looked at her, the child of the woman he loved and a man he had no respect for. How can you respect a man you've wronged and still respect yourself?

'What do you want for your birthday?' he asked.

Imogen paused in her eating, spoon halfway to her mouth, her elbow sticking out.

'That depends,' she said.

'Depends on what?'

She didn't answer, took another mouthful.

The toast popped up. He put the slices, one, two, hot, hot, on his plate and sat down. At the end of the table at right angles to her. The silence grew. He buttered the toast, spread one of the pieces with Marmite.

'Depends on what?' he asked again.

'On what my father gets me.'

'Oh? Why's that?'

'Erm.' She looked at him with a half-grin, impish. Anxious, too. 'He might be getting me a horse.'

Oh, shit. He could imagine what Lisa would say to that.

'Really? I guess you haven't told your mother yet.'

'Er, no.' Pulling a wry face.

'Do you want a horse?' he asked.

'Yes, I do.' Her eyes wide and shining, all that eagerness. Her enthusiasm touched him. He remembered himself when he was small: all he had wanted was his own boat, a fishing boat. Like his father and his grandfather. Now he was landlocked in a landlocked town.

'It's a lot of responsibility.'

'I know. But it would be okay. I could keep it at Dad's place.'

'When do you plan to tell Lisa?' he asked.

'I don't know.' She squeezed her eyes shut, flinched against the thought of it.

'Would you like me to be there?'

'Would you?' Pleading.

'I should warn you, I don't necessarily think it's a good idea.'

'You might stop her growling, though.'

He laughed. 'I might.' He doubted it.

'Thanks!' She pushed her chair back, stood up.

'We need to pick the right time,' he said.

'Yes.'

'This evening, maybe.'

She nodded, smiling. Hopeful. Lifting her hand, pushing the loose strands of hair back behind her left ear in the gesture he always found endearing. The movement delicate, unconsciously precise. She was nothing like her mother. Nothing like Carla, either. But she was part of his life somehow, his real life, the one that mattered. As Vincent was. I should call him, he thought.

'Is she giving you a lift to school?' he asked.

'No. She's gone already. She's seeing somebody.'

'Come with me, if you like.'

'Thanks!' She turned towards the door.

'Five minutes,' he called after her.

'You busy?' It was Ward standing in the doorway, leaning into the room like someone on the edge of a swimming pool.

Colin swung in his chair to face him, turning his back on the computer, his forearm resting on the top of the desk. Then he realised that he had moved, half consciously, to hide the screen, to cover up the figures it displayed. So he sat up straight, folded his arms. Be a man.

'No,' he said. 'Come in. Sit down.' He gestured towards the sofa and chairs by the window, the spot where he talked to visitors.

Ward crossed the polished floor, through the air, through the space that had once been a bedroom all those years ago.

Half out of his seat, Colin glanced back at the screen, at the cell at the bottom of the spreadsheet which was an incriminating red. Another rush of shame. But there was nothing for it, was there? Too late now. *It's a blue day, Colly. You'll just have to put up with it. See it through.*

'Well, me old fruit.' He sat down next to Ward and smiled, took a deep breath, felt his confidence begin to grow again, like a hardening erection.

'Couple of things,' Ward said. 'Not important.' He was leaning back in the chair, his tie draped over the side of his belly, the white shirt puckered into horizontal pleats around the buttons. 'First up, what do you know about Monty Kerrington?'

'Financier. Development and Mercantile. He's my neighbour.'

'I know, that's why I'm asking. Good bloke, is he?'

'He's all right. Bit of a talker. Bit of a bore, to be honest. Why?'

'Someone suggested we should invite him to join the Club. Get him involved in the local community sort of thing. And then, well, that house is a bit of local history. They might be interested in the cultural side.'

Ah, so Maddy was behind it. Might have known.

'I've got nothing against him,' Colin said. 'Or her.' Thinking of that blue stare, the sculptured face, the taut body. 'She might make an A-grade president of the Arts Society, for all I know.'

'Good. I'll call him.'

'What about a nomination? And the membership committee?'

'Oh, we don't need that. It's all agreed. Subject to references.'

'He gave me as a referee?'

'No. I did.' Ward laughed. Puff, puff, puff. Like a steam train starting up.

A little fuzz of puzzlement. He had underestimated Ward again, that ability to get things done with a word here, a nod there. Joining the Club was a cumbersome process that usually took months, yet here was Monty Kerrington being wheeled in through the back entrance because Ward wanted him. Not that Colin cared much either way.

A tap on the door. Marie was there, with a sheet of paper in her hand. Ward turned his head, craning his neck to look at her.

'Do you want to sign this?' she said. 'And I can get it to the courier.'

'Sure.' Ward made a little beckoning gesture.

She came in then, her quick-stepped walk, bouncy on her platform soles. Bending beside them, handing Ward a sheet of paper. A letter, was it? Short, tight skirt riding up a little over the back of her thighs. Plump thighs, creamy. Colin could have reached out and touched her there, stroked the smooth warm skin. The thought wasn't lustful, though. Nothing so simple. A need, a fear, a flick of dread. The stirring in his loins was a half-hearted impulse. It made him want a drink.

Ward had the letter on the table and was leaning forward reading it. His right hand rested on it like a paperweight. Colin felt a little shock at the sight of the hand with its curled-up fingers and the flaming pink of the wrist protruding from the white shirtsleeve, the filigree of burn scars like frost on a window, red frost. He remembered that night in the tent, the moment when he knew, the moment of terror when he saw that the primus was going to blow. And then Ward moving. Ward had never moved so fast either before or since.

If it hadn't been for Ward, then Colin and Larry and Ward himself might all be dead. Or, at least, great swathes of their flesh would be decorated like Ward's wrist. Colin did not know what he felt about it now. Gratitude? Yes, of course. And obligation. There was a debt to be paid. There always would be. It was the debt that had made him go into partnership with Ward when, perhaps, he and Lisa might have done something else, taken off as they had so often talked of doing. Maybe it was the debt that caused the other thing he felt when he thought about that night. Resentment. He was not sure why he should resent Ward but he did. Ward had robbed him somehow. Of his freedom? No. It was stranger than that. Ward had robbed him of his right to feel the pain that would have followed the terror. He should have died that night twenty-seven years ago. Why hadn't he?

'Good.' Ward looked up. Marie gave him a pen and he signed the letter in a quick spasm. 'Thank you,' he said, holding pen and paper out to her.

'You're welcome.' A little nod of her head, a little smile. She turned away.

Colin watched her go, the tight buns wriggling in the red skirt.

'And the other thing.' Ward was watching him, calling his attention back. 'It's Larry and Syl's twentieth anniversary next week.'

'Is it?'

'Maddy and I thought we should put on a do for them.'

'Good idea.'

'Friday. At The Little Frog. You know, just the Tribe. Us and them. You and Heidi. Lisa and Tom.'

'Great.' But did he mean that? Did he want to be at an event like that with Lisa there? The energy in her, the fervour in her dark eyes, had come to seem an accusation. See? This is me. The real me. Not that vicious little bitch you were married to. He could almost hear her saying that. And Tom? Well, the thought of Tom just left him feeling bleak.

'Amazing, eh?' Ward was saying. 'Twenty years. We'll be next. Maddy and me. Next year.'

And then? There won't be a twentieth for Colin and Lisa, will there? Because she fucked off with the gardener like Lady Chatterley.

'Well,' he said. 'We'll be there. Of course.'

'Fantastic. You know, everyone together.' Ward looked at him, eyes shining. Tears of emotion nearly. That's what Ward liked most of all, wasn't it? Everyone together. Like a family. A twitch of his gingery moustache, a grin.

Colin twisted in his chair. A writhing sensation up from his guts into his chest. Like a squirming rat. *Don't be stupid, boy. Don't be such a drip!* He thought of the bottle of whisky in the third drawer of his desk, and the need for it opened in him, warm drench of oblivion.

16.

MADDY IN A WHIRL. She had a million things to do and she was very angry. That afternoon she had been to see Silkington, the headmaster, about Donny and the bullying, and it had not been an experience to give her a warm glow of satisfaction. What a prick! That smirk! Sitting there behind his desk with a concerned expression on his face.

No, no, of course the school didn't find such behaviour acceptable. Could she give him the names of any of the boys concerned? Or the form they were in? Maybe he should talk to Donny himself. No? Well, without names there was not much he could do except, perhaps, have a word to the prefects. I mean, an announcement in assembly, without any other measures taken against the culprits, would merely tell them that they'd got away with it. Could she see that?

Of course she could see that! What she could also see was that the culture he condoned or encouraged in his miserable school meant that Donny couldn't or wouldn't give up the names they needed. Silkington did not, of course, take kindly to such an observation, perhaps because it was far too intelligent for any mere mother to be capable of, so he fought back. Ever so politely.

— What you might consider, Mrs Lorton, is encouraging Damien to exercise himself a little more on his brother's behalf.

— I don't understand.

—Well, Damien's a popular boy. If he took Donny more under his wing, as it were, then I'm sure the results would be beneficial.

— How do you know that he doesn't?

— I don't know, of course. But, in my experience, that's how these things work.

So not only did Donny get beaten up but it was Damien's fault. Her fury made her speechless for a moment. Just as well. Best to say nothing in a state like that. Best to calm down, think it through. That would be Ward's advice. Well, thank you for your time, Mr Silkington. Not at all, Mrs Lorton. What a prick!

Anger means action and action means decision. For Maddy decisions came in two forms. Either she knew instantly and with the utmost clarity what she was going to do, in which case she went ahead and did it, or else she didn't have a blind clue, in which case she went ahead and did it anyway. Well, not *it* but something. Anything, really. Just to keep moving, just to keep talking so that eventually the way forward presented itself. Her first move in such a situation was to call her friends.

Lisa was at work, of course, and when Maddy ripped right in and told her about Silkington, she got pretty angry herself, as Lisa would, and immediately wanted to write a story on the subject. That was a help because Maddy realised almost straight away that she didn't want any publicity, not yet, not quite yet, which seemed to imply that she had a long-term goal here, whatever it was. So she found herself in the odd situation of calming Lisa down, despite her own feelings, and reassuring her that it was best not to do anything in the meantime, and she finished up talking about next Friday, the dinner for Larry and Sylvia. Were Tom and Lisa free? They were. Lisa thought so. She was pretty sure. Well, for something like that she was sure she was sure. Which was good, great, fantastic.

Sylvia had just got home from work. She sounded tired. Yes, well. That stupid job. Being dead would be more exciting and it would probably pay more too, but Sylvia had this social conscience thing about taking a part in the economic community, as if earning a pittance at a job that used none of your capabilities were somehow making a contribution, not to mention all the other people in Durry, poor people, who could really do with a job like that.

Maddy, of course, said none of this. (Apart from anything else, Sylvia knew it all already. She'd said most of it herself.) Instead, after they'd chatted a bit, she asked about Larry, how was the case? And Sylvia said they were summing up today and maybe the jury would be out by evening. Maddy asked if Polly Drafton would get manslaughter and Sylvia said that Larry wasn't sure any more. He thought she might not. Which got Maddy going again. Because what was that case about if it not bullying and injustice?

So she ripped into Silkington once more, only this time she was more measured, more controlled, a great deal more sarcastic, and as she talked she began to see what she was going to do. Not writing to the Ministry of Education, as Sylvia suggested. Still less to that duh of a woman who was the local MP. No, she didn't want anything that Silkington could weasel out of and she didn't just want to make him uncomfortable either. She wanted to change things, and the only way to make a change was through the school's board of trustees and the best way to influence the board was to get elected to it. It was time she and Ward took an interest in the college, anyway. It would be another place to fly the flag, with the elections coming up.

Thus she came to a decision, with the help of her

friends, and, as always, she was full of gratitude. Thank you, Syl. That's brilliant. That's really great advice. I don't know what I'd do without you.

So that Sylvia was left wondering what exactly she'd said that Maddy found so wise and helpful.

17.

'ARE YOU GOING TO stay here all night?' Tracey asked.

'No, just a couple of minutes.'

'You working on something?' Hovering.

Lisa hated that, people looking over her shoulder. 'No,' she said, swivelling in her chair, forcing Tracey back a step or two. 'To be perfectly honest, I'm too scared to go home.'

'What?'

'Tom's cooking.'

'Ah. That bad, huh?'

'No, it's not him. He's fine. He enjoys it. It'll be pasta, of course, but, hey, that's in his genes, so who's complaining? No, it's me. I can't leave him alone when he's in the kitchen. I really get up his nose.' The tone, the jocularity, seemed false even as she spoke.

Tracey laughed. 'You should have said. We could have gone for a drink. As it is, I've just called Josh to give me a lift.'

'No, it's all right. I've some things to tidy up.'

'Okay. I'll see you then.' Turning to go. Then an idea struck her and she stopped. 'Oh, by the way, do you know any hunters?'

'Hunters? No, why?'

'The council's reviewing the gun licences. I need some vox pop.'

'Talk to the rifle club.'

'Are they into killing things or just shooting targets?'

'Both, I think.' She tried to remember. Colin had belonged to the club for a little while. He had bought himself a gun and some other gear and had even gone out on a couple of trips until he'd found out how tough it was physically. Typical Colin.

'It's a really sick argument, isn't it?' Tracey said. 'They claim they need all the hunting to get rid of the pests like possum and deer but the only reason the pests are there in the first place is because the hunters brought them.'

'Ironic, yes,' Lisa answered. But then she thought of Max Hosche walking across the Kerringtons' place to get meat for his dinner. Did he shoot his hare and his possum? Was that the problem with the Kerringtons? An old man wandering around with a gun. The more she thought about that story, the more she realised there was nowhere to go with it.

'Well, see you then.'

'See you.'

She was hardly aware of Tracey leaving because suddenly she had remembered Colin with the rifle in his hands, how odd it had made her feel. A thing she could see for real that had only ever been in photos or movies before. He had offered it to her, wanting her to hold it, grinning in a way that made her uneasy, and she had refused. Man the Hunter. Was that it? The gleam in his eye was strangely like the look he gave her when he wanted sex. Kind of eager and pleading and hungry all at once.

— Don't be scared. It's just a piece of equipment, like a screwdriver or a blender.

But it wasn't, not at all. She had turned her back, walked out of the room with a tiny, momentary shudder at the thought of a bullet coming after her.

Something nasty there, something not quite right.

In the early days, when they first met, he had seemed so

civilised. Not like the other boys with their leering eyes and their creeping hands, like spiders trying to get into your clothes. Colin was handsome, well-bred, with perfect manners. He was polite and respectful and he seemed genuinely interested when you talked to him. He had courted her for weeks in an off-hand sort of way, staying close but keeping just a little distant, as if he were scared she might not want his attention and he didn't want to force himself upon her. It made her feel important and desirable. And then they got to kissing and petting and he still didn't grab at her, so that she began to want it for herself: a whole world of new sensation just around the corner. And then he told her the story, that awful story about the puppy he had had when he was seven years old, and she had felt a lurch inside her, a need to protect, because he was so matter-of-fact about it. At that moment, he could have asked her for anything and she would have done it. And, of course, he didn't ask and the need grew stronger, until finally she decided that she loved him for ever and dragged him off to bed, only to discover that he didn't have a clue.

He was awkward, fumbling. She lay there with him in the dark, feeling hurt, feeling miserable. Did they do it? Was that it? Had it happened?

— What's wrong?
— Nothing.
— Did I do something wrong?
— No, no. It just didn't feel right. Not a good time.

That's what girls were supposed to say.

— I'm sorry.

Sorry, sorry, sorry. Miserable failure. As a wife. As a woman. First love? Oh, shit, it was a sad, sick business.

Didn't have to be that way, though, did it? Look at Sylvia and Larry, Maddy and Ward. They seemed to get it right first time. Although maybe they weren't such a good example. If it hadn't been for them, if it hadn't been for the friendship, the Tribe, the six of them, she would have left Colin years before she did. There wouldn't have been a partnership with Ward, and they would have gone overseas and gone their separate ways. Although, maybe not. Maybe she would never have had the wit to think of it. Because she cared about him, pitied him. That's why Tom sometimes made her angry. He dragged back into that, feeling sorry for someone. It scared her.

Six o'clock. The rolling globe that was her screen-saver did a double bounce in the top left-hand corner and headed down in a slow dive. Outside, the sky was darkening. Tom would be starting on the dinner. With a bottle of red wine open on the bench and an opera CD at ear-throbbing volume. Mirella Freni sings Puccini. *Un bel di vedremo* or *Si. Mi chaimano Mimi*.

She reached out, moved the mouse and the story she'd been working on sprang to life. Click by click she began to exit the files.

The phone rang.

For a moment, she thought of ignoring it and letting the answer service cut in. But no.

'Hello. *Advocate* newsroom, Lisa Cairnes speaking.'

'Hi.' Sylvia's voice.

The ticking of the computer disk as the system closed down.

'I wasn't sure if you'd still be there,' Sylvia said.

'I was just packing up.'

'I need to talk to you about something. Donny's been a victim of some bullying.'

'Yes. Maddy told me. I offered to do a piece on it but she wouldn't let me.'

'No, it's not Donny. It's about Carla.' And Sylvia started into a story of how she'd talked to James and Josie and found out the reason Carla had gone to the river.

Lisa listened with a growing sense of dread, she did not know why, and at the end she could think of nothing to say.

'I just thought you . . . he should know,' Sylvia said.

'Of course.' It was dark now, outside. The windows had begun to reflect the interior of the building, the newsroom, neon strips in the ceiling.

'I'm sorry,' Sylvia said. 'To bring it up.'

'No. God, no, that's all right.'

'I guess there isn't any way it doesn't keep on hurting. I feel that myself, but it must be so much worse for Tom. And you.'

'No, it isn't that.' Oh, dear God, she thought, of course it is. But not just the hurt, not just that. She needed help. She needed wisdom.

'I just thought it would be best coming from you, not me.'

'Well,' Lisa said, 'that's the problem, really. I'm not sure I should tell him.'

'Oh?'

'It's just beginning to settle down. He's getting counselling and for the first time since it happened he's focusing on other things. He's even talking about going to see Ward to get advice on expanding the business. I'm just scared that if he knows about this he'll be off again, obsessing about who did it. It can't do any good, can it?'

'It won't bring Carla back, no.'

'Do you know this child's name?'

'Merry Gibbitson.'

Lisa wrote the name on her pad. 'Where does she live?'

'I don't know. The kids might know. Or I could check. At the library. She might well have a library card.'

'No, no, no. Don't do that. I mean, that's probably illegal, isn't it?'

'Yes,' Sylvia admitted.

'Oh, God. This is difficult. I mean, it just goes against all my principles to keep it quiet.'

'You don't have to say anything. Not immediately. You can wait. See how things are in a day or so.'

'What if he finds out from somewhere else?'

'I can't see that he will, can you?'

'Josie might say something.'

'No. I don't think so,' Sylvia said. 'She was kind of embarrassed about the whole business.'

'Embarrassed? Why?'

'I don't know, really. Maybe because she didn't tell me before.'

'The problem is that not deciding is deciding not to, in the end.'

'Yes,' Sylvia said, 'but only in the end.'

Lisa could hear the concern, the love in her voice, and she was glad of it. It was as if Sylvia were here, in the same room, and had leaned forward, touched Lisa on the knee, a little touch, a quick stroke of her fingers, but alive in its reassurance.

'God,' Lisa said. 'This is ridiculous, isn't it? It sounds like one of those conversations that teenagers have. Is it ever right to tell a lie? Would it be right to steal food if you were starving?'

'It doesn't seem ridiculous to me.'

'Thank you.' A sudden flood of relief. Just to have the matter taken seriously. She realised that people tended not to take the problems she and Tom were having seriously. They took Carla seriously. They took that so seriously they ran away. But Tom and Lisa, they were the loving couple, they were made for each other. They were solid, weren't they?

'I won't say anything,' Sylvia said. 'Not until you tell me it's okay.'

'I could talk to Stan.'

'Stan?'

'Stan Andreissen. He's a cop. They may well have interviewed this child already. It may all be nothing.'

18.

A NICE WINE, COLIN thought. A touch of cassis and blackberry and the scrunch of tannin, a good cellar life by the feel of it. He looked at the label, plain cream paper with a drawing of a wine press, *Manawai Vineyards* in a flowing script. He imagined how Ward would react, saw him peering at the bottle.

— Manawai? That's impossible. You can't get a decent red out of Manawai. The soil's all wrong.

— Just try it mate.

Ward, then, with the glass in his fist, the twisted fist, only his first two fingers wrapped around the stem. Sniffing, tasting.

— Hmmm. Well, you've got me there, mate. You really have.

Ah, yes, he thought, taking another gulp, topping up his glass. If I had all the money I'd spent in my life on drink, well, I'd spend it on drink.

He looked over at Heidi, curled in her chair, as usual, a book in her lap, as usual.

'Tell me something,' he said. 'Amuse me.'

'Amuse?' She looked up. 'Are you ill?'

'No, I'm fine.' Not so good actually, given his mistake with the Siezmann accounts. But he didn't want to think about that. You could control your thoughts if you tried. You could keep the yellow. It was all a matter of discipline. Right now, there was the evening to enjoy. And the world beyond it. Darkness outside with just the hint of sky above the hills. I'll drink to that.

'We should do something,' he said.

She shrugged, looked up again. 'What?'

'We could invite Larry and Syl over. Ward and Maddy.' Except that Larry wouldn't be home yet. The jury was out. He'd be waiting. For another victory? Of course. A flush of pride in knowing Larry, in the fact that his best mate had been called the best barrister in the country. Larry's eyes and his smile, the humour in them, the wit and the intelligence. Laughter was like sex. Just as good. Or better even.

'We see them all next Friday,' Heidi said. 'The big night.'

The Twentieth. Twenty Years.

'We should get them something,' he said.

'Yes, that's a good idea.'

'What is it, twenty? There must be a substance. Silver?'

'Maybe.'

'No, silver's twenty-five. What comes before silver?'

'Lead?'

'Don't be dumb. Not lead.'

'I don't know,' she shrugged. 'We do not have such things in my family.'

'Too cheap.'

'Hey!' Warning him. She didn't like him making cracks about the Swiss, but it was true. In her case, anyway. She was tight when it came to money. It was one of the things he liked about her, actually, the way she had style without spending up large.

The phone rang. A second of hesitation and then she got up, padded in her barefoot way across the carpet to the table in the corner. She had painted her toenails, he noticed. Odd. Why should she do that?

'Hello,' she said, her back to him, standing there with

her weight on her right leg, hand on her left hip. Long legs, nice butt.

She turned, walked towards him, phone in her right hand hanging by her side. 'For you,' she said, holding it out.

He took it.

'Hello?'

'Is it true that you promised Imogen a horse?' The voice calm, too calm. He knew it well enough to sense the threat beneath it. Fight? Or let her have her way. Apologise. Agree with her.

'No,' he said, 'I didn't promise anything.'

'Where did she get this idea from, then?'

'She asked me and I said I'd think about it.' He could feel his irritation rising to meet her. He'd done nothing wrong. Why should he feel guilty?

'And have you thought?' she asked, barely a hint of sarcasm.

'I'm still considering it.'

'Why?'

'What do you mean "why"?'

'Why are you stringing her along?'

'I'm not stringing her along.' Yes, angry. He had a right to it.

'Then you intend to buy her a horse, do you?' Sharper now.

'Tell me,' he said, choking off the acid in his tone, 'why shouldn't she have a horse?'

'Where will she keep it?'

'Here.'

'You've got stabling, have you?'

'Why would it need stabling?'

'Oh, for God's sake!' Letting it show now, letting him see how weak she thought he was. 'Who buys all the feed and the gear, the saddle and stuff? Who pays the vet's bills?'

'What if I do?' He caught Heidi's eye, saw her wariness, or maybe not that, maybe something else.

'Fine,' Lisa said. 'We've been through this situation before, though. You shell out for the grand gesture and we're left to pick up all the ongoing expenses.'

'What if you're not?'

'Look, I —'

He cut her short. 'No, no, listen. What say I pick up *all* the costs? What say it's just something between me and her? *Then*, would it be all right?'

A pause. He felt a little surge of triumph at her hesitation.

'It's an indulgence,' she said at last. 'She'll get sick of it in five minutes.'

'What's wrong with an indulgence?'

'Okay. It's up to you. It's entirely up to you. I don't want to have anything to do with it.'

'Fine,' he said. 'I never asked you to.'

She hung up.

Carefully, slowly, as if it were a delicate object, he put the phone down on the table beside him. Picked up his glass, drank. You could control your thoughts if you wanted to. He lifted the bottle, offered it to Heidi.

'More?'

'No. Thank you.' Looking at him, wanting an explanation.

He was not sure there was an explanation. He had just argued himself into spending hundreds — shit, it might be thousands, for all he knew — on his daughter's birthday present. Not what he intended. Or was it? He didn't understand. The little sense of triumph, the feeling that he had beaten Lisa in an argument, was poisoned by the thought that she had rolled him over. Yet again.

'Imogen wants a horse for her birthday,' he said.

'Ah.'

A pause. She was waiting for more. He didn't want to give her more. He wanted them all to go away and leave him in peace.

'You will buy her one?' she asked.

'Maybe.'

She put down her book, uncurled her legs so that her feet rested on the floor. White feet. The red nails puzzled him.

'You talked on the phone like you have decided,' she said.

'Well, what if I have?'

'No business of mine.' A little gesture pushing him away. 'Except you talk on the phone like you will keep it here.'

'What if I do?'

'There is no room.'

'What do you mean there's no room? There's acres of room.'

'We lease to McCracken.'

'Not all of it. There's the paddock up behind the greenhouse. That's big enough for a whole herd of horses.'

'Ah, well. We agree that was for me. If I wanted it.'

'And?'

'Maybe I want it.'

'Maybe?'

'Maybe. Probably. I haven't decided yet.' Calm, cool.

Jesus, it annoyed him sometimes, how cool she was. Explaining with little condescending wags of her head like he was a child or the family pet. Talk to me like a human being! he wanted to yell at her.

'Why do you spring this on me now?' he said, trying to compose himself.

'Spring? I think you do the spring.'

'I mean, Jesus, maybe something was mentioned, back then, about you possibly using it but, hey, when was that? Years ago. Buried back in the mists of time somewhere.

'We arrange,' she said, with a little shrug. 'That's why we didn't give all to McCracken.'

'What do you want it for anyway?'

'To grow more. To expand the business.'

'What business?' A spasm of annoyance. 'You don't have a business.'

'You're spilling,' she said, getting to her feet.

For a moment he didn't understand, then he noticed the cool of liquid on his fingers and, looking down, the spots of wine, dark like the spatter of blood across the cream wool of the carpet.

She was moving away, out through the door, leaving him staring at the space behind her, leaving him with his anger. Why? Why did she needle him like this? How was it possible? Stay calm, get a grip. Hold it, stop it wriggling. A lump of numbness and helplessness, deep down, held tight in the cold.

She was back with a stainless-steel bowl and a cloth, coming towards him, kneeling beside his chair. He moved his legs, twisted, shrinking away, until he realised what he was doing, relaxed again. He didn't touch her though. If he'd let his leg go back to where it was, his knee would have been touching her shoulder.

She was alternately dampening the cloth from the water in the bowl and dabbing the stain, heavy jabs of her fingers, which he could hear, dab, dab, dab, and which shook her body. Vicious. Yes, she was vicious under all that coolness, wasn't she? The way she tore at you and pecked at you.

'So what is this business supposed to be?' he asked.

'Plants, of course. Wholesale supply.'

'Wholesale? Who for?'

'Tom. And others maybe.'

'Tom? Oh, fuck! Not Tom. Why are you doing this to me?' The words came before he understood what he was saying, what they might imply.

'Oh?' She stood up, looked at him. She had the bowl in one hand, the cloth squeezed tight in the other.

'I know you fancy him,' he said, 'but this is going too far.'

'I don't fancy him. He's a friend.'

'Don't give me that. I'm not blind. I mean, I watched you snuggling up to him on the sofa the other night, and now you're telling me you want to do business with him? Business, my arse! All you want to do is spread your fucking legs.'

'Pig!' She said it softly. He almost didn't hear.

'What?'

'I should. I should fuck him. Then you will see.'

'What did you call me?'

'Pig!' She yelled it this time, leaning towards him, mouth coming at him in great bites. 'Fat pig. You are stupid and dirty and you talk, kwoik, kwoik, kwoik, like nonsense. You make no sense only animal noise. You have no thinking. You are brainless. You are blind. You cannot see. You cannot understand. You spit your drink. You swear with a dirty mouth. You cannot think. You stump, stump, stump in your own shit, turning round and round and round —'

'Shut up!' he yelled, just to stop her. 'Shut your fucking mouth!'

'I tire of you. I don't want this any more.'

'Get out of my fucking house!'

'This is not your fucking house. This is my house. I make this house. I find the things. I paint the walls. This is . . .'

'I paid for every last cent of it.'

'Pay? You think money is the world. Well, go and shit on your money. Just like you piss on the floor.' She turned the bowl in her fist, a slurp of pale pink sparkling water cascading to the carpet.

'Bitch!'

The wet cloth hit him in the side of the neck.

'Bitch!' he yelled again, but she was leaving, she was gone.

'Fucking bitch.' To himself this time, almost to himself. A sob, almost a sob. God, he couldn't let her do this to him. It had to stop. Fucking bitches, all of them.

He reached out for the bottle, filled his glass.

19.

AT 2.30 P.M. ON Saturday 2 May 2003, in the High Court at Winston, after nine and a half hours' deliberation, the jury of seven women and five men found Polly Drafton not guilty of the murder of her husband but guilty of manslaughter on the grounds of provocation.

20.

HANNAH CRESWELL WAS NO longer surprised when her clients' dreams began, as if on demand, between the first and second appointments. If the analysand was positively oriented towards the therapy, it seemed, the unconscious responded. In most cases, too, the response was not just a cluster of random images. It had a structure and a set of resonances that echoed the pathology, a little drama that played out the cognitive and affective configuration of the brain that produced it. Illuminating? Well, not necessarily. Sometimes it seemed more like a bird trying to distract you by fluttering along the ground away from its nest, but there were usually enough clues to open up the space and glimpse the complexes within it.

Tom Marino was waiting for understanding, for enlightenment. His eyes were not so guarded this time. Could she help him? Sitting there, leaning forward, his hands dangling between his thighs, his fingers interlaced at the tips. He had fine hands, long delicate fingers.

Begin, she thought.

'According to Jung, the figures in our dreams aren't necessarily people from the real world but they might not be arbitrary constructions either. Sometimes they fall into certain categories, which he called archetypes and which seem to be universal across human cultures. Personally, I think the archetypes are all to do with how the brain's wired up.'

'Biology?'

'Yes. The products of our evolution, if you like. They're the conscious manifestations of what must ultimately be neurological functions. They appear in our dreams and in art and literature, too. They're like a narrative grammar that forms the basis of our stories — myths and so on. I suppose, in a sense, a dream is a kind of story, a first draft, perhaps. Or a sketch of a work of art that has some good bits and some muddle. There are parts that work really well and say exactly what the artist wants them to and others that are confused or contradictory. Does that make sense?'

He nodded, watching her.

'Now, one of the archetypes, and the one that very often appears when someone first gets into analysis, is the Shadow. Jung had a theory that in the course of our growth and development we have to choose among our traits and characteristics. Some of them we reject. These, the aspects of ourselves that we don't really like or don't really want to acknowledge, get incorporated into the Shadow. It's a kind of complement. It usually appears as a vague or incomplete figure. This is because there aren't enough traits to make a fully rounded, complete person. It's often either dark, or two dimensional, or only partially animated."

'Like the singer on the stage,' he said.

'For example.'

'So that's part of me? The part I don't approve of?'

'What do you think?'

'Well, I guess I'm not inclined to sing in public. And I wouldn't wear a clown costume. I'm not an exhibitionist.'

'You think clowns are exhibitionists?'

'They're into performing, playing a part, and they're, well, kind of confrontational. They push a certain silliness in your face.'

'Silliness?'

'A lack of reason, logic.' He gave a little laugh, a snort, and turned his head, looked out of the window into the trees outside. 'I guess that's my Shadow, near enough.' He thought about it for a moment and then glanced at her, an awkward look, like someone caught in an unguarded act. 'What about the two heads?'

'What do you think?'

'Two-faced? Yes, I guess so.'

'How would that be?'

'Well, you know, walking around as if everything is normal. And Carla's dead. I guess that's kind of artificial, isn't it? It kind of makes me a clown, in a sick way.'

Interesting, she thought, that he honed in on that directly when there were other, more conventional ways he might be said to be two-faced.

'So what about this rhyme?' he asked. 'This "promissory magic"?'

'What do you think?'

'I don't know. Promissory? Promises. IOUs. If my promissory days are done, does it mean I can't make promises or borrow money? Or I can't expect other people to keep their promises, maybe. All bets are off, is that it?'

She said nothing, let the silence lengthen into another thought.

'And the three-day corpse. It's out in the sun, in the open. Exposed. This Shadow? Is that what's exposed?' A sudden glance at her, a desperate look. All the fears clamouring for attention suddenly. 'Maybe it means I'm living on borrowed time?'

'Don't push too hard,' she said. 'There may not be an answer. Not here, today, now.'

'Yes, well. If this Shadow's like you say, it isn't necessarily going to make sense at all, is it?'

'Maybe not rational, ordinary sense.'

'I think I am living on borrowed time. It can't go on like it is, can it?'

He sat back in his chair, staring at the trees again. His fingers lifted to the side of his face, the beard, tweaking the hairs there. Thinking. Or feeling it. Feeling it was what he needed more, perhaps.

'Is a zombie a Shadow?' he asked, glancing back at her.

'It could be.'

'I feel like a zombie, sometimes. Going through the motions. It's as if my whole life before that day has been rubbed out. The living dead.'

'That, perhaps, is just a response to the trauma. A kind of shock.'

'Or maybe I want to be like her. Dead. I don't believe in life after death. I wish I did.'

'What do you believe in?'

'Nothing. There's nothing there when the light goes out.'

And yet, she thought, you have your ghost to deal with still.

21.

TOM MARINO AND KENNY Wiremu stood on the edge of the turning circle at the back of Clisserford, looking out over the flat green slope towards the stream and the distant hills beyond. Kenny was a small, nuggety man with a fringe of black beard sprouting like gorse from his jaw, a black beanie pulled down to the tips of his ears.

'What do you reckon?' Tom asked.

'Front-ender and a couple of trucks? A grader maybe. Easy.'

'How long'll it take?'

'Ooh.' A big show of figuring it out. Kenny's lips did a little put-put-put to prove the cogs were turning. Tom guessed he had already done the calculation. He was just trying for a bit of contingency. 'Ten days?'

'Eight.'

'Might rain, eh?'

'Eight days if it doesn't rain.'

Kenny didn't answer. This was the closest he would come to an agreement.

'How much?' Tom asked.

'Hmmm.' More considering. 'Sixteen grand.'

'Twelve.'

Kenny laughed. He had two teeth missing in the left side of his upper jaw. 'Fourteen-five,' he said when he'd got over the joke.

'When can you start?'

'Nineteenth. Give or take.' Rocking his hand, giving

or taking.

'How about the twelfth?'

'No way.'

'Reschedule. You can squeeze this in, only eight days.'

'Nagh,' Kenny said, but without much force. Tom took that to be a maybe.

'All sorted, then?' A silence.

Kenny looked at him. Dark eyes, sly grin. All sorted.

Tom had a feeling for the air. He came from a long line of sailors who lived and died on the water but, of course, it is the air that carries the sea's messages, the whiff of a storm, the scent of a distant shore. With Kenny gone, he started to walk away over the grass towards where the bigger mound would be; towards the hills in the west, bright, golden-grey in the morning sun. The sky above was clear blue, pale at the horizon. A puff of cloud. He sniffed the wind, the little breeze that smeared his cheeks and brow and eyes with the chill of the mountain valleys, the cold smell of growing things. His spirits lifted, a gesture towards the light.

A hopeful morning, then.

He took out his cellphone, dialled the number. Lifted the phone to his ear. The ringing tone.

'Hello,' she said. 'Mr Greenwise.' She'd picked him from her caller i.d.

'Hi. I think I have a deal on your excavations.'

'Oh?'

'A local company. PDD Earthmoving.'

'PDD? What does that stand for?'

'Pretty Damn Deep, I think.'

She laughed, her strange little gulp. 'Come and tell me about it,' she said.

'Where are you?'

'Right behind you.'

He turned. In the L-shape made by the garage block and the house was a lawn surrounded by a low hedge. It had a little fountain in the centre. Paths and borders formal in their symmetry. Most of the beds were bare, stripped for the winter, and beyond them, on the veranda, Laura Kerrington stood, white shirt and red pants bright against the shadow behind her. Mistress of the House.

'There's something you can help me with,' she said as he started to walk towards her.

'Oh, what's that?'

'You'll see.'

He stepped through a gap in the hedge, began to cross the lawn. The fountain was a concrete statue, a fake Greek thing, a woman holding an amphora on her shoulder.

'Do you like it?' she asked, in his ear.

'Not particularly.'

'I think Mountford had dreams of Versailles. I don't know. I can never decide. I might rip it out.'

Closer to her now, where she stood in front of a set of French doors, open. Right hand on her hip. He closed his phone, slipped it into his jacket pocket, walked the few metres to the foot of the veranda steps. She was already moving, turning away, stepping inside.

'Take your shoes off,' she said, over her shoulder.

He did so, although his shoes were clean, polished as always, just a little damp from the grass, that's all. He left them on the boards outside the door.

It was a long room, rectangular, stretching across the back of the house. Gleaming floors of native timber, scattered with oriental rugs. The furniture was arranged in islands: a dining table with six chairs, a lounge suite around a low table, two easy chairs at angles to one another but facing out towards the garden. The walls were covered with an embossed paper, silky sheen, and pictures, old photographs and paintings, in heavy frames. He breathed deep but couldn't catch the scent of the place. There was nothing. No smell. How could somewhere smell of nothing?

Laura was moving through a door to his right. He hesitated, unsure if he should follow her or not. Above him, hanging from the ceiling, were two chandeliers, which did not quite match, in two plaster centrepieces. Two ceilings originally. Two rooms, therefore. Two heads on a cartoon clown.

'Here.' She was in the doorway, beckoning. 'Take your coat off too.' She disappeared again.

He removed his jacket, crossed the floor. The bare boards between the rugs were slippery beneath his socks. A doorway led into a kitchen. Modern shelves and cupboards of golden wood, the stove-top and hood in stainless steel. There was an island bench in the centre and a bar with two high stools with black leather seats. On the right-hand wall a black-leaded coal range, for decoration only. It had a vase of flowers on top of it.

She was at the refrigerator, bending, taking something out.

'Open this.' Handing him a bottle. Pol Roger.

'You drink champagne every morning?' he asked,

stripping off the soft metal seal.

'Not quite *every* one.' A glance at him, a little grin.

He couldn't read her mood, but it was different from her usual restraint. Suppressed energy, a wriggle in her movements. Excited, was she? Pleased with herself?

He twisted the cork and pulled. A soft pop. Poured into one of the champagne flutes, tilting glass and bottle, pale gold of the liquid, rim of bubbles at the surface. Handing it to her, taking the other glass. She hoisted herself on to a stool, sat with her legs crossed, one heel tucked behind the spell. Left forearm lay along the surface of the bar. There was a little gold charm bracelet at her wrist. And the rings on her fingers. Bells on her toes, no doubt.

'Well, thanks for this,' he said, lifting his glass to her. 'An unexpected bonus.'

'Here's to me.' Clinking with him.

'All right. Here's to you.' Sitting down himself. He sipped the wine, the dry fruit, little zest of bubbles.

Her look, a sly expression. It didn't suit her, gave her painted lips and smooth plucked eyebrows a tawdry air. She was teasing him, he realised. She wanted his curiosity about what she was celebrating. The thought had an odd effect. He felt not interest but a mild disdain. If you need the attention of someone like me, you're in a sad way, baby.

'What's the occasion?' he asked.

'Ah!' She drank. Her glass was already half empty. She picked up the bottle from the bar between them and refilled. 'I just closed a deal,' she said. Her left hand balled into a little fist, a shake of triumph. 'I just closed my first million-dollar deal.'

'Well done.' Toasting her. 'What sort of deal?'

'Forenza. Four hundred and twenty thousand shares at seventy-nine cents. Sold them for $3.47.' She tossed back her head, lifted her fist in another clench. 'Whooo!'

'This is an interest of yours, then?'

'It's what I do. To keep my sanity.' She laughed, not the gulp this time but a little girlish giggle.

'Sanity?'

'Oh, shit. I'd go spare otherwise, wouldn't I? Stuck here by myself all day.' Then she leaned towards him, touched him on the sleeve. 'Don't tell Monty, will you?' Anxious tone. He guessed, then, that the champagne was not her first drink of the day. A lonely life. Stuck in a huge house with nothing to do except play the stock market. Waiting for hubby to come home.

'He doesn't know?'

'Oh, God, no. He thinks I'm an idiot.' She poured more wine. Hers and his. 'Interesting, isn't it? Most men do. Think women are idiots, I mean.'

He didn't answer.

'You don't, though,' she said. She was looking at him, as if the realisation had suddenly come to her.

'Don't I?'

'No.' Staring at him, an expression he could not read. 'Are you married?'

'I have a partner, yes.'

'Kids?'

Hesitation. Always a little hesitation when it came to that question. Because, every time, he had to stop himself from counting Carla. He had one child, one. He had to remove the other from his mind. 'Yes,' he said. 'I've got a son. And a step-daughter. What about you?'

'Me? No. No, no. I think that's an awful trap. The wife and mother business. And Monty's got kids. He doesn't want any more. I mean, two boys ought to be enough to satisfy his urge to breed, wouldn't you say? Not to mention the girl. Poor wretch.'

He didn't like this topic or her tone.

'So,' he said, 'this wheeling and dealing. Have you been doing it long?'

'Less than a year. About five months before we came here. I started off with fifty thousand. Haven't done badly, have I?'

'What's the secret?'

'Study. Information. Reading and listening. I mean Monty talks about it all the time, the state of the economy, business. Here, Australia, Japan. That's how I got into it, listening to him. I thought if he's going to chew my ear off every evening, the least I can do is pay some attention and put the information to good use. And you know what? I'm better at it than he is.' She lifted her shoulders, gave him a happy grin. Lips a little parted, tips of her white teeth just visible. He had an impulse to . . . He was not sure what.

'So,' she said. 'Tell me about this PDQ.'

'PDD.' Glanced at her and away, round the kitchen. Drank his wine. Confused for a moment. He didn't even like her. Why should he want her? Because she was there? Because she wanted him? He couldn't know what she wanted. The drift of secret molecules in the currents of the room.

— But I don't understand, he had said to Hannah Creswell. Is this dream about my present situation or my character?

— Why can't it be both? The one, after all, might arise from the other.

He met Laura's eyes again. 'It's a local company. Reliable. I've worked with them before.'

'When can they start?'

'I'm not quite sure. I've put some pressure on, though.'

'How much?'

'Fourteen and a half.'

"Shit." She sounded not surprised but irritated. The girlish air was gone with the reality of spending money.

'There's a lot of dirt to move,' he said. 'An excavator, two trucks, a grader, four men.' He shrugged.

'Well, all right.' Pouring wine once again. 'You know what you're doing. No point in keeping a dog and barking yourself, is there?'

'No,' he said, wondering how he should take being compared to a dog, feeling, rather, amused at how oblivious she was to what she'd said. Well, we know where we stand now, don't we? Who's the mistress, who's the servant. Click your fingers and I'll lick your hand.

22.

ONE PLACE THAT EPITOMISED the changing fortunes of Durry was an eating establishment on the corner of High Street and Cross Street. Opened in 1920 as the Sunset Café, it had survived for fifty years serving meat and two veg to the denizens of the public bar of the Durry Hotel, who were cast out every night at 6 p.m. to fend for themselves. With the changes to the liquor laws in the late sixties, an attempt was made to tart the place up. Its name was changed to Chloe's, its streetfront windows were whited over on the inside and its interior walls were painted a tasteful purple (aubergine). Thus renovated, it made a play for the discerning Durry diner. Chloe's had a licence and (astonishing!) a wine list. The meat and two veg had become Steak Diane, with Pommes Frites and salad or vegetables, to which was added Chicken Maryland and Fish of the Day (cooked in a beer batter). Chloe's lasted two decades, going through an Italian phase and a Mexican phase, and several corresponding coats of paint, from ricotta to chilli pop, along the way.

In 1996, it was bought by Gaston Brillard, a small, round man with a comic French accent and a claim to being an international chef. He changed the name to Le Petit Français which, under the spreading influence of Larry Hannerby's wit, was usually translated as The Little Frog. Gaston enjoyed this joke. Eventually, he even had small green frogs printed on the top left-hand corner of his menus. He was a man with a capacity for self-irony, a quality not always associated with the French. Rumour had it that he was not, in truth, Gaston le

Français but Gaston le Belgique. Rumour also had it that he was actually from Scunthorpe. However, if the accent was fake the claim to culinary skill was not. Le Petit Français had been shortlisted in the Grenville Awards for Best Provincial Restaurant six times in the last eight years and had won twice. Visitors came from far-away places to sample Gaston's judicious combination of Cordon Bleu and Provençal. The locals counted themselves lucky to live within his ambit. Larry Hannerby had been known to say that if Gaston went, he'd go too.

'Try this. A little.' Gaston, with a bottle, sitting down. He had glasses, three glasses, stems tucked between the fingers of his left hand.

'Oh, well,' Ward said. 'A bit early, but well . . .' He glanced at Maddy.

'Why not?' She smiled at him.

Gaston poured, a white. Three fingerfuls in each glass. Ward took his, sniffed it, sipped. A pinot gris. Fresh and light, a spring in its step.

'Local?'

Gaston turned the label to him. Wolde House.

'Ah!' Ward said, pleased that he'd picked it.

'It's okay,' Gaston sipped.

'Yes.' Maddy smacking her lips. Curious that she was drinking at this time of day. And relishing it, too. Part of the celebration already, the mood? Ward felt cosy, happy. Life was in good shape, sitting pretty. All the bad things filed away where nobody could find them. Every time the Tribe met up it made it better, more secure, more certain.

'I don't know,' Gaston said. 'What do you think? I put him in my cellar?'

'How much would you charge?' Ward asked.

'Thirty?'

'You could do thirty-five.' He laughed. 'I shouldn't tell you that, should I?'

'Oh, my friend.' Waving the remark aside, as if Ward would never have to pay for anything at The Little Frog ever again.

I wish, Ward thought.

'So,' Maddy was leaning forward, looking at Gaston. 'You called them?'

'Of course.' He grinned, sat back in his chair. 'I say I am happy that they are my very good customers for a long time and it will be very, very nice for me if they come to dinner on Friday. On the house.'

'And?' Maddy was eager, a shine in her eyes.

'Sylvie, she say, "Oh, Gaston, what a coincidence. This is fantastic. Friday is our anniversary."' He laughed, a big laugh that made his belly shake.

They all laughed.

'So they're coming?' Maddy asked.

'Oh, yes. Sylvie make the confirmation Saturday morning.'

'Brilliant,' Ward said.

He suddenly remembered the verdict and wondered how Larry was feeling, winning it, or at least having it go the way he wanted. Sometimes, Ward had noticed, a good result seemed to make Larry depressed rather than happy, especially when it was a high-profile case like this one. Perhaps I should give him a bell, he thought. Perhaps I should take him out for a session at the Club.

'So, for the menu,' Gaston said. 'You want him à la carte or table d'hôte?'

'Table d'hôte?' Interesting thought.

Gaston shrugged, a touch of modesty. 'I could do somethings a little special. You know, for Larry. There is a nice way to cook venison from St Bennet. Or goose. I could maybe give you the goose.'

'Goose?'

'I don't know if I find a goose, but if . . . There is a nice way to stuff her with orange. Or maybe Sauce de Volonne.'

'What do you think?' Ward asked Maddy.

'Yummy,' Maddy said. 'But would it work for everybody? Heidi, for instance. Isn't she a bit vegetarian?'

'Oh, well,' Ward said. 'There's always the standard menu for anyone who's like that. And goose? Well, you know. For Larry.'

'This is Sylvia's anniversary too,' Maddy told him, but nicely.

'Wouldn't Sylvia like goose?'

'She might.'

'The way Gaston would do it?' The question hardly needed answering. He turned to Gaston. 'What about wine?'

'Oh, I think Côte de Rhône. A pinot noir. I have one very, very nice. Chateau de Matecleau, you know him?'

'No.'

'This for the goose will be nice. If I find the goose. Look, maybe you leave this with me. Maybe I think, twist my brains, take a look around. Then, I get back to you, we talk again. Okay?'

'Yes, good idea. Fantastic.'

Gaston picked up the bottle. 'Thirty-five dollars, you say?'

'Let's say thirty-two.'

Gaston laughed, topped up the glasses, just the three fingers still.

'So,' he said. 'Life is good?'

'Very good. Couldn't be better.'

'Busy,' Maddy told him.

'Oh, but Maddy is always busy. Going here. Going there. You are like the angel who make everything okay.'

'Are you teasing me, Gaston?' Maddy sipped her wine. Red lips.

She has lovely lips, Ward thought. And they did nice things to you. On occasion.

Gaston laughed. 'Flattery will get you somewhere. Is that what you say?'

'Not quite.'

'Ah, but it's true. In France, it is true. I say nice things. You say nice things. We feel good. Like kisses.'

'You just want us to stay for lunch,' Maddy told him.

'Lunch? You want lunch?' Gaston with eyes round, asking as if the idea were a complete surprise.

A pause.

'Well,' Maddy said, doubtfully. 'I don't have much time.'

'You have an appointment. Of course.' Gaston was dismissing the idea of lunch.

Too quickly in Ward's view. 'Maybe . . .' He looked at Maddy and she at him. Did she have an appointment? No, not exactly.

'I make you a nice omelette,' Gaston said. 'Like the sunshine. With some herbs, just a little . . .'

'Come on.' Ward gave her a nudge with his elbow and she laughed. A merry laugh. Merry like a berry, like a cherry.

162

Tasty girl. Yum-yum.

'Why not?' she said, smiling at him.

'Bravo!' Gaston pushed the bottle to the middle of the table. 'And the wine is on the house.'

23.

AND TOM, THE ZOMBIE, two-faced clown, was another who was wine-woozy, at 12.30 in the afternoon, parking his ute in Cook Street, getting out and walking the half block to the post office. He was thinking of Astra, what he was going to say to her, because he was going to end it. Not out of a sense of duty or an act of will, not a conscious, rational decision that a man might make from the lofty height of his principles. No, this was a feeling thing, a thing of hope and freedom, of fresh air and a sea breeze. Because, for the first time, he saw the prospect of understanding. He had the sniff of a future. No matter what kind of mess he was in, how deeply mired, he felt sure now that he could escape and that he wouldn't even need to hurt or hate the woman he had used.

Odd what it must be like for her. For him, it's all been will-he, won't-he. Can he keep himself on track? Can he do the right thing? Or will he let that half-unconscious urge draw him to her, unresisting? For her, though, it's just been waiting at the mercy of his indecision and, thus far at least, she's not seemed to mind. She's greeted him with a smile and open arms. If she's felt aggrieved or bad tempered, it's been quickly kissed away. Will she fight now, will she rail, will she attempt to seduce him while he stands, like a saint, resisting her advances? He does not think so. Not today.

Up the steps and into the lobby and the room where the boxes were, the rows of little red doors. Feeling in his pocket for the keys. A young woman was crouching down in front of the box next to his. He stood, waiting for her to finish, watched the movement of her shoulders as she tugged at the letters jammed inside. She was wearing a sweater, pale mauve, closely knit, tight enough to show the knobs of her spine. He thought of Astra's back, the smoothness under his hands, the freckles like flakes of amber in the pale skin. Then another sense of goldenness. Golden light and a woman who had no name. A rush of lust and longing unattached to anyone. A flare in the dark.

'Sorry,' the girl said, standing up, a little duck of her head, self-effacing. She was clutching the bunch of letters to her chest.

'That's all right.' He smiled at her as she turned away. Carla's age. Hardly more than Carla's age.

Bending from the waist, he fitted his key into the little door, turned it. Open. A half a dozen letters inside. He took them out and then put his hand in, feeling towards the back of the box to see if there was anything there, maybe a card to indicate there was a packet to collect from the counter. Nothing. Lock the door. Keys back in his pocket. A few steps away, shuffling through the letters as he did so. The usual stuff, invoices and trade promotions, except for one: a small envelope with a local postmark and the address too far over to the right. *Mr T. Marino, Greenwise Garden Centre, PO Box 994, Durry, New Zealand.* Something odd about it, so he paused, in a shaft of sunlight from the head-high window, and opened it. A single sheet of paper folded into four. A message.

> *If you want to know why your daughter Carla went to the river, talk to Merry Gibbitson 411-2347. She went to stop them bulling her.*
> *A Friend*

He couldn't take it in at first, and then, when he did begin to understand the words, they did not make much sense. His impulse was to call the number immediately, and he had the phone out and was starting to dial before he decided, no, think about it, let's get it clear before we rush.

Merry Gibbitson. A name he'd never heard before. Was it male or female? And who was bulling who? It was an odd word, bulling. Kind of old-fashioned. People these days would say bullshitting or something similar.

His phone rang. It was still in his hand and startled him, confused him so that he just stood there looking at it until after the third ring.

'Tom Marino here.'

'Hello, Tom. This is Heidi. Can we meet?'

Meet? What was she asking? 'Yes, I guess so.'

'I have some things to talk about. Some business things.'

'All right.'

'I can drive into town,' she went on. Urgent.

'No, that's all right. I have to come out that way. To Clisserford. I can drop by.'

'Today?'

No, he didn't mean specifically today. Of course not. Not today. 'How about tomorrow?' he said. 'About two?'

'Please.'

The world, the ordinary world, was full of people with their needs and purposes, ordinary actions and reactions. Whereas he was paralysed, standing there, phone in one hand, mail in the other, the open sheet of paper with the strange message. All thought of Astra was gone. Nothing left except an emptiness, the cold of dread and hope, like dampness seeping through a wall, the heavy weight of water.

Carla had a friend, Merry Gibbitson, and one of them tried to stop the bulling.

Last time he saw her, that Saturday, intent with her bike, wheeling it down the driveway, the bag with her library books on the carrier. Swinging her leg over, riding away, without a look back, without a second thought. He hardly saw her go, it was so ordinary. And yet she had thoughts of her own, she must have had.

Call the number. No, he thought, too early. A friend of hers would most likely be at school at this time of day.

So he went to the house by the river just like all the other times. She smiled when she saw him, and they kissed and went to bed, just like the other times. And afterwards, lying there, he felt not guilty, not repulsed, but detached, as if his mind had shaken loose from his flesh.

'Are you all right?' she asked him.

'Yes.'

'Only you just seem . . . I don't know. Preoccupied.'

'Yes.' Staring at the ceiling with its flat angled cornice, the surface blank above them. There was a crack there, like a thin flash of jagged dark lightning, from the centre to the middle of the wall where the door was. It all seemed far away, though, in another world.

'Are you worried about something?' She was looking at him, her head propped on the heel of her hand, her sandy hair fluffed up into a mass of curls. Gleam of light in it from the bright window behind her.

'I don't want to take you for granted,' he said.

'You don't. I never feel you do.'

Tell her. Tell her now. If it hadn't been for the letter he would have told her already. But was that true? He didn't know. And at the moment, right now, it hardly seemed to matter whether he told her or not. Nothing mattered. Nothing that his will could want was of the least consequence.

'I should go,' he told her.

Her eyes lifted. She was glancing at the clock on the little table beside the bed. But she said nothing. Instead, she looked down at him again, to his chest, and with her free hand began to twist her fingers into the hairs there. Little pullings. Watching as if it were a delicate task she had to perform. Watching but not seeing. Preoccupied herself.

He reached up, watched his hand reaching up and coming to rest on the back of her head. The weight of it drew her down towards him so that their lips met. Love-soft lips. She made a noise in her throat, a little groan.

How can I want her if I feel nothing? he thought. Is it because she's alive and I'm not? Is that what I want, to know she's alive? To make her feel for both of us. Do I want to hurt her, is that it?

'Lovely,' she said, lifting her head.

'What's lovely?'

'This. Making love on a Monday. It sets me up for the week.'

'It's Tuesday.'

'You know what I mean.' Rolling away from him, but hanging on so that he moved with her, reversing their positions.

'Yes.' He lifted the sheet, bent his head and nuzzled her breast, licked her nipple slowly. He did want her, didn't he?

He could feel his body wanting her, coldly, clearly, surely. Was it love, though, or hatred?

'Hmmm.' She gave a little squirm. 'That's nice.'

'Maybe we should have some more.'

'Not if it's going to be a quickie. I want it slow. I don't like it when we have to watch the clock. Wondering if the boys might come home early.'

Little faces. Unsmiling, wary.

'I should go,' he said.

'Yes.' She reached out, her arm around his neck, pulling him down and lifting her head to meet him. Kissing mouth. Soft and warm.

Stop it, he thought. Stop it now and tell her it's over. You can't spare her feelings and you shouldn't. Why should you? She's in this with her eyes open. She knows what she's doing. Because whatever it is, she has it coming. It's her own fault if she needs someone like you.

He slid his hand down over her pubic bone, fingers touching damp and smooth, the silkiness that made his body come to life. The lust he felt was real and hard and far away.

'Oh, nice,' she said, a little panting breath. 'You make me feel wicked.'

'Wicked?'

'Wanting you.'

'That's not wicked.'

'No, the way I want you.'

'How do you want me?'

'I'm starting to want you very, very much.'

'That's all right. That's good. I want you to want me.'

'No, it's not.' A heavy whisper, urgent. 'I need to warn you. You need to be careful.'

'Careful? Why?' Nipple between his teeth. She gave a moan.

'When it gets nice, when it gets really, really nice. I start to want, I start to want . . . You'll think this is really mad.'

'What?'

'I want to do it without a condom.'

'Why?' A little twist. Was he afraid? Don't be afraid, a voice said.

'I shouldn't say that. I shouldn't tell you. You'll think I'm really stupid. You'll want to go.'

'No,' he said. 'I don't want to go.' Because he was not afraid of her words. This was an opportunity, a possibility. Stop pretending, the voice said. No more promises. Just let go. Give in. Come to her.

'Why?' he asked, looking into her face as if he wanted to understand. Her eyes, blue, pleading.

'I don't want anything to be between us. It isn't, you know, it isn't physical. It isn't the way you feel inside me. It's how I feel. How it makes me feel.'

'How does it make you feel?'

'Sinful, wrong, brave, lucky, open. You know, open to the possibilities. It's the risk, I suppose. I like the risk. I like to feel I'm opening up. With the right man. With a man I . . . Ooh.' She closed her eyes.

'What if you get pregnant?'

'I don't know. I like being pregnant. But . . . No, no. I'm not trying to get pregnant. I don't want that to happen. But . . . It's just the way it makes me feel. It makes me come really big time.'

He was hard, so hard it hurt. Like the concentration of his pain in a place that he had ceased to occupy.

'You want to do it like that now?' he asked.

'Oh, we shouldn't, should we?'

He reached down, rolled off the condom. Then he took her hand and guided it till she touched him.

'Like that?'

'Oh, Jesus!'

'We can do it like that.'

'Oh, Jesus!'

No more lying. No more games. He moved over her and she opened her legs. Kneeling there, supporting himself on his arms, looking down at her from far away. Her eyes were closed. The woman on the pillow, he thought. Is this the one I want?

24.

HE WAS PARKED IN the lay-by by the river, looking out through the windscreen at the cross with the ragged garland, waiting with the phone to his ear.

'Hello.' A soft, small voice.

'Is that Merry Gibbitson?'

'Yes.'

'Oh, hi. My name's Tom Marino. I think you knew my daughter, Carla.'

Silence.

'Are you still there?'

'Yes.'

'Did you know my daughter, Carla?'

'Yes.' Smaller, softer than ever. Frightened.

'Look,' he said, 'I'm sorry to bring this up. I'm sorry to call you like this but someone sent me a note, an anonymous note, which says you might know why Carla was on River Road the day she died. The note says something about bulling.'

Silence.

'Do you know anything about someone bulling someone?'

'Bullying.'

Bullying? Of course.

'Was Carla being bullied?'

'No.'

'Were you?'

Silence.

'Were you there the day she died?'

'No.' The voice breaking, twisting into a sob. Stop, he

told himself. But he couldn't stop.

'Look,' he said. 'Thank you for talking to me. I really appreciate it. I'm sure you were a good friend to Carla.'

Another sob and the line went dead. Left him staring through the windscreen at the bright sun on the eastern hills.

Carla wanted to help Merry Gibbitson who was being bullied. But why the river? And why should she go if Merry wasn't there? Someone knew. Someone knew something. Ask the child who the bullies were. He could hassle them. They deserved to be hassled. Yobs who got their jollies ganging up on other kids. Had they ganged up on Carla — no, not like that. It was a car accident, a hit and run. It didn't make sense any other way.

But someone knew.

He picked up the phone, pressed the redial button. It rang once, twice, three times, four.

'Hello.' A woman's voice. Stronger than the child's. Confused him for a moment.

'Er, yes. My name's . . .'

'Did you call here a minute ago?'

'Yes. My name's Tom Marino. I . . .'

'What do you want?'

'I understand Merry might know something about my daughter's death.'

'What?'

No, he thought. This isn't going well.

'Look, I understand Merry was being bullied by someone. All I want to know is the name of the person, the child who . . .'

'We don't know anything. Don't call here again. All right?'

25.

IT WAS A SILENT meal in the Fuchs-Wyte household. A silent evening to come, no doubt. The third in a row. All weekend, they had avoided each other. Heidi had spent the daylight hours outdoors. Colin had gone to the Club on Saturday and played bridge with people he hardly knew and cared about even less. On Sunday he had picked Imogen up from Lisa's house and taken her to a movie in the city. *The Lord of the Rings: The Two Towers*. She had not liked it much, other than the horses. Too many battles, too many animals in danger. She had gone all sulky on it and he wondered if she was disappointed in him, if he somehow could have made more effort to amuse her.

Afterwards, over coffee, because he could not avoid it any longer, they talked about her birthday. The languid look of boredom disappeared immediately. She was all smiles and eagerness. The change gave him a sick feeling. He was caught between Heidi and his daughter and he knew he wasn't supposed to let that happen. Be yourself. Stand up for yourself. Your destiny is in your hands. Well, yes, of course. Absolutely. Have to make it clear, have to insist on what you want. But what did he want? He didn't know, except that he needed people to like him, especially Imogen. And sitting there, in Stratos, seeing the question that trembled in her eyes — Was it possible? Was it really possible? — the willow man did what he so often did, he bent with the wind of the moment. Yes? He didn't actually say yes, but he let her push him closer to it.

— Why don't we give it serious consideration? he said. Next weekend. Let me make some enquiries and then, if it all seems to be okay, we could go and talk to some people.

— People? What people?

— I don't know. Who do you talk to about buying a horse?

— The Pony Club. The secretary's called Alison Mossmen and her phone number's 535-4761.

All figured out. And, shit, why shouldn't it work for her? At least one person in this shitty world could get what they wanted, could have something of her own that was alive and loved her. Yes, he supposed that horses were like dogs, they could love you as much as you loved them.

And so here he was, now, at his own unloving dinner table, supping his wine, staring deep into the bottom of the glass.

'Colin?' Heidi looking at him. The first time she'd initiated an exchange since Friday.

'Yes.'

'I wish to talk.'

Yes, he thought. It's about time we sorted it out, came to our senses. The atmosphere had thawed a bit. He was feeling better, a bit better. He could apologise, if he had to. If she apologised, he could too. He could make some promises, like paying her more attention, cutting back on his drinking. Maybe, with a few concessions, they could kiss and make up.

'Shall we talk here or in the other room?' she asked.

'Oh, in there.'

He took his wine and got up, moved away, out into the living area, turned on the lights, the soft glow, patches on the walls reflected into the room, the tan leather lounge suite, the blonded wood. He went to the sofa, thinking perhaps she would join him, but she didn't. Took her usual chair. Sat in it straight, feet together on the floor, hands curving over the ends of the arms. Like a queen on a throne.

'So you want to talk,' he said.

'Yes.'

He waited. She said nothing. Was he supposed to apologise first?

'I meant what I said,' she told him, at last.

'When? What did you say?'

'When we had the fight on Friday.'

'Oh, that. That's all right. Lovers' quarrel.'

'No.'

'What do you mean "no"?'

'I meant what I said. I don't want to fight any more. I want that we should divorce.'

What? He didn't take it in for a moment.

'We can't get divorced,' he said. 'We're not married.'

'The law says we are. Six years.'

A cold flood of truth. Skin cold. Like it was turning inside out and exposing him, his insides bleeding in the air.

'It doesn't make sense,' he said. 'It's crazy. We have a little argument and you want to leave?'

'No,' she told him. 'I want you should leave.'

'What?'

'We will divide the property. This place is less than half of everything, so, I think this is fair. I take this —' she gestured about her — 'and you keep all the rest. You go. I stay. We call it quits.'

'Jesus,' he said. 'You've been thinking about this, haven't you? You've been plotting.'

'I've been thinking three days.'

She was serious. She meant it. Fuck her, his anger said. Fuck her, let her go. But he knew, somehow, that he did not want her to because this time there would not be enough bottles in the world to drown the misery. Be reasonable, he told himself, be rational. Stay calm.

'Surely,' he said, 'there's a way we can work this out.'

'I don't think so.'

'Do you really mean that a little thing, a silly argument about a horse is worth splitting up over? If that's all it takes, I'll just say no to Imogen. You can have the paddock, no problems. She'll get over it.'

'It's not the horse. You know that.'

'What is it, then?'

'Everything.'

'Everything?'

'We are not good together any more.'

'You mean sex.'

'No,' she said. 'Not sex. Why do you always think sex?'

Because, he wanted to say. Because it matters. Because you make it matter.

'What, then?' he asked.

'You think I am nothing.'

'I don't.'

'Maybe you think so for all women.' She shrugged. It was a gesture of indifference, as if she didn't care what he thought about anything any more. He felt a punch of rage but managed to control it. Stay calm. Be reasonable. *I will have calm and quiet, you understand me?*

'Look,' he said. 'This takes some getting used to. Can we not make a decision right now? Can we just let it rest on the table and see how it goes over the next few days?'

'Okay.' Looking at him. Blue eyes. What was she feeling? Sad? She couldn't even feel sad? Nothing at all.

'For a week?' he said. He heard the note of pleading in his voice and hated it. Because it was too late. He couldn't stop it now. Did he need to be humiliated? Must that happen, too? He remembered the rifle in the hall cupboard, the box of shells in the drawer in his study. I'll kill myself, he thought. Is that what you want? I'll put a bullet through my head and then you'll see.

'Okay,' she said. 'But we don't sleep together. I want you should sleep in the spare room.'

'Fine,' he said. 'Fine.' Because those were the words you spoke when you were helpless, when you wanted just to delay things, not to have the final moment come.

She picked up her book from the table beside her chair, tucked her feet up underneath her in her reading pose, opened the book at the leather bookmark. Started to read. She didn't even glance at him. Not for a second. Water pouring, rush, into the laundry sink, the bounce of flying drops like bullets in the air. Please, Daddy. Please don't hurt him. *Let me make this clear. I will not have the peace disrupted. You understand me? I will have calm and quiet.*

26.

TOM DREAMING OF A house, an old house, and it was leaking somewhere, water dripping from the ceiling, big wooden beams and the strips of floorboards. He was in a cellar and the water was running down one of the walls, a dark patch, damp and shiny, and the floor was earth, mud, and the water was carving out a channel as it flowed across the dirt and out through the door.

Then he was standing on the veranda at Clisserford and pointing out to Laura Kerrington how the work had come along. Because the project was finished, there were two big mounds, like hills. No, they were real hills because they were covered in tall pine trees, dark green against a pale grey sky, and there was a road winding off into the distance between the mounds. And the woman, maybe it wasn't Laura although she had the same shaggy blonde hair, was standing close to him, and he wanted her. She wanted him too but there was a word they needed. He couldn't think of it but he knew it was her name, or the name of the place that she came from, where they were going.

Then, they were in a bed, naked, dusty brown light. His cock had grown enormously long so that it came up nearly to the level of his shoulders, and it was growing very thin, stretching like treacle, like an exclamation mark, and he was afraid that it would stretch so much it would become detached, that it would break off altogether.

What were the chances? Good. No, that was the wrong word — not good, the opposite. Bad. High. The chances were high. Tom didn't need to figure it out. He didn't need to remember back to the time when he had last thought about such things. The days with Annabelle before Carla was conceived.

Astra's reaction had told him. Lying there beside him after he had rolled off her, slipped out of her, aware of her as the world came back to rights. She was staring at the ceiling, taking long, slow breaths through her open mouth. Left hand came up to rest with the wrist on her breast bone. Right palm on her belly. Rise and fall.

— Are you all right? he had asked.

— Oh, yes. I'm fine. I feel . . . I feel . . . My God, I'm sorry. We shouldn't have done that. Don't hate me, will you?

— No, he said. Of course not.

She rolled towards him then, gathering up the sheet, wrapping herself in it. Lay there with her eyes closed, head pressed into the hollow of the pillow. He bent over her, the ginger curls.

— Please go, she said. Just leave me, please.

So she was ovulating about now. So she would get pregnant. Of course. It had happened before, hadn't it? Twice before. Two boys with two different fathers. All because she liked the way it made her feel to do it without contraception. Guilt and fear and hope. Did she hope? Was she wanting it to happen? Or, perhaps, more to the point, was he wanting it to happen? Because afterwards, since then, since he left her yesterday, he had not behaved like someone who was desperately fearful of the outcome. He had not been dwelling on the awful consequences for his life, for his relationship with Lisa. If he had thought of her at all in his preoccupation with Merry Gibbitson, it was the compulsion of his flesh that he remembered, Astra's cries and her body moving under him in the rhythm of their lust, as he looked down at her from a million miles behind his eyes.

27.

LISA CAIRNES, IN A brisk walk down George Street, tension in her shoulders against the chill in the bright air, reached the steps of the building that housed the *Durry Advocate*.

'Oy! Lady!'

She turned and saw him, Max Hosche, crossing the road towards her, odd sideways shuffle as if his right shoulder were turned against the wind. There was no wind.

'Max. Good morning.'

'I got a story for you.'

'What?'

'They killed Bessie.'

'Bessie?' She stepped down, back on to the footpath, looked at him curiously.

'The dog. They killed my dog. I found her yesterday, down by the creek. Dead.'

'How did they kill it?' She presumed he was talking about the Kerringtons.

'Poisoned her.'

'How do you know?'

'She was dead.' His eyes, peering at her, meeting hers for the first time. She saw the pain in them, the hurt, the plain, dumb, old human confusion.

'Oh, Max. I'm sorry.' Seeing so clearly what the dog meant to him, the loss, and feeling just that wrench of love and pity. And the outrage.

'What you going to do about it?' he demanded.

'You know Bessie was poisoned? You got an autopsy done?'

'Autopsy? I don't need an autopsy. She'd thrown up and there was foam on her mouth. Dribble everywhere.'

'Where's Bessie now?'

'I buried her.'

Oh, shit! 'You need an autopsy, Max.'

'I'm not digging her up again.'

'But we need proof. We need a vet to say what she died of. Without that, I don't know what we can do.'

'Write a story. That's your job, isn't it?'

'It'd just be hearsay, Max. If you went to the police, they'd tell you . . .'

'I'm not going to the bloody cops!'

'Without an autopsy . . . I can't help you. I'm sorry.'

His face twisted, eyes with a flash of anger. 'You're just a selfish slut!' he snarled. 'Like her! Like all the rest of them!'

'And you're a stupid old fool!'

For a moment he seemed about to laugh, but it turned into another snarl instead. 'Nargh!' A flap of his hand as if he were waving off a fly. He turned away.

She watched him go, as her anger drained from her. An impulse to call after him: Max! But what could she say? This is the second time I've let him down, she thought.

A Dead Dog. She remembered Colin and his father.

— What happened?

— He drowned it.

— What?

— He took it into the laundry and he drowned it. Held it under while the sink filled.

— Because it was making too much noise?

— Yes. He couldn't stand noise. Because of the war.

— What was its name?

— Rexy.

Then she remembered something else, another thing she hadn't done. Stan Andreissen. She had to call him about the girl, Merry Gibbitson. She had been dithering about that, feeling guilty because she wanted to ignore it, have it go away. Do it now, she thought. Go on.

28.

A BREEZE FROM THE hills, soft but cool against their faces. Big puffs of cloud like clumps of fungus floating in the stream of the air. Tom and Heidi, side by side, with their backs to the greenhouse, looked out over the cultivations, the rows of beds with narrow gravel paths between, the whole protected by a windbreak of macrocarpas along the northern and western edges. There was a big plastic water tank over to their left, a pale green cylinder with a domed top, a little pumphouse beside it. The pump drew water from the bore and filled the tank. In dry weather, the water was released through soak hoses along the beds, a gravity system. She had explained it to him once before, on an afternoon a year or so ago when the friends had been given a tour. Everything looked pretty much as it had then, except that the trees were taller and there were more beds. Yes, she said, there were some she hadn't used yet. A good chance, really, for there was plenty of room and, if they were planning for the future, they could plant a windbreak for the paddock here (pointing) behind the greenhouse. That was another tenth of a hectare there. Nothing on it now but a few sheep to keep the grass down.

They turned, walked back together, side by side, went into the greenhouse, into the warm air, under the angled roof that was bright above them with refracted sunlight. Heidi unzipped her jacket, began to talk of how this was all ready, they could begin with seedlings anytime. Certainly, there was room here too. It was good to look at it, to sense the reality of the space, the grey-brown wooden benches, the concrete floor, to breathe the warm air rich with earth smells. She had a few exotic things, some begonias, a couple of orchids, but mostly this was a functional place. Some winter tomatoes and lettuce, and a mass of trays and pots filled with dark brown, dirt-brown mix. And empty bench space, plenty of it.

Heidi explaining everything, which didn't need to be explained, slowly drew him down the length of the building. Finger pointing. She had nail polish on, and he wondered if he was noticing because it was unusual or for some other reason. She was wearing lipstick, too, maybe just a touch, a scarlet touch, which was why, perhaps, his eyes kept on being drawn to her mouth as she formed her words. The white of her teeth, the tip of her tongue, the little push of her lips as she made the oo and the ow sounds. Who and how and where and what and when. She was talking in her usual way, carefully, efficiently, saying what she meant, no more and no less, but he felt there was something odd about her manner. I'd better learn to read her, he thought, if we are going to be partners.

'So,' he said into one of her pauses but then couldn't go on because he was not sure what he wanted to say, just to stop her, maybe, and move the conversation into another place.

'Yes?' Smiling.

'This just seems such a sensible idea that I wonder why we didn't think of it before.'

'Yes.'

'And we don't even have to have a formal arrangement to begin with.'

'No.' She looked away. Something in her tone and in the movement caught his attention. Uncertainty?

'You talked to Colin?' He did not know where the

question came from and whether he even had a right to ask it.

'Yes.' This time the doubt was more obvious.

'A problem?'

She gave a sigh, lifted her hands and touched her temples for a moment, looked at him.

'No,' she said. 'I don't think so. I think that will be okay. But I know I want to be very open and honest with you at this time and I can't. I have many confusions.'

'What sort of confusions?'

'Ah, well.' She turned with her back to the bench, leaned, half sitting on it. Hands in her pockets, arms rigid so that they pushed the edges of her jacket out like twin deflecting shields. 'I have lived in Durry seven years. About like you.'

'Yes.'

'But I am not a sociable person. I do not have friends. It is bad to have no friends, I think.'

He was tempted to tell her that of course she had friends. There was Sylvia and Maddy and Larry and Ward. There was himself. And Lisa. But he knew this was not what she meant because in the sense that she meant he did not have friends either.

'But I live here.' She spread her jacket in a little gesture of inclusion. 'This is my life. It's a good life. I make things grow.' A pause. She looked down at her feet. 'When I was at university I studied science —' she glanced up at him. 'You too, I think?'

'Yes. Maths and computing.'

'For me it was biology. My parents are very religious. They think God made the world for a big purpose. Me, I have no illusions. I think it is all just an accident. We have not special privilege. We get along as best we can. We have minds that think and hands that do clever things but mostly we are just big complexities of instincts that have come about to reproduce, to have babies. I don't want to have babies but the instinct is still there. I control the instinct but I still have it. It is feelings. It is needs. It is emotions. We can stop the outputs, if you like. But we cannot stop the process. I think you understand me?'

He was not sure that he did. The words seemed to come from a great height, like pebbles rolling down a mountainside, but the look she gave him was close and compelling, pulling at him in a way that he hadn't expected, a way that he was waiting for. All it needed was the flick of a decision.

'I watch you,' she said. 'You are like me, I think. You are a lone one. The others are together but we are not. We are alone and we take our chances when we can. And for me, right now, I am wondering what my chances are. And so this is my confusion. I do not know if I want a business partner or a lover. Or maybe I do know. But I am not sure which is the one available.' The look again, not pleading, just waiting.

What could he do? He was too far away, too remote, to stop the movement. It was already too late. Three steps towards her. She stood up to meet him. His hands slipped inside her jacket and around her back, and her arms came up around his neck. Mouth to mouth. Open mouth. Her tongue pressing urgently against his. And suddenly he was alive with need and gratitude and wonder. Is this the one? His fingers smoothing down over the thick hem of her sweater and up underneath it, searching for her skin. He wanted her skin. But there was only some other fabric, softer than the wool and slippery like silk. It slid over the muscles of her back.

'Come into the house,' she said, breath hot in his ear.

But no, he knew they could not do that. There would be no time.

'I have to go somewhere,' he told her. Because there was one thing in the world stronger than she was at this moment. 'I'm sorry.'

'That's okay.' Leaning back from him, wrists still on his shoulders.

'No, I really am sorry. Bad timing.'

'No. It is good. We should think about it, maybe.'

'If we think, we may decide it's a bad idea.'

She smiled, the little dimples creasing into her cheeks. 'It is a bad idea. Everyone will tell you. But you, I think, you are a bit wild. You don't care.'

Was it true? He didn't know. He cared, he thought he cared, but there were things that were stronger than responsibility. Her golden hair in the sunlight. A little strand of it had come loose and was hanging, like a lure, over the pale skin of her brow. He smoothed it back with his fingers.

'Wild and silent,' she said, and kissed him again.

29.

THE GIBBITSONS LIVED IN East Durry, on one of the bundle of streets tucked under the hills on the other side of the river. Cold in the mornings with the damp from the water rising up to meet the mist from the range above, but now, at 3.30 on an autumn afternoon, the air was bright, almost warm. He sat in the ute with the window down, watching, waiting. Flowers Avenue was a street of old state houses, which were set back from the roadway, each with a stretch of lawn in front and a concrete path leading down the side of the house. Number 18, ahead of him and to his right, had yellow weatherboards and a roof of grey moss-covered tiles. The windows were closed and misted over with net curtains. There was a garage stuck in the front garden with a big viburnum beside it. A white metal letterbox on an iron post.

There were kids in the street. Primary school kids of varying ages. One or two had bicycles, another couple skateboards. In front of number 20, two little girls crouched on the grass verge, poking at something with a stick.

Why was he here? The only good reason was to get away from Heidi and stop himself doing something stupid. Except that this was stupid, too, in its way, sitting here waiting for someone he didn't know. How would he recognise her? If and when she arrived, he would not know it was her until she turned into her house, and by then it might be too late to catch her. He couldn't chase her up her own path, could he? Just a word, just a word, just a name. All I want is a name.

The house looked empty. The garage was open and there

was nothing inside. Maybe no one was home. So, if Merry Gibbitson did come, she might be alone and he could call her on his cellphone. Talk to her without upsetting her. Dear God, he didn't want to harass the kid. The last thing he wanted was to upset her.

He checked in the driving mirror. There were some bigger kids there now, wearing the college uniform. A boy on a bicycle. Another boy, running. Then, around the corner, a group of them, four or five. A bus crossed the end of the street. The school bus maybe. The boy on the bike, doing slow, lazy loops across the road and back, came towards him, passed by. Not a glance, not a look. The running boy had gone. Into one of the houses, he supposed. The group was still coming, though, five girls. Or maybe it was two groups, one with three and one with two. They were sauntering, dawdling, turning to talk to one another. Yes, it seemed like the two at the back were separate. They were crossing the road, moving over to the side where the even house numbers were. Three others were staying on the odd side.

He reached for the controls of the outside mirror and angled it so he could keep a better watch on the two. One was small and skinny with frizzy, gingery hair. The other was dark and plump and had a fluorescent-green schoolbag slung across her front and hanging down over her left thigh. They were walking side by side and the little one was talking, gesturing like she was scooping something in her right hand and lifting it towards her mouth. The plump one glanced at her and then looked across the road to the three girls on the other side. They were all close behind him now. If he turned his head, he could see the two clearly. The plump one was Merry Gibbitson, he was sure. Her size and shape and her slow manner seemed to go with the soft voice on the phone. Now they were very close, outside the path to number 16.

He opened the door, went to get out. The plump girl looked at him. Just a glance at first but then a strange, fearful expression, as if she knew who he was. She spoke to her friend. A stare from the little one and then they both turned aside. He hesitated with the door half open, his foot dangling towards the road. They were going into the wrong house. But it had to be her, didn't it? The look was proof. The frightened look. But why should she be frightened of a man in a ute? How could she know it was the same person who had called her yesterday?

He got back in the cab and closed the door. Think. Either he went and asked at number 16 or he gave up. He could come back tomorrow. But why? That was useless. All he needed was a name. A name to follow up, a name of someone who was there, who went there.

He pictured the stretch of road beside the river. The gorge was narrow at that point. The hills on the eastern side, the side opposite the road, crowded down close so there was no room for buildings, just the rough scrub to the water's edge and, in some places, bare rock. On the western side there were spots to climb down the bank through the grass and scrub. But not there, not right where she was found. It was steep just there. Stand at the road's edge with the wind in your hair. Why would anyone go? What was there to do?

His phone rang, noise in his jacket pocket. Took it out without thinking.

'Hi, bro. Kenny. That job down Cox's Line, eh? Monday all right with you?'

'Monday? Next Monday?'

'That's the one.'

'Yes, great. That's fine. Fantastic.'

'Eight o'clock?'

'I'll be there.'

''Kay. See ya.'

'Thanks, Kenny.'

Closed the phone up. Sat. Staring. What now?

A shadow beside the car. A looming figure.

'Hello, Tom.' A deep voice, broad shoulders, peak of a policeman's cap. It was a moment before he recognised the man. Stan Andreissen.

A jolt of surprise, curiosity at the strange coincidence of Stan being here, now, in this street but then, no. It was no coincidence. Obviously not. A sudden wave of shame and foolishness swept through him.

'Hello, Stan.'

Stan leaned one elbow on the open window of the ute, not looking into the cab but turned away, his eyes fixed, like Tom's, on the street ahead, the empty street, as if the two of them were mates contemplating this problem together.

'What brings you here?' Tom asked.

'We dropped by to see Merry Gibbitson.'

'Why?'

'Same reason you're here, I imagine. I talked to Lisa this morning.'

Lisa? What did Lisa have to do with it?

'We had it on our list of songs to pop around later on today. But then we got a call from Mrs Gibbitson to say some bloke in a ute was parked across the street and she was worried about him. Seems her anxiety was because her daughter'd received an intrusive phone call. Well, she called it "threatening", not "intrusive", but we took that as exaggeration.'

Tom sat there, feeling like an idiot, like a little boy admonished for his thoughtless behaviour. Eyes drifting, flicking to the left and down to the dashboard, and up, not seeing. Then he noticed, in the rear view mirror, that behind him, parked, was a patrol car, white with the blue word POLICE painted across the bonnet. Another cop standing beside it by the driver's door. A woman.

'Why don't you go home?' Stan said. 'Why don't you go home and I'll drop by later after we've had a word to Merry?'

'She's not there. I think she's in number 16.'

'We'll find her.' Stan straightened up. His left hand, resting on the door of the ute, gave a double pat, tap, tap, as if it were a horse that he wanted to gee-up.

'Thanks.' Turning the key. Engine firing.

Stan stepped away, raised his hand. Don't mention it.

30.

'Look, sweetheart. It may just not work out, you know?'

'It will. It will work out. We're going to the pony club this weekend. To talk to them. To make arrangements.'

'Your dad said that?'

'Yes. On Sunday.'

A week's a long time in your father's life, she was tempted to say. Instead she sighed, sipped her gin and looked at her daughter, sitting there, leaning forward with her elbows tucked into her sides, crouched around herself as if something hurt inside. Which it did, maybe. Because hope hurt. Wanting hurt. Is it that bad, sweetheart? Do you want it that much?

'I just don't like to see you disappointed, you know . . .' It's happened before, hasn't it? She didn't say that, though.

'He wouldn't. He knows how much . . . He loves me.' Equal stress on the first two words of the last sentence, which gave it an odd ambiguity. He *loves* me and therefore he wouldn't let me down. Or *he* loves me and you don't, do you? Because if you did, you wouldn't object, you couldn't object to what I want. And thinking of that, thinking of the love, Lisa began to understand why she did object. It wasn't the extravagance. It wasn't Colin's blatant attempt to buy his daughter's affection. This whole thing was a test of everyone's commitment.

'I love you too,' Lisa said.

'Why aren't you pleased I can have what I want, then?'

'Just because I love you. Two things will happen. Either your father will disappoint you and you'll be hurt and I don't want that to happen. Or . . .' Raising her voice to stave off any objection to the first alternative. 'Or you'll get your horse and then one of two other things will happen. Either you'll lose interest in it and it'll be a waste of money and you'll get nagged at for being a selfish little bitch, or . . .' Louder this time and with a warning lift of her hand. 'Or you'll love your horse to death and you'll spend all your time with it and you'll finish up living at your father's. And that would make me a selfish bitch because I'd feel I'd lost you.'

Big brown eyes like moons staring at her. Something in what she had said had touched the teenage soul. The look called up a like response. A surge of love and yearning, sadness, welled up inside her. She put down her drink and hauled herself out of the chair, on to the sofa beside Imogen, arms around her child, her lovely child. She felt the bony body in its clumsy uniform, the thin arms wrapped around her back, the drift of silky hair against her cheek. Lisa felt her tears start to come and fought against them, patted her daughter's back and was patted in return.

'It's okay.' Lisa let go, looked into Imogen's face and reached out, smoothed the dark hair back from her forehead, kissed her there, on the curve of her brow below the hairline. 'We'll work it out.'

'He is my father.'

'Of course.'

'You don't have to hate him.'

'I don't hate him, sweetheart. How could I hate him when he's part of the reason I've got you? But, you know, there are other things, too. Like I really don't want you riding your bike out to Cox's Line every day to see your horse. That would scare me to death.'

'Oh, Mum!' Another hug.

'I know I have to let go a bit. I know you're growing up. It's just uncomfortable having you expose my inadequacies.'

Imogen laughed then. Thank God. It was time for a laugh.

'What's so funny?'

'Oh, I don't know.' A giggle. 'It just seems funny.'

'Look, why don't you go and get out of your uniform and we can sit down and watch the news together?'

'All right.' Hauling herself upwards, gangly limbs extending.

Lisa went back to her chair, picked up her drink. Nothing was resolved. Maybe nothing could ever be resolved. She just had to give in. Colin had won. This time. She hated the thought that it could be expressed as winning and losing, that her emotions still forced that on her. Grow up, woman! God, your daughter's more mature about it than you are.

'Mum.' Imogen was back, hovering in the doorway. 'There's a man here. A policeman.'

'Stan. Hi. How are you?' Wondering, why? Why are you here? Scared. Because she knew this situation. She'd been here before.

He was looming in the doorframe, dark figure with the gathering dusk behind him. He had his cap off, holding it in front of him in an awkward kind of way.

'Come in,' she said.

'I was hoping to have a word to Tom.'

'He's not home yet.' Which was a little odd, she thought.

He was late. Just a bit.

She ushered Stan down the hall and into the living room. He sat in Tom's chair, putting his cap on the floor beside him. His hand smoothed over his dark hair.

'Would you like a drink? A beer?'

'No, better not,' he said, glancing past her at Imogen. 'A glass of water, that'd be fine.'

'Get Stan a water, will you, sweetheart?' Lisa said and then went and sat.

'Well,' Stan said, leaning back, 'maybe it's better if Tom isn't here.'

'Oh?'

'We had what you might call a tricky moment this afternoon. It seems he's been making his own inquiries about Merry Gibbitson.'

'But he doesn't know about . . .' Stopped herself. Trying to pick through the confusion.

'You didn't tell him?'

'No.'

'Ah!' A realisation for him, too, then. She waited for him to go on.

'Well,' he said, 'he knows now that you know because I told him this afternoon.'

'Oh, shit, Stan. I'm sorry. You don't need to get involved in our nonsense.'

'It's okay.' Raising his hands to push it all away. 'Not my problem.'

Imogen there beside him with a glass. He reached up, took it from her. 'Thanks, love.' He drank and then set the water on the table beside the chair.

Imogen stepped back but hovered there. Wanting to

know what was going on, wondering if she would be allowed to stay and listen. Let her, Lisa thought. She's a big girl now.

'We talked to Merry,' Stan said. 'And yes, she was the subject of a bit of intimidation. And yes, it seems Carla was sticking up for her. She gave us a couple of names and we talked to them too. It seems there was a time, last year, when a bunch of kids fooled around down by the river. There was some talk, some nonsense about taking Merry down there. They never did. None of them went near the place.'

'But Carla went.'

'Yes, it seems so. She was going to meet Merry at the library but they missed each other. It looks like Carla went to the river to check. The timing would fit.'

Lisa turned to Imogen. 'You don't know anything about this, do you?'

'No.' Of course not. She would have said, wouldn't she?

'Do you know Merry Gibbitson?'

'No, not really.'

'Carla never mentioned her?'

'No.'

'So we're no further ahead than we were,' Lisa said, turning back to Stan.

'Maybe. Maybe not. There were always some odd things about the accident. The scene was a bit of a mess, what with the ambulance and so on, but even so the crash site boys couldn't quite make it add up. The skid marks. And where the bike was. The bits of glass in the road. Carla's body. Maybe she wasn't near her bike at all when it was hit. You know, if she'd parked it by the side of the road and gone down to the river. It would explain why she wasn't wearing the bike helmet.'

'You mean she came back up to the road and the car hit

the bike and then her?'

'The other way round, maybe.'

A silence. Imogen perched on the arm of the sofa. Stan sitting forward, staring at his hands that were loosely cupped between his thighs.

'Does it get us any closer to catching anyone?' she asked.

'Probably not,' Stan said.

31.

'Why?' Tom asked.

'Why what?'

'Why didn't you tell me?'

'Because I was scared you might do something stupid. Which you did,' Lisa said.

He sighed, closed his eyes. She could see the tension in him and the humiliation. It shocked her to realise how strung out he was, how close to the edge. She was afraid for herself and for him.

'I'm sorry,' she said. 'I guess I wasn't being that open and honest.'

'I needed to know.' Looking at her, haunted eyes.

He wasn't going to forgive her, she could see. He wasn't going to forgive her here and now, just because she asked him to. Oh, God, she thought, don't let it damage anything. Don't let it matter. Because she knew that situation, the slow accumulation of unforgiven wrongs, like crimes concealed, ignored, covered over with a layer of concrete, and then another layer, made smooth, and each one didn't matter, each one was just a small thing, insignificant, except that gradually the floor gets thicker until, in the end, you can't stand upright any more.

'We could fight, you know. We could yell and scream,' she said.

'No.' He sounded too tired to fight. And fighting didn't necessarily clear the air, did it? She had fought with Colin.

'We could get drunk.'

'Maybe that's the answer.'

'It would be Larry's answer.'

'Yes.'

'Good old Larry,' she said. Her voice felt too bright, too cheerful. She was already running away, changing the subject. 'We should buy them a present. We haven't got long. Two days. What's a twentieth anniversary?'

'China.'

'China?'

'Yes.'

'How do you know that?'

He shrugged. 'I just know.'

'All right,' she said. 'I'll go to Hardy's. Do you want to come too?'

'No. You do it.' They're your friends, he might have said. She heard it in his tone. God, she thought. We're growing apart. This is really serious. What do I do? Panic. She felt the panic, but that was no good. That was pathetic.

'Are you all right?' she asked.

'Yes. I'm fine. Just tired.'

'Are we all right?'

He looked at her, the same haunted look, and she thought, Don't say no. Even if you think it, don't say it. Because words are magic sometimes and saying it might just make it true and meant.

'We need to look after ourselves,' she said. 'And each other.'

'Yes.' But he sounded empty, way past caring.

Well, she thought, if we have to, we'll part, won't we? Go our separate ways and never see each other again. I can run to Sylvia and Maddy and cry on their shoulders, and you can do whatever it is that blokes do in such circumstances. But the thought did not give her comfort. It was not bleakness she felt, not fear of the future, because without Tom there didn't seem to be a future.

'Can you talk to me, please?' she said. 'I need to know.'

'Know what?' Looking at her.

'What's going on with you?'

A moment of hesitation and she felt a quick stab of fear at what he was going to say.

'Nothing much,' he told her.

'Is this counselling doing you any good?'

He sat up then. A twitch of his shoulders, awkward, embarrassed even. Has he been lying? she thought. Has he even been to the counsellor?

'Yes,' he said. 'I guess so. At least, I thought it was. She's a Jungian. We talk about dreams and archetypes.'

What? But she kept quiet. Held her cynicism back.

'I guess the idea is to provide a theoretical framework in which you can understand yourself.'

'And?'

'It kind of makes sense. It's like language. Just as the brain is wired up in a way that makes all languages the same deep down, it's also wired up with certain kinds of images and symbols that we use to process our experiences. If you can understand how it works, you can process your problems.'

Like blended vegetables. Baby food. This was not the conversation she wanted to have. She didn't need a lecture on psychoanalysis.

'I guess it just seems to start from a long way off,' he went on. 'So far off that it's hard for it to connect with the present. I thought it was beginning to make sense, but then this thing with this kid comes along and everything blows up again. I'm kind of back where I started.'

Of course. A rush of love and pity.

'How do you feel?' she asked him.

'I don't know. Unreal. I just feel unreal. I think maybe I'm going mad. '

'Don't do that, please.'

What a thing to say. What a feeble thing to say. But this is the problem when you love someone. You are at their mercy.

32.

IT WAS EASY TO find once you looked for it. It began not where Carla had died but twenty or thirty metres north, closer to town. A steep, narrow path, no more than a strip of dirt maybe fifteen centimetres wide, led down through the green, tufted grass of the verge. As he descended, the strange silence of the river enveloped him. Above, to his left, was the road where, from time to time, a car passed with a quick, smooth growl. Below, to his right, the water. He felt the suck of the cold, like a force, as if he were a lifeless thing, light and floating on the air, and the river was pulling at him, drawing him towards its surface.

After about twenty metres, the path turned back on itself and plunged more steeply. Three crude steps had been cut into the dirt. Even with their help he had to cling to the trunk of a small mahoe to stop himself falling. He could hear the water now, and its grey-brown surface there below him was no longer flat but scored with little folds and ripples, flexing like muscle. Flowing smoothly and quickly. Bits of flotsam, green or yellow leaves, dragged past and away. The water was close to the bank right here. On the further side was a stretch of grey-white shingle with a layer of rounded stones beyond. Rough shrub clinging to the cliff face, a steep slope lifting to the sky.

Then, suddenly, ahead of him a small tree, a taupata, with shining, dark green leaves clinging to its gnarled and knotty branches, and below it, at the edge of the water, a rock. It was a big rock, the size of an armchair and, as he got closer, he heard the water lapping at it, clucking and complaining. Beyond it, on its downstream side, was a little beach, a strip of river stones and gravel, maybe two metres long and almost a metre wide. This, it seemed, was where the path went. Nothing more than this: a small cramped space, not much bigger than a coffin, tucked between the water and the grassy slope. There were a couple of empty beer cans lying among the stones. No other sign that the path meant anything.

So he stood, with his hands in his pockets, listening to the river, looking across it at the further bank a dozen metres away. The air was cool, the light bright. Sun on his face in a pool of warmth, which emphasised the chill of the rest of him. Blood beat through the head. The drift of air in breathing lungs. A kind of stillness, but it was not peace. It was waiting. Waiting without purpose, without reflection. Because he knew that there was nothing here. No answers. No leads. A dead end that he had been drawn to because there was nowhere else to go. Love, hope, rage and shame stopped here. Behind him and above him was the road where Carla died. In front of him the river and beyond it the wilderness. What to do? Just wait. For something to happen. Some tick of the clock, some trick of the cells. Wait and watch. For a sign, a meaning somewhere. You search for it, but without a purpose, as if the will has stopped, as if the conscious mind is paralysed, stung by a spider, but the body goes on, trying to make its own kind of sense of things, looking for comfort, looking for sensation to fill the emptiness. He had become the skin of a thing, an illusion, a ghost that scarcely existed, grabbing hold of anyone who came within reach. Are you the one? Please, please help me. Can you see me? Am I real?

A display cabinet full of china, white and bright with spots of colour, gold. Too clean, Lisa thought. Too cutesy. She could imagine what Larry would say to a Lladró figurine. Of a shepherdess. Something about haystacks and the ploughman's son and the sentimental bullshit of the upper classes.

'Can I help you?' A slim young woman with her hair in a bun. Round-rimmed glasses that enlarged her innocent expression. The little Hardy's name tag on her left breast said Brenda.

'Yes, I'm looking for something for some friends of mine. It's their twentieth wedding anniversary.'

'Ah, yes. You're wanting a single piece, are you?'

'Well, not a dinner set. No.'

'Only some people, for an occasion like that, they arrange with us for their family and friends to each buy something from a set.'

'No, not these people.'

'Ah. Well, what about a vase? For flowers.'

'She might like a vase but he wouldn't. He's more a toby jug sort of person.'

'Oh, well.' Brenda turned, with a sudden look of hope in her eyes. 'We have some toby jugs over here.'

'She would hate a toby jug.'

'Hmmm. A bowl, then? A fruit bowl.'

'Yes, that might do.'

'Traditional or modern?'

'Good question.'

'You're thinking he might be traditional and she might be modern?' Brenda looking at her, bright bird expression behind the lenses. This girl's sharper than she seems, Lisa thought.

'I'm thinking I don't really have much idea what I'm doing. Why don't you point me towards the bowls and leave me to it?'

'Well, over there, behind the pillar, there's some rather nice stoneware. More contemporary. And the traditional styles will be around here. They're arranged by pottery.'

'Thank you.' Lisa moved towards the more contemporary, picking her way between the display tables and cringing back from the fragility around her.

On the other side of the pillar, standing looking at the stoneware, was a man. Colin. He was dressed in dark-grey pants and a maroon polo-neck. Tall and straight. His right hand in his trouser pocket.

Her first impulse was to turn and walk away, keep on walking, but then, no, she thought, we are civilised beings, aren't we?

'Hello. Day off?'

He turned, saw her. A pause as he registered who it was, monitored his reactions as she had monitored hers on seeing him. 'Yes,' he said. 'Couldn't be bothered. Mental health day. You're obviously here for the same reason I am.'

'Leaving it late,' she said. 'Disorganised.'

'Impossible job.' He gestured towards the display. Bright summer colours. Yellow things covered in gaudy fruit and flowers. 'I mean, if it was just Larry it would be easy. You could buy him a quart of Haigh's in a commemorative bottle and be done with it.'

'Yes.'

A pause.

'How are you anyway?' she asked.

'I'm okay. I'm well.'

She was not sure he looked well. Strain in his face, puffy round the eyes. She turned away. It was hard to look at him, she realised. Was it the business of the horse? She could have fooled herself, maybe, that it was no more than that.

'Imogen is coming to you tomorrow?'

'Sunday,' he said.

Of course. He would be hung over tomorrow. They would all be hung over tomorrow.

He glanced at her. He seemed anxious about something. Their argument. Don't bring it up here, she told herself. Don't let's have a stand-up in the middle of Hardy's china department. It might be just too tempting. And her anger dragged at her again like a child tugging at her sleeve. Do I hate him? God, maybe I do. Maybe it's necessary, essential to the arrangement.

'How about you?' Colin was asking. 'Are you well?'

'Yes.'

A pause as she felt the awkwardness of that. The lie in it. For a moment she thought he was going to touch her and she flinched. Like a wire, which you were sure was dead but just might not be.

'Well,' she said. 'I don't think I'm making much progress here. I might try High Street.'

'It is supposed to be china, isn't it?'

'So I believe.'

'Dumb idea.'

'Would it be easier if it were wood? Or stainless steel?'

'Or plasticene. Probably not. One could always ignore tradition, of course.'

'But that's the curious thing about Syl and Larry. They wouldn't agree on anything *except* the tradition.'

'Yes,' he said. 'You're right.'

So that was it, then? No more? What more could there be?

'Well, I think I'll leave you to it,' she said.

'Happy hunting.'

'Best of luck to you too.'

33.

THE LADY AND HER hired man, her gardening consultant. He brings her catalogues, suggestions. She listens, she looks, she chooses. He notes down her wish, lest he forget. This is part of a transaction, circumscribed by their business arrangement. And, of course, they trust each other. There would be no point otherwise.

'Yes,' she said. 'I like that.' Leaning forward in her chair, right hand resting on the table beside the plan, left hand at the top of her thigh. The gesture pushed her chest out, curve beneath the fine knit of her beige sweater. She turned her head and looked at him, blonde hair shifting. Blue eyes.

'Of course, there's some pruning to do,' he told her, 'but that's about all in terms of maintenance. And you'll have colour all the year.'

'White.'

'White?'

'Yes, I want all the blossom to be white. Or pink. Pale pink.'

'Plum blossom.'

'If you say so.'

'A magnolia I'm thinking of would be quite dark, black or purple, when it started to flower but then later white, a creamy white.'

'That's fine.' Another look. 'How much?'

Lips seemed to hold the last sound, stayed half open.

'I'll have to cost it. I guess a thousand. Not more than two.'

'Good. And your man starts Monday?'

'Yes.'

'Good.' A little smile. 'Shall we drink to that?'

'All right.'

She stood up, moved away, heading across the big room towards the kitchen. After a moment, in which he felt the sudden vacuum of her going, the drop in temperature, he followed her.

She was bending down, looking into the refrigerator.

'How's the stock market?' he asked her, pausing by the breakfast bar, leaning on it, watching her. The sweater riding up and exposing a little patch of skin, mouthshaped, above the waistband of her jeans.

'Oh,' she said. 'Boring.' Standing up with a bottle of wine in her left hand.

'You lost,' he said.

She laughed. 'Yes. Not much. But it spoilt my record run. Nine straight weeks with a profit, and this time?' Moving towards him, bottle in one hand, corkscrew in the other, holding them out to him. 'Here.' Fingers touched. The warmth of her skin and the cold of the bottle. She turned away again.

Nothing happens if you wait. There is safety in stillness.

He split the seal with the sharp end of the corkscrew, running it round the top of the neck and lifting off the little black cap. Screw then into the yellow-brown of the cork, winding it in.

'What did you do before this?' he asked.

'Before what?'

'Clisserford and the stock market.'

'I'm not going to tell you that,' she said.

'Why not?'

'Why not?' Standing there a metre or two away, a glass in each hand. 'Because I don't like that sort of thing.'

'What sort of thing?' Levering the corkscrew, little pop as the cork came free.

'Information about people. Background. Confession. I don't like the past.'

'This place is the past.' He gestured up and about at the space around them.

'This is different. This is a style. You can confront a style.'

'You like confrontation?' He held out his hand for a glass and she gave him one.

'Yes. I like confrontation. At least, I don't like my reactions cluttered up with useless facts.'

Pouring wine, giving it back to her. Taking the second glass, filling that one also. Raising it. 'Here's to confrontation,' he said.

'I thought we were drinking to all the white blossom.' Touching glasses with him.

A mouthful of wine, cold, slowly letting it trickle round his teeth and down his throat. He put the glass down on the breakfast bar. He thought about the river, the grey force. Do you sink or do you swim? Do you go down like a stone or are you carried off by the rush of water, laughing, to the city, to the sea and the sky? You'll never know until you jump.

A woman here with hair like gold.

She went to move past him, perhaps to sit on one of the stools. Not touching but close enough that he felt the movement of the air against his hand. He didn't think about what he did next, it was just something to do, to see what would happen. Because although the hired man, drinking wine with the lady, knows his place and knows his job is to yearn for her from a hopeless distance, the madman does not. Reaching out, gripping her wrist. No feeling for a moment. But, when she didn't pull away, didn't twist and yank herself free, but merely paused and then turned to him and reached around him, putting her glass down on the bar beside his, her eyes on his, he began to want her.

'Well,' she said, 'I see you like confrontation too.'

He reached for her, pulled her towards him, found her mouth. She pressed in close, hard against him, and his hands slid down her back to her buttocks, gripped her. He felt the muscles tense and wriggle under his palms. Her mouth was chewing at him. He breathed a scent of musk and lemon, clean and sharp and dragging at him like a hook. And the need, the familiar need, that was new with the eagerness of each new body, began its demonstration, the empty logic of desire.

'Ah.' Mouth twisted aside from his. Her voice hot against his neck. 'Down, Fido,' she said. Her fists on his chest, pushing him away. 'I think we should just sit here and drink our wine. Like good little children. All right?'

34.

THE SEATING WAS A problem. Maddy was not the sort of person who got into a flap about such things, but this was an occasion, something special. It took her back to her childhood, with her mother worrying about cutlery and canapés and who should talk to whom to best advance her father's latest scheme. And, in any case, she knew that if she left it to chance it would be a disaster, with all the men at one end of the table and the women at the other. So it had to be formal: boy, girl, boy, girl. Larry and Syl at the ends: they were the guests of honour and you couldn't have them in the middle of a side because, with three per side, there was no middle pair. And Colin and Lisa probably wouldn't want to be next to each other and maybe not even opposite. Although, of course, *some* couples had to be next or opposite. It couldn't be done otherwise. Was there a way? Well, eventually she found one that kind of worked: Larry, with Lisa on his left, and then Tom next to Lisa and Maddy herself next to Tom. Then Sylvia at the other end with Colin on her left and Heidi next to Colin and then Ward. Ward would want to sit next to Larry as Colin would, too, probably, but then they both couldn't be there.

She had written the cards out in black ink with a calligraphic pen and she placed them carefully on the table among the silverware and the gleaming glasses, little twinkles of the light reflected from the open fire that flickered pale brown shadows on the walls. The room had a chill but it was growing warmer. The lights were turned down to a cosy gloom. It was

The Little Frog's back room, kept for special functions or for when the main restaurant was exceptionally busy. There was a table and a sideboard for the wine and for serving the food, and space, too, so that the ones who arrived early could mill about for a while, and some extra chairs if they wanted to sit.

'All right?' Ward standing by the fire with a glass in his hand. He was quality-testing the champagne. Or so he said.

'Yes.'

The table looked fantastic. Gaston had found a silver serving dish for the centrepiece, long and narrow with a handle at each end, and Maddy had bought some flowers from Belles Bouquets in High Street, just some princess lilies, creamy white with a purple blush in the throat, a mound of them, up and spilling out with a few spiky leaves to give the extra definition. Less was more with such things. So the flowers and the glassware, the silver cutlery and the white linen, the glow of the fire and the dim lights, all made it seem like an occasion. She wanted it to be an occasion. Something to remember.

Ward looked at his watch. 'Almost kick-off,' he said.

'How's the wine?'

'Fine, fine. Just a little . . .' He lifted his hand and rubbed his thumb and forefinger together, searching for the word. Then he realised. 'Would you like some?'

'Yes, if you don't mind.'

'Sorry, Poppet.' He took another mouthful from his glass and headed to the sideboard. 'There's a sauvignon blanc here, if you'd rather.'

'Of course not.'

'Only asking.' Light tone. 'Who's going to be first, do you suppose? Col and Heidi?'

'Lisa and Tom.'

'You think?' Coming back towards her, bearing the two glasses, handing her one. 'Cheers.' Raising his. And hers to meet him. Touch. Like a little bell.

'Well done,' he said.

'Not me. Gaston mostly.'

'No, but your idea. Your initiative. You're a good organiser, Mad. You know? You get things done.'

'Thank you.' Happy at the compliment. 'I do wonder if we should have had the kids here.'

'What? All of them?'

'Well, Josie and James, anyway.'

'No. Time enough,' he said. 'Time enough when we're all old and grey and they're grown up. They can organise things then. They can run around and make sure poor old grandma's got her slippers.'

She laughed. 'Stop it, you're depressing me.'

'It'll happen, though. Old age. I mean, do you suppose we'll all be here in another twenty years?'

'You mean here? Celebrating Larry and Syl's fortieth at The Little Frog?' It was a strange thought. Not depressing exactly because it seemed so improbable.

'Would it be so bad?' Ward asked. Because, of course, it would be exactly what he wanted.

'Twenty years is a long time and we have things to do. I mean, once you're Mayor, you might think about Parliament.'

'Oh, I don't know about that, Poppet.' Looking doubtful and amused at the same time. But then a thought struck him. 'You could, though.'

'Me?'

'Yes. Why not?'

Smiling. She could feel herself smiling. Why not?

Colin held the front door to let Heidi through first. She stepped past him, brief press of her elbow against his stomach. He followed her inside into the main room of the restaurant. The door by which they entered was in the middle of one long wall. There were maybe a dozen tables, most of them in the space to the left. To the right was the kitchen and, in front of that, a counter where the till was. A woman there. Gaston's hostess, Annette, looking up as they came in. Dark hair and a narrow bony face, a big mouth, smiling when she saw who it was, walking towards them now.

'Bonsoir. Nice to see you.' A heavy French accent on the English phrase. She held out her hands, waiting for their coats. Heidi's first, draping it across her arm. Colin tried to juggle the package as he removed his own but, in the end, he gave it to Heidi.

'We're in the inner sanctum, I guess,' he said.

Annette smiled, tipped her head to one side. A lean woman, slight build. Not much in the way of breasts. A bony ride.

'Of course,' she said.

Was she really French? He could never quite decide.

Annette gestured for them to precede her towards the counter, towards the door almost hidden away there. It led into a narrow corridor. An arrow on the wall in front of them pointed down the passage to the right: Toilets. To the left a wooden door, kauri panels, knob down at thigh level. Heidi turning it, moving on through.

Voices, warmth. Here they were. Ward and Maddy. Lisa and Tom. Faces turning as they came in.

'Hello.' Ward drew out the word and raised his hand, his good hand, like someone waving at you from the other side of the road.

Heidi moved towards him, allowed herself to be hovered over, kissed on the cheek. Colin, watching, waited to find out what she would do with Tom, but before he had a chance to see, Maddy was there in front of him.

'Hello.' Smiling at him, that little Maddy smile that lifted more on the left of her mouth than the right. He leaned towards her, touching her elbow, kissing her on the cheek.

'You're looking gorgeous,' he said.

'Thank you.' Touch of her fingers at his wrist. Heidi and Ward were over by the sideboard. She was putting the present there, with the others.

'I expect you'd like a drink,' Maddy said, waving him forward.

'I would indeed.'

Tom and Lisa were to the right of the fireplace but he ignored them, mostly, didn't catch their eyes.

'Apéritif,' he said to Ward's big back.

'Ah, Colin.' Turning. 'Yes, yes. It's nothing special. Just a Deutz.' He had the bottle in his hand, a flute in the other, pouring, handing it to Heidi. 'And one for monsieur.' He pronounced it 'messier'.

'Thanks, me old boot.'

'You're well?' Ward asked.

'I'm all right. Better for a day not thinking about other people's financial crap.' Taking the glass, drinking. He would really rather have had a Scotch, a couple of Scotches. There was a bottle there. Laphroaig. Unopened. For Larry's benefit, no doubt. Patience, he told himself.

'How about you?' he asked.

'Million dollars,' Ward said.

'I should hope so.'

Together, he and Ward turned towards the others. Heidi was over by the table, looking at the flower arrangement. Maddy standing with Tom and Lisa. Colin raised his glass to the three of them. Tom and Maddy responded in kind. Lisa just smiled. He remembered their encounter in Hardy's this morning. It had felt strange, talking to her like that, almost as if they were a couple, together. And he had thought, just for a second, was it possible? Could he have her back? If things fell apart with Heidi, could he go to Lisa and say, hey, you know, why don't we try again? The idea appealed to him, not because it would happen (how unlikely was that?) but because just thinking it was possible gave the world a hopeful spin, a yellow tone.

'Oh, by the way,' Ward said. 'Monty Kerrington. All signed up. I've invited him Tuesday, to meet a few of the members. You might like to join us.'

'Sure. Why not? Will Larry be there?'

'I'm not sure. He . . . Ah, speak of the Devil!' Attention suddenly towards the door, which was opening. Sylvia was coming in, Larry behind her.

'Surprise!' Ward moving forward with arms spread wide in welcome.

'Good Lord!' Sylvia laughed.

'Happy anniversary!' someone said. Was it Maddy or Lisa?

When they finally got to the table, there was a fuss about the seating arrangements. Ward didn't care but Maddy was annoyed. A couple of her labels had got switched somehow. Colin wasn't supposed to be next to Lisa and opposite Heidi. He was supposed to be next to Heidi with Tom next to Lisa. It didn't seem to bother Lisa, though.

'Come on,' she said, grinning at Colin. 'We can do this, can't we?'

Bad luck. Maddy didn't like her plans getting out of whack. Ward could see the little lines between her eyes deepening as people ignored the fact that the labels were wrong and sat down, telling her, Look, how good we're being, taking our places exactly where we're told, like good boys and girls. She didn't like being teased. He caught her eye, winked at her, gave her a little shrug of his shoulders to show he understood. She deliberately deepened her frown for a second and lifted the corners of her mouth in a pretend smile. It was all right, basically. Of course it was.

In actual fact, Ward preferred the new arrangement. It would be easier to talk to Colin sitting there, opposite and one along, and he would rather talk to Colin than Tom. He tried to like Tom but it was hard. Tom didn't make small talk. You could chat away to him and he would say nothing at all back to you, as if you were talking drivel. Ward always felt that Tom disapproved of him, not morally, but intellectually. Well, morally, too, if you counted the other thing, but Tom didn't know about that. Nobody knew about that and Ward didn't want to think about it either, not tonight, not ever. He had put that from his mind, locked it up and thrown away the key. Except he hadn't quite, had he? A feeling of doom, a feeling of panic.

He turned, looked at Larry, who was supping on his wine. Ward caught his eye.

'How now, my pretty knave! How dost thou?' Larry grinning at him.

Ward lifted his glass in the toast. 'Buttocks!'

'Trees!'

Laughing, then. Made him feel better.

'Right,' Larry said. 'Where's the tucker?'

'Hang on a minute. Calm down. Gaston's still working his wizardry.'

'Wizardry?'

'Something special.'

'What? I can't have Civet de Lapin à Languedoc?'

'Tonight it's table d'hôte.'

'But I always have Civet de Lapin à Languedoc.'

'No, you don't,' Lisa said, joining in. 'You didn't have it the last time we were here.'

'That can only have been because there were no lapins. Où sont les petits lapins?'

'Gone to stewpots, every one,' Lisa said.

'Stewpots?' Ward was lost already. They were always too quick for him and French, of course, was not his subject.

'Stewpots are brothels, right?' Colin said.

'No. Strictly not.' Larry with his serious tone. 'A stew is a brothel. Comes from the fact that public baths used to be used for immoral purposes. A hot bath was a stew. As was a room heated with a fire.'

'Like this one,' Ward said.

'Yes, indeed. We are dining in a stew.'

'In a brothel?' Colin asked.

'Well, I don't doubt that some people would say that

Gaston lives off immoral earnings but . . .'

'Please,' Ward said. 'There are ladies present.'

Lisa caught his eye. He smiled at her but she didn't really respond. Gave him a look he couldn't read. Didn't she like being called a lady?

'Ladies — where?' Larry looked about him, pretending curiosity.

'No,' Colin said. 'That's the whole point. Ladies don't swear.'

'You mean only men swear?' Ward said.

'That's right,' Colin said. 'Like Matchett's in High Street. Only menswear.'

'Keep your filthy mondegreens to yourself,' Larry told him.

'What . . .' But Colin never had a chance to finish whatever it was. There was the waiter, Brian, hovering next to Lisa with a plate, bending, offering.

"Soup, Madame?"

French onion soup with a crust of parmesan.

'Thank you,' she said, leaning back a little so he could set it in front of her.

'Monsieur?' To Larry.

'Yes, of course. Bring it on.'

A waitress, too, someone Ward had never seen before. She had the rolls. Silver tongs from a basket.

Larry bending over his bowl, sniffing. 'Ah. Mouth-wateringly good.'

'Like Pavlov,' Colin said.

'Pavlov? That name rings a bell.'

'The Salivation Army.'

Lisa, of course, had forgotten, when she said Colin could sit there, what it would be like. She shouldn't have forgotten. She had been in that situation enough times, trapped in the middle of them while they rattled on like schoolboys, cracking puns and trying to one-up each other. Except, of course, that Ward never one-upped anybody, just trundled after them like a big clumsy bear, occasionally making comments that the other two poked fun at and then looking all injured innocence. What? What did I say? He enjoyed it, she thought. He enjoyed being the butt of their jokes, their intellectual whipping boy. Well, he must do. He had been at it for long enough. It was strange because he owed them nothing. On the contrary, they owed him. But it didn't seem to make a difference. He was the one who tagged along behind, deferring to them. Like she had done in the days when she was Mrs Wyte. Admiring them, listening to them talk, watching them show off. Laughing sometimes because they were funny. Sometimes.

She glanced at Tom sitting there, diagonally opposite her. Lifting his spoon to his mouth, sipping soup, dabbing at his whiskers with his napkin. His eyes fixed on Maddy and Syl, who were talking. He liked that, listening to people. And he liked being surrounded by women. It was something she had taken a while to notice about him, the way he preferred women's company to men's.

Maddy and Syl. And Heidi next to him. Heidi, too, was listening. Eating her soup. She put down her spoon, picked up a piece of roll and popped it in her mouth. Picked up the spoon again. In her left hand. That was odd, Lisa thought.

Heidi wasn't left-handed, was she? Caught her eye, then. As you do when you stare at someone. Heidi looked startled for a moment and then smiled at her, a little humourless grin. Her right hand came up and lifted the edge of the soup bowl, tilted it away from her. Maybe it was a thing Swiss people did, ate soup like that with hands the opposite way round. She had never noticed it before.

Lisa picked up her wine, sipped at it. Larry, on her right, was quiet for a moment, staring at his plate. She turned to him.

'How did the sentencing go?' she asked.

He said nothing, took a big gulp of wine, but he held up three fingers. Three years.

'Is that good?' The thought of it appalled her. Polly Drafton locked away. But then, maybe gaol would be wonderful compared to life with her husband.

'She'll be out in eight months. She's served ten already,' Larry said.

Lisa could not tell whether he was pleased by the result or not.

'It doesn't seem fair,' she said.

'Fair? No, my pet, it isn't fucking fair.' His stress on the obscenity was harsh and bitter. Bitter look in his eyes and flush of anger along his cheekbones, broken veins there in the reddened skin. She couldn't remember when she had last seen Larry angry, or if she ever had. Not like this, at least. She wanted to reach out to him but she was afraid to. Too much rage there, all held in. But then, without warning, he laughed, throwing back his head and hooting at the ceiling.

'Buttocks!' he said, raising his glass to her and then to Ward.

'Trees!' Ward answered.

'Bushes!' Colin joining in.

It was an old toast. The buttocks had something to do with 'Bottoms Up!' but she didn't know about the rest. Maybe none of them knew any more. She clinked with them anyway, four glasses lifting, bright in the light. She wanted to say something more to Larry but he was turning away from her, leaning towards Ward. She was left with Colin.

He caught her eye and gave an extra little lift of his glass in acknowledgement. 'Nice,' he said, meaning the wine.

'Yes.'

A moment when he might have said something more, something significant, but all that came was, 'Did you find a present?'

'Yes. In the antique shop.' She glanced at Larry, making sure he wasn't listening. 'Got them a Royal Doulton plate. Dickens.'

'Ah, good. I got them a breakfast set. Fitz and Floyd. Cost a fortune but . . .' Shrugged like he had no option, did he? He had to mention money, of course.

'So,' he said. 'Everything all right? With you?'

'Yes. Sure.' The question surprised her, just a little. 'And you?'

'Oh, yes. Of course. Couldn't be better.' He blinked and then she noticed something odd. A little tremor under his right eye, flick, flick, flick. Like a small fly jumping in a spider web. He knew it was happening but he couldn't stop it. Coughed instead, turned away. 'So, Sylvia,' he said loudly. 'What's it like to be married to this reprobate for twenty years?'

A sudden silence.

'Well . . .' Sylvia answered, slowly, thinking of something. 'They say marriage is a wonderful institution and, although I'm not sure I ever wanted to spend twenty years in an institution, being with Larry has certainly helped pass the time.'

Laughter. A cheer. Larry raising his glass to her down the length of the table, grinning.

'Response! Response!' Colin said, beckoning to him.

'All right. Marriage is property. Property is theft. Theft is a crime. In these days of zero tolerance, I think twenty years is a light sentence.'

Another cheer. Or perhaps it was a groan.

'Again! Again!' Colin turning back to Sylvia.

'Oh, well. I think the devotion of a faithful husband is a wonderful thing. It just seems a pity he gives it to his car.' And then. 'No, no, no.' Sylvia flapping her hands. 'This is a silly game. I don't mean that.'

'Larry hates cats,' Ward said. 'Colin's the one who loves his car.'

'Right on,' Colin agreed. 'Looks great, goes fast and it doesn't argue.'

'Well, well.' From Maddy, as if he had been provocative. 'What do you think of that, Heidi?'

'I think a man who loves his car makes a very good chauffeur.'

'And the woman who loves her credit card makes a good slot machine,' Colin cut back at her. Sarcastic suddenly.

Lisa glanced at him, saw the anger in his face. What was going on? Heidi looking at him. Not a glare, exactly. She was too expressionless to glare. A chill look. She hates him, Lisa thought. Heidi's gaze shifted to her plate, and Lisa felt a sudden rush of sympathy for Colin. Poor old Wyte, with another problem relationship. Another woman who wouldn't mother him enough.

Dumb, Sylvia thought. Embarrassing. She should never have let herself be provoked. Not that the joke about the car was unfunny. Or, at least, it was not its lack of humour that embarrassed her. She just didn't like those kind of cracks about marriage and relationships. They were so conventional, so stereotyped as a way of interacting. The laughter always seemed hollow, as if people were responding because they felt they had to, like the way they clapped at the end of a speech no matter how boring it might have been. And, anyway, she didn't want to be making jokes. Jokes were not her thing It was as if someone had caught her in an act of secret mimicry, like pretending to be a ballet dancer in front of her bedroom mirror.

She looked down the table at Larry, sitting as he always sat, hunched a little forward, his right hand curled around the stem of his glass, his head low, shrinking back into his shoulders so that, if you were sitting next to him, he had to look at you out of the corner of his eye. It gave him a sly, knowing expression. Like a chameleon, she thought, with a tongue that flicked out and caught you if you got too close.

'Oh, by the way.' It was Tom talking to her. She turned towards him.

'The police asked those kids about Carla and the bullying.'

'Oh?' It took a second to understand what he was talking about.

'It didn't come to anything. No new information.'

'That's a pity.'

'But thank the kids for me anyway. For the note.'

'Note?'

'Someone sent me a note about Merry Gibbitson. An anonymous note. I presumed it was Josie. Or James.'

'Oh, God. I'm sorry about that.' Except, Sylvia realised, she should probably be apologising to Lisa, not to Tom.

'No. I was grateful.'

And presumably he knew that Lisa had decided not to tell him? Shit, Sylvia thought. It's like quicksand.

'It must make you so angry,' she said. 'Having the person responsible go free.'

'The killer.' He was almost correcting her. Yes, she thought. Why not use that word?

'I mean, to know that they might be still living here in Durry.'

She was aware of Maddy on her right, leaning forward, listening.

'Yes. Every time I see a white car. And there are quite a few. Every fifth car in town is white. It's the most popular colour.' He hesitated. His eyes shifted to Maddy. 'I mean, you have a white car.'

'Yes,' Maddy said.

'And there's a good chance you were driving it that afternoon.'

'No. I wasn't actually.' A hesitation. And then Maddy began to sound just a little wary. 'I had to take Damien and three of his friends to cricket. There's no way they would all have fitted in my car.'

That was odd, Sylvia thought. It was always Ward who took the boys to sport. She glanced at Tom.

'So,' he shrugged. 'Either way.' As if it made no difference. Which it didn't. Except all this talk of who was where doing what just raised a cloud of suspicion. That was the trouble with an unsolved crime. It generated speculation, stupid, nasty speculation, so that you even started to wonder about your friends.

What did Tom feel about it? It was hard to tell. Sitting back in his chair, drinking his wine, an odd expression on his face, preoccupied. Then he was looking up towards her right, and she saw that Brian was standing there with the second course. Two plates for the ladies — Maddy and herself. Coming down in front of her, it was a little mound of vegetables, chopped and bound together in a dome by something yellow.

'Ah,' Maddy said. 'This is one of Gaston's specials. What's it called, Brian?'

'Goût du Soleil, Madame.'

'Taste of the sun.'

'Yes, Madame.'

―――

So, he thought. If Maddy didn't use her car to take the boys to cricket, then she must have used Ward's. Which meant that if Ward went out, he used Maddy's car. But then, so what? It meant nothing. Except that he had begun to churn through all that stuff again: where people were, what they were doing on that particular Saturday afternoon. Merry Gibbitson had stirred it up. Still, that wasn't Maddy's fault. Not fair to give her the third degree. Not fair to bother people on a night when they were supposed to be having fun. And he was having fun himself, in a way. He supposed it was fun, although it might have been madness. What was going on under the table. His hand on Heidi's thigh. Hers on his.

It had started almost as soon as they sat down, the glance she gave him, full of the knowledge of Wednesday afternoon. Then, after ten minutes or so of just sitting there, ignoring each other, listening to the others start in with the usual routine, their knees touched. Was it her who made the move or him? He didn't know, but somehow the touch became a press and the press persisted. God, he had thought. Do I want this? The thought of Laura Kerrington and the put-down she gave him, the lust that turned sour in his belly, left him nauseous and disgusted.

But then he felt something more, a faint brush of Heidi's fingers, tingling stroke of the tips along the top of his leg. It was quick and gone, a tiny offer. So he reached out under the table and put his hand on her thigh, the fabric of her trousers, slipped his fingers over to the inner surface, moved them back into the warmer place. Heat through the fabric. She closed her legs but his hand slipped away with the movement so she opened them again. Sitting there while Larry and Colin rattled on about brothels and Maddy talked to Sylvia about some sub-committee they were both on. Until the soup arrived. He couldn't keep touching her then, so he took his hand back but kept his leg there, next to hers, sometimes pressing just a little harder, sometimes relaxing.

And then he felt her fingers, creeping. Brushing on the outside of his leg, wriggling over his hip and stretching, reaching for him. He began to stir. Just for a moment, he shifted in his seat, turning a little towards Larry's end of the table as if he were desperately keen to hear the conversation there. It gave her a bit more room. Her fingers found his cock beneath the cloth and squeezed. He wanted more but good sense prevailed. At least, he took it to be good sense. It might just have been cowardice.

So back to sitting up straight. For a little while she kept touching him, fingers on his leg, as she ate her soup with her left hand, but then she withdrew and there was nothing but the press of knees.

That was the problem with desire. It kept on dragging you forward. You couldn't stop, because if you did you wouldn't realise the potential. Stopping was hopelessness and disappointment. Yet, in the end, you had to stop because the last act finished of its own accord. It could not go on for ever. So you never got what you wanted, because what you wanted was impossible: the woman in the dream, the perfect merging of the mind and body, death of the self so that you wouldn't feel the pain any more.

But that was bullshit. There was no merging. These were real people he was fucking around with. They had their own agendas. All those complications. God, Astra was bad enough. Laura Kerrington would have been worse. But Heidi? It was almost as if he were trying, more and more, to push his life to the limit. What bigger challenge could he pose than having an affair with his partner's ex-husband's partner? And it would happen. It would have happened on Wednesday, if he hadn't run off to go and try to talk to Merry Gibbitson. The hands under the table proved it.

He looked across at Colin, listened to his bravado as he egged Sylvia and Larry on, trying to engineer a confrontation. He felt Heidi freeze when Maddy dragged her into it and the strange stillness in her as Colin got back at her with his crack about the slot machine. And he couldn't tell which it was, the risk or the need to comfort her, but he reached out for her once again under the table, and this time when he touched her thigh she put her hand over his and squeezed it.

Colin caught a movement at the corner of his eye. Tom getting up from the table, putting his napkin there beside his plate. Off for a piss. Off to wave his dick around. Heidi oblivious, staring at Maddy. Still as a stone. Oh, fuck it, Colin thought.

Washing his hands, staring at his face in the mirror above the basin. Staring back. The face is real, the body real. A solid thing like the wood-panelled wall, the cork-tiled floor. Yet it wasn't the solid things that mattered but the feelings. The madness.

He cupped his palms and held them under the cold tap, scooped water up and into his face. Chill of it, a shock on his skin, dribble in his beard. Again. The water worming its way through the hair on his chin and the underside of his jaw, down his collar.

You have to stop it, he told himself. You have to cease to be this way. Especially with them. With Laura and Heidi. But saying 'especially' meant that it was perhaps not so bad with other people. Astra, say. Who might be pregnant. Jesus, in some ways that was the worst of all. The worst possibility, the most irresponsible. I don't care, part of him said. The words were there, formed, in his head. What sort of voice had uttered them? Something self-destructive. Or maybe not.

Maybe it was the voice of his true self.

He pulled a couple of paper towels from the holder, wiped his face and his hands, threw the crumpled mess into the basket on the floor beside the basin. Turned to go. The panel door with the low knob, white china. He switched the lock, turned the knob. Opened.

Heidi was standing outside.

For a moment, just the stare and the silent corridor. The noise from the restaurant and the room where the party was. Then she lifted her hand, pushed the door. He stepped back and she moved toward him, came inside. He closed the door and locked it again. Standing in the small space, close. Her arms coming up around his neck, her mouth lifting. He pulled her in to him and kissed her. Felt her mouth eager. Hugging her tight, his lips against her ear, the side of her neck.

'Ah.' Her breath.

Tongue on her throat and down into the V of her blouse, the rounded knobs of her breast bone. There was a necklace there, a thin chain, hard on the smooth skin. His hand down her back, her hip, sliding up her waist and her side, cupping her breast, firm and spongy in the bra. He wanted suddenly to free it, have her naked. Reaching for the buttons of her blouse.

'No,' she said.

Stopped.

Breathing, warm breath, she kissed him on the forehead.

'We are mad,' she said.

'Yes.'

'They will miss us.'

'Yes.'

'And I don't want we should make love in a toilet.'
'No.'
'Oh, God.' Pulling him close to her, kissing him again. Their tongues pressing together. She turned her head aside. 'I'm sorry.'
'Why sorry?'
'I don't want to be the cock-tease.'
'You're not.'
'I just want to touch you. To say thank you.'
'Thank you?'
'Yes,' she said. 'Now maybe you should go.'
'Yes.' Moving away.
She gripped his wrist, held him back. 'You will come and see me?' she asked.
'Yes.'
She smiled, a sad little smile. He pulled against her grip and she released him. He turned away towards the lock on the door.

35.

'Oh, fantastic!'

'Wonderful. Wonderful time.'

'Gaston, you're a genius.'

Gaston with a little bow. Annette behind him, grinning. Ward felt the glow of his own genius — well, not genius exactly but satisfaction. And a flush of love and gratitude for Maddy.

Outside, spilling out into the night. The cold. Even with the wine it felt cold out here. Lisa turning up the collar of her coat. Colin stepping away, almost as if he wanted to run to keep warm, but coming back then. Standing a bit aside from the others. Ward moved to be near him.

'Worked out pretty well,' he said.

'Yes.' Colin wriggled his shoulders.

Heidi was talking to Larry and Syl, saying how nice it had been and very lovely to be sharing the occasion. Maddy and Tom and Lisa there behind them. Heidi turning then towards where Colin and Ward were, looked at them, seemed to hesitate.

'Let's go,' Colin said.

She stepped towards him.

'Thanks,' Colin said. 'Great dinner.'

'See you, Ward.' Heidi smiled.

'Take care now,' Ward said, and then to Colin, 'See you Tuesday.'

'Tuesday?' Colin pausing, looking at him, puzzled.

'Monty Kerrington.'

'Oh, right.'

He and Heidi walked away.

Ward shivered. 'Well, then.'

'Thank you so much.' Sylvia looking at him, turning to include Maddy too. 'We've had a wonderful evening. You know, really special.'

'Thanks, mate,' Larry said, holding out his hand. He had a problem doing it because he was carrying two presents, boxes, wrapped in fancy paper, bows on them, one gold, one silver, that gleamed in the street lights.

'Not at all,' Ward said, pleased. He shook with his good hand, the upside-down grip. Feeling happy. A plain and simple thank you from Larry was something special.

Sylvia came close and reached up her face, kissed him. Then she hugged Maddy, but one handed because she was holding a parcel as well. The one Ward and Maddy had given them, the Lladró figurine of the travelling player, which Maddy had not been sure about but Ward had insisted on. Quality, that's what counted.

'Bye, bye, then.' Sylvia turning to Tom and Lisa.

'Happy anniversary!' Kisses, hugs. Larry shaking Tom's hand too, making a joke about the cold night air.

Goodbye! The two of them crossing the street, walking close together. Larry bending his head to hear something Syl was saying and she reaching up, putting her arm around him to give him a hug because she was the only one with a free arm.

'Aren't they cute?' Lisa said.

'The happy couple. Just like newlyweds,' Maddy added.

'Well, thank you for that.' Lisa smiling from one to the other. 'Both of you.'

'No, no problem.'

'You must let us know what we owe you.'

'No, no.' Ward pushing away the thought of money. Some other time.

The four of them, two by two, walked together to the carpark, not saying much. The sky was dark above the street lamps.

'Maybe it'll rain,' Ward said.

'Yes.' Tom standing beside the four-wheel drive, looking up at the sky.

'What are you doing over the weekend?' Maddy asked.

'Don't know. Imogen's going to Col and Heidi on Sunday.' A pause. 'That bloody horse.'

'Oh, it'll work out,' Maddy said.

'I'm sure it will.'

Maddy turning away. 'Well, call us if you get bored.'

'All right.' Lisa waving, climbing into the vehicle.

Their own car was just a bit further on.

'You okay to drive?' Ward asked.

'Well, I don't think *you* are.' She had her keys out. Door release. Beep. He went round to the passenger side and climbed in. Put his seat belt on, sat back. A nice, cosy feeling. Done just nicely. And the wine was very, very good.

Maddy starting up, moving off.

Tom and Lisa were ahead of them, turning left outside the carpark, whereas they went right.

'You don't suppose there's a thing going on between Tom and Heidi, do you?' Maddy asked.

'What?' Looking at her. Her face was turned forward, staring out ahead.

'Well, you know, I could have sworn they were holding hands at one point, and then they both went off to the loo at the same time and they were gone for . . . well, I guess it wasn't that long.'

'No,' Ward said. 'And it wouldn't make sense, would it? Tom and Heidi?'

'You okay?' Lisa asked.

'Yes,' he said.

'How's Heidi?'

'Don't really know. Didn't talk to her much.'

'I noticed that.' She stared out of the windscreen down the funnel of High Street. 'Colin seemed his usual. Hyper one minute and depressed the next.'

'Bipolar tendencies.'

She laughed. 'That shrink's getting to you.'

'Maybe.'

'You want to watch it. You'll be discovering you've got a complex next.'

'We've probably all got complexes.'

'Yer. And I suppose some are more complex than others.'

'Doubtless.'

'It's not an excuse, you know.'

'What isn't?' Glancing at her.

She caught the movement out of the corner of her eye but didn't turn towards him. 'Complexity,' she said. 'Neuroticism.'

'Who's neurotic?'

'I don't know. You? Me?'

'It's probably what makes people interesting.'

'Interesting?'

'Sexy.'

She laughed. What else could she do but laugh in response to that sudden flick of need, the little rush in her belly?

'Keep your hands on the wheel,' she said.

'Yes, boss.'

Sylvia was at school. A bell was ringing. It was a fire. The school was on fire. No. Waking, struggling up through the pitching darkness, she realised it was the telephone. Red numbers of the digital clock: 2.30. God, what was going on? She reached out for the receiver, picked up. Blessed silence for a second.

'Hello.'

'Syl?' A scared voice, a little-boy kind of voice, but one she recognised. She thought she recognised.

'Colin?'

'Is Larry there?'

'He's asleep, Colin.'

Larry behind her. She could hear him snoring quietly.

'I need to speak to him, Syl.' He sounded terrified, helpless. 'I need to speak to him now.'

She didn't answer, wondering what to do.

'Is that okay?' he asked, a pleading, querulous tone.

'Wait a minute. I'll see.'

She put the receiver down on the bedside table, turned on the reading light. Larry gave a grunt. He was lying on his back, mouth half open. She leaned over him, shook him. Gust of wine and whisky, sour on his breath.

'Wa?'

'It's Colin,' she said. 'On the phone. I think he's in trouble.'

Another groan. He tried to roll away from her but she kept her grip on his shoulder, pulling at him.

'Wake up, love. Wake up. It's Colin.'

She had done this before, in the middle of the night, when one of his clients did something stupid. Maybe not so often when he was as drunk as this.

'Who?' He was blinking at her, eyelids screwed up against the glare.

'Colin's on the phone. I think he's in trouble.'

'Colin? Jesus.' Struggling upright into a sitting position.

She pulled back the covers and swung her legs out of bed so he could reach across to the receiver. Stood up, took her dressing gown from the chair there, put it on. Wondering, anxious.

'Col?' Fingers through his hair, wispy hair on his bald pate. 'What?'

She stood there, arms across her stomach, hugging herself. Waiting.

Silence. Then he said, 'Okay, keep calm. They're coming. Right?'

A pause.

'Don't worry about that. The important thing is don't say anything. Nothing at all. All right?'

Another pause.

'That's okay. I'll be there as soon as I can. Remember, say nothing. Tell them that's what I told you to do. Right? . . . Good. Hang on in there, mate.'

He reached over then, slipped the receiver back into its

cradle. Then he turned and stared at her. His eyes, the expression on his face. She had never seen him look like that before.

'Something's happened to Heidi,' he said.
'What?'
'I think he's killed her.'

36.

HEIDI MIRA FUCHS, AGE thirty-four, died at approximately 2 a.m. on the morning of 10 May at the house she shared in Cox's Line with her de facto husband, Colin Wyte. Cause of death was a single shot to the head from a 5mm Schnauzer rifle. The victim was sitting up in bed at the time and her assailant standing about two metres away. The bullet entered the left eye on a downward trajectory, resulting in severe damage to the lower brain and brain stem. The injuries sustained would have resulted in massive disruption to neurological functions, producing paroxysm and loss of consciousness followed by general paralysis. Death would have occurred in a matter of minutes.

Mr Wyte dialled 111 at 2.24 a.m. On his advice that Ms Fuchs had been shot, the operator alerted not only emergency services but also the police. Constables Matakana and Grainger reached the house at around 2.40 a.m., by which time Ms Fuchs was already dead. Mr Wyte was in a distressed condition. At first he said he wasn't supposed to say anything, then he volunteered the information that Ms Fuchs had been killed by an intruder. However, he then retracted this statement and said that he had done it. He then directed Con. Grainger to a Jaguar car in the garage, the boot of which contained the Schnauzer rifle. Mr Wyte also said that he had already called his lawyer, Mr Lawrence Hannerby. Mr Hannerby arrived at 2.55, and at 3.05 Mr Wyte was arrested on a charge of recklessly discharging a firearm and taken to Durry Police Station for further questioning.

Extract from an interview with Colin Wyte taken by Detective Sergeant Vince Petters, Saturday 10 May 2003

CW   . . . We must have left the restaurant around eleven, maybe a bit before, and we drove home. Didn't talk on the way, not much. I was pissed off and I was trying to be reasonable. I guess it made me a bit depressed, too.

VP   Why were you depressed?

CW   Well, because we'd had this fight earlier in the week. She said she was going to leave me. We kind of agreed that we wouldn't decide anything until the weekend. This weekend. I thought, you know, the dinner, a night out with friends, I thought it might smooth things over, change her mind. I guess it was pretty obvious that that hadn't happened.

VP   Why?

CW   Because of how she behaved. She was all over Tom.

VP   Tom Marino?

CW   Yes. They were playing footsie all evening. I didn't realise at first but then, at one point, he got up and went out of the room. A couple of minutes later she followed him. It kind of alerted me, and when they came back I could see what they were doing. Groping each other. Under the table.

VP   Did any one else notice what was going on?

CW   Maybe. It was obvious enough.

VP   And when they left the room? How long were they gone?

CW   I don't know. Seemed a fair while. Long enough.

VP   What did you think they were doing?

CW   (laughs) What would you think they were doing? Having it off. Rooting. The beast with two backs. I already suspected it was going on. I just didn't think she'd throw it in my face like that.

VP   So tell me what happened when you got home?

CW   Well, when we got inside, she went straight to the bathroom. She was in there quite a while and, I don't know, that kind of upset me too. I thought, God, you know, what's she doing? Douching herself, taking a shower, doing her toenails. It all seemed calculated to put me in my place.

VP   Did she normally take a shower in the evening?

CW   Yes. She's very clean. On the outside. But she didn't normally take this long over it. It was almost like a reminder. She'd been a long time in the bathroom at the restaurant and now, here she was, doing the same thing again.

VP   What did you do?

CW   I had a drink or two. I ignored her. Tried to. I figured the relationship was all over, finished, so I'd better get used to it. But thinking that just got to me even more. And . . . I don't know, I couldn't just sit there. So I went to talk to her.

   She was in the main bedroom by then, sitting up in bed, reading a book. She said she didn't want to talk to me and asked me to leave. I said it was my house, my bedroom, too. She said no it wasn't. We had agreed not to sleep together and this was where she was sleeping so it was her room.

VP   Was she angry?

CW   No. Not then. Calm. She can be so calm sometimes, icy calm. You think of the Ice Queen. That's her. I pleaded with her. I said couldn't we talk, try to make it up. No, she said, she wanted out.

> — It's Tom, isn't it? I said.
> — No, she said. It's got nothing to do with Tom.
> — Why then?
> — Because I don't want to live with you, she said. I want to be on my own. I want to lead my own life. So I asked her if she cared about me any more and she said, no she didn't. Any feeling she had had was gone.
> — I suppose you want me to beg you to stay, I said. I suppose you want me to get down on my knees and beg.
> — No, she said. Not at all.

So I did. I got down on my knees beside the bed.

> — There, I said. This is what you want, isn't it? You want to humiliate me.

She told me to get up because I looked foolish and she went back to reading her book. It was like there was no feeling there, no emotion. Like she didn't care at all. You know, we've been together nearly seven years. I mean, I know that's not a lifetime, but it ought to count for something. And I got angry. I guess I got angry, although it didn't really feel like that. I felt I was floating, in a kind of a way. I just wanted to make her react. I just wanted to see that she felt something.

So I went and got the rifle. I took it out of the case and I got one bullet as well, just one. I didn't put it in the breech, I held it in my hand. I wanted to show it to her, to scare her with it. So I pointed it at her. And she did look sacred then, really scared.

— It's all right, I said. It's not loaded. Don't be frightened.

And I showed her the open breech.

— Just tell me you're not fucking Tom, I said.

And then she lost it. She just started yelling at me. She said it had nothing to do with me who she was fucking because our relationship was over and that I was stupid and insensitive and that she was sick of my games and my bullying and that it served me right if she was having it off with Tom because I drank so much our sex life was dead and she went on and on saying things, really vicious, nasty things about how inadequate I was, how useless and stupid. She wouldn't stop. She was screaming and screaming. I asked her. Please, please. Because it was like I was being invaded. Her words were in my head. They were ripping me, like claws. And I don't know why, I must have put the bullet in the gun and pointed it at her, not really aiming, I wasn't aiming. I didn't mean anything. I didn't realise it was loaded. I just kept asking her to stop, please stop. Please, please, please, please.

(A pause)

VP Then what happened?

CW It went off. I don't know how. (Sobs) Heidi was

thrashing around on the bed and making a kind of moaning noise. And her eye was gone. And there was blood there, all over. I went to her and took her hand and she gripped me hard. I kept telling her I was sorry. Then I thought, I have to get an ambulance but I couldn't. The phone was on the other side of the bed and I couldn't reach it. She was holding me so tight. I couldn't get her fingers off my wrist and I thought, I have to, I have to hit her hand to break her grip. But I couldn't do that. I couldn't hit her. Then, in a minute, she started to relax. She lay still and her hand just went weak and I didn't know. I didn't think, you know, she might be . . . I just made a dive for the phone and called 111. And then . . . Well, you pretty much know what then.

VP   You stayed there.

CW   Yes. I stayed with her. I tried to feel her pulse and I thought there was one. A little one. I thought she, well, I thought there was a chance.

VP   When did you put the rifle in the boot of the car?

CW   I don't remember.

VP   It wasn't in the bedroom when the police arrived.

CW   Really? Well, I guess I moved it. I must have.

VP   And where was it originally? Where did you keep it?

CW   Where? I don't know. I think it was in the wardrobe.

VP   The wardrobe in the main bedroom?

CW   Yes. I think so. It was right there, in my hands.

VP   What about the shells?

CW   They were there too.

VP   We found them on the desk in the study.

CW   I must have moved them. I suppose I did.

37.

LISA FELT NUMB. THE swelling light, like a cold flash-burn, swept up into her face and prickled over her skull. She sat down at the kitchen table as the sensation passed on by. She could hear the hum of the dishwasher. She could see the shadows from the morning sun, the brightness of the window, in a skewed angle across the surface of the kitchen cupboards. She could feel the table under her hands, if she tried, if she thought about it. There were other things to anchor her, too. Like the realisation that she had been through this before. Something like this. The day Carla died. Except that then, under those circumstances, the first thing she had felt was that she had to look after Tom. Now, it was Imogen.

The phone started ringing. Slowly, she got to her feet, moved across to where it sat on the bench beside the refrigerator, picked it up.

Hello?'

'Lisa?' It was Maddy.

'Hi.'

'You've heard?'

'Yes. Sylvia just called.'

'My God. Isn't it awful? Do you know what happened?'

'No. Except that he shot her. And that he's been arrested.'

'For murder,' Maddy said, as if it were impossible.

'Yes, well. You'd expect that, wouldn't you?'

'Look, do you want to come over? Or I thought we might go over to Larry and Sylvia's. For company. Larry's still in bed. He didn't get home till after six apparently. But, you know, I thought . . . Ward is taking this really hard. He needs you. We need each other. At a time like this.'

Why? Lisa wondered. Then she saw that it made sense. They were all in this together, in a way. The Tribe. The idea gave her comfort. Just a little.

'I'm not sure,' she said. 'It'll depend on Imogen.'

'Oh God, poor kid. This must be hell for her. How is she?'

'Not good. She's in her room.'

'Give her our love. Give her a hug from us.'

'Yes.' A little pause. 'And I have to call Tom. He doesn't know yet. He's gone to Greenwise.' The words were as much a reminder to herself as information for Maddy.

'Are you all right?' Maddy asked.

'Yes. A bit dazed.'

'Call me later. If I'm not here, I'll be at Syl's.'

'Yes.'

'I know this must be extra complicated for you.'

'Thanks, Maddy.'

She hung up, wondered for a moment what to do and then found herself walking out of the kitchen, down the hallway. She knocked on Imogen's door. No answer. Turned the knob.

The room was full of light. Imogen was lying on the bed, fully clothed, with her arm across her face, shielding her eyes from the brightness. Lisa went to the window to dim the Venetian blinds. Then she crossed to the bed and sat down beside her daughter. Imogen didn't move, kept her arm where it was, the bony elbow sticking up under the navy blue sweat-shirt. Lisa reached out her hand, watched it stretch the distance and begin to stroke the child's hair. The touch, the smoothness of those silky strands, brought a sudden stab of pain through her numbness. Her own pain and Imogen's, and with it came the bite of love and the fierce urge to protect. He should have killed himself as well, she thought. He should have done the decent thing and left us cleanly, without any mess. He's lost her now. A sob lifted in Lisa's chest. The tears swelled and pushed at her.

Imogen moved her arm, looked up at her. Big eyes. Helpless, frightened. Lisa swung her legs on to the bed and lay down, folding her daughter into her arms. The girl began to weep softly too. Lisa didn't move, just held on.

'Greenwise Garden Centre, good morning.' Tom's voice in the receiver, confident, matter-of-fact.

'Hi, it's me,' Lisa said. 'Something's happened.'

'What is it?' Alarm under the cool surface.

'There's been an accident . . . Well, I don't know if it's an accident. Heidi's dead. It looks as if Colin killed her.'

'Jesus!' Just the one word and then a silence. Something about the word, the tone, that stopped her speaking. Force, the force of it. An explosion.

'Are you okay?' she said, at last.

'Yes. I . . . Billy isn't here yet.' He sounded vague, helpless suddenly.

'Don't worry. We're okay. We might go over to Larry and Syl's. Ward and Maddy will be there.'

'Yes.' As if he hardly heard her.

'Okay . . . Well, then . . .'

A pause. What did she want of him? To rush home and be with her and Imogen? To utter words of shock or comfort? Anything. Anything at all, as long as it was not this paralysing silence.

'Are you okay?' she asked again.

'Yes,' he said, cold and distant now.

'All right. See you.'

38.

WARD LOOKED AWFUL. ALL his flesh seemed to be sagging on his big frame, his face grey, as if he were suffering from a wasting disease. He and Maddy sat side by side on one of the sofas, not lolling there relaxed, but tense, drawn into themselves, like witnesses waiting to be called into the courtroom. Sylvia made them coffee. It was something to do, something to keep her own hands busy, to stop her mind whirling around the sick, empty feeling in her stomach. This was why Ward and Maddy were here, of course. To pass the time. It was the only thing you could do when something like this happened, something big and awful and personal. You had to submit to the process. You had to endure, as best you could, and help other people to do the same. Make coffee, sit, talk, repeat the words, over and over, until the feelings were worn out, exhausted, until there was nothing left to do but go on living.

'Here we are.' Putting the tray on the table. Four faces looking up at her. Ward and Maddy. Josie and James. Sylvia wondered whether the kids should be there but they seemed to want it. They were bound up in it, of course, like everyone else. They had their feelings to deal with, as well, perhaps, as their curiosity.

'Thank you,' Maddy said.

Sylvia sat down. 'How are the boys?'

'Oh, they're okay. They have things to do. Things arranged. And they thought, well, yes. They may as well just do them.'

'How's Larry?' Ward asked suddenly, almost cutting off the end of Maddy's sentence.

'He's still asleep.'

'Don't suppose he got any at all last night.'

'A couple of hours before . . .' The words she wanted were 'before Colin called', but she found it hard to say his name.

'So do you know what happened? Why?' Maddy eager for information.

'Only what I told you on the phone really. What Larry said this morning when he got back. It seems they had an argument. He got the rifle, for some reason. She lost her temper when she saw it. Crazy, yelling, apparently. She said all sorts of things, horrible things. He pointed the gun at her to make her stop. It went off.'

'Oh, God,' Maddy said.

'Just one shot?' Ward asked.

'Yes.'

'In the head?'

'Yes.'

'Well,' Maddy said. 'At least she didn't suffer.'

'How do you know she didn't suffer?' Josie's voice, suddenly there. Sharp, accusing.

'She would have died instantly. With a head wound,' Maddy said defensively.

'Why? People can have really bad head wounds and not die. There was a man in America who had a crowbar through his head. It went in here,' — pointing to her cheek — 'and came out here . . .' Pointing to the top of her skull above her eye.

'Don't talk nonsense!' Ward said sharply.

'It's not nonsense. His name was Phineas Gage and he . . .'

'Josie!' Sylvia stopped her.

Josie glared, a little glare, in place of an apology.

James, of course, was just sitting there, very still, taking it all in.

'We're all upset,' Maddy said. 'Of course we are.'

Sylvia pressed down the plunger on the coffee, poured into the three mugs, handed two of them to Ward and Maddy.

'Do you kids want something?' she asked.

They shook their heads in unison.

'No,' Josie said. 'Thank you.'

A silence. Strange how they had come together to talk about it and now there was nothing to say.

'Have the police been in touch with you?' she asked.

'No.' Maddy looking surprised at the question.

'They probably will. About how things were last night.'

'They were fine. We had a great evening. I thought everybody did.'

'Yes,' Sylvia said, remembering the warmth and the love and the laughter. 'We did.'

'That's what makes it so terrible. Everything can be going along the way it should and then, suddenly, something happens. Something that makes no sense.'

'It was an accident,' Ward said.

'Yes,' Maddy agreed.

'Colin couldn't possibly mean to kill anyone.'

'Of course not.'

'It's manslaughter, then. He'll be out in three years.'

Was that all he cared about? Sylvia wondered. The length of time Colin would spend in gaol?

'It might not work out that way,' she said.

'Of course it will. With Larry defending him.'

'Larry doesn't think he can take the case.'

256

'Why not?'

'Because he's involved.'

'But he has to.' Ward looking appalled that there could be another possibility.

Sylvia felt sick at the thought of Colin's defence. 'Nobody seems to be thinking very much about Heidi,' she said.

'Poor woman.' Maddy looking suddenly upset. 'God, it's awful.'

All we've got is clichés, Sylvia thought. Appalling, awful, sad, poor woman. Words too weak to get a grip. But maybe that's the way it should be, had to be. The event lumbered on, like a rolling boulder, and none of their talk seemed to affect it at all, just flutterings of rags against its grinding surface. But maybe enough flutterings would stop it in the end. And maybe, if you could get a purchase, it would simply rip your arm off.

'Yes,' Ward said. 'But we can't help Heidi now, can we? It's Colin we have to worry about.'

He was right, perhaps. This was not a time for judgment and condemnation. Friends couldn't do that. Friends stood by you when you were in trouble. They didn't ask questions. They didn't point the finger. They didn't think of themselves. They were just there. Except that Sylvia wondered what would it be like if things were the other way around. If it was Colin lying in the morgue and Heidi in a cell at the police station. How would it all seem then?

39.

TOM PARKED THE UTE beside the garages, leaving as much room for Kenny and the machinery as possible. As he got out and began to walk back to the corner of the house he saw a man coming towards him. Monty Kerrington, it must be. Plump with sloping shoulders. Wavy brown hair and a well-cut suit with a white shirt and lemon-yellow tie. A handkerchief to match the tie in the breast pocket of his jacket. All smart for a Monday morning.

'Greenwise?'

'Yes,' Tom said.

'Kerrington.' Holding out his hand.

Tom took the hand, looked into the face. Monty had brown eyes and a narrow, finely sculptured nose, a pointed chin, scrubbed-pink shaven. A small, sad mouth with turned-down corners. Innocent. The husband. Did she talk to you? Did she mention what happened on Friday? No, of course not. Nothing happened, did it?

'Hi,' Tom said.

'Your bloke's starting today?'

'Yes. They should be here any time now.'

'Good, good.' Monty nodded, setting the pouching flesh at his neck aquiver. His attention drifted away past Tom's shoulder, floating over the land perhaps, his land. Glance back at Tom. He had a question to ask.

'Did you drive past the neighbours'?'

Ah, of course. Tom felt a surge of rage. Why should that bastard be alive and she be dead was the thought that came with it.

'Yes.'

'Police still there?'

'No.'

'You know what happened?'

'No, not really.'

'Murder.' Monty offered the word without expression, without comment. He wasn't trying to impress. He didn't even seem to be taking a ghoulish interest. A curiosity, was it? 'He murdered her. Odd feeling, having that in the neighbourhood. I know him, you know. We've had them over for drinks. It makes you think.' A pause. Another glance.

Tom tried to find the words that would disengage the two of them but there was nothing there, not readily. And he couldn't just turn away. You kiss a man's wife, you have to be polite to him.

'What makes somebody do that?' Monty asked.

'I don't know.'

'Bizarre. Bizarre to think about. I mean, you read about crimes in the paper, you see them on TV, but none of it's real. Even the real things don't seem real, if you know what I mean. And then, well, it happens just up the road, next door, virtually. And the police are interviewing you. And, what's more, it's somebody you know. I mean, I've shaken the hand that pulled the trigger. Makes you think.'

'Yes.'

'Hmmm.' Thinking. Fishing around in his trouser pocket. Then, suddenly, he had his car keys in his hand and was clicking at the black remote attached to them. The garage door began to open.

And then there was Kenny, walking towards them

from the corner of the house.

'Morning,' Tom said.

Kenny didn't answer, responded only with a grin and an upward flick of his head. Monty turned and saw him, though.

'You the fellow with the machinery?'

'That's me.'

'Are you blocking my drive?'

'Not yet,' Kenny said.

'Well, let me get out of here first then, will you?' Turning, heading towards the garage. A big grey car. A Mercedes.

The front-end loader nudged at the earth like a butting animal. Roar of the diesel motor as the forks lifted, bucket full of brown dirt. Turning, trundling towards the mound that was to be. Kenny had gone, but Tom still stood there, watching, trapped in the safety of the noise.

'Good morning.' She had come up beside him.

'Hi.' He did not look at her, kept his eyes on the machines.

'Do you want a coffee?'

'No,' he said. 'I have to go.' Which was true. There were orders to get out. Stock replacement.

'You heard what happened at our neighbours'?'

'Yes.' A pause. He felt the words coming and decided not to stop them. 'I knew her.' There was more to say. A lot more. 'She was a friend.'

'Really?'

He could feel her looking at him but he did not respond

to the attention. He just let her register whatever was obvious, what might have shown in his face. Which could have been anything. Or everything.

'How does that make you feel?' she asked.

'Angry.'

'Yes, I guess it would. How angry?'

The loader was full again, turning, lumbering up over the rim of the crater it was making and heading towards the rudiments of the mound.

'I want to kill him,' he said, the words like a sudden certainty, a realisation.

'Could you do that?' She did not sound shocked or surprised. She seemed interested, as if he had just laid claim to an unusual ability.

'I don't know. I doubt I'll get the chance to find out.' Because they had put Colin in gaol. Gaol protected him; gaol took away your right to vengeance and gave it to a system.

A roar from the machine as the bucket tipped and dumped its contents. Three buckets to the cubic metre. Brown earth tumbling, slithering, a fraction added to the growing volume.

'When will you be back?' she asked.

When? In a day or two, he supposed. To check how it was going.

'Later in the week. Friday, maybe.'

'No,' she said. 'Make it sooner than that. I want to talk to you.' A touch on his sleeve and she was gone, walking away, back to the house.

40.

COLIN FELT THERE WAS a barrier now, a thick shield, like safety glass, between himself and the events. It all seemed bright still. He could hear the words, replaying in his head in cuts and snatches, loops of meaning, twisting flakes like the ash from a fire. Yet, despite its vividness, he felt almost nothing. The pain was deep inside. It had become part of him.

Larry came to talk about what he called the First Appearance. He had another lawyer with him. A woman called Fiona. She had short-cropped sandy hair and was dressed in black. Larry explained that he could not represent Colin in court because the police had interviewed him about what had happened at the dinner. They probably would not call him as a witness, but the fact that they could made it impossible for him to appear for the defence. Fiona was here instead. She was from Larry's firm. She was a first-class barrister.

'But you'll . . . You know. You'll keep an eye on things, won't you?' Colin asked, looking at Larry.

'We'll work together,' Fiona said.

'Good. That's great.' Nodding. It was all the same really, wasn't it?

'Now, this morning, you won't have to enter a plea,' she told him.

Plea? 'I should plead guilty,' he said.

'Oh?' Larry raised his eyebrows.

'It would be easier, simpler.'

'I don't think so.' Larry was dressed in a pinstripe suit, a red tie with small animals on it. African animals, a little safari park.

'I won't get off.'

'No,' Fiona told him. 'But we could get you manslaughter.'

'How?'

'On the grounds of provocation.'

'She provoked me.' Voice, the voice of hatred. That's what hurt the most, the hatred in the way she spoke, except that he couldn't really feel the hurt. It was too deep down.

'The choice is this. If it's manslaughter, you might be out in two to five years. Maybe less. You can do something with the rest of your life.' Larry's voice was crisp, businesslike. Nothing like the evening Larry with the drawling wit and the glass in his hand. Colin listened without really understanding. The rest of his life? It seemed an impossible achievement.

'If it's murder, you might do ten to fifteen. That's a long time inside.'

'Pleading guilty wouldn't be easier, then?'

'Not to murder, no. You might want to plead guilty to manslaughter, when the time comes.'

'What do I have to do?'

'You have to listen to Fiona. She's your counsel. I have to keep out of it. I'm going to leave you now so that she can talk to you and tell you what to expect. Okay?'

Standing up. Larry was standing up, about to leave. There was an ostrich on his tie and a lion and a giraffe. There was an antelope with pointed horns. But there wasn't a gnu and there wasn't a zebra. Why wasn't there a zebra?

'Are you angry with me?' Colin asked.

Larry laughed, the old familiar Larry-laugh. 'You've

fucked up somewhat, mate. You're not exactly on my list for citizen of the year.'

'I don't want people to be angry with me.'

'Nil carborundum . . . Don't let the bastards grind you down. Take care.' Larry shook his hand, turned, walked to the door. Tall figure waiting for the guard to let him out. And then he was gone.

'Nothing's going to happen this morning,' Fiona said. 'You'll just be charged. I don't think we should even ask for bail. I think . . .' She began to explain about psychological reports and something about a bail hearing in a week's time. He didn't understand. Didn't hear. Just kept staring at the door. A grey door with a spyhole in it. Larry had gone out that door.

'Do you want to know what happened?' he asked Fiona.

You stupid man. You stupid, stupid man. You don't think. You don't feel. You feel nothing for no one but yourself. You are insensitive. You play games. You manipulate, manipulate. You stupid man. Always, always you manipulate me. You are nice, you buy me presents, then you go quiet on me, you say nothing for hours, or else you shout because I don't do what you want, because I have my own life, and you think what I do is nothing. You hate what I do because it's mine. So would it be a surprise if I go with someone else? Someone who listens? Someone who is nice to me? Would it be a surprise?

No one is ever nice to Colin, though. Poor Colly. Poor, poor Colly. He gave you a house. Gave you a place to grow your plants. He didn't laugh. He didn't say how silly they were. He tried to make it work. He tried. He did his best. He worked hard and he made money. Maybe if you were nice, if you were nicer, it could all be fun again. Because it's you that stops him. You that makes him small and weak. If you were nicer, it would all be fun. You could make love together in the bed in the morning and he could make you smile. Like he used to. A yellow day, instead of this one. A lovely yellow day.

41.

SHE WAS AT THE bench in the workshop, the pokerwork iron in her hands. Thin drift of blue smoke, smell of burning wood. Head bowed, intent on her work, she did not see him, so he stood and watched her. The concentration held her still. Lit by the skylight above her, white round of her shoulder, copper-coloured curls. She was dressed, as usual, in T-shirt and overalls, like a country girl, face fresh from the clean air. As he looked at her, he remembered the sharp cry, intensity of pleasure, scream of love, the thought that she wanted him to impregnate her, that he wanted to do it, not because of what would happen, neither of them wanted that, but because of what they were. Physical creatures, living bodies. Submitting. Did you come alive when you submitted? Could you reattach yourself to the real world? He was afraid of her now, he realised. For the first time.

She paused in her work, moved back a little to examine it, and saw him. Smiled.

'Hi,' he said.

'How long have you been there?' She switched off the iron, placed it on its rack so that the hot end was not touching anything.

Moving towards her, around the end of the bench, reaching out for her, folding her to him, her solid weight, relief just in the presence of her but a kind of sickness also, like nausea.

'Are you okay?' Pushing him away a little, looking at him in concern.

'Yes.'

'That bloke who shot his wife, you knew them, right?'

'Yes.' There was no escaping any of that. It was all his world was right now. 'He's Lisa's ex-husband.'

'Oh, Jesus. Is she all right? How's Imogen?'

'Not good.'

'Poor kid!' She hugged him suddenly. As if he, too, were a poor kid. Which he was, perhaps. At least, he could feel that he was and let her treat him that way.

'How about a cup of tea?'

'I think I just want a cuddle.'

She laughed. 'You might change your mind given the state I'm in.' Moving back from him, looking at him, grinning, but unsure of herself. 'Although that's good in one way. No little babies in the offing.'

'I'm sorry about that.'

'You're sorry I'm not pregnant?'

'No.' But maybe he was, a little curl of disappointment. 'I'm sorry about what happened. Last week.' That long ago? Was it a whole week since he was last here. 'And I'm sorry I didn't call. I should have called. To see how you were.'

'I was fine.' She took his hand, tugged at it, began to lead him towards the house. The door into her kitchen with the tongue-and-groove walls and the black and white linoleum worn through in brick-red patches.

'Go and lie down,' she said. 'I'll make you some tea.'

He did as he was told, walked through into her living room, clean and tidy, the hooked rug on the floor in front of the TV, the quilted cushions piled in the old sofa. In her bedroom he took off his jacket and shoes, lay down on her bed with his hands behind his head, stared at the ceiling. Thinking nothing. Seeing nothing. But then the scent of her began to rise out of the bedclothes, the pillow. Like toffee, like something good cooking on a stove, but sharper too, more primitive, hooking into the head. He turned, rolled on his side, took the second pillow in his arms and buried his face in it. Breathed.

'You hiding?' She was standing there with two mugs of tea, looking down at him.

'Smelling. Smelling you. Wonderful smell.'

She laughed. Put the mugs on the bedside table, kicked off her shoes and sat, lay down beside him. The sag and lift of the mattress was a beckoning, rolling him towards her. He let it happen, reached out, arm around her, pulled her over so that her face was above his, kissed her. Let his hand rest in her hair, the spring of the ringlets. He had once said she looked like Shirley Temple. She hadn't liked it.

'I've told you before,' she said, moving back a little. 'You don't need to worry about me. I can manage. I mean, this is a convenient arrangement for me. A little company, great sex, no ties. What more could a girl want?'

'Certainly not a baby.'

'Noooo.' Drawing it out, her lips rounded like the offer of a kiss.

'But it was nice.'

'Oh, God!' Rolling her eyes.

The high pitch of pleasure, which had come to nothing. What to do now then? Where to from here?

'Drink your tea,' she said.

At the top of the drive he paused, put the handbrake on. The road was empty both ways. No. To the left, from the south, a car. He could have got out ahead of it but he didn't. Waited, watched it. It was a white car. Small, moving fast. Too fast. Growing. The hum of its motor, like an insect. Flash in front of him. A two-door. Toyota. Like Maddy's car but a man driving. Ward? Could it have been Ward? Hard to tell with the ripple of reflection across the side window.

He eased out into River Road, turned towards town. Feeling puzzled. More puzzled than he understood. Ward driving Maddy's car along River Road, what was wrong with that? If it was Ward, of course, which it might not have been. The speed, then, was that it? He remembered Friday evening, at the dinner. Ward leaning across the table, saying something to Colin, the two of them laughing, and the look in Lisa's eyes, the expression on her face, which said they were berks, both of them. Colin the Killer and Ward the Wet. The thought came with a strange sense of bitterness. He had nothing against Ward, except, of course, that he and Colin were such bosom buddies.

Then he remembered the snatch of conversation with Maddy.

— Were you driving it that afternoon?

— No. I wasn't actually. I had to take Damien and his mates to cricket. They wouldn't have fitted in my car.

So who was driving your car? Ward? No, he thought. That's crazy. Yet here they were, the man and the car, in the very spot.

An intersection coming up to his left. Pigskill Road. He braked, swung into the turn. A hump through a little cutting and then he was up on top where the roadway widened. He pulled over on to the verge. Reached in his jacket pocket for the cellphone. Pressed the double-digit code for Ward's number.

'Good afternoon. Wyte and Lorton, Accountants. This is Marie speaking.'

'Is Ward there please?'

'No, I'm afraid he's out. Can I take a message?'

'Marie, this is Tom Marino. Do you know when he'll be back?'

'Hi, Tom. He shouldn't be too long. I can give you his mobile if you like.'

'Please.'

A pause. She read it out to him.

'Thanks,' he said.

He hung up and dialled the number she had given him while it was still in his head. One ring. Two. Three.

'Lorton here.' Noise in the background. Street noise. Ward was walking somewhere.

'Hi, Ward. This is Tom.'

'Tom, how are you, mate?' Concern in his voice, and something else. Weariness. 'How are Imogen and Lisa?'

'Coping.'

'Tough on Imogen.'

'Yes, she's taking it hard.'

'Bloody dreadful business.'

'Yes.'

'God, poor old Col.'

No! But he didn't shout that, didn't even say it. Just stayed silent, swallowed. Stared at the road ahead of him, arrowing off between the fields on either side.

'Was there something I can help you with?' Ward asked.

'No, not really. Just a thought. A quick question. On the afternoon Carla was killed, were you out driving Maddy's car?'

'Me?' A pause. Just a little pause. 'No, I wasn't.'

Lying bastard.

'Thanks, Ward. Sorry to bother you.'

Hung up. Didn't even think then. Rang directory service. Got the number, got connected.

'Hello, this is Maddy Lorton.'

'Hi, Maddy. It's Tom.'

'Tom? Oh, God, how are *you*?'

'I'm okay. Look, I know this is a bad time to be bothering you with my obsessions but I just have one quick question.'

'Yes?'

'On Friday evening, at dinner, you said you weren't driving your car on the day Carla got killed. I just wanted to know if Ward was driving it.'

'What's this about, Tom?' Suspicion.

Allay it, he thought. Lie to her.

'Nothing really. A couple of people I talked to mentioned a car like yours. I'm just trying to decide if there were two white Toyota Starlets around town that day or one.'

'My car wasn't anywhere near River Road.'

'I know that.'

'Ward took it out. He ran up to Kaimata. On the way back he stopped off at the service station on Longbush Street.'

'To get gas?'

'I think he used the car wash.'

'Thanks, Maddy. Look, that's really helpful.'

'That's okay.' Suspicious, still suspicious. But he didn't care. He had what he wanted now.

Lying bastard.

Heart beating hard. The rush of certainty, the confidence. It was like desire. Take it easy, he thought. Be careful. Think it through.

42.

'Are you all right?' Sylvia asked.

'Yes,' Larry said, looking at her.

'Come. Sit here.' She patted the space next to her on the sofa.

For a moment it seemed as if he would refuse, as if he couldn't be bothered moving just for the sake of her proximity, but then he stood up, a sort of twist and heave with one hand on the arm of his chair and the other balancing his glass, and moved over, sat down. The leather creaked. She felt the warmth of him close to her. She reached up her arm and slipped it behind his neck, smoothed her palm over the side of his head, the ribbed texture of his hair, the fleshy flap of his earlobe.

'You look tired,' she said.

'Not tired. Just stuffed around.'

'Who's stuffing you around?'

'Nobody. Me.' He took a big gulp of his whisky.

'Is it Colin?'

'Yes. Mostly. Well, professional distance isn't always my long suit, is it? Even harder to achieve in cases like this.'

'Even though you can't represent him?'

'Especially when I can't represent him.'

Well that made sense, in a way. All the care and none of the responsibility.

'Does he have a defence?' she asked.

'Everybody has a defence.'

'What will you do?'

'Go for provocation. It'll be mostly up to him. The only version of what happened is his. If the jury believes him, then we have a chance. If they don't, he's had it.'

'Do you believe him?'

He turned his head to look at her, a little grin on his face that had no humour behind it.

'Honest answer?' he asked.

'Yes.'

'I don't think he knows what the truth is.'

And no one else knew either. No one would ever know. Colin could say anything about Heidi now she was dead, any lies at all, and if people believed him, that would become the official version. It seemed obscene, a travesty of the way a life ought to end. The least you ought to do for her was to try to understand. How could you give her anything like full value otherwise?

'I'm sorry,' she said, 'I can't help asking. Usually, with your cases I'm curious but there's no real urgency, no real need. This time it's different.'

'Ask away.'

And suddenly, of course, all the questions seemed footling or prurient and she felt pathetic for wanting to ask them. Except that they pushed. They insisted.

'Where was the rifle?'

'In the wardrobe.'

'In the wardrobe?'

'That's what he says.'

'Why? Lisa says he never used it.'

'Who knows why?' A shrug. 'Isn't there a frisbee on the top shelf of my wardrobe?'

'And he just took it out and shot her?'

'No. When he first pointed it, it wasn't loaded. He wanted to scare her. Then she started yelling.'

'She started yelling when he pointed it at her?' That doesn't sound right, she thought.

'Yes.'

'Why would anyone do that? Surely, if someone points a gun at you, you'd stop yelling, not start. And what was she doing while he was taking it out of the wardrobe? Just sitting there?'

He shrugged. Because that's what Colin said happened and there was nothing to prove it wasn't so?

'It's all crazy,' she said. 'It makes no sense. The police seem to be asking everyone if she was having an affair. Why?'

'Colin thinks she was.'

'That can't be right.'

'He says she admitted it.'

'Who with, though?'

A silence. He was thinking. He was weighing up the pros and cons of giving her the information. She wondered how he made such decisions, what criteria he applied. Whatever they were, she did not really understand them. Sometimes he told her things that seemed very indiscreet. At others he withheld what seemed like completely trivial information.

'In the strictest confidence,' he said. 'For the time being at any rate.'

'All right.'

'It was Tom.'

'Tom?'

'Colin says Heidi and Tom were having it off.'

'And what does Tom say?'

'He denies it. Of course.'

'It's ridiculous,' she said. 'You believe it?'

'I don't have to. Colin believes it.'

'And you're going to drag it all out in court?'

'Out of my hands,' he said.

'Here you are then.' Ward was standing over her with a glass of wine. She reached up, took it, watched him as he turned and moved to his chair. He sat down with a sigh, leaned back. Then, he lifted his own glass to her in a little toast, winked.

'How was your day?' Maddy asked, smiling at him.

'Just a day.'

There was something in his response that reassured her. No need to talk, no need to analyse and dissect things. It was enough to sit there comfortably together, with the boys away in their rooms, a little communion at the end of the day. She felt lucky, privileged, to have such a moment in the current turmoil, trying to keep all her activities on track with this hideous thing with Colin going on as well. They were both lucky. To have each other.

'I called Catherine Lynyard,' she said.

'Oh? What about?'

'She's on the board of trustees. I'm going to see her about what happened to Donny.'

'Good.'

He didn't seem very interested, perhaps because bullying was not so important in the greater scheme of things. She was tempted to say that it was bullying that caused the big problems later when kids grew up.

'Have you talked to Larry and Syl?' he asked.

'No. I think she went round to see Lisa. Imogen's taking it very hard.'

'Yes, Tom said so.'

'You saw Tom?'

'No, he called me.' A little pause. 'A tax problem.'

'Curious. He called me, too.'

'Oh, what about?'

'The usual thing. You know what he's like. He just can't leave it alone.'

'Carla?' The question was quick and then he had to clear his throat. Something stuck.

'Yes.'

A little pause. He took a sip from his glass. 'What did he say?'

'Oh, nothing. He wanted to know if you were driving my car that afternoon.'

Another pause.

'And?'

'And what?'

'What did you say?'

'I said you went out to Kaimata. Why does it matter?'

'No, no. Not at all.' Something in his tone, though.

'You did go out to Kaimata, didn't you?'

'Yes,' he said, looking at her. 'I did.'

'It's just Tom.'

'I know.'

'It's hard for him,' she said.

'It must be, yes.'

'Especially now. It isn't fair, is it, how some families seem to just get all the crap piled on them and others have none at all. Apparently Imogen refused to get up today. Just stayed in bed. Too frightened.'

'I guess life isn't fair.'

'I just feel so lucky sometimes that we're all right.'

He didn't answer. He was staring into his glass as if there were something floating in it. Was the wine corked? No. He would have said so. He would never drink corked wine.

'Catherine Lynyard also said she might join my Visual Arts Committee. She's quite knowledgeable.'

A second before he reacted. 'Oh?'

'I thought we should have them to dinner. Her and John. They'd be good allies.'

'Yes,' he said. 'They would.' Looking at her. Smiling. Nodding. 'That's a really great idea, Poppet.'

43.

THERE WAS PLENTY OF parking along the Esplanade this early in the morning. Tom got out of the ute, shut the door and turned away, began to walk along the footpath. The grass verge still had a scattering of dead leaves, the smell of autumn, fresh and rotten, cool. The bright sunlight on the left side of his face, flutters of warmth as it flickered through the bare branches.

The old house with Ward's office. There were brass plates beside the door: Brian Blenkinsop, Lawyer, and Wyte and Lorton, Chartered Accountants. Yes, well. You could strike the Wyte out now.

The stairs with a tan carpet, wood-panelled walls. He walked up towards a landing. Creak. There was always a creak on the fourth step. Louder today. In the morning. In his present state of mind. Would Ward be here yet?

The door at the top was open. The PA, Marie, sitting at her desk. Twenty-something, with black hair cut so that it fitted her skull like a crash helmet. Dark red lips.

'Good morning,' he said, approaching.

'Hi.' A smile. A nice smile, head on one side in a coy gesture.

'Is Ward in?'

'Do you have an appointment?'

It wasn't quite a question because it tailed off on the last word and her eyes flicked to the side, looking past him, back out into the corridor. Ward was standing there on the landing beside the open door of his office.

'Tom,' he said. 'Come in.' A gesture. Ushering. Wave of his twisted hand. Not a gracious gesture. It was reluctant, grudging, but Ward gave a grin as Tom approached, a stretching sideways of the big moustache.

So he sat down in one of the armchairs. Ward too. Here we are then.

Ward looked at him. Didn't speak. Neither of them spoke for several seconds.

'I thought you might pop by,' Ward said.

'Yes.'

'After yesterday.'

'Yes.'

'I owe you an apology.'

'An apology?' He could feel the rage, like vomit, surge to his throat.

'Yes. I think it's probably the worst thing I've ever done in my life.' Then, seeing the expression on Tom's face, he looked very frightened. 'No, no, no. Don't think that. I didn't . . . I wasn't the one. It wasn't me.'

Tom didn't move. He was scared to move because of what he might do.

'I was there that day. I was driving Maddy's car. I came round a corner and there was this bike by the side of the road. It was up on its stand and it was badly . . . Well, its back wheel was sticking out into the roadway. It gave me a fright, and I guess I was going a bit fast. I braked but I hit it, just clipped it. Sent it flying, though. I stopped, of course. I had a good look. There was no one there. No one at all. The bike was lying on the grass, well out of the roadway. I drove on.'

'Did you get out of the car?'

'No. It wasn't me, Tom. She wasn't there. I swear to you.'

Ward swallowed, lifted his hands and briefly pressed them to his face, the left one covering his eye, the right, with the two curled fingers, in a grotesque peep-o gesture. Then he took a deep breath.

'I went on. I was going to Winston and I'd decided, I don't know why, I'd decided I'd take River Road that Saturday. For the drive, I suppose. Anyway, when I got into the city I had a look at the car. There was no damage, hardly any, just a scuff mark, a bit of a scratch on the left side. I went to a service station and bought some tinted wax, polished it up.'

'You didn't break the headlight?'

'No. But you see, the worst thing, the thing that makes me feel bad, is that on my way to Winston, about 10 k after I hit the bike, I saw another car, going in the opposite direction. It was travelling really fast.'

'What sort of car?'

'I don't know. Something sporty. It was yellow.'

'Yellow?'

'Yes, yellow.'

'Who was driving?'

'I didn't see. I guess I was kind of distracted by hitting the bike.'

'And you didn't tell the cops about any of this?'

'No. I just didn't realise, at first, that there was any connection with Carla. It was really a whole day later and, by then, I'd already polished the car, and I don't know . . .' A heavy sigh, an admission. 'I mean, I'm not supposed to drive a stick shift because of this . . .' Lifting his right hand, waving it. 'And I guess I was thinking of what people would say. You know, me disobeying the conditions of my licence and so on. And the fact that I'm on the council. I didn't want people to think I was that kind of person, someone who'd wreck a kid's bike and just drive off, the kind of person who'd cover up the evidence.'

But you are that kind of person.

'Why did you cover up the evidence?'

'I don't know.' A look, a helpless, hopeless look.

'And why didn't you say anything? To me. Or Lisa.'

'I don't know, mate. I should've. I was confused. And every day it got harder. I thought they'd find the yellow car. And when I finally realised, maybe, they weren't going to, it seemed impossible to tell you because, you know, it might have ruined everything.'

'Everything?'

'The Tribe.' A miserable look on his face, and then the eyes covered again.

I'm supposed to feel sorry for him, Tom thought. I am supposed to feel sympathy and forgiveness because he's confessed his fault and admitted he's wrong. He's been a good boy and wants Mummy or Daddy to say, There, there, dear. It's all right.

'So what are you going to do now?' Tom asked.

'I suppose I'd better go and talk to the police.' A little rise in the intonation that made it almost a question, as if he wanted, hoped for (would it be possible?) a response that said, No, no, Ward, you don't have to do that. You don't have to put yourself through that.

'I think you'd better,' Tom told him. Was there more to say? Was there more he could say without losing it?

He stood up, turned away. In his peripheral vision, he could see Ward staring at him helplessly.

Didn't meet his eyes, though. Just walked out.

44.

HANNAH CRESWELL SAT IN her usual chair looking out of her window into the trees, her enchanted forest. From here the illusion was not as convincing as from the other chair, where the patients sat. Through the branches she could see the glimmer of light and the flicker of movement as people walked along the footpath above the house. From the patients' chair you gazed into a tangled gloom that narrowed into darkness. You were suspended in the trees, like some small creature lost in arboreal vastness, sent forth on a perilous journey. Hannah let everyone choose which chair to sit in on their first appointment and she had noticed over the years that the few who didn't take the patients' chair were the ones who needed to keep control. They were the least successful in solving whatever problem it was that had brought them here. In most cases they did not come back after the first or second appointment.

Tom Marino hadn't seemed like that, which was why she was surprised that he was so late today. He had seemed committed to the process. She would have expected him to return with another dream, something reflecting his ongoing discovery of the Shadow, perhaps, or a specific reference to the terms of his situation. It was impossible to predict just how an analysis might develop but she had felt confident that she knew, in a general way, what would happen to Tom. He was self-reflective and intelligent enough to sketch a picture of himself that made sense to him. This would then be followed by the much slower process of understanding how this picture connected to the deeper needs that drove him. He would have to venture far into the forest. In search of his soul? It was not a stupid word. Hannah had never believed in a conventional religion, in God and Life Eternal, but she understood that the notion of the spirit was as relevant to human biology as the chemistry of the blood. The soul was just one expression of the mystery of consciousness — a mystery only from the perspective of the conscious, of course. Tom's soul, the centre of his being, his reason for living, was lost to him. In a sense, it had always been lost. It was just that he had never missed it till now. So he must seek it, like the heroes of legend, through many dangerous adventures, and when he found it he would see that it was something precious, like a jewel. Maybe it would be given to him by a woman and maybe, for a time, he would think that it was the woman he wanted. Only gradually would he realise that she was just a means to an end. Hannah did not know exactly how this story would go, only that she must help Tom extract it from the tumbling chaos of his thoughts and his feelings, his actions and his dreams. There were a thousand versions, but they were all based in a single fundamental pattern. If Hannah had an article of faith it was this.

The empty chair concerned her, therefore. She looked at her watch. It was five to nine. Too late now. She was sure he wasn't coming. She supposed there was a good reason, and that he would call her and apologise and make another appointment for next week. She would charge him for her lost time, of course. It would be unprofessional not to do so and, in any case, payment was a measure of commitment and without commitment the whole exercise was futile. Her next patient was due at a quarter to ten. There was time for something else, perhaps. A few moments of stillness.

45.

SO, WHAT HAPPENS? THE members of the Tribe go on talking, they go on drinking coffee, the coffee being the measure of the talk. For the time it takes to get it and drink it they are bound together in a conversation. For that long, the custom says, they will listen and contribute. They will engage in the appropriate exchange, the gossip and the affection that binds them together. Sometimes, of course, in special circumstances, there is an extra interest, a greater need and intensity.

Thus, Madeleine Lorton and Sylvia Hannerby sat in the bay window in the mid-morning assembly at Stratos and sipped their lattes. Maddy had bought biscotti, too. Crisp sticks of tan-coloured biscuit, chocolate-tipped. She took one between thumb and forefinger and chopped the end off with her white teeth. A fastidious woman, Maddy, despite her arty, flamboyant air, and always healthy-looking with her rosy cheeks and thick brown curls. Today she was dressed in black but with a silk shawl around the shoulders of her coat, rippling peacock colours, blue and green and gold.

Sylvia looked paler, more subdued. A white shirt and grey wool skirt, a black coat, which she had taken off so that it lay around her hips on the bench seat. She was on her way to the library, the job that bored her and that she felt guilty about having.

What were they to talk about on that particular Tuesday? It was the fourth day since the murder. Was it possible to move on? Was it possible to return to the business of ordinary living like the doings of children and the politics of Durry? Not quite.

'Apparently she has no one,' Maddy said.

'No family?'

'Not here. There's a sister in Zurich but she has no money. She can't afford to come. Well, she says she's not going to come.'

'You spoke to her?'

'Ward did. And he talked to the undertakers, too. They called last night. Apparently they asked Colin, and Colin said to talk to Ward. About what to do. That's the way it works. If there's a friend who can take over, then that's who they ask.'

'Well, we *are* her friends.'

'Like I said, there's no one else. No one who wants to know, anyway. Apparently she used to be in a crowd before she moved here. She worked in a bank somewhere. But she lost touch with them.'

'It's up to us, then.'

'Yes.'

A pause, as they both thought about it, both contemplated the mess of emotion and conflicting loyalties. But what did loyalties have to do with it? Wasn't it just a matter of being decently human?

'So, what happens?' Sylvia asked.

'We'll have to wait until the coroner's finished with the body. Then it goes back to the undertaker. That may be tomorrow. Or the day after. Then, we'll need to organise the funeral.'

'Which undertaker is it? Not Anlaby. He's such a slimy man.'

'Chapelgate,' Maddy said.

'Cheme? Is that his name?'

'Yes, Michael Cheme.'

Maddy sipped her coffee, took the last bite of her biscotti. 'Do we need a church?' she asked.

'No. I don't think so. Heidi wouldn't want a church.'

'You can't always tell what people would want. When it comes down to it.'

'No,' Sylvia said. 'But you have to go on something. What you know about them. In any case, a church would make it a public thing. It would be full of prurient people wanting to gawp. If it's down to us, we want a small, simple ceremony. A private ceremony.'

'We could do it at Chapelgate.'

'Yes.'

'We could put a discreet ad in the paper saying friends and family only.'

'In the *Advocate*?'

'Yes. If the timing's right.'

'We could do it next Monday.'

'Good. I'll talk to the undertaker, if you like.'

'All right,' Sylvia said. 'But we need to find out when the body's going to be released.'

46.

CURIOUS HOW EASY IT was for Ward to talk about it, once he had decided. The police didn't even criticise or want to know why he hadn't come forward before. They just took his statement and thanked him. Did he still have the car? they asked. Yes, of course. Good, fine. They may wish to examine it further.

Walking out of there, walking away into the clear, bright afternoon, he felt that a weight had been lifted from him. It was always possible, of course, that they could charge him with something, although he couldn't think what. Withholding information? Causing the police to waste their time? He didn't think so, and although he knew that there were other potential difficulties (especially if the media got hold of the story) the relief at having come clean was just too strong to make him worry about any of that. He felt light. He felt happy. Even with the thought of Colin still hanging heavy on him, he felt happy. And, given that it was already four o'clock and he had no more appointments that day, he felt like knocking off and celebrating.

The Businessman's Club was almost empty. He stood looking at the main room: the polished wood of the tables and the gleam of the clean glass ashtrays, panelled walls hung with the photographs of past presidents, a thick blue carpet with its angled rows of tiny golden swords. The committee had argued about that. Whether it should be swords or fleurs-de-lis. The swords had won for no good reason that Ward could see. What difference did it make? At the bar, he bought himself a Cuban and a glass of shiraz, a big, fat shiraz from South Australia, and he sat in an armchair in the corner, the usual corner. Satisfied. Not complacently satisfied. He was still too aware that he had made a fool of himself and still too anxious about the consequences to feel complacent. But he had always had a capacity for getting over things. For not worrying or, at least, for not worrying so much that it ruined his palate. The wine was as good as it should be and it wrestled with the fine tang of the tobacco like a lusty whore. No, whore was the wrong word. It was less worn, less shop-soiled than that. Like a widow, maybe. A young widow, strong and sexy, with eager limbs, who had had it before and who missed it, wanted it.

Good God, he thought, as a smoke-ring drifted from him and dissolved in the air, I'm excelling myself. And then he thought of Maddy or, rather, didn't think, just felt the need. Tonight, perhaps. He should tell her about the accident, of course. And he would, at the right moment. But there was time enough for that and, right now, he didn't want to think about the awkward stuff. Right now he wanted just to sit and enjoy the wine and the cigar, and in a little while there would be someone to talk to and around 6.30 Larry might well show up. And then, of course, it was Tuesday and Monty Kerrington was supposed to be here and be introduced to the other members. Whoever was around. They'll all be around, he thought. It'll all be fine. And, as he sometimes did when he was here by himself, he counted the presidents, all thirty-seven of them, and wondered how it would feel in a year or two when his own portrait was up there too.

Lorton makes his mark. Who would have thought it, eh? Back then. A dull boy, a pudgy boy. Good-natured? Yes.

Phlegmatic? That's a word for him. He bumbled along all through the third form and the fourth form, trailing after those other two, the bright sparks, Wyte and Hannerby. You wondered what they saw in him, why they put up with him. Until the incident, that is, the fifth form general science field trip, overnight to the Waitangiruru State Forest. What happened? Nobody's quite sure because nobody's said, exactly, but they had a primus in the tent. Wasn't supposed to be there but one of them had brought it along and they were cooking up something (pun intended). Seems it was faulty, though. Seems it had a crack in the tank or a broken seal of some other defect, because all of a sudden it was a mass of flame. Two of them sat there staring, paralysed, knowing what was going to happen but helpless to stop it, and the third, the dumb one, the slow one, the one too thick to rub two sticks together, was on his knees and grabbing it and hurling it out through the tent flap, out into the night. And just in time too. Wham! The thing exploded, half a second out, before it hit the ground, and burning alcohol and chunks of brass were flying everywhere. There were six little fires they had to extinguish and one of them was Ward's right hand.

The funny thing was that afterwards he couldn't remember what he had done or why he'd done it. So uncharacteristic, although the effects were real enough: the weeks in hospital, the fourteen operations, the problems as he learned to write left handed. There were good things, too, though, like his picture in the paper. Ward the Hero! That was when Maddy first noticed him, that photo in the *Winston Evening Mail*, as he sat in hospital with a sheepish grin on his face and his fair hair flopping over his left eye. Maddy was drawn to heroes, perhaps because her Dad had won an MC fighting Tom Marino's relatives in North Africa. When she met Ward a couple of years later, she remembered him and fell in love — with his story, with his hand, with the fact that his father owned a fair-sized chunk of Taranaki, but most of all with his sweet-good nature. Such a decent fellow. So easy-going. Wouldn't hurt a fly.

47.

AT FIRST, WHEN HE told her, Lisa couldn't believe it and, then, when she saw that he was not making it up (and, God, why would he make up anything like that?) she got angry. Not the sharp, energising anger that she felt at an injustice, although there was a bit of that, but the heavy kind that came as a response to stupidity. So stupid, to waste everybody's time like that, to cause people, and especially Tom, needless suffering that could have been avoided. If Ward had opened his fat mouth sooner, they'd have spent the last six months looking for the right person — the person, perhaps, who was driving the yellow car. And, of course, her usual reaction to stupidity, when it was about something like this, was to expose it, hold it up to ridicule (well, you didn't have to do anything to ridicule it except hold it up). Her first reaction was to write a story.

It took her a while to come up with the idea, though, and when she did she immediately had doubts, and the doubts made her annoyed with herself. Moral dilemmas often made her annoyed, because she didn't like situations where she couldn't decide and took any kind of wavering as a sign of her own weakness or her lack of clarity. That's what principles were for, wasn't it? To make things clear? But it would be hard to write a story about Ward, to show people what an insensitive, selfish clod he had been, not only because he was a friend and you were supposed to forgive friends their faults, just as you were supposed to forgive your children's, but also because Maddy was even more of a friend and Maddy was an even bigger friend of Sylvia's and Sylvia was just about the one person, other than her immediate family, whom Lisa felt she could never do without. Exposing Ward would threaten all that. How could she?

Yet, if she didn't write the story, she would be denying everything she stood for in her working life. It was no good saying that, well, it was just a little tin-pot paper and who really cared if it avoided things other than the last meeting of the local chapter of the Embroiderers' Guild. If it was a worthless paper, it wasn't worth working for, and she was wasting her time by being there. If, as she had always believed, it could make a difference and, in fact, had made a difference over the years she'd been involved with it, then it had done so only to the extent that it avoided niceness and coyness and did not upset people and stuck to the truth. Lisa believed in the truth. Without truth there was no trust, and if you couldn't trust people human life just fell apart, didn't it? The paper encapsulated that idea. It was all about keeping people informed, keeping them honest — the one being the flip side of the other.

She asked Tom about it while they were making dinner. Should she write the story?

'You don't have to do that for me,' he said. He was at the cupboard, taking out plates and bowls. The clatter and scrape of china, she could hear it over her shoulder as she sliced the beef.

'I wouldn't just be doing it for you.'

'Well, if it's for your own benefit, go ahead.' Which wasn't the kind of answer she wanted. It was the kind of answer that would have upset her at another time. It was dismissive, almost as if he thought she was to blame somehow. Now, though, she didn't get annoyed. She just felt puzzled.

'Doesn't it upset you?' she asked, glancing at him.

He was at the table, laying forks down next to the bowls.

'Yes,' he said. 'I want to bash his stupid head in. But I'm relieved in a way, too. I always knew there was something more, some other clue to be had. Perhaps now we might catch the bastard.'

So calm, so cold. He might have been offering a problem in logic that you could work out if you thought about it hard enough. She didn't understand how he could talk about being angry in such a cold voice. It scared her.

She bent down to the cupboard under the bench, pulled out the wok and set it on the stove. Oil and a dash of soy, the sliced ginger. Sizzle. Tiny beds of steam in frantic clamour about the little discs. The first whiff of the aroma lifted to her face.

'If we print a story, then it's more likely some member of the public will come forward. Someone who saw the yellow car.'

He didn't answer for a moment. Perhaps he hadn't thought of this possibility.

'Then write it,' he said.

'It's not that simple.'

Ward had acted like the lowest of the low, but could she really imagine herself ripping into him in public, in print? Would that really help to find the driver of the yellow car?

'I'll talk to Stan,' she said. But would there be time? Deadline at noon tomorrow.

'Frank! How are you?'

Frank Drummer, turning at the words.

'Ward!' he said, grinning. 'Good day to you, my friend.'

'Let me introduce you to Monty.'

They were standing at the bar, or rather sitting perched on the high stools. It was more convenient here than at one of the tables. Easier for people to come up and meet Monty and then move on.

'Monty, this is Frank Drummer. Frank, Monty Kerrington. New member.'

'Well, then. Welcome aboard,' Frank said.

Ward watched them shake hands. A hearty shake like good blokes should.

'Monty's in finance,' he said to Frank and then, turning to Monty: 'And Frank runs Hardy's. You know, the department store in High Street.'

'I know.' Monty pulled a sour face but not for real. 'I see it often enough on my wife's Visa statement.'

Frank laughed.

'About time you gave me a volume discount,' Monty said, and he laughed too.

'Are you new to Durry as well as the Club?' Frank asked.

'Been here six months. Bought a bit of property. Land up the end of Pigskill Road and the old house down Cox's Line.'

'Ah, you'll be close to recent events, then.' Frank glanced at Ward to see if this topic of conversation was all right. He was good that way, Frank was. He understood people. Sensitivities. Ward winked at him to show it was okay. It was fine.

'Brings you up with a start, that's for sure,' Monty said. 'I know the bloke, you know.'

'Yes, we all know him. He's a member,' Frank replied.

'Not the sort of member you'd want to advertise.'

'Terrible business,' Ward said. 'But you have to stick by

your friends.' Feeling bad about poor old Col.

'Well, fair enough.' Monty knocked back the last of his Scotch, put his glass on the bar with a little smack.

Ward signalled to the barman for another round.

'Let me,' Frank said. 'What'll you have?'

'Whatever that was.' Monty flicked his finger at the glass.

Two more Scotches coming up. The amber twinkle in the diamond of the cut glass.

'On my tab,' Frank said. 'And I'll take a G and T.' Then, turning to Monty, he went on. 'So you've bought Clisserford.'

'Yeees. Bloody stupid name, don't you think? Always makes me think of some bit of the female what's-it.'

'Well . . .' Frank wasn't sure but Ward laughed.

'I should change it,' Monty said. 'Tell you what, we could run a competition for the best name.'

'What would the prize be?'

'Don't know. What do you think? On second thoughts, though, it would be a waste of time. I already have the winning entry.'

'What's that?' Ward asked.

'Pumpkin.'

'Why "Pumpkin"?'

'Peter, Peter pumpkin eater
 Had a wife and couldn't keep her
 Put her in a pumpkin shell
And there he kept her very well.' Monty threw back his head and laughed.

Ward wanted to join in but he couldn't quite. Was it because it wasn't funny? It was funny, in a way. It kind of was. But it was such an odd thing to say that it had to be kind of serious, too. But what did it mean if it was serious?

'Well,' Frank said, with a little nod towards Monty. 'Great to meet you. I dare say we'll have many more opportunities.'

'Dare say we will.' Monty offering his hand again, Frank taking it.

Then, just as Frank was turning to go, Larry was there. Lanky, smiling.

'Ah!' Ward felt his spirits lift, although there was also another brief thought of Colin. Wondering where Colin was right now, at this moment. Thinking the last time they were all here together, only a couple of weeks ago, sitting at the table in the corner, the three of them. Now there was Monty instead of Colin. It didn't work, somehow. It wasn't right.

Still, he introduced them, Larry and Monty, and he suggested that they go over to a table now. So Larry got his usual and they went. Not to the corner table because Blenkinsop and Pete Gilligan were there and, apart from anything else, Larry and Blenkinsop didn't get on. Well, it wasn't Larry's fault, of course. It was Blenkinsop. Professional jealousy. Although it wasn't quite that either, because Blenkinsop wasn't a barrister, only a solicitor. That was a thing between lawyers, Ward supposed. The people who did the court work were the glamorous ones and the others were jealous of them. It was a bit like surgeons and doctors, maybe.

'Buttocks!' Larry said.

'Trees!'

'Here's to her fair and slender thighs.' Monty did his own thing, which Ward liked.

'Now,' Monty went on, turning to Larry, 'are you defending my friend and neighbour in Cox's Line?'

'No, I'm afraid not.'

'Then I don't suppose you can tell us anything about the case.'

'No, I can't.'

'Then how's a bloke to satisfy his curiosity?'

'You'll just have to wait for the trial,' Larry said.

'That could be months.'

'Could be a year. That's getting to be pretty standard these days. I imagine the police talked to you?'

'They did.'

'And could you tell them anything?'

'No. Didn't even hear the shot. Not that we would. We're not that close.' Monty sat there, looking keen and eager, but Larry didn't reply. Supped his whisky. Looked at Ward, looked at Monty.

But Ward wasn't paying that much attention. Talk of the police reminded him of this afternoon, the statement he'd made, and now, this time, he suddenly felt not so comfortable about it. Would it all blow over? Could it be allowed to? Maybe the papers would get hold of it — not the local rag, because Lisa wouldn't let that happen, he was sure of it — but the dailies, the *Winston Evening Mail* or the *Chronicle*. Would they think it a big enough story to do anything with?

'It's early for this time of year, don't you think?' Larry was saying. Was that what he was saying?

'Could be.' Monty answered.

'Yes. It's darker than usual, heavier. I guess it's the humidity. It tends to make people want to do strange things. Like selling their Demergena shares. Do you think I should sell my Demergena shares?'

'Oh, I get it.' Monty nodded. 'Very good.'

Quite what Monty got, or thought he got, Ward wasn't sure. He was feeling disoriented all of a sudden, as if the good feeling, all the optimism he'd been running with, were a sham. A weird sensation, sick and dizzy, like a man who thought he was walking along a street and suddenly finds himself at a cliff's edge, looking down. A long way down. Step back, go back, but where to?

'Well,' Monty was saying, 'like the ski-field owner said, "There's no business like snow business."'

'White on, my friend.'

48.

FREE TIME. NOTHING TO do but sit and think. That was the irony of it. They took away the space and they gave you the time. Before, in that other life, there were so many pressures, so many demands, that thinking was always interrupted, always cluttered. Now, it was possible to think clearly. Because there was no booze either and oddly, strangely, he didn't want any. He liked the clarity. Because he knew the truth about himself. He was guilty. Yes. Make no mistake. And although it seemed, in a way, that it had all happened to someone else, he knew it was not so. If he thought for a moment, he could still feel the kick against his shoulder as the gun went off. His shoulder, no one else's. No other person felt that kick. No other person saw her thrash around, as if her body had gone mad, as if all the parts of her were fighting amongst themselves to get away, to run away. No other person felt the iron grip of her hand, hanging on, as if he were her last hope. He had done that to her.

But it wouldn't have happened if he hadn't aimed at her, if he hadn't loaded the rifle, if he hadn't gone and got it, if she hadn't yelled at him like that, if she hadn't been fucking Tom Marino, if she hadn't, hadn't, hadn't walked into his life that day back then, seven years ago.

Seven years? And, of course, she didn't walk into his life, he walked into hers, in a sense. One morning, coming up the stairs to find her sitting there at the reception desk. From the temp agency because Claire (was that her name?) had walked out in a huff the day before. Such smooth, pale skin with a touch of colour at the cheekbones, such big blue eyes, such golden hair so tightly, strictly tied back and under control. Her voice cool, like mountain air. That was the thing about her, in a way, her Swissness. She was bright and fresh and clear, the blue sky, the snow-white mountains. Had she smiled? No, not on that first morning. It had taken several mornings and several little bits of wit, before he had made her smile. But every day, every one of those early days, he had looked forward to seeing her. At first the looking forward had begun when he opened the door to the building, and then at the moment he drove into the carpark and then somewhere around Victory Bridge and then stepping out of the house, drinking his coffee, shaving, waking up. His first thought on waking up. Heidi. That was love. Ward had wondered why they didn't hire someone else, someone permanent, why Colin kept saying no, no. Because I need her in the mornings. Because I think of her when I wake up.

She was his first thought on waking up now too. The bitch. No, how could he call her a bitch when he'd done that to her? It was his fault, all his fault. Except if she hadn't yelled at him, it wouldn't have happened. The words, her voice. He could still hear it. It was burned into his brain.

You are stupid, stupid. You are a stupid man. You don't think. You don't feel. So is it a surprise that I like Tom? He listens. He is nice. He understands me. And if I have sex with him whose fault is that? Whose fault? Your fault. You drink too much. We are not a couple. You are not a man. You ruin yourself with drinking. Tom is a man. He can do it. Not like you. Drinking makes you like a baby. Go and drown yourself, you stupid man. Go and drown yourself in your wine and your whisky.

No, no, no. Why can't you be nice to me, the way you were in the old days, when you first moved into the house. When I gave you the house, the garden you always wanted. Was that why you moved in with me? Were you using me? No, no, I don't want to think that. That isn't fair. And I'm sorry, I'm sorry, I'm oh so sorry. But why did you yell at me? I just wanted peace. I just wanted quiet in my own house. If you hadn't yelled, it would all have been fine. We could have made up. We could have gone back to how we were and I wouldn't have to drown like Rexy. Wouldn't have to squirm and shit when he held me under. Silver bubbles, rubble-bubble, blip, blip, blip. *Let me make this clear. I will not have the peace disrupted. I will have calm and quiet, you understand me?* Calm and quiet, that's all I wanted. You can't blame me. I just wanted the bitch to shut up, that's all. If only she'd done that, it would have been fine. Everything would have been all right. So whose fault was it, in the end? You tell me that.

49.

WARD AND MADDY AND Larry and Sylvia, Lisa and Tom. All together now in Maddy's house, which was Ward's house too, of course, except that anywhere that Maddy lived was Maddy's house. In Maddy's living room, the pale, pale walls like washed-out daffodils, the dark green paint, the prints by Maddison, the Dansworth quilt, the original Shaw (that's Basil Shaw, the father. Where did you get that?) and the comfortable, plumped-up, loungey furniture, with the throws and the rugs and the pottery pieces on the shelves and little tables. Tasteful and stylish (according to the eclectic Maddy canon) and warm now, with the night outside, the French doors rain-spotted, streaked with drops. They all sat there in a big circle, quiet, in a sombre mood so even Larry hadn't quipped or cranked, and Ward served wine with bowed head and sober mien, holding back the big smile of open, honest self-satisfaction that usually accompanied a broaching of his cellar.

Well, here we are, then. Maddy looked around at them all. It was her job to do this, her meeting.

'Well,' she said. 'I asked Michael Cheme to come along so we could start things going with him.'

'When?' Lisa asked.

'Seven-thirty.' Maddy paused, just in case there was any criticism. It was always best to anticipate the criticism so that you could nip it in the bud. 'Is that all right?'

Lisa shrugged as if it didn't matter. Was that the problem here, that nobody cared really? Nobody cared about a woman shot in the head? No, how could that be? Maddy herself had felt sick, sick at the thought of it, of what Colin had done. A person she liked. As they all liked Heidi. A friend.

'When will the body be released?' Lisa asked.

'Tomorrow,' Maddy answered. 'Is that right, Larry?'

'You know more than I do,' he told her.

'Funeral when then?' Lisa asked.

'Monday.' Maddy glanced at the others to show that she was actually consulting them.

'Yes.' Sylvia nodding. Nods all round.

'Michael can do it at 11.30,' Maddy said. 'Is that all right?'

No one said no.

'I thought we should have it at Chapelgate. Just something very small. You know, not to make a big public thing of it and have it full of spectators.'

'Somebody will have to say something,' Lisa said.

'Yes, of course.'

'Who?'

Nobody answered. Larry and Ward were studying their wine glasses, like judges at a tasting. Sylvia sitting looking drawn, looking sick at the thought of it all. Tom stony-faced. Did he ever feel anything, that man? Maddy remembered what she knew of him, what she'd learned today from Catherine Lynyard after they'd talked about the board of trustees. She wasn't even sure she wanted Tom in her house, but what could she do? She hadn't had a chance to tell Ward about it yet.

Lisa was staring from one to another, waiting for an answer to her question.

'I will,' Sylvia said.

'Maybe we all should,' Maddy added.

'No, no.' Lisa shaking her head. 'We don't want a procession.'

'Maybe we need a celebrant,' Ward suggested.

'Michael can do that,' Maddy answered.

'No.' Lisa firmer than ever. Was she getting angry? Why was she angry? 'Nobody deserves an undertaker talking at their funeral.'

'He's very good.'

'They all sound insincere.'

'We can do it ourselves,' Sylvia said. 'I'll talk. And Maddy can. And maybe one of the men too. What about you, Ward?'

She didn't suggest Lisa, of course. That would hardly be appropriate. And not Tom either. Doubly inappropriate, although maybe he would want to. There he was, just sitting there. Still, silent, like a snake. And Lisa didn't even know.

'Of course,' Ward said. He had spoken at a fair few funerals over the years. It went with being a councillor. 'Only . . .' He looked round the room. He was worried, Maddy realised. She wondered why. 'Only, I think, you know . . .' Ward seemed to take a deep breath. 'There is Colin to consider.'

'What?' Lisa said it so loud that Maddy jumped.

'I wouldn't like anything to be said against him,' Ward answered.

'I don't believe this!'

'Please, don't shout,' Maddy said. It was the wrong thing to say, of course.

'It's a matter of loyalty,' Ward persisted.

Lisa turned on him. 'It's sexist crap.'

'No, it's not. He's a friend.'

'He's a murderer.' The voice, Tom's voice. Not a shout — it was a whisper almost. Something strange, something strange and cold, so cold that the hairs on the back of her neck stood up and the room fell silent.

'It's just . . .' Ward tried again.

Larry cut him off. 'We hear you, mate.'

'Well,' Maddy said, 'I'll say something and Sylvia will. And Ward?'

'No,' Tom told her. 'I'll do it.'

Really? Maddy thought. I don't think so.

Lisa was turning to Tom as if she were going to object to him too. Did she know? What did she know?

'That's one from each of the three couples,' Sylvia pointed out.

'Let's leave it for now,' Maddy said. 'We can decide that later.'

'Jolly good.' Ward seemed happy. But that was Ward. He never took offence. He was such a good-natured man.

Michael Cheme was tall and thin, with a smile so heavy it seemed to drag his chin down to his chest whenever he used it. He sat there looking sadly round the group. Did he understand the circumstances? Sylvia wasn't sure.

'Music?' he asked.

Music? Sylvia didn't know. Did anyone know? The appalling thing about all this, the thing that made her feel guilty and sad and angry all at once, was the way no one, not any of them, seemed to know much at all about Heidi.

'Bach,' Tom said suddenly.

'Bach?' Maddy staring at him.

Jesu Joy of Man's Desiring.

'Of course.' Cheme nodding, writing it down in his little flip-top notebook with the black cover. 'And would anyone want to come to Boulder Hill, to the crematorium?'

Nobody responded.

'There is, of course, a small chapel there,' Cheme went on. 'Very small, but perhaps an opportunity for a few people to spend a last moment or two?'

Another silence.

'I don't think so,' Sylvia said at last. Only because no one else seemed inclined to say anything.

'Fine. Good. Very good.'

Another pause.

'What about Colin?' Ward asked.

'Oh, for God's sake!' Lisa said.

'I only thought . . .'

'Leave Colin out of this, you drongo!' Lisa, shouting at him. The burst of temper surprised Sylvia, and the others too. Lisa's eyes bright with fury. 'Can't we just think of Heidi for a few moments. Can't we just try and give her some value. We're all she's got. Here.'

Cheme gazing at her with a look of sympathy. He probably looked at his breakfast the same way.

'We're all upset,' Maddy said, giving Lisa a reassuring little smile. Then she turned to Ward, leaned towards him, reached out and squeezed his wrist.

'Lies and hypocrisy,' Lisa said.

'Hey, now. Steady on!' Ward was indignant.

'I just hate hypocrisy. And people who can't face up to their responsibilities.'

What? What was this about? Sylvia caught Larry's eye, saw his surprise and curiosity. Lisa's words hung there like a challenge. Ward seemed to have shrunk away, sitting with his shoulders hunched. Maddy was staring at Lisa and looking puzzled and hurt.

'You don't know, do you?' Lisa said to her.

'Know what?'

'What I know is . . .' Larry said suddenly, loudly. A pause as he drew all the attention towards him. 'A bloke could die of thirst before he gets a drink round here.'

'Sorry, mate.' Ward lumbering to his feet, picking up the bottle, seeing it was empty.

'As me dear old white-haired auntie used to say . . .' Another pause. Longer this time. Larry's face contorted, twisted into an expression of mock despair. 'I've forgotten.'

Laughter, feeble laughter. But there was no more than a smile from Maddy. And Lisa was still furious, jaw clenched, blaze in her eyes.

'More wine.' Ward headed away with the empty bottle, off towards the door.

Larry turned towards Cheme. 'Our brains cease to function after eight o'clock. GJF. It's a chronic condition.'

'GJF?'

'General Judgement Failure. And, of course, anyone who can say that without slurring is certifiably sober.'

'Ha, ha.' Cheme with a polite laugh, mystified by Larry's nonsense. 'Well,' he went on, 'we're probably just about done here, I think.' He turned his head, looked towards Maddy for confirmation.

'Yes, yes. I think so.'

'Well, then . . .' Standing, his body flicking into upright

like a stick man. Maddy, too, got to her feet. 'Good. I'm sure everything will be just fine.' Cheme moved to his right, bent at the waist and offered Sylvia his hand. Looming over her like a crane.

'Thanks,' she said, taking the thin, limp fingers in her own. She wanted to wipe her palm on her skirt when he let go.

Slowly he circled the room, shaking hands with each person there. Coming back at last to Maddy. And Ward, who had returned with a new bottle.

'Sure you won't stay for another?'

But Cheme, at least, had more social sensitivity than to accept.

'No, thank you,' he said, offering Ward his hand.

'Jolly good.' Ward grinned, gave Cheme his twisted fingers, that cautious shake that always seemed a pity because Ward was such a hearty man.

'Nice to meet you all.' Cheme with a smile and another, general bow. He headed for the door with Maddy there to guide him. Sylvia pictured them out in the hall. Maddy would apologise and Cheme would pooh-pooh any suggestion that he had been discommoded.

Ward poured the wine, hesitating over Lisa's glass, and Tom's too. The two of them sitting there, side by side, looking ... Hard to say how they were. Lisa with her arms folded. Tom with his fists resting on his knees. He seemed relaxed except for the fists. They were tight and white at the knuckles. Ward, back in his seat, raising his glass in a little silent toast.

Maddy returned, briskly walking to her chair but not sitting. Standing there, looking indignant, looking puzzled. Ward, seeing her, started to make a move to say something but he was too slow.

'What was all that about?' Maddy demanded, glaring at Lisa.

'Ask him!' Pointing at Ward.

'I think,' Ward said, gazing up at his wife, his hand reaching out to her in a half gesture of appeal, 'we should take this discussion off line. You and I.'

'Absolutely not,' Maddy told him. 'I'm not stupid and I don't like rumour and muddle and innuendo. We need to get this sorted out.'

'Tom and Lisa are annoyed with me,' Ward said.

'I can see that. What I don't understand is why.'

Ward sighed, a heave in his big shoulders. 'Sit down, Poppet,' he said.

She sat down and Ward began to talk, an extraordinary story about how he had been driving down River Road in Maddy's car on the day Carla was killed and how he had hit her bike (but not her, but not her) and had polished up the scratch on the car and hadn't told anyone. Even when the police were asking people to come forward, he hadn't told anyone.

It sounded incredible, especially so when coming from Ward who was so reliable, so dependable, so guaranteed to do the right thing and stick by the rules. But that, perhaps, was just the point, just the reason why he had tried to hide it.

While he talked, Tom and Lisa sat, unmoving, as they had before, and Maddy too was very still, listening with her head bowed a little so that you couldn't see her face, looking down at the floor to her left, her hands in her lap, folded neatly. She might have been in church, listening to the sermon.

'And that's it, really,' Ward told her. 'Not much more to say.'

'What about the yellow car?' Lisa demanded.

'Oh.' Ward glancing up at her.

'There better have been a yellow car,' Lisa said.

'Yes, there was.'

'Because this week's *Advocate* will have it on the front page.'

'There was!' Ward more firmly, almost a break in his voice. He turned to Maddy. 'Further down the road, coming the opposite way, I saw a yellow car,' he said. 'A sports car. It was almost raining by then so I didn't get a good look, and anyway . . . It was going very fast.'

'And that's all?' Maddy asked quietly.

'Yes.'

A silence. Waiting to see what Maddy would do. She was in charge. She sat almost primly, with her spine straight, not touching the back of her chair, her head on one side, her mouth twisted in a little smile, a half smile that had more determination than it had humour. Her eyes looking down to the floor, somewhere towards Ward's feet.

'Well,' she said at last, with a sudden bright glance around the room. 'I'm glad we got that sorted out. Would anyone like a cup of coffee?'

'Wait a minute,' Lisa told her. 'You can't just ignore it.'

'I'm not ignoring it. I just don't see any point in talking about it.'

'No point?'

'What good will it do?'

'Well, he might at least apologise.'

'Why?'

'Why?' Lisa's voice climbing close to a shriek.

'He's sorry. You can see he's sorry. Full of remorse and

shame and all the other things a criminal is supposed to feel. Isn't that enough?' Sudden glare of anger in Maddy's eyes.

Ward now, leaning forward to placate her. 'It's all right, Poppet. It's all right.'

'It's not all right.' Turning on him. 'They want to humiliate you. Over a little mistake.'

'No, no.'

'And other people have done worse things. Much worse things.'

'Let's go,' Lisa said, standing up, turning to Tom. He didn't move for a moment. 'Come on,' she said. 'I'm not staying here.'

'It's cold outside.' Larry looking up at them. 'There may be no room at the inn.'

'Stop being a smart arse,' Lisa told him. She turned back to Tom, who was getting to his feet. 'Come on.' Walking to the door. Tom following.

'Why don't you tell us all about Astra Bridge?' Maddy called after them.

Sylvia didn't understand. She expected Maddy to make a move to stop them leaving but she didn't. Someone had to do it, though. Quickly, putting down her glass, she got up, ran after them.

'Wait!' she called, out in the hallway.

They had their coats on and the front door open.

'Don't go!' Hurrying up to them.

'I can't stay,' Lisa said. 'I can't stand it. I can't listen to crap like that.'

'She's angry. She's upset. I think she's angry with Ward as much as anything.'

'She's just lining herself up alongside the male bullshit.

The little-boy bullshit. Poor Wardy does something wrong. There, there, Wardy, don't feel bad. We still love you. It's like Heidi, for God's sake! The bloody woman's dead and all we're supposed to do is feel sorry for Colin. I can't stand it. It's lies and hypocrisy!' Furious. Eyes dancing.

Sylvia took a step back. She glanced at Tom. His eyes too. Dark and calm and cold and wild. The eyes of a wild animal. A silent animal, watching, waiting for an opportunity. She felt a sudden shiver of fear.

'All right,' she said, turning back to Lisa. 'You go. I'll talk to her. I'll call you tomorrow. Maybe coffee?' She reached out, touched Lisa's arm. Then she moved closer to her, kissed her on the cheek. Lisa gave her a little tense hug in reply.

'Bye, Tom,' Sylvia said, tempted to kiss him too, but not quite wanting to, held back somehow.

The two of them left. Sylvia closed the door behind them, walked back to the living room.

Ward and Maddy and Larry were sitting as before. All of them looked up at her as she entered and took her seat again.

'And then there were four,' Larry said.

'She's upset,' Sylvia said, stating the obvious.

'We're all upset,' Maddy answered. She let out a breath. Suddenly, she looked as if she were going to cry. 'I just don't think it's right to accuse Ward like that. It's not as if he did anything really bad. Just a mistake. A silly mistake. Wasn't it, Pookey?'

He nodded slowly, miserably.

'And calling him a hypocrite and a liar, my God. With Tom sitting there. I mean, I should get credit for my restraint, don't you think?'

'How do you mean?' Sylvia asked.

'We all know what Tom and Heidi were up to. That's being a liar. That's being a hypocrite.' Maddy with a jab of her finger to make her point.

'I don't think we know anything about Tom and Heidi, do we?' Sylvia answered.

'I do,' Maddy said. 'I saw them at your dinner, even if you didn't. They were all over each other. Then, the next thing, they were off in the bathroom together. What do you suppose they were doing in there? Reading the newspaper?'

'I can't say I noticed,' Sylvia said, thinking about Tom Marino's eyes. She turned to Larry. 'Did you notice?'

'Leave me out of this, I pray you.' He lifted his hands, pushing off the subject.

The gesture annoyed her. 'Do you believe they were having an affair?' she insisted.

'I . . .' He looked at her, a warning look, a look that meant he was not going to say what she wanted to hear. 'I think it's not beyond reasonable doubt.'

The bloody case! Colin's defence! Even now, even here, he couldn't bring himself to think in any other terms.

'God,' she said. 'Can't you stop being a lawyer, just for a moment?'

All he could do to that was shrug.

Believe, believe. You had to believe, if you possibly could. If you believed, there was a much better chance of winning. So believe in it, even if you can't. The thought made her feel sick, as if twenty years of marriage had all been a lie.

'Whatever went on between Tom and Heidi, I'm sure Lisa knows about it,' she said. Because, she thought, at least there, in that relationship, there is some honesty and candour.

'But she doesn't know about the rest of it, though.'

Maddy was indignant still. 'I had coffee with Catherine Lynyard this morning. We were talking about Colin and Heidi and she asked me about Tom. Was there something going on? No, I said, I didn't think so. Well, she said, you might be wrong about that. It seems that she and Paul own this property on River Road and the tenant is a woman called Astra Bridge. She's a solo mother, who gets by on the benefit and bits of handicraft. Pokerwork, stuff like that. Catherine found out that for the past few months this Astra has been having an affair with a man who drives a truck with Greenwise on the door, a short man with black hair and beard. Now you tell me who that might be.'

Silence. Sylvia couldn't take it in. It didn't make sense and then, of course, it did, and she thought, Oh, Lisa, my poor, poor Lisa.

'That,' Maddy said, 'is what I call lies and hypocrisy.'

50.

SO WHAT CAN TOM do but confess? The game is up. He heard what Maddy said, even if Lisa didn't. He knows that she knows. Won't it be worse if Lisa hears from someone other than himself?

He begins with the words they always begin with, the sinners.

'I need to talk to you.'

'Now? I'm tired.' And angry, too. She was furious, still furious. And some of her anger was on his behalf. That would not make things easier.

'There's talk going around that I was having an affair with Heidi.'

'I know there is.'

How? How did she know?

'It isn't true.'

'I know it's not.'

'I've been round there a couple of times lately. We were discussing how I might take more of her stuff. You know, other than dahlias. Last week . . . It may have been Tuesday we were in her greenhouse and she was upset. I gave her a hug. For comfort.'

'I don't need to know this. Not now. It's not important.'

'There's something else.'

A pause.

Go on. You have to go on. But this is the last point for turning back. Once the first words are spoken they will lead to the rest. It will all be said.

'I've been having an affair with someone else. Someone different. Not Heidi.'

51.

POLICE SEEK YELLOW CAR IN ACCIDENT PROBE

Bold headlines on the front page, along with the picture. The same picture. Won't the readers be getting sick of this picture? The white cross by the roadside, the garland of flowers. The case of Carla Marino.

— You remember. That young girl who got killed by a hit-and-run driver; sixteen she was. Nice kid.

— Yes. My sister's girl, Karen, was in the same class as her.

— Hope they catch the bastard.

Will they catch the bastard? Maybe not. Not now. Too long ago. Too hard to remember. Someone must have seen it, of course. Back then. Last year. Someone must have noticed it, a yellow sports car with a broken headlight, maybe more, maybe badly damaged. It's surprising how much damage you can do to a car if you hit a human being. Someone must have seen it, driving towards town. If it came on into town, into High Street or Victory Road, it would have been obvious, so obvious. So it turned off somewhere. Into Ridge Road, heading for the motorway. Could it hide there? Ridge Road or Pigskill. Where could it hide on Pigskill Road?

———

The Sundrift Motel was on Ridge Road, a hundred metres or so from the service station. The proprietor knew him, had bought rhododendrons off him only last year. Tom said nothing, no explanation. Took the keys to unit 9 and the little carton of milk. The room had a queen-size bed and a TV; a brown Formica table with two chairs, black wrought iron, mustard-coloured fabric on the seats and the padded backs to match the mustard- coloured carpet. On the wall was a picture, an old poster for a bullfight. He picked up the phone, called Greenwise, told Billy sorry but he couldn't make it today. No, he was all right. Tomorrow maybe. Or Saturday, at the latest. No, truly, he was all right. Thought of Billy's house, a little brick place tucked under the hill, with the garden blooming. Billy worked hard for his life, all the way from Hull. Wouldn't go back for a million pounds. Well, a million, maybe.

He sat on the bed and thought, or tried to. Wondered if he should call Hannah Creswell and apologise for standing her up. Sorry, just forgot completely. Got distracted. Could he say that? The problem was not the apology but what happened next. She would expect him to make another appointment. Did he want one? Did it matter? It was ridiculous to think that anything could make a difference now. Nowhere to run to, no help for it.

He thought of Vincent, his lost son. Someone should call him. Someone should tell him what was going on. And Annabelle. He should talk to Annabelle. But why would that matter? Except that somewhere, back there, the days when they first met, was the reason. Our cells combined and it was Carla. How could that be? How could a chemical reaction become those years of loving? A chain of cause and effect. Or a string of random events. There was nothing in it any more. No purpose. Just a meaningless concatenation of pain and impulse.

Made another call then.

'Hello.'

'Hi there. It's Tom.'

'Hi there, honey. I'm glad you called.' An edge to her tone, anxiety. It pierced his weariness, the buzzing lack of sleep.

'Are you okay?' he asked.

'Yes, well . . . Something happened, though. Somebody knows. About us. I had a visit from the welfare people.'

'What did they say?'

'Nothing. They don't say anything specific, just remind you of the law.'

'What law?'

'About cohabiting.'

'You're not cohabiting.'

'No, I know. It's just the hassle. If they stop the benefit, it takes weeks to get it put back on. It's happened before.'

A pause. Wondering what to say.

'We might have to cool it for a while,' she told him. 'Is that all right?'

'Yes, of course. How long?'

'I don't know. A few weeks.' More, she meant more.

Tell her, he thought. Tell her Lisa's found out and given you the boot. Tell her you can come and move in with her, look after her, care for her little boys, offer her your hassles, your emotions, all your messy, shitty, rag-bag, rotting life. Yeah, right.

'That's okay,' he said.

'Are you mad at me?'

'No. No, of course not.'

'We could have coffee in town or something. Lunch. I

don't know, maybe we can work something out.' A pleading tone.

'I've got some things to do. I have to go out to Cox's Line and check on a job.'

'Please, don't be mad at me. It's just . . .'

Get out of her life, you idiot!

'It's okay. I'll call you later maybe.'

'Yes, please. Do that.'

Hung up.

Stared at the wall. The matador with twirling cape on tippy-toes, his back-arched, tight-buttocked lift. Bull with tasselled lances in its hump, red streaks of blood. Poor bull. Poor blind, dumb, bleeding bull.

52.

THE FIRST MOUND HAD grown. It was over a metre high, a flat convexity, like the surface of an eyeball. Beyond it a big brown scar, a long gouge in the green paddock. There were two trucks now as well as the loader, one waiting while it was filled, the other carting dirt to the mound. Three days' work and, he figured, the job was about a third done. Kenny's estimate was pretty close.

As long as it didn't rain. The sky, if he cared about it, was not reassuring. A grey band above the hills to the north-west. The wind from there was soft and cold. The smell of damp in it. If it rained, if it rained hard, the whole site would be a swamp. The gouge, where the loader was currently working, would become a lake a metre deep. Well, then, he thought. She can have goldfish and water lilies.

He turned towards the house, the long veranda, the blank, dark windows. Where was she? Did she know he was there? Was she watching him? A vanity, to think he was being watched, that he was not invisible. *Come and see me. Soon. I want to talk to you.*

He walked across the grass and up the steps to the veranda, tried the French doors. Unlocked. He stood there with the door ajar, listening, waiting. For what? For the call of reason and good sense? Don't make me laugh. He's waiting only for the next breath, the next click of the chemical cogs, the compulsion. He wants the impossible, and the more he fails the more he needs to risk, to try again. He's the hero. Or the beaten dog that comes creeping back.

He slipped off his shoes and stepped inside. Closed the door and the noise of the machines was muted suddenly. Silence from the room and the spaces beyond it. But no, there was music somewhere, faintly. Slowly, softly, he crossed the floor to the kitchen. Nothing there except the smell of coffee, but the sound was louder, just a little, coming from the other door. It led out into a long hallway that ran to the front of the house, the big front door with its stained glass panels, blue and gold and yellow and green, Art-Deco flowers, tulips on the point of opening, curling stems and spatulate leaves. He walked towards it, down the length of mushroom-coloured carpet runner, with the polished floorboards on either side. What does he feel? He feels nothing. Body moves because the body leads. He does as he's told, dragged forward to the point of impact.

The music was upstairs, so he turned, with his hand on the polished newel post, and began to climb. The kauri banister and brass stair-rods. If someone found him here, what would he say? Nothing to say. He had no words, no reason to be here. Just the lust or the craziness, or nothing much at all.

At the top of the stairs was a landing that opened to a corridor at right angles to the one below. It ran the width of the house, its longest dimension. Doorways on either side in both directions, all closed except, perhaps, the one down the end to the right, an angle of light there, an upper-case kappa, and the music. He walked towards it on another mushroom-coloured runner. The pale walls were hung with dark pictures, and here and there, along the length of the corridor, were little tables holding china bowls and vases. Dried arrangements, flowers and leaves and peacock feathers. Offerings, perhaps, along the way.

The door was ajar. He pushed it further open. A room full of light. She was wearing a black leotard and sitting on a mat in the centre of the floor in the lotus position. Her eyes were closed. Around her, polished wooden floorboards, empty space except for an exercycle, a portable stereo and a small rack of hand weights. Three of the walls had big sash windows looking out over trees and fields and, to the south, the distant mass of buildings that was the town. Along the fourth, either side of the door, were big mirrors, floor to ceiling, with barres across them at waist height.

He stood there, looking, his eyes gradually settling to the still figure on the mat. The music swelled and drifted. It was romantic, lush and steeped in sentiment, full of feeling that floated like a sweet, ripe smell in the currents of the room. Having got here, having found her in the empty house, he felt a little jolt, reality confronting him, and an impulse to turn and run, but the sight of her and the sound of the music held him. He could not leave and yet he could not speak either in case he startled her, so he stood there, trapped like a fly in honey, waiting for her eyes to open.

Which they did after a minute or so. They opened slowly, almost sleepily, and then she saw him and they flicked wide with shock. Then they closed again and she smiled.

'Well,' she said after several more seconds, 'it's Mr Greenwise. Angry Man.'

He didn't answer, just stood and waited, until the music shifted, sliding into a darker, more sombre tone and, as if in response to the new mood, she began to move, unfolding her legs, standing up with a slow, graceful twist of her body. She walked across the floor to the stereo, bent from the waist and pushed a button with the tip of her finger. Quiet. Walking then on soft, bare feet, pink feet with painted nails, she crossed to one of the mirrors, stood before it with her hands on the barre.

'Come,' she said. 'Stand behind me.'

He did as he was told, like a good dog, looked over her shoulder at their faces in the glass.

'You can touch me,' she said.

He reached out and his hands, in the mirror, slid over her belly. Feel of the tightly woven cloth like a false skin, dry and smooth, under his fingers. Only his hands were alive. He pressed himself against her, felt the push of her backside against his pelvis. His right hand slid up to her left breast, squeezed it, as his left slid down to the space between her bare thighs, smoothness, heat beneath the fabric. Eyes on hers reflected as he felt for her there. He didn't see her, though. What he saw was the subject of his lust, his dream queen, hair like gold.

She laughed.

'Do you like to watch? Do you like to see what you're doing? I do. I've always wanted a mirror on the bedroom ceiling.' She rocked her hips, pressing back against him harder. 'Except that it would look so tacky most of the time. And then I'd have to wake up and see myself first thing in the morning. And Monty. Lying there.' Her little gulp. 'Oh, God! I couldn't stand that.'

He bent his head, mouth to her neck, pushing the hair aside so he could kiss her and bite her, breathe her smell that was perfume mingled with her sweat. Watching from a distance, his dog-self sniff.

'Did I invite you?' she said. 'I don't remember.'

'Maybe.' He pulled at the strap of the leotard, trying to

get it to slide down her shoulder, but she made it impossible. Kept her hands on the barre, her shoulders squared.

'Maybe not. But I might have done. It was when you talked about the murder, when you said you wanted to kill him. You sounded as if you meant it. Did you mean it?'

Did he? Of course, but it was hard to think now, hard to find that emotion. The anger was fused into the rest of it, a sickness, a certainty. He reached out, winding his arms inside hers and up so that he held her wrists. He pulled. She resisted but he pulled harder and broke her grip on the left side. Immediately she let go with the right. He held her hands in front of her at the level of her crotch. Her eyes reflected, fixed on his, were amused, teasing, scared. No, not scared. Not scared at all. She was in control, and it was a kind of control he understood, the sense of power that comes from not caring what happens, from giving yourself up to what's going to happen. It can't touch me, can it? It can't really touch me.

'Could you kill someone?' she asked.

'I don't know.'

'What would you say if I told you I'd killed someone?'

'Who?'

'I couldn't tell you that, could I?'

'When, then?'

'Oh, a while ago. It might be a long time ago. It seems like another life. And I've killed animals. Big animals. Dogs, horses.'

'How did you do it?'

'I can't tell you,' she said.

'A gun?'

'No. I don't have a gun.'

'A blunt instrument?'

'I'm not strong enough.'

'Poison?'

'I'm not going to tell you. I want you to go on wondering if it's true or not.'

'I know it's not true.'

'Don't be so sure.' She pulled with her arms, trying to break his grip. 'Let me go.'

He might have refused, might have dominated her, but there was no winning in such a contest. He couldn't hold her for ever.

He released her. Immediately she reached up, pulled at the left shoulder of the leotard, slipping it off her shoulder, wriggling and pulling at the other strap. The garment fell loose from the upper half of her body and she pushed it down over her hips, stepped out of it. He reached for her.

'No,' she said. 'You too.'

So he undressed himself. Jacket, shirt, singlet, jeans, underpants, socks. While he did it, she stood there, naked, looking at herself, at him, in the mirror, left hand on her hip, head tilted to the right. He moved behind her again, reached around her, slid his hands over the smoothness of her electric skin, watched in the mirror as they moved as before, the right one up to her breast, the left one down. She pushed back against him again: the hardness of her coccyx hurt.

'Angry Man,' she said. 'How can I make you angry?'

He pressed his teeth against the side of her neck.

'Like this?' She reached behind her with her right hand and dragged the nails, hard and painful, up the back of his thigh. He bit the muscle at the top of her shoulder.

She laughed and then twisted in his arms, pushed away from him.

'Not here.' Walking away towards the door.

He bent down and took his wallet, with the condoms in it, from the back pocket of his jeans. Followed her.

She was halfway towards the top of the stairs, walking, body upright, shoulders back, a stride full of purpose. Then, turning aside, opening a door, entering, without looking back at him. Knowing he would follow. Of course he would follow. With his tongue hanging out.

A room done in blue and white, with frills and flounces. Blue and white curtains held back with ties at the window. A brass bed with a blue-and-white quilt trimmed with ruffles, lace trim on the matching pillows. A white dressing table with a triple mirror. She was standing there in front of it.

'Lie down,' she told him, and he did so, on his back, on the quilt.

'Do you know who this room belongs to?' she asked, looming suddenly above him, lifting one knee on to the bed. 'Monty's daughter. Monty's little girl. She never stays here. She hates it here. Weird, don't you think? To keep a room for a child who hates you.'

Her gaze travelled down his body. He couldn't move. He was helpless.

'You're a hairy man, aren't you? I don't think I've ever had such a hairy man before.'

'How many men have you had before?'

She laughed. She wasn't going to answer that. 'Men count, don't they? They tell me men count. It's a trophy thing.'

'Maybe.'

'Do you count?' she asked.

'No.'

'If I counted I'd have to remember. Even the ones I'd prefer to forget.' Her fingers trailed against his thigh. Then she gripped his cock and squeezed it. 'What do we do with this?'

So he gave her his wallet, watched as she opened it and took out a condom. Then he lay back, with his hands behind his head.

'There we are,' she said. 'All dressed up and no place to go.'

He reached out, gripped her upper arm.

'It's all right.' She was laughing. 'I'll give you what you want. What you seem to want.'

Climbing on to the bed. She straddled him, knees either side of his hips, and then rocked forward, reaching down with her left hand, manipulating, rocking back, sliding down on him, smooth and warm. He lifted his palms to her breast but she pulled away, pressing with her clenched right fist on his chest. Rocking back, looking down, a smile, a girlish kind of smile. He humped his hips, pressing into her.

'So,' she said, 'you're fucking me. Your heart's desire. And it doesn't mean anything. Nothing at all. You fuck me and you come. Maybe I come too. But then what? It's a pointless, pointless exercise. We might not even remember it tomorrow. Will you remember? Do you want to remember? I bet I can make you.'

And suddenly her arm was swinging, her right arm, up and down, a small bright flash, and thumping with the side of her fist on the top of his shoulder. Stab. He yelled out. Her arm again upward, but he stopped her this time, caught her round the wrist. Protruding from her clenched hand was a little metal spike about two centimetres long. A pair of pointed scissors.

Looking down at him, grinning, little flick of her tongue against her top lip. She reached out with her free hand, and he felt the rub of her fingers there where she'd stabbed him, lifted them to her mouth. There was blood on them. Licking. It was his anger she had there, his hatred, seeping out of the hole in his shoulder. Hurting? Yes, it was coming now, a rush of pain, right there where Lisa had bitten him that evening. When? How long ago?

'Do you want some?' Offering, reaching, touching him on the lips, rocking back again. Smiling down at him with blood on her mouth, her chin. And the eyes were cold, blue eyes, nothing. No one. Flick of her tongue, a snake-flick. And the wound began to throb with the pulse of his hatred, beating hard. She was his. He had her. Wrist in his grip. She couldn't get away. And he loathed her.

Slowly, her hand opened and the scissors fell, a small prick on his bicep.

'I'm defenceless now,' she said, reaching out again for the blood, fingers rubbing. She showed him her palm, red with it, and then she began to smear it on her breast. 'You want to kill me, don't you?'

He couldn't speak. He was choked, dammed up, the pressure building. And she was a vile thing, looking down and smiling with her bloody mouth like a bright good morning, eyes like blue stones, opal glitter.

She pouted. 'Ooo,' she said. 'Poor diddums. Go on, kill me. Try.'

And it was coming, the rage. It would consume them both. Except a voice was calling him from far away, a clear voice in the mountain air. His name. I have a name. They gave me a name.

A yell. A roar. He swung his arm, dragging her, hurling her away from him so that she sprawled across the bed and tumbled off the other side. A scream, as her hand clutched, useless, at the quilt and waved for a moment, like the last grasp of a person drowning.

Tom!

53.

NOT THE WHITE CAR going south. That was Ward. It was a yellow car and it was heading north. Martin Wraggles didn't see it because it was in front of him. A yellow car, smashed up, with a broken headlight. It might have had blood on it. It must have been noticeable. Someone else must have seen it, then. Unless it turned off. Into Ridge Road or Pigskill. Ridge Road led to the motorway. Lots of traffic there. Lots of cars. Past Riley's Service Station, past the Sundrift Motel, and on up to the top of the range. Rangi's Farm and Paragon Road. Somebody would have seen it there. So it turned down Pigskill, then. Pigskill Road led nowhere.

'Lisa?'

'Syl.'

'Where are you?'

'Caddis Park Drive.'

'What are you doing?'

'Well, actually, I'm going to interview an old man who wants to make a donation to the local school because some of the pupils helped him after he was robbed.'

Something in her tone. Sarcasm, almost.

'Are you all right?'

'No, I'm not. Tom's left me. No, that's wrong. I kicked him out. No, that's wrong too. We agreed not to be together and he left. In deference to my feelings. I would have killed him otherwise.'

'Why?'

'Why what?'

'What happened?'

'He told me he'd been fucking some woman in River Road.'

'This is all Maddy's fault.'

'No, it is not Maddy's fault! It's Tom's! Why can't you people get the responsibilities right?'

A pause. Shock. Sadness.

'I don't want to be "you people", Lisa. I never was before.'

'Oh, God, Syl. I'm sorry.'

'Would you and Imogen like to come over? This evening, for some company.'

'Just so long as Ward and Maddy aren't there.'

'They won't be. Neither will Larry. He's staying over in town.'

'Yes, then. I really would like that. I really think I need that.'

'Lots of love, then.'

'Thank you.'

Damage. Ward knew there was damage. The only question was how much and how permanent. It was hard to think about it right now, hard to get a perspective because of all the things that were happening. Panic in the partnership, for one thing. All Colin's clients wanting to know what was going on. Who was looking after their interests? Audits? Tax payments? Profit and loss? Yes, yes. But Ward found it difficult to sympathise.

Of course it was a problem, but couldn't they see how much worse it was for Col? Compared to what he had to deal with, their concerns were pathetic, weren't they? Couldn't say that, though. Just had to get on with it, try to sort it out.

So he went down to Winston to talk to Colin. Well, not just for the business, obviously. As a friend. Poor bugger. Sitting in that room with the cream-coloured walls and the brown lino on the floor and you knew there were cameras going, watching your every move. Ward couldn't say Colin was all that focused on what was happening with the Balder Trust. Couldn't say he was all that focused on anything, to be honest. Staring straight ahead. Looking at something that Ward couldn't see. A ghost maybe? Ward didn't like that thought.

— You're all right, mate?

— Yes, Colin said. I'm all right.

— You missing anything?

— Missing?

— Do you need anything?

— No.

— Best to try and come to terms with it, you know. Somehow.

— Oh, yes.

— Anything we can do . . . Just you let me know.

— You know what? I haven't had a drop since I've been in here. And I don't miss it. I really don't miss it one little bit.

—That's good.

— Oh, yes. I can be good. When I want to be.

Poor old Col. Not much for it but to soldier on, eh? All he could do, as he said to Maddy, was to get in some help. A contract accountant. Some young gun who was fresh out of university. The sooner the better. Because a quick look had told him there were some funny bits and pieces in Colin's way of doing things. Perhaps not the best. Perhaps some corners cut here and there. Nothing untoward, of course. He hoped not. He fervently hoped not.

'I don't like this, Maddy.' He liked it so little that the wine had lost its taste. A good bottle of Trelissic 2000.

'It's all right, Pookey.'

'Did you talk to anyone today?'

'Alistair Oxeley. And Trevor Steely.'

'No, I mean like Sylvia.' Or Lisa. But he didn't want to say that. He didn't want to bring that up directly.

'No. Not today.'

'I don't want it to make a difference, Maddy. I don't want it to spoil things.'

'What's going to spoil things?' She looked at him with a little smile, her special little smile, all innocence. He knew it well. It was the smile she gave him when she was absolutely determined to get her own way.

'You know. All this.' Waving his hand to indicate the plague of viciousness, the difficulties, the humiliations, the grudges and offences that might sap the health of their shared existence.

'I will not have Tom Marino talking at the funeral, that's all.'

Was that what she cared about? Why?

'Oh, Maddy. Does it matter?'

'Yes, it matters to me. I will not have you humiliated by someone who is far, far worse than you are.'

'I don't care. Truly, I don't. I just don't want us to lose everything. Everyone.'

'Really? Good God, Pookey, I have a feeling it's too late for that.'

The end then. Sour wine.

54.

CRISIS BRINGS OUT THE worst in people. And the best. Thus it is with Josie Hannerby, who had always despised Imogen Wyte, taking her to be the worst kind of mincing young female: a spoilt brat, for ever shamed into insignificance by her elder, more forthright step-sister, Carla Marino, now deceased. On this day, in these circumstances, whether through pity or common decency, Josie took Imogen under her wing and invited her to her room to view the menagerie, and Imogen, who had little interest in animals that were not horses and certainly did not like to be closer than one metre to any arthropod larger than a housefly, went. And after a brief inspection of the funnel-web spiders and the ant farm and the terrarium with the wetas in it, a conversation was struck up concerning a pop band called Screaming Fragrance in which Imogen discovered that Josie was not the stuck-up know-it-all she had always assumed and Josie found that Imogen had a great deal more wit and critical intelligence than most fifteen-year-olds of her acquaintance. In such moments are friendships forged. Indeed, it was during just such a seemingly random encounter twenty-seven years previously — in a fifth-form common-room during a wet lunch-hour — that Josie's mother, Sylvia, and Imogen's mother, Lisa, found a common, if fleeting, interest in a punk rock band called Stinking Lips; an interest that sparked a feeling that became a mutual fascination that grew into a commitment that had lasted ever since. Thus, the two girls, upstairs, sat cross-legged on Josie's bed and chatted about school and music and boys and the meaning of life, while their mothers, downstairs, side by side on one of the fat leather sofas, drank wine and contemplated the possibilities of a failed relationship, another failed relationship.

Men. They're bloody idiots.

Lisa, tight-jawed, white-knuckled when she stopped to dwell too closely on it, spoke with the hard edge of suppressed fury, laughed with the harshness of bitter truth. She hadn't cried yet and Sylvia thought it might be a good thing if she did, except, of course, that Lisa didn't cry any more than Sylvia did herself, at least not as a result of her own misfortune. She got angry, and anger did not always help in getting a clear picture of what was wrong or of what one ought to do about it.

'So, where's Tom now?' Sylvia asked.

'I don't know. Some motel, I suppose. Or maybe he's run off to her.'

'Do you know her name?'

'No.'

'Do you want to?'

No answer and then a realisation, a look of surprise and puzzlement.

'You mean you know her name?'

'Yes,' Sylvia said. 'She's the tenant of a friend of Maddy's.'

'Bloody Maddy! She knew?'

'She only found out yesterday. By chance.'

'Oh, God. I hate it! I hate this creeping around. This gossiping behind people's backs!'

'Yes.' Sylvia might have pointed out that gossiping behind people's backs helped you learn the truth, but it was not the sort of judgement that came readily to her.

'Her name's Astra Bridge,' she went on.

'Sounds like a fortune teller. What do they do? Sit around and read tarot cards? When they're not fucking, that is.'

'She's a solo mother. She's got two kids.'

'Oh, shit!' Lisa sighed, a tired, angry, teeth-gritting sigh. 'I don't want to know, Syl. I really don't want to know that she's a real person, with struggles and problems.'

'I just wondered, you know. If that wasn't part of the attraction. I mean, he's lost Carla.'

'Instant family?'

'Could be. It mightn't mean anything, really. He's been under a lot of stress since Carla died. It's obvious to anyone. This thing, this relationship. It might just be a result of the state he's in.'

'You think I should try to understand?'

'Well, perhaps.'

'Forgive and forget?' A look. Lisa's dark eyes. Was it a real question or just her sarcasm, the cold edge of fury?

'Maybe it would help to talk to him. That's all.'

'Swallow my pride, eh? Don't you see, Syl. I can't do that. It hurts too much. Oh, God!' And suddenly she folded over, arms clutching her stomach, face twisted, lifted, agonised, as if the pain were physical and there now, tearing at her.

Sylvia moved closer to her, reached out, laid her arm across the rigid back, gripped her, held her. She leaned forward herself until their heads were touching, hard press of bone on bone. Then Lisa began to shake, a steady tremble, a quiver through her frame, the little rasp of hair on Sylvia's temple. There, there, Sylvia wanted to say. Tut, tut. The kind of words she might make if Josie were upset, or James.

'Bastard! Fucking bastard!' A throat-stripping curse. And then it fell apart. Lisa, turning, clutching at her, sobbing, clinging, face pressed into the angle of her shoulder, arms about her, hugging tight.

'Oh, oh, oh,' Sylvia murmured. 'Oh, my love, oh, dear, my love.' While Lisa shook and cried for who or what or how much hurt you couldn't guess. Sylvia held her, just held her, feeling only the need, the yearning of a giver. Pain ebbing, breath drawn in a long, shuddering intake, Lisa drew back a little. Her eyes, wide, helpless, hopeless, wanting, cheeks wet, nose run, lips. That mouth, wide lips, that laughed and spoke and flicked out wit and indignation, bruised now, swollen by the pain. Its hurt and its need so undemanding. Sylvia reached out with her hand to the back of her friend's neck and drew their heads together, mouth to mouth, the warmth and snot and tenderness, the sweet pain of loving that had been there, bedrock under all these years.

Lisa moved after a moment, pulled away, sniffed loudly. Gave a laugh, a kind of laugh, and wiped her nose on the side of her hand.

'I need a tissue.' Bending for her bag and burrowing in it.

Sylvia, her mouth so suddenly bereft, looked at her as she leaned forward, went to touch her, hand lift reaching out towards the arch of spine, but then withdrew. The feeling, the need in her, so simple, so daring, settled back into secrecy. She picked up her wine from the table, lifted it, pressed her lips to the hard glass rim.

55.

So here's how it might have gone. Carla goes down to the river to see what's happening to Merry Gibbitson. She leaves her bike at the top of the little track with the helmet resting on the bag of library books. A mistake. There's not much room there and the rear wheel sticks out into the roadway. Ward, driving Maddy's white Toyota, comes along from town, from the north. He's going too fast. He clips the bike. The blow knocks it aside and sends the bag of books and the helmet flying partway down the bank. Ward checks that no one has been hurt and drives on. Meanwhile, Carla has heard the noise and comes back up, or perhaps she has already discovered there is no one there, down by the big rock. She finds the books beside the road, and the bike damaged and unrideable. She wonders what to do. Then she notices her helmet is missing. She begins to hunt for it. It starts to rain. Should she leave the helmet and come back later? She hunts some more. She's a rational person. It makes more sense to find the helmet now if she can. It doesn't seem to be on the river side of the road, though. She turns and looks over towards the other side. Something there, perhaps, buried in the bushes? Has the helmet flown all that way? She begins to cross the road to investigate further. What with the rain and her urge to hurry, she doesn't pay enough attention to what might be coming. The yellow car, travelling north, much too fast. Around the bend and it hits her. Throws her flailing over the bonnet and away. Does the driver stop? Perhaps, as Ward did. Does he see her lying there or dragging herself, in a last half-conscious effort, to the side of the road? He sees there's damage to the car, at least. Obvious damage. A broken headlight. Go on into town? Turn back? Ridge Road? Pigskill? Perhaps the driver lives in Pigskill. Almost home, if he does. Another fifty metres. Turn left. Out of sight. Almost.

Pigskill runs back into the hills, towards the west, for two or three kilometres. A shallow valley. Farmland. To the south, a rough-cut jumble of broken slopes, eroded, crossed by little water courses. Grazing for sheep but not much else. No roads. To the north and west, the ground rises steeply. Ridge Road winds its way up there, crossing the range towards the main highway. There are walking tracks from the valley up to the crest of the ridge but nothing that a vehicle could manage. Even a trail bike would find it hard going. Any car that drives into Pigskill either comes out the way it went in or it stays there.

The house stood on a knoll with a curving drive leading up to it. North facing, to catch the sun. It was two-storeyed with white walls. It had a roof of dark brown plastic tiles and an elaborate TV aerial that looked like a node in a satellite navigation system. There were flower beds on either side of the door with pansies, early morning bright.

Tom rang the bell, a musical chime. A dog began to bark, around the back somewhere. A pause. A click. The door opened. A woman dressed in jeans and a dark green sweatshirt. She had mousy-coloured hair, and spectacles with round lenses and wire frames.

'Hi,' he said. 'My name's Tom Marino. This is an odd

sort of inquiry but you may be able to help me. I'm looking for a car. A yellow car. Probably a sports car. I think it came down here or is owned by someone who lives in the valley. Do you know it?'

'No.'

The woman moved back just a fraction, her hand gripping the edge of the door. Ready to slam it, he thought. Beside her left knee a face appeared, a round face with rosy cheeks and curly blond hair.

'Hello,' he said, smiling at it. 'What's your name?'

The child stared at him. The woman placed a warning, protective hand on its head.

'It would have been a while ago. Six months,' Tom said, looking back at her. 'You might not have seen it for six months.'

'No,' she said, shaking her head, pulling a helpless kind of face. 'Can't help you, I'm afraid.'

'Well, thanks anyway.' He turned away.

The door closed.

Moving back to the ute, wondering just what kind of place this was. A farm house? There were no buildings, no machinery. Just a house in the middle of nowhere at the end of a long drive.

He looked up at the sky, a breath of something there. Rain on its way? Or the nor'wester?

Keep going. Don't stop. I can find it.

And, of course, there was Imogen to think of. And work. The daily round. The habit of living when you didn't have a reason. Except that Imogen and work, too, to a lesser extent, were a reason. And if motherhood, at the moment, was a fraught business, full of doubts and uncertainties, then recording the life of Durry and the sundry goings-on of its citizens was comfortingly dull. There were ructions in the council about the condition of High Street. There was a production of *The Best Little Whorehouse in Texas* in rehearsal at the theatre. A Durry College fifth-former had won a scholarship to London to study violin. Everything as it should be. Almost.

Tracey standing beside her desk. 'There's a bloke here to see you.'

'Who is it?'

'Won't give his name. He looks like Worzel Gummidge. In reception.'

Max Hosche. Sitting there, looking uncomfortable, arms folded, the floppy hat squeezed tight in his right hand.

'Hello, Max.'

'Ah.' Standing up.

'What can I do for you?'

'Cuppa tea would be nice.'

'How do you like it?'

'Black. Three sugars.'

She showed him into the interview room and went and got him a tea.

'Here you go.'

'Thanks.' Reaching out with hands in fingerless gloves, thin hands. The winter would be cold in his caravan. How long could he go on living there? she wondered.

Sipping. Lips pushed out into a suction kiss. 'Ah!'

'Enough sugar?'

'It'll do,' he said. Looking at her, enjoying her curiosity.

He would not, of course, apologise for calling her a slut. She did not want him to.

'I've got a story for you,' he said.

'Oh?'

'Only I'm not going to give it to you unless you write it up.'

'That won't work. I can't make any promises. You know that.'

'Hm.' Another long sip of the tea. Then he smacked his lips, looked at her. 'Yellow car,' he said.

'What?' Just a phrase, a pair of words, but the shock of them was like cold water.

'You had a story in your paper about a yellow car.'

'Yes, yes. That's right.'

'A sporty kind of car, would it be?'

'It could be. Yes. Very likely. Do you know of one?'

'I did. Only saw it a couple of times. Then it disappeared.'

'When was this?'

'Last year. November.'

'Who was the driver? Do you know?'

'Oh, yes.' Another sip at the tea. 'It was her.'

Her? 'Laura Kerrington?'

'Ah, now. This is a story, right? You'll print this one.'

———

A weatherboard house, a paint-peeling grey. An iron roof, once blue, now streaked with rust. There was an old rusting ute with four flat tyres in a paddock out front. Slack-wire fences, rutted driveway. He stopped, got out. Picked his way through the puddles to the front door. Windows all covered, whitewashed over on the inside. He mounted the concrete step. Knocked. No answer. To his right a movement. A chicken had come round the corner of the house and was pecking in the mud. He stepped down to its level and moved towards it, followed it as first it walked and then ran zigzag ahead of him.

Round the back was a yard, empty except for three forty-four-gallon drums, rusty and painted red and white. A big shed or a barn, or maybe it was a double garage from which the doors had been removed. An old Bedford truck in the left-hand side and, in the right, something else, covered in a blue tarpaulin. He walked towards it. Into the dark beneath the tin roof.

It was a car all right, judging by the shape, and the tarp was tied securely to the bumper at the front. He took a few steps along the side of the vehicle, bent down, lifted the edge of the blue material. Hard to see in the gloom. But it wasn't yellow.

'You looking for something?'

He stood up, turned. A man there, jeans and a blue checked shirt, his hair wispy, brown. There was stubble round his chin. In his right fist he held a long-handled shovel.

'Hi,' Tom said, moving towards him. 'I didn't think there was anyone here.'

'You're trespassing.'

'Sorry about that. I was looking for something, actually. A yellow car.'

'No yellow car here.'

Tom turned, flicked his head towards the tarp-shrouded shape. 'I guess that was never yellow, was it?'

'Nope.'

A pause. The man stared at him.

'You know of anyone round here who owns a yellow car, then?'

'Nope.'

'Have you seen one on the road? A few months ago. November, last year.'

'I got better things to do than watch the road.'

Another pause.

'Why don't you bugger off?' the man said, taking a step backwards, opening up the way towards the driveway.

'Well, thanks for your help.'

'Don't mention it.'

'No,' Dart said. 'Nothing. According to Frank, the LTSA database has a grey Mercedes and a dark green Rover registered to the Kerringtons. Both of them in the husband's name.'

'What about previously? Last year?'

'Nothing. Another Mercedes, a Ford Mondeo. Nothing sporty. Nothing yellow.'

'She borrowed it? Hired it?'

'How reliable is this source of yours?' Dart said.

Lisa looked at him, saw his suspicion, felt angry for a second that he would doubt her judgement. 'He's an oddball,' she said. 'But I don't think he makes things up.' But, of course, that mightn't be true.

'Maybe you should just give it to the cops.'

'There's no story if we do that. They'll keep the lid on it until the investigation's done.'

'I'm not sure it's our story anyway.'

Why not? But before she could follow that thought too far, it was overtaken by another, a flash of an idea.

'She changed her name! She married Kerrington and they moved here. The car's in her maiden name. How do we check that? Can we get at the Births, Deaths and Marriages Register?'

'Maybe.' Dart reached for the phone.

The end of the road. A turning circle. A gate made of metal tubing and wire mesh above a concrete cattle-stop. He got out into the sunlight, silence. Green swathe of grass beyond the wire fences. Hills around him, covered in pine trees. Sky above was blue, white puffs of cloud. A chain and padlock on the gate. Beyond it a dirt road in a graceful curve around a stand of poplars and off towards the head of the valley. Turn back? Give up? It's here somewhere. I can find it.

He moved to the fence, swung his leg through between the top two strands of wire.

'No,' Dart said. 'No record of them ever being married. He married somebody called Jocelyn Munrow in December '86. They were divorced in '91. That's it.'

'She's just using his name, then.'

'What about the electoral roll? She'd have to use her legal name on that,' Tracey said. Everybody on to it now. Everybody listening, paying attention.

'We'd never find her. It's alphabetical.'

'Isn't there an online version?' Tracey asked.

'Must be,' Stevie said. 'The council would have one.'

'They could do a search. For the address.'

'Clisserford. Yes.'

'And what about the real-estate database,' Lisa said. 'Who owns the house?'

The road in lazy loops, like a river. Nothing here but trees and grass and sky. The hills drawing closer, gradually, as he walked. A strange place, like a park almost. Except the grass was uncut. Waist high in places. No one came here, not even cows or sheep. Somewhere a bird was singing. European bird. A thrush, maybe. No other sound except his feet on the gravel. The winding road. Then there was a sudden gust of wind, a whoosh of leaves and bending grasses, and ahead of him, appearing in the widening angle around a stand of young pinus radiata, was a building.

It was a barn, with a red rusted roof and sides, corrugated iron. Standing there in the middle of nowhere.

'No, no database. No way they can do a search in reverse.'

'And the house is in his name. That's it then.'

No! She wouldn't have that. There must be a way.

All of them looking at her in a suspended moment, waiting for the time to stretch into a decision. Give up?

Sylvia!

She grabbed the phone, dialled the library.

'Syl, it's Lisa. I want some information. About Laura Kerrington.'

'Yes?' Sylvia uncertain, doubtful. Caught in the rush of Lisa's words.

'It's important, Syl. I want to know if that's the name she's registered under. Her legal name.'

'Hang on.'

Silence, a long silence. Although perhaps not. Just a little drift of voices in the distance. She strained her ears after the sounds. Dart and Steve and Tracey were watching her. Dart at his desk. Steve at his workstation. Tracey standing with a cup of coffee.

'Here it is,' Sylvia said suddenly. 'I've got it on the computer. "Laura Jean Camble, Stylist, Clisserford, Cox's Line, Durry." That's C-A-M-B-L-E.'

'Thanks, Syl. That's fantastic.'

'What's a stylist, do you suppose?' Sylvia asked.

The double doors were closed with a hasp and padlock. Nothing to see when he peered through the gap. Something in there? He stepped back, pulled at the door, trying to get it open. Movement on the hinges, back and forth a few inches, but it held. Feeling in his pocket for his knife. A strong blade, a screwdriver. Screws could be rusted in or rotten. Leaning on the door, pressing it steady with his shoulder. First screw. Twisting, and then a quick jerk. Yes.

'A 2001 model Mazda MX 9, daffodil yellow, registered to Laura Jean Camble,' Dart said.

'Yes!' Lisa's fist clenched. Tracey and Stevie, both grinning.

'Reported stolen on 22 November last year.'

'Fuck!' No, wait a minute. The twenty-second? That was the day Carla died. 'She did it.'

'Hey, now. Wait a minute!' Dart with his hand up, pushing away the idea.

'She did it, the bitch! Oh, don't worry. I'll be careful. I'll be very careful.'

Second screw. Coming away, falling into his palm. He folded the knife, put it (and the two screws) into his pocket, gripped the edge of the left hand door, swung it back. A wall of light fell inwards. A car, parked with its rear towards him. A sports car with its top up. Covered in dust. It was yellow, though, underneath. He moved down towards the bonnet, squeezing between the car and the side of the barn. The pop-up headlights were half open, the one on the driver's side more than the other. The flap was twisted, bent back on itself. Dents to the wing too. Then he saw the windscreen, cracks like a spider web, the point of impact high up in the corner. Leaning on the back wall, creak of iron, looking at it. The lens of the headlight broken.

He was afraid of it. Afraid of the certainty. There were dark marks around the headlight. Streaks along the top edge of the wing. His hands were trembling. He lifted them to his face and pressed them against his eyes, to steady them, but the quivering ran down his arms and into his shoulders. Pain there from the stab wound.

What do I do now? He looked again at the car. Let himself see it and realise what it was. Her last moment. Her last thought. Here.

'Good morning. This is Laura Kerrington.' The voice.

'Oh, hello. I was wanting to speak to Laura Camble. Is she there?'

A pause. A long moment of doubt. 'Who is this?'

'I'm doing a survey on stolen vehicles and was wanting to talk to Ms Camble, who . . .'

'You're that reporter, aren't you?'

Shit!

The line went dead.

Well, she thought, only one thing left. Call the cops. Call Stan.

On his way back down Pigskill Road, he passed the Bedford truck just emerging from the driveway that led to the house with the car under the tarpaulin. He drove past, not thinking, and then, about fifty metres further on, he came to a narrow bridge, a culvert across a stream. Had an idea. Braked, backed up so that he was in the middle of the bridge, blocking the road. Stopped, opened the door, got out.

The truck was pulling up behind him.

'What the fuck are you doing?' the driver said as he

approached. It was the same bloke. The one with the brown hair, blue checked shirt.

'I need some information.'

'You'll get nothing out of me.'

'Then you're not going anywhere.'

'Move it! I ain't got all day.'

'Well, I have. All day. For ever.'

'Fuck!'

'All I want to know is who owns the property at the end of the road.'

'How would I know?'

'Of course you know. They're your neighbours.'

'Nobody lives there.'

'I didn't say who lives there. I said who owns it.'

'A bloke called Kerrington.'

'Kerrington?'

'Yes. Fat cat from the city.'

'You're sure?'

'Course, I'm fuckin' sure. Now move your arse.'

56.

THE WIND WAS UP. It had come out of nowhere as it sometimes did, a burst of energy from the north-west that sent the clouds running for cover. Sylvia, as always, wanted to be out in it and today, for once, she followed the impulse. It didn't matter that the kids would soon be home from school and that she had to cook dinner. She needed space today. She needed out.

A pair of jeans, her walking shoes, a waterproof jacket over her woollen jersey. She set off up Acacia Drive while the trees hissed in the gardens and the wind pushed the cold into her right ear. There were reasons to go, reasons to get away. She had been restless all day and the call from Lisa about Laura Kerrington hadn't helped. Lisa's voice had been tense with eagerness and she had barely paused to say thank you before she was gone. Sylvia was not inquisitive but she could get caught up in other people's excitement, wanting to be active, on the move, darting here and there for no particular reason. Although today she had a reason, of her own.

From Acacia Drive she turned into Aspen Close, a cul-de-sac, steeply curving round the side of the hill. Here, for now, she was sheltered from the wind. No noise, no movement, but a kind of expectation in the air, a shift in pressure maybe, that made the world seem bright and fragile like fine-blown glass. She leaned into the slope and started to climb. She had to hurry. There was only one place to go on a day like this, and it was over an hour's walk there and back. She had not much more than that before it started to get dark.

Five minutes to the top of the street. Between numbers 27 and 29 was a narrow path leading off behind the houses into the Reserve, the bush-covered slope on the south-west of Dogwatch Hill. Under the trees now, darker, with the threat of the wind like a whisper all around her.

She thought of Larry, her reason. She had been thinking of him all day, on and off, since he had called her mid-morning. Strange for him to do that and she had felt a moment's panic, thinking that something had happened.

— Are you all right? she had asked.

— Yes, I'm fine. I just wanted to hear your voice.

— Are you sure you're all right? She had said it teasingly, laughing at his romantic impulse, which was so unlike him.

— I've had enough, Syl. I'm sick of it.

— Of what?

— The law. I want to get out.

— What will you do?

— I don't know. But there's enough money.

— I don't care about money.

— Why don't we just go? Take off somewhere.

— What about the kids? she asked.

— They could come too. We could buy a yacht.

— You always said you hated yachts.

— I do. But we've got nothing here, have we? Nothing but obligations and bad habits. We would get a bike. A big one. A Suzuki 1000.

— You're crazy.

Thinking, though, that yes, that was just what she wanted. The two of them together, taking off somewhere. Ripping through the air like they'd done when they were nineteen. I like it, she had told him. I like the speed. And then, later. How fast did we go? *150*. That's nearly a hundred miles an hour. *95*. We could have died. *If we'd crashed, yes.* But we didn't, did we? We made love, instead. Under a tree above the beach, with the sound of the sea and the speed still throbbing in her blood.

The path led up and around the hill under the shelter of the trees towards the east. The steep slope was broken every now and then by flights of steps, with wooden facings, cut into the brown clay. Wind again now, the branches and the fern fronds thrashing around her, light dancing, the air too quick, too urgent to smell of much. She pushed herself, breathing hard, striding into the slope and driving down with her leg to take the rise of each step. She was growing warm, the sweat beginning across the top of her breasts, so she unzipped her jacket and let the air flow around her, let the wind soak into her sweater and smear itself over her skin like a chilling balm. And she thought, why not? Why not a bike, the two of us like this in the open air?

Brightness, a break in the bush. She was nearly there. A few more steps and the path turned back on itself. Grass now and the first gorse bushes. The wind pulled at her hair and wrapped itself around her face. If she paused here and turned she would be able to look out over the town and the river towards the hills beyond, but she didn't want that. Not yet. She wanted the top.

She could see the trig station ahead of her, upper third of it jutting above the brow of the hill. No scrub now, only grass, clumps of tussock, tossing and flowing in the stream of the air. Rush of it round her, pulling at her face as if it wanted to steal her breath. She thrust her hands in her jacket pockets and strode forward, the last few metres to the crest.

And then a gust, the wind grabbed her, flung her, sent her sprawling, hands and knees, and tossing her over as she grabbed at the ground, the grass, and held on tight. She lay there on her back, looking up at the sky, the marching clouds, and gasped for breath, and then, when the shock had faded, she started to laugh. Laughed again when she tried to stand and the wind threw her down again. The trig station was five metres away, a pyramid of wooden struts, painted red and white. She began to crawl towards it, clambering through the thick clumps of tussock, every breath a pain as her jacket rattled round her ribs and threatened to fly up over her head.

Here then, over the concrete base, grabbing at the wood and hauling herself upwards, leaning, clinging.

To the south the valley, green of the pasture on the western side of the river, a scatter of houses along the thin ribbon of road and the river itself, a grey, bright snaking band, and the dark green of the eastern hills and there, in the farthest distance, scarcely visible in the haze of the moving air, was the city, just a dove-grey blur on the horizon.

And she looked at it and laughed and closed her eyes and clung on tight as the wind tried to tear her breath, her hair, her clothes from her body, and she knew suddenly that this was the happiest she ever wanted to be.

57.

TOM WOKE. HAD HE been asleep? No, not asleep, thinking. Hardly slept for two nights now. He was in a chair, a leather chair, in the big living room of the big house, with the two chandeliers and the rugs on the polished floor. He could see out over the veranda and the little lawn with the fountain to the two half-finished mounds of dirt. It was evening, darkness coming down, and the wind was blowing, sweep of it from the hills and the puff and quiver against the French doors. The noise of it lulled him, stilled his senses. Not asleep but thinking, if it could be called thinking, this maelstrom of words and images and feelings. Carla and Heidi. The yellow car. Laura Kerrington. Pain there in his shoulder. Blood on her body. *Angry Man, don't be foolish. I might call the police. Have you thought of that? I might tell them you raped me.* Pleading. Was she pleading? *We could have a lot of fun, you know.* She had been driving the car. Who else could it have been? And if it were her, he had to kill her. Except, if he were going to kill her, he should have done it then, when she stabbed him. There was enough reason, then, enough hatred. How could there be more hatred than that? Hatred of her. Hatred of himself. So although he knew now who was responsible (or almost knew), the knowledge was useless to him. Knowledge left him helpless, enfeebled, undirected. Tom, the fool, the idiot, the object, the guilty one. Sitting there waiting.

Almost dark now. Somewhere outside, the noise of a car. Was it a car? He didn't notice. Too far gone and the wind sound blurred the world. He didn't hear the garage door, the key in the lock, foot on the floor. He didn't notice anything until the light went on. Bright light. Blinking, hand up to shade his eyes.

'Who are you?' A man coming towards him across the polished floorboards. Monty Kerrington wearing a suit and overcoat, overcoat flapping with his stride. 'What are you doing here?' Stopped a metre or so away.

'Waiting,' Tom said.

'Where's Laura?'

'I don't know.'

'How the hell did you get in? Who turned off the alarm?'

'No alarm,' Tom told him. Staring, looking at Monty, at his black shiny slip-ons with their little gold buckles. Wasn't he supposed to take his shoes off?

'What are you doing? Why are you here?'

'Do you own a yellow sports car? A Mazda MX 9?'

'That's Laura's car. It was stolen.'

'Stolen? It's in a barn at the end of Pigskill Road.'

'Rubbish.' Monty took off his coat, threw it over the back of a chair.

'It's there. I've seen it.'

'Does Laura know this? Where is she?'

'Search me.'

'Get out of my house,' Monty said. He had a cellphone in his right hand.

'No.'

'I'll call the police.'

'Yes, do that. Who was driving the yellow Mazda on the twenty-second November last year?'

'How would I know? It was stolen about then.'

'It was involved in an accident. It killed someone. Now

it's in your barn smashed up, with a broken headlight.'

'Jesus!' A look on his face, so sudden. Dazed. Hand in his nut-brown hair, fingers pushing back through the waves. He turned away, walked across the floor. Tom pivoted in the chair, craning his neck to watch him. Standing there at a sideboard, Monty lifted his head, gazed up at the ceiling. Then he seemed to slump, look down again. 'Do you want a drink?' he asked, without turning round.

'Were you driving that car?' Tom asked.

'No.'

Relief, then. Why? Because he knew for sure now.

'I'll have a Scotch.' He turned back again, face to the windows, to the reflection of the room in the shimmer of the wind. His own shadow figure in the shadow chair, Monty behind him, in the distance. Why did I ask for a Scotch? he thought. I don't drink Scotch. That's Larry's drink. And Colin's. A drink for bastards. Monty's shadow, moving, coming forward, looming larger. There beside the chair, holding out a glass, fine, bright crystal.

Tom took the whisky. Monty went and sat in the other chair.

'What do you want?' he asked, crossing his legs, leaning back. 'Is it blackmail?'

'How could I blackmail you?'

'I don't know. You may think you've got something on Laura.'

'I just want to know if she was driving that car.'

'She wasn't.'

'Can you be sure of that?' Tom asked. 'How well do you know her?'

'I know her.'

'Did you know that she's made over a million dollars on the stock market over the last few months?'

Monty opened his mouth to answer and then shut it. A big gulp from his drink, and then he took out his phone again, opened it, pushed a couple of keys. Holding it to his ear, listening.

'Hi,' he said. 'It's me. Where are you? . . . Don't play games, please. There's a bloke here who says he's found your car. In our barn on the Pigskill property . . . It's what's-his-name, Greenwise. The guy from the garden centre . . .' Then Monty was leaning forward, holding the phone out. 'She wants to talk to you.'

Taking it, lifting it.

'Angry Man,' she said in his ear. 'You found me out. Was it you who told the newspaper woman? And the cops?'

'No.' What newspaper woman? Lisa, was it? 'You killed someone.' Watching Monty, watching his eyes, the fear in them. And feeling a sudden stillness in himself.

'Yes. It was bad luck. It wasn't fun.'

'What happened?' He could scarcely get the words out.

'I was coming back from Winston. I wasn't used to the car. I'd only had it a few weeks. It started to rain and I turned on the wipers, only I got it wrong. It was the headlights, the pop-ups. I was confused for a second and I couldn't see because of the rain, and then this person was right there. I hit her.'

'Do you know who she was?'

'No. She had a name, I suppose. I might have heard it, I don't remember. After it happened, I put the car in the barn and I hiked up to Ridge Road and hitched a ride into town. I went to the police and reported the car stolen. Then I hid.

I went to Australia. Just in case. It had all blown over by the time I got back.'

'It was my daughter,' he said. And the words came from deep down.

'Really?'

A pause. Silence. Monty's eyes wide, face drawn. Waiting.

'That's a weird coincidence, don't you think?' she said. 'Very strange.'

Another pause. He couldn't speak. He couldn't move.

'I expect you want something,' she went on. 'I don't know. I can't see what I can do, really. Can you?' Then, suddenly, her tone changed, quickly urgent. 'Look, sorry. I've got to go now. Tell Monty I couldn't wait. Tell him I won't be back.'

Silence. He closed his eyes. And the darkness seemed to suck at him. He felt the first small shift in his blood, a throb of anguish, and suddenly it was all moving, pouring through him, into his chest and his groin, down into his arms and legs, through flesh and bone, a flood of pain so swift and so complete that there was nothing left of him to feel it. And the whisky glass exploded in his hand.

58.

AND SO HE SLEEPS, this wounded dog, in the bed in the room with the picture of the bleeding bull. And he dreams. Of course, he dreams. He's in the hallway outside Carla's room and he's afraid. He knocks and there's no answer, and so he turns the knob, opens the door, wondering what he will find. And there she is, in bed. She's two years old. Lying there asleep. Her small face, with its pointy chin, dark hair on the pale pillow. He reaches out and touches her. And she's awake. She was just pretending. And she starts to giggle and he tickles her and she writhes and twists and then she bites him. Sharp teeth on his hand in a playful way. And he puts his hand over her face, loosely, and she keeps on biting, or trying to. He can feel her teeth scraping on his palm. And suddenly, she's not a child any more, she's not a human being. She's a strange thing, a giant grub and she's gnawing at him, tearing at his flesh, and her eyes are small and dead, like blobs of wax.

— No! he says. And Carla starts to cry.

On the afternoon before she died, as she was leaving school, she came upon Margot Riley and Tina Greene and another girl, a younger kid, year nine maybe, who she didn't know. They were standing under a tree beside the school drive. Slutty Margot, with her blouse hanging out and her tie undone, was chewing gum and leaning on the trunk of the tree and looking down her nose at the younger kid, who was overweight and had black hair and sloping shoulders. Tina, as always, hovering there, looking pinched and rat-like, bright little eyes and grinning little mouth, ready to run away at the first sign of trouble. Carla, with her bike, was going to walk on past, but as she got close to them the plump kid gave her a look that stopped her. Scared and pleading, both at once.

'Hi,' Carla said. 'You guys all right? What are you doing?' Keeping it cheerful, keeping it innocent. There were streams of other kids wandering past, going home.

'Nothing to do with you,' Margot said.

'We're on rubbish duty,' Tina told her. 'Cleaning up rubbish.'

'Yer.' Margot reached out and stroked the plump kid's shoulder. Then, she pulled a face and gave a shudder, wiped her fingers on her skirt.

'Rubbish stinks!' Tina wrinkled her nose. 'Pooh!'

'It's a fat pig, that's why. Pigs stink, don't they?' Margot shoved the plump kid hard, so that she staggered.

'Hey!' Carla told her. 'Cut that out!'

'Fuck off!' Margot glaring at her, threatening.

'No. You fuck off. Leave my friend alone.'

'She's not your friend.'

'Yes, she is. We're going down to Baxter's to have a coffee.' Carla looked at the plump kid. 'Aren't we?'

'Yes.' A soft voice, frightened, little whisper.

'You're not allowed to go there in school uniform,' Tina said. Typical. Tina the hypocrite, keeping all the rules that didn't matter, the public rules.

'Who cares? You don't care, do you, Margot?' And then she had a thought, a sneaky thought. 'Hey, why don't you come too? We can all go. The four of us.' She turned from one to the other, hoping she'd guessed them right. Tina looked worried all of a sudden, screwing up her face and showing her ratty teeth. Good.

'Nagh,' Margot said. 'Who wants to go to a dump like that?'

'We do,' Carla said, relieved. She beckoned to the plump kid. 'Come on.'

So the two of them walked away. Easy as that. Although the plump kid seemed to have to drag herself as if she still thought it was going to be impossible.

'What's your name?' Carla asked her.

'Merry.'

'I'm Carla.'

'I know.'

'You don't have to take any crap from them. They're pus-bags.'

Merry didn't answer.

'They're inadequates. You should feel sorry for them.'

'They're going to take me down to the Rock,' Merry said.

'When?'

'Tomorrow.'

'Well, don't go.'

'I guess I could stay home.'

Something about the way she said it made Carla see that she didn't want to have to stay home.

'What are you supposed to be doing?' she asked.

'There's an art class at the Community Centre. I go to that on a Saturday afternoon.'

'Well, you should go to it then,' Carla told her. 'Don't let them stop you.'

'But they know about it. They hang around the Mall.

They're going to get me.'

Now, by the main gates. Two buses there, with the kids piling into them.

'You like art then?' Carla asked.

'Yes.'

'Are you any good at it?'

'Oh, a bit.' Merry closed her eyes tight, as if she might have told a lie, as if she were hoping what she'd said was true.

'I'm not. I'm hopeless. I can't even draw a wiggly line. My sister's good, though. She can draw.'

'I like making colours,' Merry said.

'What time is this class?'

'Three o'clock.'

'Look, I have to go to the library tomorrow. I can be there at three o'clock if you like.'

'Really?' Soft brown eyes looking at her, pleading and grateful, all at once.

'Sure. Not a problem.'

'Wow. That's great. Thanks.'

The buses were full now. The last stragglers squeezing on board. Merry glanced towards them. 'I have to go,' she said.

'Don't you want to come to Baxter's?'

'I can't. I have to get home.' Looking worried, as if Carla were going to stop her somehow.

'Whatever.'

Merry turned away towards the bus, a knock-kneed kind of walk.

'See you tomorrow then,' Carla called after her.

And the dog-man dreams. Of a howling wind that strips the trees. The iron of the roof is coming loose and bits of the house are flying away and he's out there trying to secure it, clinging on to a ladder and banging in nails, but as fast as he secures something another bit comes free. And then he's falling, through the house, as if it were an unreal thing, dissolving all about him. And he's there in a garden with a wide lawn that slopes down to a lake that stretches out as far as the horizon and it's dusk or maybe dawn with a darkened sky above and thin layers of grey cloud, striations through the brightness where the light is, beyond the water. And the lake is blue grey, paled with silver. And there are voices somewhere, faint, high voices. Children playing. He sees them there, down at the water's edge. There are three of them and they're launching a boat.

And so he wakes in the dark and his hand is throbbing. Five stitches from the broken whisky glass. He lifts it to his chest and lets it rest there, in the half-sleep, softly breathing, and the pain seeps into him, filling his body, and he welcomes it because it's real.

59.

THE CHAPEL AT THE crematorium had stained glass windows, two of them on either side of the door. Each showed a lighted candle in a red holder. Each with a yellow flame, like a thick lick of blond hair. A symbol of eternal life. The coffin lay on a raised platform, on rollers. There were two little double doors ahead of it, closed now, but doubtless at the flick of a switch they would flip open and the rollers would start to turn, and the box would glide off into whatever place it was back there, with its oven and its men in overalls.

Tom alone, stood there looking, wondering why he had come here, wondering why he had not just done as the others and gone through the motions at Chapelgate. Waste of time really, standing here, trying to say goodbye, trying to think of words, of thoughts, that would move you on to somewhere else. A girl on her bicycle, with her library books strapped to the carrier, cycles off into the afternoon. That was goodbye, that was the chance, if only he'd known it.

— Bye, Dad. I'm off now.

— See you later, sweetheart. Take care.

So she rides away and you look at the sky and think that it might rain.

And in the end it all just gets packed up into a box, less than two metres long and a fifth as high and a quarter as wide at its widest point. A box of shiny wood veneer with fake brass handles. A box that's heavy with the dead weight of waste and loss. You can cry over it, this box, standing here for the second time in six months, with your hand on the smooth, cold surface and your shoulders shaking. Tears; these are tears. He doesn't know why he is crying, unless it's for his little girl. He has to turn away.

The door opens. He doesn't notice. He doesn't see Lisa step inside and close it behind her.

She stands there, looking at him. He is facing the wall, with his head bowed. She sees his misery from a long way off. She doesn't go to him, she doesn't touch him. She can't bring herself to touch him. She is not sure what she feels. The pity and the sadness and the rage have gone. But she can't find the love either, not just now. Nothing but the circumstance, the being here.

'Tom,' she says.